Praise

LYNNE GRAHAM

Born of Irish/Scottish parentage, Lynne Graham has lived in Northern Ireland all her life. She grew up in a seaside village and now lives in a country house surrounded by a woodland garden, which is wonderfully private.

Lynne first met her husband when she was fourteen. They married after she completed a degree at Edinburgh University. Her first book, written at age fifteen, was rejected everywhere. But she began writing again when she was at home with her first child. It took several attempts before she sold her first book and the delight of seeing that book for sale in the local newsagents has never been forgotten.

Lynne always wanted a large family and she now has five children. Her eldest, her only natural child, is in her twenties and is a university graduate. Her other children, who are every bit as dear to her heart, are adopted: two from Sri Lanka and two from Guatemala. In Lynne's home, there is a rich and diverse cultural mix, which adds a whole extra dimension of interest and discovery to family life.

Lynne loves gardening and cooking, collects everything from old toys to rock specimens and is crazy about every aspect of Christmas.

Lynne Graham

The Arabian Mistress

The Contaxis Baby

TORONTO NEW YORK LONDON
AMSTERDAM PARIS SYDNEY HAMBURG
STOCKHOLM ATHENS TOKYO MILAN MADRID
PRAGUE WARSAW BUDAPEST AUCKLAND

Recycling programs
for this product may
not exist in your area.

ISBN-13: 978-0-373-68831-9

THE ARABIAN MISTRESS & THE CONTAXIS BABY

Copyright © 2011 by Harlequin Books S.A.

The publisher acknowledges the copyright holder
of the individual works as follows:

THE ARABIAN MISTRESS
Copyright © 2001 by Lynne Graham

THE CONTAXIS BABY
Copyright © 2002 by Lynne Graham

Printed in U.S.A.

CONTENTS

THE ARABIAN MISTRESS

Lynne Graham

CHAPTER ONE

IN HIS villa in the South of France, Prince Tariq Shazad ibn Zachir, paramount sheikh and ruler of the oil-rich Gulf state of Jumar, tossed aside the cellular phone and turned his attention to his most trusted aide, Latif.

Shrewd at reading others, Tariq noted the strain etched on the older man's face. 'Something wrong?'

'I regret that I should have to disturb you with this matter...' Latif settled a folder down on the desk with an air of profound apology '...but I felt it should be drawn to your attention.'

Surprised by the other man's discomfiture, Tariq swept up the folder. The opening document was a detailed report from Jumar's chief of police. Tariq scanned the name of the foreign national, who had been imprisoned for bad debts. He froze, his superb bone structure clenching, narrowed dark eyes hardening with angry incredulity. It was Adrian Lawson, Faye's elder brother!

Yet *another* Lawson guilty of dishonesty and deception! As he read the explanation of the events which had led to Adrian's arrest his lean, strong face hardened in disgust. How could Faye's brother have dared to set up a construction firm in Jumar and rob the very citizens that he, Tariq ibn Zachir was sworn to protect?

Powerful memories were stirring, disturbing memo-

ries which Tariq had spent twelve months endeavouring to forget. What male wished to recall his own worst
mistake? Faye with her fake innocence, who had laid
a snare to entrap him as surely as any seasoned gold-
digger. The bait? Her beautiful self. The threat after the
trap had snapped shut? *Scandal!* The paramount sheikh
of Jumar might exercise feudal power over his subjects.
But, even in the twenty-first century, Tariq ibn Zachir
accepted that it was his duty to maintain a conservative lifestyle. And a year ago his choices had been few
for his father, Hamza, had been dying...

Snapping back to the present, pale with bitter anger
beneath his tawny skin, Tariq slowly breathed in deep.
Unlike many other scions of Middle Eastern royal families, he had not been educated in the West. Tariq had
been raised much like his ancestral forefathers. Military school, tutors, desert survival exercises with the
British special forces. At the age of twenty-two, a pilot
and an expert in every possible form of combat, Tariq
had finally convinced his father that, while the ability
to lead his future people into battle was naturally important, one hundred years of peace within their borders
and with their neighbours might suggest that a business
degree could be of rather more imminent use to his son.

Tariq had duly discovered a natural talent for the
business world and had enriched the swollen coffers
of a state already so fabulously wealthy that he and his
people made the highest per capita charitable contribu-
tions of any country in the world. And with his entrance
into the more liberal culture of Europe, Tariq had also
received an unparalleled education on the ways of West-

ern women. Yet even in the grip of his subsequent cynicism, he had *still* been slaughtered like a sitting duck when he'd met Faye Lawson…

'How do you wish me to act in this matter?' Latif enquired.

Tariq flashed him a questioning glance. 'There is no action to be taken. Let the process of law take its course.'

Latif studied his feet. 'It seems unlikely that Adrian Lawson will be able to produce the money necessary to obtain his own release.'

'He may rot.'

After a very long and tense silence, Latif cleared his throat with deprecatory hesitance.

Tariq sent him a look of grim amusement. 'Yes, I *know* what I do…'

Uneasy though he was with that response, the older man bowed and departed again. Well aware of the source of Latif's anxiety, Tariq considered his own position with grim disfavour. Realities he had sidestepped now confronted him. His fierce pride, his fury at being set up and trapped, had come between him and common sense. But it was time to sever his connection with Faye Lawson and move on.

It *should* have been done a year ago. It was not a situation which could be left unresolved. Particularly not when he now had the responsibility of bringing up three young children, orphaned by the plane crash which had decimated his own family circle. He needed a wife, a warm, maternal woman. It was his duty to marry such a woman, he reminded himself. However, it could not be said that he was eager to embrace that duty.

Thrusting aside the folder on Adrian Lawson, unread beyond that first enlightening page, Tariq lounged back in his chair like a restive tiger, brooding dark golden eyes hard as iron. The Lawson siblings and their boorish stepfather, Percy, were a sly and greedy trio, who allowed no moral scruple to come between themselves and financial profit. How many other men had Faye played for a sucker? How many lives had Percy ruined with blackmail and dishonest business practices? And now it was evident that even Adrian, the only one of the trio whom Tariq had believed to be decent, was equally corrupt. Such people *should* be punished.

Tariq pictured the hawk that was the emblem of his family soaring high above the desert in search of tender prey. A chilling smile formed on his well-shaped mouth. There was no reason why he should not strike a blow for natural justice. Indeed there was no reason why *he* should not take advantage of the situation and have a little fun at the same time…

FAYE SAT BESIDE HER STEPFATHER in the back of the taxi in total silence. Small and slight of build, she was dwarfed by the bulk of the man beside her.

It was only mid-morning but it was hot and, after the long night flight from London, she was exhausted. The cab speeding them through the wide pristine streets of Jumar city was taking them to the prison where her brother, Adrian, was being held. Had she not been so worried about Adrian and had money not been so tight, she would have refused to share even a cab with Percy Smythe.

It still shook Faye that she could feel such intense dislike for any living person. Family loyalty had always been very important to her but she knew she would never forgive Percy for dragging her down into the dirt with him and utterly destroying any faith that Prince Tariq ibn Zachir had ever had in her. Nor could she forgive herself for being so infatuated that she had refused to allow herself to question Tariq's sudden unexpected proposal of marriage twelve months earlier.

'This is a waste of time.' Percy's plump, perspiring face was full of exasperated impatience. 'You've got to go and see Prince Tariq and ask him to have Adrian released!'

Beneath the pale blonde hair which merely served to accentuate her present lack of colour, Faye's delicate profile froze. 'I *couldn't*—'

'Well, how are you going to feel if Adrian picks up some ghastly Middle Eastern infection and pops his clogs?' Percy demanded with brutal bluntness. 'You know he's never been strong!'

Her sensitive stomach churned for there was more truth in that melodramatic warning than she liked to credit. As a child, Adrian had had leukaemia and, although he had recovered, he still tended to catch every passing bug. His uncertain health had finally destroyed the army career he'd loved, forcing him to rethink his future and plunge into the business venture which had led to his current plight.

'The Foreign Office assured us that he was being well treated,' Faye reminded the older man tautly.

'Insofar as he's been locked up indefinitely! If I was a superstitious man, I would believe that your desert warrior put a hex on us *all* last year,' Percy complained bitterly. 'I was riding high then, making money hand over fist and look at me now—I'm practically broke!'

Just as he deserved to be, Faye reflected heavily. Her stepfather would walk over anyone and do anything to feather his own nest. But there was one surprising exception to that rule: Adrian had somehow become as dear to Percy as any flesh-and-blood son. It was ironic that Percy should have sacrificed his own security in trying and failing to keep her brother's business afloat.

The prison lay well outside the city limits, housed in a grim fortress surrounded by high walls and lookout towers. They had to wait for some time before they were shown into a room where a line of seats sat in front of a sturdy glass partition. Faye only then appreciated that neither privacy nor physical contact were allowed between inmates and visitors.

But a bigger shock was in store for her when Adrian appeared. He had lost a lot of weight and his prison clothes hung loose on his thin frame. The drawn pallor of his features alarmed her: her brother looked far from well. His bloodshot eyes were strained and reluctant to meet hers.

'You shouldn't have come, sis,' Adrian groaned on the phone provided for communication. 'This is *my* mess. I got too cocky and over-extended myself. I let

Lizzie spend like there was no tomorrow. It's the way people live here…you go a bit mad trying to keep up—'

Percy snatched the receiver from Faye and growled, 'I'll go to the press back home and kick up such a *stink* they'll let you out of this hell hole!'

Adrian studied his stepfather in open horror. 'Are you crazy?' he mouthed silently through the glass barrier.

Faye retrieved the phone, her violet-blue eyes full of anxiety. 'We can't raise the kind of money you need to get out of here. Your lawyer met us off our flight but he said that he could no longer act for you and that the case was closed. You have to tell us what else we can do to fight this.'

Adrian gave her a bleak defeated look. 'There *is* nothing. Didn't my lawyer tell you that there is no right of appeal in a case like mine? How are Lizzie and the kids holding up?'

At that reference to his wife, Faye tensed for she had no good news to offer. After the experience of having her luxurious home in Jumar repossessed and being deported with her twin toddlers because she no longer had any means of support, her sister-in-law, Lizzie, was feeling very sorry for herself.

'Like that, is it?' Adrian read his sister's evasive gaze. 'Lizzie didn't even send me a letter?'

'She's pretty down…' Faye hated adding to his misery with that admission. 'She asked me to tell you that she loves you but that right now she's having a problem just coping with being back home without you.'

Adrian's eyes filled with moisture and he twisted his

head away, swallowing hard to get himself back under control.

Faye blinked back tears at her brother's distress and hurried to change the subject. 'How are you managing?'

'Fine…' her brother mumbled curtly.

'Are you being treated all right?' Faye was intimidated by the suspicious appraisal of the two armed officers watching their every move.

'I have no cause for complaint…just that it's hell because I hate the food, speak rotten Arabic and keep on getting sick.' Her brother's jerky voice faltered. 'But whatever you do, don't let Percy go screaming to the media because that will make me a marked man in here. The locals see any criticism of Jumar as criticism of their lousy womanising ruler, Prince Tariq—'

In an abrupt movement, one of the armed officers strode forward looking outraged and wrenched the phone from Adrian's grasp.

'What's wrong…what's happening?' Faye surged upright in a panic.

But on their side of the restrictive glass, she and her stepfather might as well have been invisible. Adrian was escorted back to the doorway through which he had earlier entered and vanished from view.

'I bet those thugs are taking him away to beat him up!' Percy was as aghast as Faye at what had happened.

'But neither of those men put a hand on Adrian—'

'Not in front of *us*…but how do you know what they're doing to him now?'

They waited ten minutes to see if Adrian would reappear but he did not. Instead a severe-looking older man in uniform came in to speak to them.

'I want to know what's going on here,' Percy demanded aggressively.

'Visits are a privilege we extend to relatives, not a right in law. Your visit was terminated because we will not allow our most honoured ruler to be referred to in offensive terms.' As Percy swelled like a ripe red fruit ready to burst in messy rage, the senior prison officer added loftily, 'Let me also assure you that we do not abuse our prisoners. Jumar is a civilised and humane country. You may request another visit later this week.'

Registering then that every word spoken during such visits appeared to be monitored and that Adrian must have been equally unaware of that reality, Faye hurried her stepfather out of the room before he could add to her brother's offence.

Percy raved in frustrated fury all the way back to their small hotel in the suburbs. Faye was grateful that the taxi driver did not seem to understand a word of Percy's vitriolic diatribe against Jumar and all things Jumarian. Taking Tariq's name in vain in a public place might well be tantamount to inviting a physical assault. As her stepfather headed straight for the residents' bar on the ground floor, Faye got into the lift and went back up to her hotel room.

In her mind's eye, all she could see was the look of naked despair on her brother's haggard face. Just six short months ago, Adrian had believed he would make his fortune in a city reputed to be a building boomtown. Faye sat at the foot of the bed staring at the challenging reflection of the telephone in the dressing mirror facing her.

'The number is easy to remember,' Tariq had told her once. 'We owned the first telephone in Jumar. You just dial *one* for the palace switchboard!'

Momentarily Faye shut her swimming eyes, pain and regret and bitterness tearing at her. However, like it or not, Prince Tariq ibn Zachir seemed to be the only option they had left. In most other countries, Adrian would have been declared bankrupt, not imprisoned for debt as if he were a criminal. She had no choice but to approach Tariq and plead her brother's case. Tariq was all powerful here within his own country. Tariq could surely do *anything* he wanted to do...

So what if the prospect of crawling to Tariq made her cringe? How could she value her pride more than her brother's welfare? Tense as a cat on hot bricks, Faye paced the room. Would Tariq even agree to see her? How did she beg such a massive favour from a male who despised both her and her stepfather? She was out of her depth here in Jumar where the very air seemed to smell of high-powered money and privilege, she thought bitterly. A year ago, she had been even more out of her depth with a male as exotic and sophisticated as Tariq ibn Zachir. And bone-deep foolish to imagine that anything lasting might come of such an inequal relationship. But, no matter what Tariq had chosen to believe, she had played *no* part in Percy's sordid attempt to blackmail him!

Reminding herself of that essential truth, Faye reached for the phone. Dialling that single digit to be connected to the palace was easy. However, in the minutes that followed, she discovered that the palace switchboard was tended by personnel who spoke only Arabic. Breaking off the call in frustration, Faye reached for the purse in her bag. From the central compartment, she withdrew a slender gold ring etched with worn hieroglyphic symbols.

Her hand shook. For a split second, memory took her back to the instant when Tariq had slid that ring onto her finger in the Embassy of Jumar in London. She shivered, assailed by a tide of choking humiliation. How stupid she had been to believe that that was a *real* wedding ceremony! It had been a farce staged solely to combat Percy's threat to plunge Tariq into a sleazy media scandal. But only when that cruel farce was over had Faye realised what a complete clown Tariq had made of her.

Making use of the hotel stationery, Faye dropped the ring into an envelope and dashed off a note requesting a meeting with Tariq. She went down to Reception and asked how to have an urgent letter delivered. The receptionist studied the name on the envelope with widened eyes and extended her interest to the additional words, 'PERSONAL, PRIVATE, CONFIDENTIAL' taking up half of the space. 'This…it is for Prince Tariq?'

Faye reddened and nodded.

"One of our drivers will deliver it, Miss Lawson.'

Back in her room, Faye went for a shower and changed. Then she lay down on the bed. A loud knock, recognisable as Percy's calling card, sounded on the door. She ignored it. He thumped again so loudly she was afraid that the hotel staff would come to investigate. She opened the door.

'Right…' Her stepfather pushed his way in, his heavy face aggressive and flushed by alcohol. 'You get on that phone now and contact Tariq. Hopefully he'll get a kick out of you grovelling at his feet. And if that's not enough to please His Royal Highness, warn him that you can *still* go to the newspapers and give them a story about what it's like getting married and divorced all in the space of the same day!'

Faye was horrified. 'Do you really think that wild nasty threats are likely to persuade Tariq to help Adrian?'

'Look, I may have miscalculated with Tariq last year but I know how that bloke ticks now. He's a real tough nut to crack—all that SAS training—but he's also an officer and a gentleman and he prides himself on the fact. So first you try licking boots and looking pathetic…' Percy subjected her navy blouse, cotton trousers and her clipped-back long hair to a withering appraisal. 'Look pathetic *and* beautiful!'

The light rap that sounded on her door at that point provided a merciful interruption. It was the hotel manager, who had greeted them on their arrival. He bowed as if she had suddenly become a most important guest.

'A limousine has arrived to take you to the Haja place, Miss Lawson.'

Faye swallowed hard. She had not expected so speedy a response to her request for a meeting.

'Don't you worry…she'll be down in two minutes.' Percy turned back to his stepdaughter to say appreciatively, 'Why didn't you just *tell* me you'd already started the ball rolling?'

Keen to escape her stepfather's loathsome company, Faye went straight down in the lift. She settled into the luxurious limousine, feeling like a fish out of water in her plain, inexpensive clothes. And she was, wasn't she?

She had lived in a quiet country house all her life, rarely meeting anyone outside her late mother's restricted social circle. Percy had married Sarah Lawson when Faye was five. Disabled by the same car accident in which her first husband had died, Faye's mother had been confined to a wheelchair and desperately lonely. She had also been a well-to-do widow. After their marriage, Percy had continued to use a city apartment as his base and, pleading pressure of work, had spent only occasional weekends with his new family.

Faye had never gone to school like other children. Both she and her brother had initially been taught at home by their mother, but once Adrian had overcome leukaemia Percy had persuaded his wife that her son should complete his education with other boys. At eleven years old, hungry for friends her own age, Faye had finally worked up the courage to tell her stepfather that she too wanted to attend school.

'And what's your mother going to do with herself all day?' Percy's accusing fury had shaken her rigid. 'How can you be so selfish? Your mother needs you for company...she's got nothing else in her life!'

Faye had been devastated at eighteen when her gentle mother had died. But only then had she appreciated that some people believed she had led an unnaturally sheltered life for a teenager. Indeed, at the interview for the nursing course she was hoping to begin in the autumn, several critical comments had been made about her lack of experience of the *real* world. Had she felt like baring her soul, she might have told them that, with Percy Smythe in the starring role of stepfather, she had had ample experience of life's nastier realities...

Having traversed the wide, busy streets of the city to a gracious tree-lined square, the limo pulled up in front of a vast old sandstone building with an imposing entrance. Spick-and-span soldiers stood on guard outside. Faye clambered out, flustered and unsure of herself.

Climbing the steps, she entered a vast and imposing hall crowded with people coming and going. Frowning, she hesitated. A young man in a suit approached her and with a low bow said, 'Miss Lawson? I will take you to Prince Tariq.'

'Thank you. Is this the royal palace?'

'No, indeed, Miss Lawson. Although the Haja fortress still belongs to the royal family, His Royal Highness allows it to be used as a public building,' her companion informed her. 'The Haja houses the law courts and the audience rooms, also conference and banqueting facilities for visiting dignitaries and businessmen. While retaining offices here, Prince Tariq lives in the Muraaba palace.'

So this was *not* Tariq's home and he had chosen a more impersonal setting for their meeting. Her eyes skimmed over the fluted stone pillars that punctuated the echoing hall and the wonderful mosaic tiled floor which gleamed beneath the passage of so many feet.

The Haja was a hive of activity. An elderly tribesman was sitting on a stone bench with, of all things, a *goat* on a string. She saw women veiled in black from head to toe, other women in elegant western clothing, their lovely faces serene, clusters of older men wearing the traditional male headdress, the *kaffiyeh*, sharply suited younger ones bare-headed and carrying files and attaché cases.

'Miss Lawson...?'

Forced to quicken her steps, she followed her escort under an archway. Tribal guards armed with both guns and ornate swords stood outside the door which was being spread wide for her entrance. She forced her feet onward, heart thundering, throat tightening. Perhaps what she least expected was to find herself standing alone in a beautiful inner courtyard, lush with islands of exotic greenery and embellished with a tranquil central pool. She blinked. Hearing the sound of footsteps, she turned and saw Tariq coming down a flight of steps about twenty feet away.

To disconcert her yet further, Tariq was clad in riding gear, a white polo shirt open at his throat, skintight beige breeches outlining his narrow hips and long powerful length of leg, polished brown boots on his feet.

Her tummy muscles clenched. She had forgotten quite how tall Tariq ibn Zachir was and how dynamic his presence. He stilled like a lion on the prowl. Magnificent, hugely confident, his silent grace of movement one of his most noticeable physical attributes. In the sunlight he was a golden feast of vibrant masculinity. His luxuriant black hair shone. His tawny skin glowed with health and his stunning bronze eyes gleamed like precious metal, both brilliant and unreadable. Indeed, he was quite staggeringly beautiful and it was an appalling challenge for Faye not to stare at him. Her mouth ran dry, a slow, painful tide of pink creeping up to dispense her pallor. Her heart hammered against her breastbone so hard she could barely catch her breath.

'I appreciate your agreeing to see me so quickly,' Faye muttered dry-mouthed.

'Unfortunately, I haven't much time to spare. I have a charity polo match to play in an hour's time.'

Tariq came to a halt at the stone table by the pool and leant back against it. He angled his arrogant head back and studied her with a bold, all-male intensity that made her feel horribly self-conscious. His expressive mouth quirked. 'Surely Percy did not advise you to wear trousers to this meeting? Or is that sad outfit supposed to be a plea for the sympathy vote?'

At that all too accurate crack about her stepfather, Faye turned as red as a beetroot and stammered. 'I c-can't imagine why you should think that.'

'Don't play innocent.' Tariq gave her that advice in a tone as smooth as glass. 'I had a surfeit of the blushing virgin act last year. I should have smelt a rat the instant you ditched it and appeared in a plunging neckline but, like most men, I was too busy looking to *be* cautious.'

Writhing with chagrin under such fire, some of which she knew to be justified, Faye snatched in a stark breath of the hot, still air. 'Tariq...I *very* much regret what happened between us.'

Tariq dealt her a slow smile which chilled her to the

marrow for it was not at all the charismatic smile she recalled. 'I'm sure you do. It could not have occurred to you *then* that your precious brother would soon be locked up in a prison cell in Jumar.'

'Of course, it didn't.' Faye took that comment at face value, striving to be grateful that he had rushed them straight to the crux of the matter. She curled her hands together. 'But you like Adrian. You know that he's been gaoled through no fault of his own—'

'Do I?' Tariq broke in softly. 'Is our legal system so unjust? I had not thought so.'

Recognising her error in appearing to criticise that system, Faye said hastily, 'I didn't mean that. I was only pointing out that Adrian hasn't done anything criminal—'

'Has he not? Here in Jumar it *is* a crime to leave employees and tradesmen unpaid and clients with buildings that have not been completed according to contract. However, we are wonderfully practical in such cases.' His shimmering smile was no warmer than its predecessor. 'To regain his freedom, Adrian has only to satisfy his creditors.'

'But he's not able to do that…' As she was forced to make that admission, Faye's discomfiture leapt higher still. 'Adrian sold his home to start up the construction firm. He plunged *everything* he had into the venture—'

'And then lived like a king while he was here in my country. Yes, I am familiar with the circumstances in which your brother's business failed. Adrian himself was foolish and extravagant.'

As Tariq completed that brief but damning indictment, Faye lost colour. 'He made mistakes…*yes*, but not with any bad or deliberate intent—'

'Surely you have heard of the principle of criminal irresponsibility?' Indolent as a sleek jungle cat sunning himself in the sweltering heat that she was finding unbearable, Tariq surveyed her. 'Tell me, why did you send me *this*?'

That switch of subject disconcerted Faye almost as much as his complete lack of emotion. The last time she had seen Tariq he had been hot with dark fury and outrage. Now she focused on the ring in the extended palm of his lean brown hand and her tummy twisted. He tossed the ring into the air where it caught the sun and glittered, exercising the strangest fascination over her. Catching it again with deft fingers, he then tossed the ring with speaking carelessness down onto the stone table where it finally rattled into stillness.

'Were you hoping that I might have some sentimental memory of the day I put that ring on your finger?' Tariq asked with cold derision.

Faye studied his superb riding boots until they blurred beneath the fierceness of her gaze. A wave of deep shame enveloped her and roused a terrifying lump in her throat. How very hard it was to accept that he had caused her such immense pain yet deprived her of any real right of complaint. True, he had misjudged her, but he could hardly be blamed for that when her own stepfather had tried to blackmail him. Nonetheless, unjust as it might be, Faye hated Tariq for believing that she was as calculating and mercenary as Percy Smythe.

'Tell me…' Tariq continued with awesome casualness, '…do you think of yourself as my wife or as my ex-wife?'

Reacting to that light and, to her, inappropriate question as if it was the cruellest of taunts, Faye's pale head flew up and mortified pink warmed her cheeks afresh. 'Hardly. At the time you made it very clear that that wedding ceremony was a charade! I know all too well that I was *never* your wife.'

His dense black spiky lashes lowered over dark deep-set eyes for once unlit by any lighter hue. 'I was curious to find out how you regarded yourself.'

'I'm only here to discuss Adrian's position—'

'Adrian doesn't have a position,' Tariq interposed without hesitation. 'The law has already dealt with him and only repayment of his debts can free him.'

He was like a stranger. Neither courteous nor sympathetic, neither interested nor perturbed. This was Tariq as she had never known him. Hard, distant, forbidding. Terrifyingly impersonal. A male whose cool authority of command was so engrained that it blazed from him even in casual clothing. Faye's slim hands closed in tight on themselves. 'But surely *you* could do something…if you wanted to…'

'I am not above the law,' Tariq stated, ice entering his rich dark drawl.

Her desperation grew. 'But, even so, you can do exactly as you wish…isn't that what being a feudal ruler is all about?'

'I would not interfere with the laws of my country. It is a grave insult for you to even *suggest* that I would abuse the trust of my people in such a way!' Hard golden eyes struck hers in a look of strong censure.

Faye tore her shaken gaze from his and tried not to cringe. She fully understood that message but did not want to accept it. Even though she was standing in partial shade, she was perspiring and wilting in the suffocating heat that he seemed to flourish in. But knowing that she undoubtedly only had this one chance to speak up on her brother's behalf, she persisted. 'Adrian can't work to pay off his creditors from inside a prison cell—'

'No, indeed, but how is it that you and your stepfather find yourself so poor that you cannot rescue him?'

'Percy used up all his surplus cash trying to *save* Adrian's business. And don't tell me that you weren't aware of that.' Faye could not conceal her bitterness at the brick-wall reception she was receiving. It was now clear that, even before she'd approached him, Tariq had known all the facts of her brother's case but had already decided not to interfere. 'I'm only here begging you to find some way to help my brother because I have nowhere else to turn.'

'You have yet to explain *why* I should wish to help Adrian.'

'Common decency…humanity…' Faye muttered shakily. 'Officer and a gentleman?'

Tariq elevated an aristocratic dark brow. 'Not where your self-seeking, dishonourable family is concerned.'

'What can I *say* to convince you that—?'

'Nothing. You can say nothing that will convince me. Tell me, were you always this obtuse? Or was I so busy looking at your angelic face and divine body that I failed to notice a pronounced absence of brain cells?'

His ruthless mockery lashed red into her tense, confused face. 'I don't know what you're getting at—'

'Why don't you just ask me under what terms you might persuade *me* to settle Adrian's debts?'

'*You* settle them?' Faye studied Tariq in bewilderment. 'That idea never even occurred to me—'

That disclaimer fired an even more sardonic light in his level gaze. 'We're running out of time. So I shall use plain words. Give yourself to me and I will buy your brother out of trouble. There…it is very simple, is it not?'

Her lips parted. *Give yourself to me.* Her dark blue eyes huge, she stared back at him in disbelief.

Tariq absorbed her reaction with a cynical cool that sent her shock level into overdrive. 'Sex in return for money. What you once used as a bait to set a trap for me but *failed* to deliver.'

Hot, sticky and stunned by that blunt condemnation, Faye raised her hand to tug at the constricting collar of her blouse. A trickle of perspiration ran down between her breasts. His keen gaze rested there and then whipped up to connect with her shaken eyes. The charged sexuality of that knowing look scorched her sensitive skin like a taunting flame. A helpless flare of response gripped her taut body without warning. Thought had nothing to do with the sudden ache in her breasts, the throbbing tautness of her nipples or the curl of dark secret heat darting up between her thighs.

Appalled self-loathing trammelling through her, Faye

dropped her head, fighting and denying the physical sensations which threatened to tear her inside out. She needed to think, she *had* to concentrate for Tariq could not possibly mean what he was saying. This could only be a cruel power play at her expense. At the same time as he let her know that he would not lift a finger to help Adrian, he was trying to punish her for the past. Punish her with humiliation.

At that energising thought, Faye lifted her head high again. Her fine-boned features were pink but stiff with angry, injured pride. 'Obviously it was a mistake to ask you for this meeting.' Struggling to keep her voice level, she thrust up her chin. 'Whatever you may think of me, I don't deserve what you just said to me.'

A caustic smile slashed Tariq's lean, powerful face. 'What a loss you have been to the film world! That look of mortally offended reproach is quite superb.'

'You ought to be ashamed of yourself!' Undaunted by the incredulous blaze that flamed in his spectacular eyes, Faye gave him a scornful glance. Spinning on her heel, she stalked back out of the courtyard without lowering herself to say another word.

CHAPTER TWO

FAYE shot like a bullet back into the crowded concourse again, cannoned off someone with a startled apology and backed away into one of the pillars.

She was in shock. She knew she was. But she was furious to find that her eyes were awash with tears and she couldn't see where she was going. Gulping back the thickness in her throat, she whirled round to the back of the pillar and struggled to get a grip on herself again. What was she? Some wishy-washy wimp all of a sudden?

'Allow me to offer you refreshment...' an anxious male voice proffered.

Frowning in surprise because she recognised that voice, Faye parted her clogged eyelashes and focused on the polished shoes of the little man standing in front of her. Latif, Tariq's most senior aide, whom she had met in passing on several occasions the year before. Slowly she lifted her bent head. Latif bowed so low that she got a great view of his bald patch. Indeed she honestly thought he was trying to touch his toes and could not immediately grasp what on earth he was doing until it occurred to her that the older man might well be granting her a tactful moment in which to compose herself.

'Latif...'

'Please come this way...'

Latif led her through a door and across a hall into a charming reception room furnished in European style. Grateful for the blessed cool of the air-conditioning there, Faye collapsed down on a silk-upholstered sofa and dug into her bag in search of a tissue.

The reserved older man stayed by the door at a respectful distance and Faye averted her attention from him. Latif was kind. He had seen her distress and brought her here to recover in privacy and, unfortunately for him, good manners forbade leaving her alone.

Jingling with jewellery and barefoot, a procession of maids carrying trays entered the room. One by one they knelt at her feet to serve her with coffee and proffer cakes and sticky confectionery. Beneath her astonished scrutiny, they then backed away across the whole depth of the room with downbent heads before exiting again. Presumably all visitors, many of whom would naturally be VIPs, were treated with such exaggerated attention and servility but it made Faye feel extremely uncomfortable.

'I believe the heat may have made you feel unwell.' As Faye finished the bittersweet coffee in the tiny china cup, Latif broke the silence with exquisite tact. 'I hope you are feeling better now.'

'Yes, thank you...' Faye bit at her lower lip and then took the plunge for she had not the slightest doubt that the discreet older man knew all about Adrian's predicament. 'Have you any idea how I can help my brother?'

'I would suggest that a second approach might be made to Prince Tariq tomorrow.'

So much for inspired advice from an inside source! Faye tried not to release a humourless laugh. Surely Latif could not have the foggiest clue of what had passed between her and Tariq? *Give yourself to me.* Pretty basic, that. No room for misunderstanding there. She was still shattered that Tariq could have made such a suggestion to her. It was barbaric.

Yet no sooner had she made that judgement than an unwelcome little voice spoke up from her conscience. Hadn't she once offered herself to Tariq in no uncertain terms? Hadn't she once made it quite clear that she'd been willing to sleep with him? And hadn't she then got cold feet when she'd seen how that unwise invitation had altered his attitude to her? Without a doubt, Tariq now saw her as the most shameless tease! Tears lashed the back of her eyes again. Wasn't it awful how one mistake could just lead to another and another? From the instant she had departed from the values she had been raised to respect, she had learnt nothing *but* hard lessons.

Eager now to leave the Haja, Faye rose to her feet. 'Thank you for the coffee, Latif.'

'I will send a car again for you tomorrow, if I may.'

'I'd be wasting my time coming again.'

'The car will remain at your disposal for the whole day.'

Latif evidently wanted her brother released from prison, Faye decided. Why else was he getting involved behind the scenes? She returned to the hotel in the same style in which she had departed. As she crossed the foyer, slight shoulders bowed with exhaustion, Percy emerged from the bar to intercept her.

'Well?' he demanded abrasively.

'All I got was…was an improper proposition.' Faye could not bring herself to look at her stepfather as she admitted that but she hoped that that honesty would satisfy him and save her from an interrogation. Percy was a bully. He had always been a bully. Just then, she did not feel equal to the challenge of standing up to him.

'So what?' Percy snapped without hesitation. 'You've got to do whatever it takes to get Adrian home!'

Once again, Faye was shocked. But as she hurried into the lift and left her stepfather fuming, she asked herself why. Percy had never had much time for her. It had been naïve of her to believe that he might be angry on her behalf. For Percy, the bottom line was Adrian. And shouldn't that be *her* bottom line as well?

Knowing it was past time that she ate something, Faye rang room service and ordered the cheapest snack on the menu. Then she made herself face facts. But for her, Adrian would not have got to know Tariq and would never had thought of setting up business in Jumar. It was also her fault that Tariq now regarded her and her brother in the same light as their stepfather. Like it or not, *she* had put Tariq into a compromising position where Percy was able to threaten him. Her foolish infatuation, her lies and her immaturity had led to that development. Adrian was suffering now because Tariq despised and distrusted all of them. Who could ever have imagined that from one seemingly small lie, so much grief could have flowed?

Faye swallowed hard. When she had first met Tariq, she had pretended to be twenty-three years old, sooner than own up to being a month short of her nineteenth birthday. Tariq's subsequent outrage at the lies she had told had been extreme and succinct. She might as well have set out to trap him for the end result had been the same. Retreating from recollections that still made her writhe with guilt, Faye returned to the present and the grim prospect of what she ought to try to do next to help her brother...

That evening, her stepfather came to her hotel room again but she opened the door on the chain and said she wasn't well. It wasn't a lie: she was so tired, she felt queasy. In her bed she lay listening to the evocative call of the muezzin calling the faithful to prayer at the mosque at the end of the street. With her conscience tormenting her, she got little sleep.

At half-past eight the following morning, wearing a loose dress in a pale lilac print, Faye climbed into the limousine which Latif had promised would be waiting. The day before she had made serious errors with Tariq, she now conceded, newly appraised humility weighing her down. She had tried to save face by talking only about Adrian. But, mortifying as it was to acknowledge, Tariq had good reason to think she was a brazen hussy, who had set him up for a sleazy blackmail attempt. Perhaps an open acknowledgement of that reality, a long overdue explanation and a sincere and heartfelt apology would take the edge off Tariq's animosity. Maybe he would then consider *loaning* Adrian the money he needed to settle his debts and let bygones be bygones...

This time the limo whisked her round to a side entrance at the Haja fortress where Latif greeted her in person. Quiet approval emanated from the older man.

Ushered straight into a large contemporary office, Faye breathed in deep and straightened her shoulders. Sleek and sophisticated in a pale grey business suit of exquisite cut that moulded his broad shoulders, lean hips and long powerful legs, Tariq was standing by the window talking on a portable phone. He acknowledged her arrival with the merest dip of his handsome dark head.

Taking the seat indicated by Latif, who then withdrew, Faye focused on Tariq. His classic profile stood out in strong relief. She watched the long, elegant fingers of his free hand spread a little and then curl with silent eloquence as he spoke. Memories that hurt assailed her and she dragged her attention from him and folded her hands together on her lap to stop them trembling.

But she remained so aware of his disturbing presence that she was in an agony of discomfiture. She knew that lean bronzed face almost as well as her own. The slight imperious slant of his ebony brows, the spectacular tawny eyes that had such amazing clarity, the narrow bridge of his aristocratic nose dissecting hard high Berber cheekbones, the strong stubborn jawline, the passionate but stern mouth.

Only the day before, she had felt the humiliating pull of his magnetic physical attraction. Her soft full mouth compressed. That had unnerved and embarrassed her. But he had caught her at a weak moment. That was all.

She was no longer an infatuated teenager, helpless in the grip of her own emotions and at the mercy of galloping hormones and foolish fantasies. She had got over him *fast*. She might not have dated anyone since but that was only because he had truly soured her outlook on men.

'Why are you here?'

Shot from her teeming thoughts without due warning, Faye jerked. Then she lifted her head and tilted it back. 'I believe I owe you an explanation for the way I behaved last year.'

'I need no explanation.' Derision glittered in Tariq's steady appraisal. 'Indeed I will listen to no explanation. If you think I'm fool enough to give you a platform for more lies and self-justification, you seriously underestimate me—'

In one sentence thus deprived of her entire script, Faye breathed, *'But—'*

'It's very rude to interrupt me when I'm speaking.'

Faye flushed but she was already so tense that her temper sparked. 'Maybe you would just like me to lie down like a carpet for you to walk on!'

'A carpet is inanimate. I prefer energy and movement in my women.'

Her humble and penitent frame of mind was already taking a hard beating. Cheeks scarlet at that comeback, Faye nonetheless tried afresh. 'Tariq...I need to explain and apologise. You wouldn't give me the chance to explain at the time.'

'If that is your only reason for being here, I suggest you leave. Sly words and crocodile tears won't move me. The very thought of your shameless deceit rouses my temper.'

Faye swallowed hard. 'OK...you have the right to be angry—'

'Grovelling insincerity makes me angry too,' Tariq incised even more drily. 'Cut the phony regrets. I made you an offer yesterday and that's why you're here now. Only a tramp would accept a proposition of that nature, so stop pretending to be a sweet, misunderstood innocent!'

Faye, who usually had the mildest temper in the world, was appalled to feel a river of wrath surge like hot lava inside her. She rose from her seat in an abrupt movement. 'I won't tolerate being called a tramp! What do you call a man who *makes* such an offer to a woman?'

'A man with no illusions...a man who disdains hypocrisy.'

Faye trembled. 'My goodness, you insult me with a proposition no decent woman would even consider and then you turn round and you flatter yourself from your pinnacle of perfection—'

'You are *not* a decent woman. You lie and you cheat and there is nothing you would not do for money.'

'That is not true...it all started because I told a few stupid white lies and I know it was wrong but I was crazy about you—'

'Crazy about me?' Tariq flung back his arrogant dark head and laughed out loud, the sound discordant in the thrumming atmosphere. 'You let me go for a mere half million pounds. You were so blinded by greed, you were content to settle for whatever you could get!'

Almost light-headed with the force of rage powering her, Faye now fell back a step and gaped at him. 'I let you go...for half a million pounds? What the heck are you trying to accuse me of doing now?'

Tariq centred his brilliant golden eyes on her, his beautiful mouth hard as granite. 'You were a cheap bride, I'll give you that. You may have come with no dowry but I was able to shed you again for a pittance.'

Faye was no longer sure her wobbling knees would hold her upright and she dropped down into the chair again, all temper quenched. Evidently, Tariq had handed over money to somebody, money she knew nothing about. She did not have to think very hard to come up with the name of the most likely culprit. 'You gave money to Percy...?' She swallowed back a wail of reproach at that appalling revelation.

'I gave it to *you*.'

And like a flash in the darkness, Faye finally recalled the envelope which Tariq had flung at her feet after their fake wedding that dreadful day. Did he recall that he had been talking in Arabic at the time? Didn't he realise that she had naively assumed that their marriage certificate had been in that envelope? And when she had finally stumbled out of the Embassy of Jumar, heartbroken and with her pride in tatters, she had thrust the envelope at Percy in revulsion and condemnation. 'Are you satisfied now that you've wrecked my life? Burn it...I don't want to ever be reminded of this day again!'

How many weeks had it been before she'd finally forced herself to see her stepfather again and ask for the certificate in the hope that he had not after all destroyed it? She had believed that she might need that certificate to apply for an annulment in case the extraordinary ease of Jumarian divorce was not actually recognised by English law. But Percy had laughed in her face when she'd mentioned that fear.

'Don't be more dumb than you can help, Faye,' her stepfather had sneered. 'That wasn't a legal marriage! It wasn't consummated and he repudiated you straight after the ceremony. Your desert warrior was just saving face and trying to protect himself with some mumbo-jumbo. Why else did he insist it took place in private in the embassy?'

Percy had followed that up with the explanation that embassies fell under the legal jurisdiction of the countries they belonged to, rather than that of the host country. Faye had felt too mortified by her own obvious ignorance to counter his charge of 'mumbo-jumbo'. An Arab gentleman dressed just like a Christian vicar *had* presided over the first part of that ceremony but he had spoken only in Arabic and there was no denying that Tariq himself had called their wedding a complete charade.

Repressing that slew of memories, Faye focused her bemused thoughts back on the cheque which Tariq had said was in that envelope she had blithely surrendered. She closed her eyes in stricken acknowledgement of yet another insane act of foolishness on her part. She had handed a cheque for half a million pounds to Percy

Smythe! But if the cheque had been made out to her, how on earth had he cashed it? For she had not the slightest doubt that it *must* have been cashed!

'Tariq...I didn't know that envelope had a cheque in it.' Her taut temples were pounding out her rising stress level. 'I don't know why you would have chosen to give me money either.'

The silence stretched and stretched.

Overwhelmed by guilty self-loathing and the most drowning sense of sheer inadequacy, Faye stared into space. No wonder Tariq ibn Zachir thought she was a trollop. No wonder he believed that she had conspired with her stepfather to set him up for blackmail. No wonder he was so certain that she was greedy for money. What had Percy done with that half million pounds? Percy, who had been outmanoeuvred in his blackmail attempt by Tariq's announcement that he would *marry* Faye. Whatever, that huge sum of money was evidently long gone.

'I can't believe that you would want a woman with such low moral standards,' Faye said finally.

'You'll be a novelty.'

'A woman who doesn't *want* you?' Faye was past caring about how she sounded. Here she was guilty as charged it seemed on every count. Guilty of serial stupidity. Guilty of being a teenager madly in love and doing all the wrong things in her efforts to make him love her back. She had done a marvellous job on him, hadn't she? Thanks to her own lies, he thought she was the most dishonest brazen hussy he had ever met!

'Is that a challenge?'

Faye gave him a dulled look. Tariq gazed back at her with a sizzling force that penetrated her veil of numb defeat. 'No!'

'You will be my mistress for as long as I want you.' Tariq surveyed her as if he had just stamped a brand of ownership on her, his male satisfaction unconcealed.

Seriously unnerved by that statement of intent, Faye leapt back out of her seat again, her hands clenched into fists. 'You can't *still* want me...you never wanted me that much to begin with! This is just a giant ego-trip. It's mindless revenge—'

'*Not* mindless. I never act without forethought.' Tariq stretched out an imperious hand. 'Come here...'

Faye went into retreat rather than advance. Shark-infested water might as well have separated them. 'I didn't say I agreed.'

'Then make your mind up.'

Faye folded her arms in a defensive movement. 'Adrian?'

'He goes home to England on the first available flight.'

Faye shook her head, tried to still the nervous tremor in her lower limbs. 'I'm not what you think I am. I can't imagine being any man's mistress. I won't fit the bill—'

'You underestimate yourself.'

Tariq extended his hand again, glittering golden eyes fixed to her with intimidating cool and expectancy.

'If you think I'm going to come running every time you snap your imperious fingers—'

'Sooner or later, you will. I have immense patience.'

That quiet confidence took Faye wholly aback and froze her to the spot. 'You're crazy…'

A slight smile curved his lips. 'You're scared.'

'Like heck I am…I'm just fed up with all this nonsense!'

The smile acquired amusement, veiled eyes resting on her slight, taut frame with an intimate intensity she could feel as surely as if he had touched her. 'I didn't sleep last night. I *couldn't* sleep, not even after a couple of cold showers. I knew you were mine then.'

'But you…you hate me!' Faye slung back at him in vehement protest.

'Hate? Too strong a word.' Tariq strolled closer like a hunter set on closing in for the kill but doing so at his own leisure. 'Is that why you look sick with fright? Is that fertile imagination of yours throwing up images of gothic whips and chains? Do you really think I would inflict a single bruise on that perfect skin of yours? You'll cry out with pleasure, not pain, in my bed.'

Faye was so mortified by that assurance, she whirled away from him. It was a mistake. He closed his arms round her and turned her back to him. With one hand, he loosened the clasp at the nape of her neck and cast it aside. Gazing down at her with scorching golden eyes, he threaded long fingers through her long pale blonde hair and tugged her head back in a gentle motion.

'Tariq—'

'You *want* me.' A lean hand pressed to the shallow indentation of her rigid spine and curved her into intimate contact with his long muscular thighs.

Suddenly it was a challenge to talk and breathe at

the same time. She stared up at him, trying to hold herself rigid but awesomely conscious of the all-pervasive strength of his powerful physique. *'No—'*

'You're trembling—'

'I'm cold!' Faye scarcely knew what she was saying any more. That close to Tariq, her mind was a sea of confusion and her own physical reactions took over.

'Cold?' Tariq lowered his proud dark head, his breath fanning her cheek, the evocative timbre of his low-pitched drawl sentencing her to stillness. 'Who are you trying to fool?'

Feeling weak as water, Faye mumbled, 'Please…'

'Please what?' Tariq brought his wide sensual mouth within inches of hers and somehow made her lips part in invitation, her very breath catching in her throat, her slender length instinctively stretching up to his to get still closer. 'Tell me, please, what?'

The scent of him enveloped her like a sneak invasion by an aphrodisiac. So familiar, so special, so…*him.* Her nostrils flared, head spinning on a released flood of sensuous recall from the past, heat forming in her pelvis, breasts lifting and swelling within the constriction of her cotton bra. It was as if her whole body were burning and melting from inside out, a blind sense of fevered anticipation enthralling her, pitching her high.

'What?' Tariq prompted soft and low, even his dark sexy voice sending a darting quiver of hot response through her.

'Kiss me…' The instant she actually yielded and formed the words, Tariq released his hold on her.

She staggered back on cotton-wool legs, ill-prepared

for staying upright without his support. She blinked like a woman wakening from a disorientating dream.

'As a people we prefer to keep intimacy behind closed doors,' Tariq murmured smooth as silk. 'This office is too public but there is no greater privacy available than that within the harem quarters at Muraaba.'

Faye pressed an unsteady hand against her tingling lips as if she might quiet the sheer craving which still held her taut. 'Harem quarters—?'

'To be a mistress in Jumar is no sinecure and no ticket to freedom or excess. To be *my* mistress is, above all, to be an invisible woman,' Tariq said with a regretful sigh. 'To live behind high walls and locked doors and centre your whole being and your every thought on the man in your life because he truly will be *all* that is in your life. Say goodbye to the world that you know for the foreseeable future.'

Faye was slower to recover from that near embrace than he had been. She had only just reached the point of dying a thousand deaths over the recollection of how she had swayed against him, reached up to him on tiptoes of yearning, begged for his kiss like a brainless programmed doll. He had *made* her want him. With effortless ease and within seconds. She was devastated by that discovery.

'On the other hand, since an aversion to me would not appear to be a sticking point…' Tariq surveyed her with the predatory gaze of a hawk '…you may well be inconsolable when I get tired of you.'

'Harem…you think you're going to put *me* in a

harem?' Faye parroted in a wobbly voice. 'Are you out of your mind to suggest such a thing?'

Tariq lounged back against his polished desk. 'Very much in it. Furthermore, since I cannot trust you, your brother will *not* walk free from his prison cell until you have moved in—'

'Tariq—'

He made an unapologetic play of studying the slim gold watch on his wrist. 'I'm afraid your time is up. Unfortunately, I have other people waiting to see me. A car will now convey you to my home—'

'Now?' Frowning in absolute disbelief, Faye just gaped at him.

'Your hotel room was cleared within minutes of your departure from it. Having been informed that your brother may soon be released, your stepfather is already waiting at the prison. You will see neither of your relatives again until our arrangement comes to an end.'

Faye attempted to swallow but the lead weight of incredulity sat like a giant rock at the foot of her throat. 'You're not serious…you can't be serious about *any* of this stuff—'

Tariq strode past her and opened the door for her departure. He gave her a lethal smile that tied a cold hard knot inside her. 'How much of a gambler are you?'

Faye turned pale.

'And how well do you think you ever knew me?'

CHAPTER THREE

FAYE saw a stone bench sited near the side entrance.
From there, she could see the now familiar limousine
waiting outside. To take her to the Muraaba palace? Or
to the airport? Her choice, wasn't it? Essentially, she
was free as a bird. Sitting down, she tried to calm her
seething thoughts.

How well do you think you ever knew me? A body-
blow of a put-down from the male who had almost destroyed her. In spite of her attempts to suppress it, angry
bitterness welled up inside Faye and she laced her trembling hands together. Was it *her* fault that her stepfather
was a con artist? Her own mother had died penniless
but for the roof over her head. Within weeks of Tariq's
defection, Adrian had decided their childhood home
should also be sold.

'OK, sis?' It had been a rhetorical question.

Adrian had had no desire to hear that his sister's heart
had been breaking at the prospect of losing her home.
Nor had he wanted to be reminded that she had hoped
to set up a riding school there or that, deprived of both
stables and paddock, she would have to sell her beloved
horse as well.

But then Faye was not used to putting herself first.
Growing up, she had not been encouraged to think her

needs or wishes should carry the same weight as other people's. But that didn't necessarily mean she was a doormat, did it? How *could* she have argued about the sale of their family home? Her clerical job had not paid enough to cover her share of the maintenance costs. So Adrian had sold house, contents and land to raise capital for his construction firm. He had promised that she would share in the fruits of his success, would undeniably have shared those profits generously had there been any...

And what had Percy done with that half million pounds from Tariq? Pocketed it by forging her signature? Or had Tariq made it even more simple for Percy by making out that cheque in her stepfather's name? Tariq, who thought all women leant on the nearest man for financial support. A 'goodbye and get lost and keep quiet' payment.

Was that what that cheque had been, on his terms? Faye shuddered. Compensation for the wedding that had filled her with pathetic joy and then concluded in the cruellest farce? She folded her arms tightly round herself. She could not bear to think of that day at the embassy. She had truly believed it was her wedding day. But after the ceremony Tariq had turned on her as though she were the lowest form of human life, stamping on her pride, her hopes, her love, devastating her.

'Divorce is easy in my culture,' Tariq had delivered. 'I say in Arabic, "I divorce thee" three times and circle as I say it. Do you want to *watch* me reclaim my freedom again? Do you want me to demonstrate what a sham this ceremony was?'

The savage hurt and humiliation of that day would never leave Faye. The unwilling bridegroom, the arrogant and autocratic prince, outraged even by a wedding that *was* a charade. He had just stomped all over her feelings as if she were nothing, nobody worthy of any consideration. Was it any wonder she hated him?

Yes, she hated Prince Tariq Shazad ibn Zachir. Yet the same frightening physical longing which had deprived her of her wits before still lingered like a bad hangover. Why? She refused to think about that. However, she had not the slightest intention of taking up residence in any harem! Thought that was a good joke, did he? Well, she wasn't quite as wet as she had once been.

Adrian had to be freed from prison before he fell seriously ill. No choice on that count, she told herself. No matter what the cost? And then her strained eyes widened on a sudden realisation: the instant Adrian was on his flight back to London, he would be safe! Tariq had called her a liar and a cheat. So why should she act any differently? Tariq deserved to be double-crossed. Tariq *deserved* to be cheated. For the sin of having the stepfather from hell, she had already paid a high enough price.

'May I be of assistance?'

Faye glanced up to see Latif and she stood up. 'I'd like to make a phone call.'

The little man looked uneasy.

'Even a criminal usually gets one phone call...but maybe not in the civilised and humane country of Jumar,' Faye conceded in a bitter undertone.

Latif flushed and bowed his head. 'Come this way, please.'

He left her alone in an office a few doors down the corridor. She called her stepfather on his portable phone.

'Faye?' Percy demanded loudly. 'Whatever stunt you've pulled, it's working! I haven't had the final word yet but it looks like our Adrian may be walking free this afternoon—'

'Just answer one question for me,' Faye interrupted in a flat little voice. 'The day of the wedding, I gave you an envelope. What did you do with the cheque inside?'

Total silence buzzed on the line.

Percy cleared his throat.

'You took the money, *didn't* you?' Faye pressed in disgust. 'You let Tariq think he could buy me off as if I was a blackmailer too!'

'Adrian's had most of the money without knowing where it came from and stop talking about blackmail, Faye. All I did was try to protect your interests and, if Tariq wanted to pay us off to keep us quiet, why shouldn't I have accepted the money?' her stepfather protested. 'It's all in the family—'

'You're a con man and a thief. You robbed my mother and you ripped off me. Don't insult my intelligence by talking about family!' Faye sent the receiver crashing down again.

Slowly she retraced her steps and walked head held high out into the hot sunshine to climb into the limousine. 'How well do you think you ever knew me?' Tariq had asked. Well, some day soon he might be asking himself just how well *he* had ever known *her*!

The drive out to the Muraaba place took much longer than Faye had expected. Once the city limits were behind them, the desert took over for miles. It was the emptiness that fascinated Faye, then the rise of the rolling shadowed dunes baking below the remorseless heat of mid-morning. Sand and more sand...what a thrill! Had she really been so crazy about Tariq once that she had fondly imagined she could live with all that sand?

In the distance she saw a massive sprawling building surrounded by fortified walls that got higher the closer they got. As the limo approached, a cluster of tribesmen squatting in the shade jumped up to open the gates. Two sets of solid iron gates, Faye noted, one shorter inner pair, the outer so tall they could have kept the sun trapped, she thought fancifully.

Within the walls, terraced gardens of breathtaking beauty stretched up the hillside in every direction. She was blind to them. She was noting the number of guards on duty and reckoning that Tariq's desert palace appeared braced to withstand both imminent seige and invasion. Her heart sank. Her nebulous plan to stage an escape within the next twenty-four hours would be more of a challenge than she had naively hoped.

Shoulders straight, chin tilted, ignoring the curious eyes and the whispers that accompanied her passage, Faye entered the palace. On her way past, soldiers snapped to attention, presented arms and saluted. She drifted on. It would be so easy to develop delusions of grandeur in Jumar, she decided. The Muraaba was a really ancient building, she registered with a grudging stirring of interest. Fantastic mosaic panels in glorious turquoise, green and gold covered every inch of the walls in the great hall that echoed from her footsteps.

A startling cry of pain followed by the shout of a child smashed the tranquillity and made Faye first freeze and then hurry on in search of the source. If a child had been hurt...

Faye came to a halt on the threshold of a room. So appalled was she by the scene which met her gaze, she could not initially accept what she was seeing. Three servants were huddled by the wall wailing and a fourth, a woman, was down on her knees while a small boy struck at her back with a switch. For an instant, Faye waited for one of the staff to intervene and then she realised that nobody was going to intervene and that the victim seemed too scared to protest such treatment.

Faye stalked forward. 'Stop that!'

The little boy in his miniature robes stopped for an instant in surprise and then started again.

'Stop it right this minute!' Faye ordered icily.

The next thing the little horror rushed at *her* with the switch! She bent down and gathered him to her. The switch fell from his hand. Then she held him at a distance from her to let him kick out his tantrum without hurting her or anyone else. He was very young but his little face was screwed up in a mask of uncontrollable rage. 'Let go of me!' he bawled at her. 'Let go, or I will whip you too!'

'I'll put you down when you stop shouting.'

'I am a prince...I am a prince of the blood royal of Jumar!'

'You're a little boy.' But Faye stiffened, now picking

up on the stricken silence surrounding her. She studied the exquisite silk embroidery on the clothing the child wore. He spat at her and she grimaced. '*No* prince of the blood royal would behave like that,' she told him without hesitation.

His bottom lip came out. His big brown eyes suddenly filled with tears. 'I am an ibn Zachir. I am a prince. You do what I tell you…why you not do what I tell you?'

And in that instant he went from being a little monster to being a child, and a distressed and frightened child at that. As he went limp, Faye slowly released her breath in relief that she had won the battle and drew him close. He could not have been more than five years old, maybe not even that. 'Does the prince have a name?'

'Rafi…'

Belatedly conscious that an outraged parent might descend on her at any minute, that she was in a foreign country with a very different culture and that for all she knew even the tiniest royal children were encouraged to beat servants all the time, Faye attempted to set the boy down again. Disconcertingly, he clung like a limpet.

Faye felt something touch her toes. She peered down over Prince Rafi's back. His female victim was sobbing at Faye's feet. The other servants were now lying face down on the floor as if they were waiting on a bomb dropping or someone shouting, 'Off with their heads!' She felt like an alien set down without warning in very dangerous territory.

'Sleepy…' Rafi told her round his thumb.

'Will someone put Rafi...I mean, His Royal Highness down for a nap?' Faye asked with the weak hope that someone spoke some English.

'Nurse...I am nurse.' It was the lady cowering at her ankles.

'It is wrong and unkind to hurt people, Rafi.' Faye sighed.

'He no mean hurt,' his nursemaid muttered fearfully.

'Rafi sleepy...' He snuggled his silky dark head under her chin. 'Lady take Rafi to bed?'

Well, hopefully that would get everybody up and moving again, Faye decided.

'My horse flies faster than the wind,' Rafi told her sleepily as she carried him from the room.

She resisted the urge to ask if he beat the horse too. 'I love horses.'

'I show you my horse.'

It was a long trek through passageways, a positive procession for they seemed to gather servants and grow into a crowd on the way. And with every covert marvelling look that came her way, every awestruck appraisal that suggested she was doing something extraordinary, Faye's frown grew. It was one weird household. She might possess the stepfather from hell but Tariq had got nothing to boast about on his *own* home front. Did he beat his servants too? Her tummy turned over at that image.

Finally they arrived in Rafi's bedroom which was just stuffed with every imaginable toy and indulgence. Spoilt little brat, Faye thought, refusing to be softened by the child's sweet innocence asleep. But some adult must surely first have taught such brutality by example, she conceded heavily. A parent? Evidently, Tariq shared his huge palace with his extended family. No wonder he was talking about stashing her like a guilty secret in a harem! No way was she staying in the Muraaba palace!

With that conviction in mind and ignoring the servants following never more than a dozen feet from her, Faye explored until she found a room literally walled with packed bookshelves. Her search took some time but eventually she found a map of Jumar which had the airport clearly marked. Noticing that the airport appeared to be a much greater distance from the city than it actually was, she assumed that it was an older map for the city had grown much larger in more recent times.

Concealing the map in her bag, she settled down in a magnificent reception room on a low traditional divan. Refreshments were brought to her there. More grovelling, all the staff seeming so scared and desperate to please. At the same time, her dazed eyes roamed over the spectacular exoticism of her surroundings. Rich geometrical patterns of faience tiles adorned the walls, some of which were even studded with what appeared to be precious stones, and the elaborate domed ceiling far above appeared to be composed of tiny coloured glittering mirror-glass mosaics. Superb Persian rugs lay on the pale marble floor. The divan on which she sat was covered with hand-painted precious silk. This was where Tariq had grown up, she found herself thinking, against a fantastic and opulent backdrop so dissimilar to hers, it took her breath away.

A wave of what appeared to be collective anxiety sent the maids into retreat a mere minute before Faye heard a man's footsteps echoing in the main hall. Seconds later, Tariq strode in and stilled to view her.

His lean, strong face was taut. 'Latif has informed me that there had been some incident between you and Rafi—'

Eyes flaring with anger as she recalled the shocking episode she had witnessed earlier, Faye shot to her feet in full defensive mode. 'So someone has complained about my behaviour, have they? Well, let me tell you, you had better get me on a plane home because I have no plans to stand by and watch any child or indeed any adult beating servants!'

His superb bone structure clenched hard. 'Say that again—'

'You mean once wasn't enough? What sort of primitive country is this? What kind of a society allows a small child to behave like that?'

Pale with anger beneath his bronze skin, Tariq breathed. 'Are you telling me that Rafi struck one of the household staff?'

Breathing in deep, Faye described the scene she had interrupted in a few pithy words.

'Rafi is mine to deal with,' Tariq growled, the darkening of outrage accentuating his bold cheekbones. 'We are *not* a primitive country. I will have you know that assault is assault in Jumar, no matter who the victim or who the perpetrator. I am very grateful that you intervened but do not judge a whole people by the behaviour of my obnoxious little brother!'

'L-little brother?' Her cheeks were now glowing red as fire. 'Rafi is your little brother? But if what you are saying is true, why didn't someone step in to assert control over him?'

'*Who*? My father died when he was three. His mother died six months ago. She was an evil-tempered woman from another Gulf state.' His stunning dark eyes had a grim light. 'She taught Rafi to behave as he does. The servants who look after him were *hers* and the spirit was knocked out of them long before they accompanied their mistress to Jumar. They would never dare to try and restrain Rafi. It is an offence to lay hands on anyone of royal blood—'

'Is it?'

'That law was not made to allow a child to rampage out of control! I was reluctant to deprive Rafi of the nursemaids who have looked after him since he was a baby but I see now, it must be done. He *has* to be taught how to behave.'

'What age is he?'

'Four...old enough and bright enough to know better. I shall deal with him.' Tariq headed for the door like a male with a target and a definite purpose in mind.

Faye rushed after him. 'What are you going to do?'

'I can see what you *think* I'm going to do but you're wrong,' Tariq spelt out in impatient reproof as he read her anxious expression. 'I may know little about children but I hope I know enough not to repay violence with violence. I will talk to him and remove certain privileges as a punishment.'

'I'm sorry about what I said a moment ago. It's just

I was upset about the whole thing…but Rafi's awfully young and, having lost both his parents, probably very unhappy—'

'I know these things but I also fear that he has his mother's cruelty in him.'

Left standing, Faye chewed at her lower lip, wondering why she felt so troubled and why on earth she should feel so involved. It was nothing to do with her and she was certainly no authority on childcare. However, she was terribly relieved that Tariq had been furious about the episode which she had witnessed. At least, she hadn't been *totally* wrong about his character the year before when she had honestly believed that, with very little effort, he might walk on water…

FOURTEEN MONTHS AGO, Adrian had been invited to his commanding officer's wedding at which Tariq had been the guest of honour. Heavily pregnant at the time, Lizzie had decided to stay home and Adrian had asked Faye to accompany him instead.

'Come on, sis,' Adrian reproved when she tried to turn him down. 'Since Mum died, all you've done is hang out with horses. I *know* you're shy but you need to get out occasionally.'

The day of the wedding, Adrian's car refused to start and, much to his dismay, they had to use Faye's ancient little hatchback instead. A poor passenger, her brother honed her nerves to screaming point during that drive. Her less than pleasant day out then got going with a real bang when, stressed beyond belief in her efforts to find a parking space at the church, she reversed her car into Tariq's stretch limo.

As aghast as if she had killed somebody, Adrian leapt out and started shouting at her. 'What do you mean you didn't *see* it? It's as big as the blasted *Titanic*!'

Welded to the bonnet of her car to stay upright and shaking with reaction, Faye stared in even greater horror at the dark-skinned excitable men erupting out of the limo. Then the passenger door opened and Tariq climbed out with unhurried grace. Silencing his bodyguards, he strolled across the tarmac to where her brother, who had his back turned to him, was still ranting.

'How could you do something so stupid?' Adrian was seething.

But Faye's attention had already been captured by the tall, dark, incredibly handsome male smiling at her. A smile that literally *talked*. Sympathetic, concerned, charming. Her heart started beating very fast. From his wonderful smile, her gaze travelled upward to encounter spectacular lion gold eyes that made her feel breathless, boneless and pretty much mindless too. Within seconds of first seeing Prince Tariq Shazad ibn Zachir, Faye was mesmerised.

Ignoring Adrian, Tariq strode straight to her side. 'You're suffering from shock. You *must* sit down.'

'B-but…but your car—'

'It is nothing. Please do not consider it.'

He urged her back to his limo where a guard already had a door open. Guiding her down on to the edge of the leather seat, he murmured something in his own language in aside and then said to her, 'Try to calm your-self. Nothing that need concern you has happened.'

'Your Royal Highness...er...' Adrian began in a strained and apologetic undertone from behind him '...Prince Tariq...my sister... er...well, I'll see to her, no need for you to be bothered...'

'Thank you but I am not easily bothered.' Tariq passed a crystal tumbler of iced mineral water into Faye's hand. He gazed down into her eyes and her heart-beat went so far into earthquake mode she felt literally dizzy. He smiled again. Straightening, he then turned to extend a hand to her brother and speak to him.

It was Adrian who then hurried Faye back out of the limo. Walking away from Tariq, all Faye was able to think about was whether she would ever get to speak to him again. She felt...*sent*, no longer grounded on solid earth. Butterflies in her tummy and excitement pulsing through her in a crazy flood.

'I've never thought about it before but I suppose you *are* quite beautiful.' Her brother treated her to a frown-ing appraisal inside the church. 'Nothing like looks sav-ing your skin, sis! You reversed into a giant stationary vehicle that a blind man could have avoided. Yet His Royal Highness chose to insist that *his* limo was parked in the wrong place, that non-existent sunlight must have reflected off your mirror and that *he* will pay for the repairs to your car!'

'Oh...is he...is he really a prince?' she muttered.

'About as real as they come,' Adrian said drily. 'Commander-in-chief of his own army and acting feu-dal ruler of the Gulf state of Jumar. Hamza, his father, is supposed to be on his last legs and Prince Tariq has already taken on all of the old man's public engagements abroad.'

Her heart sank at that dismaying confirmation for even the smallest spark of common sense warned that a male of that status was out of her reach, but still curiosity had to be quenched. 'Married?'

'No. What's that to you?'

'I was just wondering. He's awfully nice—'

'Nice?' Adrian grimaced. 'Look, I may not have actually spoken to the chap before today but, according to what I've heard, he's faster than a jump jet with women! Thankfully, you're far too young to interest him.'

'Too young? I'm nineteen next month!'

'Oh, wow…' Adrian rolled his eyes, unimpressed. 'Well, you're still safe as houses. I doubt that Prince Tariq is the kind of creep who takes advantage of starry-eyed kids!'

A fateful and unfortunate conversation which within the space of hours led to the first outright lie which Faye had told since she had outgrown childish fibbing. At the reception, Adrian soon abandoned her for the more convivial company of his fellow officers and Tariq strolled over to speak to her. 'May I join you?'

And even a year on, Faye had to admit that lying never came so easily or so naturally to her again. For the first time in her life she wanted to impress a man and *not* with the image of some starry-eyed kid, and she knew she had only that one chance for there was little likelihood that they would ever meet again.

'Hardly anybody knows you here but one who does

referred to you as a teenager.' Tariq made that lazy comment only after asking her if she was fully recovered from the episode in the church car park.

'People really do lose track of the passage of time when they don't see you for a few years.' Hugely aware of his lustrous dark golden eyes resting on her, she ran far from idle fingers through the glossy fall of her silvery fair hair. She knew he could barely drag his admiring attention from her crowning glory and she gave him what she hoped was a mature and yet teasing smile. 'I may not be that tall but I'm actually twenty-three years old.'

'You don't look it,' he murmured frankly.

'That's the fresh country girl bloom,' she told him, batting her eyelashes.

And that was it, that was how easy it had been. Her sole objective had been that she should not be excluded from attracting his interest by her age alone. She had not thought further than that, had foreseen no potential problems in the future because at that point, before he'd even asked her out, it had not occurred to her that they might *have* a future of any kind.

'I would like to see you again,' he said then.

'When?' she prompted, ditching her attempt at older woman cool.

Tariq stilled in surprise and then the beginnings of an amused smile tugged at the corners of his beautiful mouth. 'Wait and see.'

And the roses began arriving the next day. White roses every day, white roses that filled the house with their rich perfume. No card but she knew, of course she knew, they were from him and she dreamed away every hour, leapt every time the phone rang, but it took him a week to call her.

'Tell him you're booked up!' Lizzie printed on the phone pad when she realised Faye was speaking to Tariq.

Faye gave her sister-in-law an agonised look. At the shortest possible notice, she would have walked barefoot all the way to London in a thunderstorm to see Tariq!

'I'm sorry, I can't make it…'

Perhaps another time, Lizzie mouthed at her to repeat and made shocking faces at her until she did so.

'You've got a lot to learn, kiddo.' Her sister-in-law groaned when Faye was in tears after Tariq rang off without having suggested an alternative. 'If you want to be kissed off after one date, go ahead and show him how keen you are!'

Only four years older than Faye, Lizzie thought it was all a terrific laugh. When Tariq called Adrian and invited the entire family out to dinner instead, it was also Lizzie who took her husband aside before they went out the following evening to warn Adrian not to drop Faye in it with Tariq about her age.

'I don't like the fact you've lied at all.' Adrian looked at his hot-faced sister with surprise and strong disapproval.

'Give it a rest, Adrian.' Percy backed Faye up and startled her. 'It's not like this little flirtation is likely to go anywhere, is it? Not with him being a *royal* prince. Let your sister enjoy herself. If a squeaky clean night

out for the whole flippin' family is this bloke's idea of
a hot date, what have you got to worry about?'

In the weeks which followed, Faye worked very hard
at telling herself that there was no future in any relationship with Tariq but it did not stop her falling head
over heels in love with him. Indeed, realising just how
much she loved him soon made her feel very vulnerable
and increasingly desperate. Once his father died, she
was convinced that she would be ditched and forgotten about because Tariq would be spending more time
in Jumar than abroad. Believing that her time with him
was running out, believing she was never going to love
anyone the way she loved him, she reached an impulsive decision that subsequently proved to be the biggest
mistake of her life.

It was so ironic, Faye reflected in mortification as
she returned to the present in the tranquil beauty of the
Muraaba palace: a year ago, Tariq had sounded so utterly shocked when she'd invited him to spend the night
at her home and made it clear that they would be quite
alone there. But it was really his own fault that her stupid and unwise invitation had not led to *any* actual intimacy.

Nervous as she had been, she had tried to create a
special ambience for a romantic evening with the man
she had loved. The very last thing she had wanted was
a guy who showed up late and crushed her tender naïve
expectations by saying things like, 'I won't be staying
all night. I never do when I am with a woman.'

Or: 'Why must we eat now? I am more likely to be
hungry *after* sex than before it.'

And finally: 'How many *other* men have you done this with?'

At what had to have been the ultimate put-down for a virgin, Faye had spilled wine all over herself, burst into floods of tears and raced upstairs. Sticky and reeking of alcohol, she had got into the shower to wash. When she had returned to her bedroom, wrapped only in a bath towel, Tariq had been waiting there. Mere minutes later, Percy had walked in on them and the trap as such had snapped shut without her even appreciating the fact for she had fled back to the bathroom in embarrassment and Tariq had left the house by the time she'd emerged again.

Faye closed her eyes and literally flinched from her memories. What a total idiot she had been to throw herself at Tariq like that! Carried away by her own imagination, she had begun behaving as if she were involved in some great tragic love affair. She had refused to see that that affair as such had existed only in her own head. The humiliating truth was that, in spite of a series of incredibly romantic outings, Tariq had never mentioned love. Indeed, apart from a few light kisses and a little discreet hand-holding, she might well have been a platonic friend. So it was hardly surprising that, after such minor flirtation, Tariq had been pretty taken aback when she'd suddenly chosen to surrender to her own far more passionate inclinations and asked him to spend the night with her! Resting back against the comfortable cushions, Faye slowly drifted to sleep on uneasy acknowledgements that still filled her with pain and deep, deep chagrin.

FAYE WOKE UP, DIMLY conscious of motion, of being too warm, yet of feeling strangely secure in the arms that held her. *Arms?*

'Be still…' As she stirred Tariq's dark deep-timbred drawl sounded, commanding even when quiet, she noted without surprise.

'What…wh-where?' Her eyes opened in the same instant as he laid her down on a comfortable yielding surface. She had a hazy impression of a big sunlit room but the recognition of the reality that she was on a huge canopied bed hit her with more striking effect. At incredible speed, she reared up off the pillows and flipped backwards off the bed again, landing upright like a trained gymnast.

From the far side of the mattress, Tariq surveyed her with transfixed golden eyes. Then he shook his dark head slightly as if he was questioning what he had just witnessed.

'Lucky fall…' Faye was furious and embarrassed by her own instinctive and childish reaction. The couple who had looked after her late mother had at one time been circus performers. As a child, with a brother who was frequently ill and a parent who had bad days too, Faye had spent a lot of time with Pearl and Stan. To keep her amused, the kindly couple had taught her some of their skills.

His aristocratic brows drew together. 'How…and why did you do that?'

How? She didn't want to answer that for there was nothing very cool or sophisticated about circus tricks in the bedroom. But her heart hammered, her mouth running dry on that second question. *Why*? Why did he have to be so gorgeous? Why did her rebellious brain throw up a mental image of them entwined in loverlike intimacy on that silk-draped decadent bed? Lust, her conscience told her in reproof, while her gaze rested on his lean, powerful face and, without her seeming volition, widened to take in inch by appreciative inch his long, lithe, muscular physique. The heat she despised sparked a licking, taunting flame in her pelvis. She reddened, shifted her feet, pressed her thighs together in a desperate effort to quench that treacherous response.

'You frightened me,' she condemned on a sudden brainwave, hoping to shift the focus of the dialogue from her acrobatic talents.

'How did I frighten you?' Tariq threw his proud dark head back, a level challenge etched in his darkly handsome features.

He was fairly leaping for the red herring she had proffered. But, in a sense, it was true that he frightened her, Faye acknowledged ruefully. However, it was her own lack of control she feared and his power over her. She just looked at him and he sent her traitorous body haywire. Intelligence didn't get a look-in. She did not need to ask herself why she had turned herself into a lying pushover a year ago!

'Under no circumstances would I ever hurt a woman.' As Tariq made that declaration, feverish colour scored his hard cheekbones.

It was extraordinary but he made her feel guilty. Faye backed away from the bed and moved her hands in a rueful dismissive motion. 'I don't want to be here and you know that—'

Tariq now viewed her with steady cool. 'You made the choice.'

'Between a rock and a hard place?'

'Welcome to how I felt on the day of our wedding. Trapped like an animal!' Tariq spelt out, shocking her with that allusion. 'No choice but to accede to the *lesser* evil of marrying you. My father was dying. You knew that. What a comfort it would have been for him to learn in his last week of life that his son and heir had been exposed in some English tabloid as the sordid seducer of a teenage girl!'

Her lashes lowered, her lovely face bled free of colour. 'But you *didn't*—'

'I need no reminder of that fact.' Venting a derisive laugh, Tariq strolled forward to capture both her hands in his. He tugged her to him as easily as if she had been a doll. 'What are the odds of my letting you go untouched a second time? A billion to one?'

The atmosphere sizzled. Tension curled her every nerve-ending. 'Tariq…'

He released her hands and framed her flushed cheekbones with splayed fingers instead. Molten gold eyes inspected her with hungry precision. His intense gaze enthralled her. She breathed in brief rapid bursts. Excitement was shivering through her in delicious little waves. Excitement was rising in her as fast as her body temperature. Excitement that literally consumed every rational thought.

One hand pushing into her hair, he ran a sensual

forefinger along the line of her full lower lip, watched her pupils dilate, her moist pink lips part. And then he met that invitation with the hot devouring hunger of his mouth. For her, the effect was instant conflagration. Every skin cell charged up on the passion he had never shown her before and just went wild. Her hands slid beneath his suit jacket, found silk shirt, clawed it away, finally reached skin, warm, smooth skin covering hard whipcord muscles. She felt him shudder against her, all potent male power and promise, and she melted with liquid longing.

Tariq moulded his hands to the feminine curve of her hips and hauled her closer still, crushing her sensitised breasts to the hard wall of his chest. Low in her throat she moaned acquiescence to the plunging penetration of his tongue. On fire, she gasped, shivering violently, out of control, mindless...*ecstatic*. With a driven groan, Tariq dragged her back from him.

'I can't stay...' He breathed thickly.

She swayed, passion-glazed eyes locked to him. 'You can't stay?'

'I found you asleep and carried you to bed but I only came home to change. I have *Majilis* to attend this afternoon.' Stunning eyes fully screened by his lush black lashes, he was already endeavouring to straighten the clothing she had disarranged and smooth his tousled black hair.

Faye breathed in so deep she thought the top of her head might fly off to release the surplus air. Disbelief held her fast but she didn't even know what he was talking about. 'You...you have *Majilis*...you're going out?'

Tariq flashed her a rather sardonic look of amusement. He shrugged back his wide shoulders with sensual cool. His slow-burning smile mocked her. 'Only minutes ago you told me you didn't want to be here. You change direction like the wind. Even I did not expect a single kiss to win the battle...'

Faye might as well have been turned to stone by that speech. She closed her eyes: she dared not look at him lest he saw her raging mortification. She was drowning in self-loathing but still she could feel the pulsing ache of the hunger he had roused in her. How dared he speak to her like that? How dared he gloat?

'So you think you're irresistible?'

'No...*you* make me feel irresistible. Small distinction,' Tariq contradicted on his fluid passage to the door. 'You're hot for me. I'm sure other men have enjoyed the same response. But, right now, you're mine alone.'

'Do you know how much I hate you?' Faye snapped, her hands knotting into defensive fists.

'Why would I care? What is that to me?' Arrogant head thrown back, his dark deep-set gaze pierced her like an ice dagger. 'I want to possess you. I want to lie with you all through the night and make love to you as and when I want. But that is *all* I want from you.'

CHAPTER FOUR

LONG after Tariq had gone, Faye stared at the door, her fingernails still biting sharp crescents into her palms. His honesty had devastated her. Sex was all he wanted. For goodness' sake, had she expected him to confess to a tortured longing to know her heart and her mind instead? And why on earth did she feel so hurt by that admission of his? It was not as if she still *cared* about him. In fact, it was ridiculous for her to still be so sensitive!

A light knock sounded on a door at the other side of the room and she spun round. A pair of smiling young girls, who bore little resemblance to the crushed individuals in little Prince Rafi's retinue, entered.

'We are Shiran and Meyla. Your lunch is ready, my lady,' one of them informed her shyly.

Faye discovered that through that second door lay a whole host of other apartments, each as exquisitely appointed as the next. Was she in the harem? It scarcely mattered. Now that her adrenalin was leaping again, all she could think about was escape. Presented with a fabulous array of dishes all laid out on a low table in a superb reception room next door, Faye sat down to eat. Checking her watch and seeing that it was almost two in the afternoon, she then asked for a phone.

Once again, she dialled the number of her stepfather's portable phone.

'Faye? Adrian's out!' Percy sounded immensely cheerful. 'We're at the airport—'

'Good. How soon will you be on a flight home?'

'Another half-hour. Look, I can't talk long. Adrian's in a shop but he'll be back in a minute. I told him that you flew back home this morning. He wouldn't agree to leave Jumar if he knew the truth,' Percy admitted without a shred of embarrassment.

'You're really worried about me, aren't you?' Helpless bitterness tinged Faye's unusually sarcastic response.

'Come on, Faye. It's my bet you're in the lap of luxury right now and it's not like His Royal Highness is some bloke you don't fancy! Let's face it, you've been a right wet weekend ever since he dumped you—'

Faye closed her eyes and said, 'I just don't believe I'm hearing this—'

'Well, now you finally got your prince, so I don't see why you should be complaining or feeling sorry for yourself.' Percy was warming to his theme, having rationalised events to his own satisfaction. 'I think our Adrian has done you a favour.'

'Thanks…thanks a bundle!' Riven with resentment, Faye slung aside the phone in disgust.

Escaping from the Muraaba palace would be a challenge. She had two options, neither of which struck her as that promising. Borrow a horse and try to sneak out in disguise or conceal herself in a car that was about to leave. First, she asked Shiran if the palace had stables and where they were and then she made a series of requests. The maids' eyes widened in surprise and confusion at the items she asked to be brought to her but they went off to do her bidding.

Her suitcase arrived, along with the food and bottled mineral water she had requested and the set of male robes and the headdress. Those last two demands were fulfilled with a great deal of giggling curiosity. Maybe the maids thought she was going to try and dress up as a man and spring some stupid childish prank on Tariq, not to mention a less than inviting midnight feast of bread and water.

Finally alone, Faye changed into trousers and a shirt and crammed the supplies along with her passport into her capacious backpack. A courtyard lay outside her bedroom. Using the elaborate wall fountain there as a foothold, Faye climbed the perimeter wall. Never having had the slightest fear of heights, she could have walked the wall blindfold. Traversing it, she continued along the walls of the eerily empty courtyards next to her own. Forced to climb higher at one point, she crossed a balcony so that she could ease herself down onto the flat parapet surrounding a giant domed roof.

Progress was slow but only twice did she have to risk touching ground level again to cross between buildings. Perched on the low sloping stable roof, she watched a couple of grooms leading a magnificent black horse out into a big flashy motorised horsebox. Bingo! She dropped down onto the cobbles in a shadowy corner and donned the robes she had in her backpack. Then she waited for a chance to board the horsebox.

When the men paused to talk, she made a run for it. Hurrying up the ramp into the box, she saw there was only that one horse on board. Startled by her entrance, the stallion threw up his head, his hooves clattering and banging on the boards. Faye dived into the furthest stall and crouched down to hide herself as best she could.

The ramp went up with a hydraulic hiss and minutes later doors slammed and the engine fired. The horsebox rocked over the cobbles, making the stallion fuss even more. Halting, presumably for the gates to be opened, the vehicle then turned, not towards the city as she had hoped, but in the other direction. Oh, great, she thought in exasperation. So now she would most probably have to take the horse as well. No way would she try hitching a lift in a country where, outside of the city, absolutely nobody seemed to walk.

How far would Tariq go in an effort to retrieve her? Might he simply shrug with fatalistic acceptance and just let her go? Faye recalled the look on his face when he'd mentioned those cold showers and felt hot all over. No, Tariq would not be cool about her vanishing act. All over again, she would be damning herself in his eyes. Refusing to concede that she was welching on their agreement, she grimaced at the noisy fretful movements of the stallion. Arabians were highly strung and *this* was the horse she was planning to steal and ride if need be?

The horsebox ground to a slow, jolting halt. Of course, they were stopping; the stallion was becoming frantic. Standing up, she approached his stall, talking in a low, soothing voice, calming him with confident hands. He was very responsive. She heard the ramp being unbolted. Holding the stallion's reins with one hand, she undid the gate of his stall. Was she *mad* to take such a risk? But the stallion was already surging forward, eager to leave a confinement he clearly hated, and without further hesitation Faye threw herself up into the magnificent leather saddle.

What happened next was just a blur. The hydraulic ramp went down and full daylight flooded in, momentarily blinding her. She had a fleeting impression of startled dark faces but by that stage the stallion was already plunging out past them, heading like a bullet for the flat salt plain that bounded the layby in which the horsebox had parked.

Faye gave the beautiful animal his head and let him gallop. It wasn't as if she didn't know where she was for she had studied that map in detail. Basically all she had to do was stay out of sight of the road and skirt the edge of the desert until she reached the city limits. At some stage she would have to pass the horse over to someone to be returned to the palace but that was really her only source of concern.

She was surprised by the strength of the breeze that blew her hair back from her face. However, it felt wonderful after the claustrophobic interior of the horsebox. Even so, it was still incredibly hot and she stopped to open her backpack and, disdaining the male head covering, she covered her head with a scarf. She noticed then that there was a faint haze over the sun.

Within the first sweltering hour, the salt plain gave way to sand and their pace slowed, but that was only what she had expected. However, when the landscape began changing again from sand and scrub to dunes that began to build from almost imperceptible rises in ground level into gradually steeper gradients, Faye's brow pleated in dismay. She had not been prepared to see deep dunes on the careful route she had traced for the simple reason that there was none close to Jumar City. Obviously she had drifted too far out into the desert.

Stark unease assailed Faye. But for the rushing sound of the wind that was getting steadily stronger, the silence beat at her ears. The light seemed to be fading, only it couldn't be, she told herself, for it was barely five in the evening. She had at least three more hours of daylight, plenty of time in which to complete her journey. However, the sun now lay behind a peculiar reddish haze and dark clouds were gathering in a sky as grey as a stormy sea.

So it was going to rain, she thought, possibly even a full thunder and lightning job. The stallion snorted and jerked, a nervous ripple running through his powerful haunches. Of his own volition, he broke into a canter, resisting her efforts to pull him back. He was far too strong for her to hold and he plunged wildly up the side of a steep dune. That was when she heard the thwack-thwack sound of an approaching helicopter above the wind.

'Calm down, boy...' she urged as the horse began to buck.

She tried to hang on but she was thrown and she hit the sand like a stone. The silky soft grains provided an unexpectedly hard surface and she was winded. By the time she caught her breath, removed the backpack which was digging into her spine and began to rise to her feet, the helicopter had landed and a male figure was striding towards her.

It was Tariq, but Tariq as she had never seen him before. She had the momentary sense of time having slipped back for before her stood a male who was every inch an Arabian prince in his regal splendour. He was sheathed in black gold-edged robes, worn over a pristine cream undershirt, a *kaffiyeh* covering his proud head, his clothing flowed back from his hard, muscular physique in the teeth of the buffeting wind. She collided with blazing golden eyes that had an electrifying effect on her already leaping nerves. Behind him, obedient as a pet dog and now infuriatingly calm, trotted the black stallion.

'Are you insane to run into the desert in a sandstorm?' Tariq roared at her with raw force. 'But you will suffer now too for I will not leave Omeir here to die—'

'Sandstorm…d-die?' Faye stammered in shock.

Tariq was already swinging round and vaulting up onto the stallion's back. Omeir was the *horse*, she worked out. Leaning down, Tariq hauled her up in front of him in a manoeuvre that made her awesomely aware of his masculine strength, not to mention his superior horsemanship. His sense of balance was superb.

'Tariq…how did you—?'

'Keep quiet!' he bit out above her head. 'Don't you realise how much danger we're in?'

As he sent the stallion leaping forward at a break-neck speed, she caught a last glimpse of the helicopter sitting abandoned on the sand. Danger? Yet he had come for her alone. Sandstorm? The sky *was* beginning to glow the most spooky red. Involuntarily, she shivered, clutching her backpack beneath her arm. Omeir galloped full spate along a *wadi* between the dunes. The wind lashed her cheeks, carrying grit that stung and dust that made breathing a choking challenge. She bent her head, closed her eyes. *He's* not getting away with doing that, so why should you? Guilt almost ate her alive at that point.

A little while later, she squinted from beneath the scarf she had pulled down over her brow. A whirling terrifying wall of sand the height of the sky was folding in. The sand already borne on the wind was fast reducing visibility but she saw the big dark irregular shape of a rocky outcrop looming ahead. Shelter? Barely thirty seconds later, Tariq swept her up and dropped her down onto the sand and, for a stricken moment, she honestly thought he had decided to dump her because her weight was slowing him and Omeir down too much.

Plunged into craven panic, trying to stay upright in a gale threatening to blast her off her feet, she cried, *'Tariq?'*

'Move!' Tariq was already behind her and only as he thrust her forward did she register that the mouth of a cave lay directly ahead of them.

Faye stumbled into the sandy interior on legs as weak as paper straws. Omeir surged deeper into the cave to stand sweating and shivering. Faye turned round just in time to see an uprooted date palm pitch into view and land only a few yards outside the cave. She fought to catch her breath in the sand-laden air, eyes huge, shaken face pale. Until that moment, she had not appreciated just how violent and destructive a sandstorm could be.

'You might have killed us both...you might have killed Omeir. Though he knows this oasis well, he was too frightened to find his way here on his own!' Closing a hand over her taut shoulder to steady her, Tariq pressed her through a break in the rock walls. 'The ground falls steeply here...watch your step.'

The passage opened out into another cave. The first thing Faye noticed with relief was the improved quality of the air and then she recognised the unmistakable sound of flowing water.

But for the pale linen of his undershirt glimmering in the darkness, she could hardly see Tariq. Feeling her way along the rough wall with a trembling hand, she dropped her backpack and slowly sank down onto the sandy floor. The last thing she expected and probably the last thing she wanted just then was for Tariq to strike a match and light an oil lamp.

She blinked in disconcertion. Flickering light illuminated soaring pillars of ancient rock and the glimmering pool of water refreshed by an underground stream. It also showed her a sight which at any other moment would have struck her as pure comedy: Omeir virtually squeezing his girth through the same passage by which they had entered and trotting over for a noisy drink at the rock pool.

With pronounced reluctance, Faye focused on Tariq.

'Obviously you and wonder horse have been here before.'

Tariq slung aside his gold-bound *kaffiyeh*, luxuriant black hair tousled above his hard, bronzed, dusty features. She literally saw his even white teeth grit. He dropped down lithely by the edge of the water and splashed his face, using the cloth he had flung down as a towel. 'So it amuses you to be sarcastic and flippant when you have done wrong…that is no surprise to me.'

This time, it was Faye's teeth that gritted. It had been an incredibly long day and she ached in places she had not known she could ache. More galling still, that exhausting ride into the desert had been a *total* waste of time and effort. Emotions already high after what she had endured, hot temper now bolted through her at the speed of light. His tone was so outrageously pious and superior, she leapt upright again with clenched fists. 'Go on…call me a cheat and a liar for trying to—'

'Run away?'

'I wasn't running away!' Faye launched at him even louder, pride stung by that label. 'You gave me no choice. You forced me—'

'I forced nothing. You agreed to my terms.'

Soft, full mouth tightening, Faye ignored that succinct and unwelcome reminder. 'My *departure* was my way of letting you know that, just like you, I won't surrender to blackmail—'

'I did not employ blackmail in any form.' Rising to his full imposing height, fabulous cheekbones taut, Tariq subjected her to a scorching appraisal. 'Give me one good reason why I should have agreed to settle your brother's debts and demanded nothing in return!'

At that blunt invitation, Faye simply saw red. Percy's smug words on the phone earlier had stung her pride like acid. In speedy succession, she recalled every piece of hurt and humiliation she had suffered since first meeting Prince Tariq ibn Zachir. Then she breathed in so deep, she trembled and gave him on her terms what she considered to be one very good reason. 'After what you did to me a year ago, I don't think it would have been such a big deal for you to give me one free favour!'

Tariq elevated an imperious brow. 'What *I* did to *you*?'

'You turned what should have been the happiest day of my life into a nightmare! You don't even know what I'm talking about, do you?' Faye's voice shook on that realisation. 'I'm talking about my wedding day. You asked me to marry you. You let me put on a wedding dress and wear something blue—'

'Something blue?' Tariq questioned with frowning bewilderment. 'What is this "something blue"?'

'And all the time you knew that you were going to turn right round and divorce me straight after the ceremony. Not because you'd had a change of heart but because you had planned it that way from the start!' Faye's long-repressed sense of injustice was now rising as fast as her voice pitch. 'You asked me to marry you but you didn't *mean* one word of that proposal. I trusted you but you betrayed my trust.'

In receipt of that condemnation, Tariq strode forward, his gaze flaming molten gold. 'How you can accuse me of betrayal when you conspired with your stepfather to set me up for blackmail?'

'I just did accuse you, didn't I?' Finally getting to stage the confrontation her pride had demanded but been denied on the day of that wedding, Faye stood her ground. She had no intention of getting dragged down into the murky waters of Percy's opportunistic blackmail attempt because, no matter what Tariq believed, she had had nothing to do with that development. 'I married you in good faith—'

'Yet you made *no* attempt to dissuade me from divorcing you.'

'I beg your pardon?' Faye was totally taken aback by that statement.

'Did you even ask me to forgive you?'

'F-f-forgive me?' Faye got out with the greatest of difficulty, so shattered was she by the nature of that question. He had twisted the whole topic round and now he was throwing it back to her in an unrecognisable guise. Why would she have attempted to persuade him not to divorce her when divorcing her had so evidently been his intent all along?

'No, far from hanging your head in shame and admitting the truth of your greedy deception, you fled at supersonic speed with a cheque clutched in your hot little hand!' His lean, strong face was rigid with icy contempt and hauteur.

'Hanging my head in shame?' Faye enunciated in ringing tones of revulsion.

'You *had* no shame. You protest that you married me in good faith.' Tariq curled his lip. 'But a true wife, a true bride would never have left the embassy. A true wife would ultimately have followed me home.'

'What on earth are you talking about?' Faye was really struggling to comprehend but still failing to follow his reasoning. 'Why would I have followed you home? I was *never* really your wife…where do you get off saying that to me? You divorced me—'

'I did not divorce you.' Tariq's dark, deep drawl rose not one iota above freezing point.

'You didn't?' That declaration really shook Faye, who had always assumed that the dark deed of divorcing her had been done right there in front of her that same day.

'Not then,' Tariq extended with harsh clarity, wide, sensual mouth compressing into a hard, awesomely stubborn line.

Faye folded her arms, striving to look supremely unconcerned by the news that she had not been cast off by divorce quite as immediately as she had believed. 'Well, how would I have known what you were doing that day when you were striding up and down in a roaring rage and ranting mostly in Arabic?'

Tariq froze even more. In fact an ice statue might have revealed more expression than his hard bronzed features did at that moment. 'I did lose my temper to some extent—'

Omeir kept on walking between them, getting in the way of her view of Tariq. Faye circled round the stallion to hiss in retaliation, 'You lit up like Guy Fawkes' night!'

'Now I am seeing the real character you were once so careful to hide from me.' Tariq dealt her a contemptuous appraisal that served merely to heap nourishing coals on her inner fire. 'You are attacking me like a shrew.'

'If I was a shrew, you would have indelible teeth marks all over you and instead you got away *scot-free* with what you did to me!'

'We will not discuss this matter further. Control your temper before I lose mine.'

'I like you better when you lose your temper!'

Having now imposed himself halfway between them like a large clumsy buffer, Omeir snorted, threw up his handsome head and pawed the ground.

'What's the matter with him?' Faye demanded involuntarily.

'All animals react to tension. Omeir has been with me since he was a colt. He knows my every mood and at this moment...my mood is not good,' Tariq spelt out.

'Well, I only have one thing left to say to you.' Angry resentment and pain still licked along Faye's every nerve-ending but she was already regretting hurling revealing recriminations about the marriage that had not been a proper marriage. Now all she cared about was conserving her own pride. 'I was really, really glad when I thought you divorced me. In fact I wasn't out of that embassy an hour before I appreciated what a lucky escape I had had! I can imagine no greater misery than to be married to a pious, judgmental louse like you!'

Electrified tension written into every taut line of his stance, Tariq studied her. The atmosphere sizzled hot as coals. 'Is that a fact?'

Faye flung back her head, shimmering pale hair rippling back from her pink cheeks. 'Does that hurt your ego, Tariq?'

'Not at all.' Tariq strolled forward like a prowling predator, his spectacular eyes smouldering gold in his hard-boned features. 'You are mine any time I want you and I do *not* wish to retain you as my wife.'

'Any time you want me—?' Her infuriated repetition of that bold assertion broke off in a startled squawk as Tariq caught her hands in his and pulled her to him, clamping her into intimate contact with his lean, powerful frame with easy strength.

'Yes…'

Raising her to him, he brought his demanding mouth down on hers with explosive force. Heat that had nothing to do with her temper set her alight. Shock shrilled through her quivering length, the kind of sensual shock her treacherous body exulted in. She closed her arms round his neck, let her fingers surge up into the silky black hair she loved. And all the time, stoked by the raw eroticism of every plundering passionate kiss, her excitement built higher and higher. She pushed helplessly against him to ease the throbbing sensitivity of her breasts, the taunting ache low in her belly.

With an abruptness that startled her, Tariq wrenched her back from him, breathing thickly. 'This is neither the time nor the place for such self-indulgence.'

Plunged into appalled embarrassment by her own response, Faye pulled free of him. She spun away, face hot as hell-fire. Her mind was a whirl in which stricken self-loathing rose uppermost. He had told her she was *his* any time he wanted her. Had she had to bend over backwards to prove his point for him?

'Tell me, when you ran away, where did you think you were going?' Tariq demanded.

Taken aback by that question but cravenly relieved by his choice of subject, Faye frowned. 'The airport... where else?'

'The airport is many miles from here.'

'It can't be...' Faye was glad of the excuse to go into her backpack and dig out the map. Eyes evasive, she turned back to extend the map to him. 'At least not according to this.'

'This map is more than half a century out of date. It is also written in Arabic—'

'I don't need to be able to read Arabic to recognise the symbol for an airport!'

'In this case, that symbol is for an airfield built during the Second World War and long since abandoned.'

'That's not possible,' Faye drew closer to study the map again. 'There's the city—'

'We have more than one city,' Tariq delivered in a raw driven undertone. 'And that is *not* Jumar City. That is Kabeer which is on the Gulf coast. Allah be praised that I found you before the sandstorm—'

'Well, you saved Omeir the wonder horse.' Cheeks burning with huge mortification at the news that she had totally misread the map, Faye whirled away again.

A lean hand snapped round her wrist and turned her back, unwillingly, to face him again. 'This is too serious a matter to be dismissed with a facetious comment as if it is nothing. All my life I have been trained to accept responsibility yet, in the space of a moment this afternoon, I forgot my duty.'

Releasing her again as if there was now something rather distasteful about a such personal contact with her, Tariq raked her dismayed face with brooding dark eyes. 'I was in the Haja when I was told of your flight into the desert. Hearing of your acrobatics on the various roofs and walls of the Muraaba would have greatly amused me had not a severe weather warning just been announced. In defiance of all common sense, I resisted the pleas of my companions and took up a helicopter. *Why?* In such dangerous flying conditions, I would not ask any man to risk his life to save yours!'

As he spoke, a forbidding darkness clenching his taut features, Faye fell back a step, colour receding, facial muscles tightening, sudden shame at the crisis she had caused engulfing her.

'It was not a risk I should have taken, I, who have no heir other than a four-year-old brother!' Pale now beneath his bronzed skin and rigid with tension, Tariq produced a portable phone and said with savage force. 'Even worse, I've been wasting time with you while my country, to whom I owe my first duty, is in a state of emergency!'

Recognising the depth of self-blame now assailing Tariq, Faye felt terrible. Rescuing her had demanded too high a price from him. For possibly the first time she recognised that, unlike her, he had to live *two* lives, both public and private, and naturally the responsibilities of being the ruler of his country counted way above other more personal inclinations. 'I'm really sorry...'

'Not one half as sorry as *I* am to have failed in my duty...' Grave and stern as only he could be, Tariq strode back into the outer cave. Within the space of a minute, she heard the faint echo of his voice speaking on the phone. The storm had ended and the wind had dropped without either of them noticing.

Faye stooped down to splash her face as he had done earlier, a great solid wodge of conflict and guilt attacking her. She grabbed up the *kaffiyeh* he had left lying and patted her skin dry. She could smell the evocative scent of him on the cloth. Sandalwood and just *him*. Male and warm and exotically sexy. In the wake of what he had admitted to her with such haunting, seering honesty, she was even ashamed of that last utterly inappropriate thought.

From somewhere she could hear a low throbbing drone. Engines of some kind? The childish part of her just wanted to scream that she had not meant to cause so much trouble. Omeir was squeezing back through the gap so that he could stay close to his lord and master. Faye's eyes prickled with hot, hurting tears. Omeir *was* pretty special and, just then, she didn't much care if she rated much lower than the horse in Tariq's estimation.

Picking up her backpack, she slunk back out of the caves. The bright blue sky was full of military and air-force helicopters. In the distance a trio of jets flashed past leaving trailing silver paths in their wake.

'You *see* what I have caused?' Tariq gritted out in a raw undertone. 'An all-out search for me is being staged when these resources should have been concentrated on those injured by the storm!'

'I'm really…desperately sorry,' Faye mumbled chokily. 'I honestly never realised how serious a sandstorm could be. I thought they just shifted the sand around a little—'

'Close your mouth before I strangle you.' Tariq groaned.

'Where was Omeir being taken?'

'At this season the tribal sheikhs meet at a gathering in the eastern territory. Omeir would have been collected on the road and taken into the desert in advance of my arrival. Now we will both be late,' he completed half under his breath.

'I really didn't mean to cause all this trouble for you—'

'Lust brings its own punishment.'

Compressing her lips on that grim announcement, Faye backed into the shadowy depths of the cave again. From there she watched the helicopters descend to land, one after another, sand flurrying up all around them.

Without warning, Tariq turned his imperious dark head to look at her again. A slashing smile that was purebred primitive momentarily lightened his brooding tension. 'On the other hand, perhaps I have finally paid the full price for desiring you and may hope to now enjoy the rewards.'

At the sound of raised voices nearby, he swung away again, having plunged her into flushed disconcertion with that concluding statement. A surge of anxious pilots and a whole bunch of less agile older men, who had

clearly come along as passengers, were now converging
on Tariq. As they approached, they fell down on their
knees and began to offer loud and fervent prayers of
gratitude for his safety. Never would she have witnessed
such an unashamed and charged display of emotion in
the West but, once she got over the drama of the scene,
what she saw touched her to the heart.

They were so relieved that Tariq was unharmed. He
wasn't only respected, he was genuinely loved and valued. Before Adrian had turned against Tariq under the
mistaken impression that Tariq had attempted to seduce
his kid sister, her brother had told her how very well-
liked Tariq was and, indeed, that everyone he heard
speak of him believed he was a terrific guy. She too had
once held the same opinion. But then Percy had intervened and, overnight, Tariq had become a stranger. A
stranger with a dark, volatile side to his character that
she had never dreamt existed. She had lost the man she
loved beyond all reason, lost him for ever, she recog-
nized in sudden stark pain.

Yes, she *had* loved him, she acknowledged dully.
After Tariq had, without question, risked his own life
to save hers, it was beneath her to continue pretending
that she had only been infatuated with him. Pride and
pain had made her buy into that lie. He might never had
loved her but he had liked and respected her. That was
what she had truly lost and her bitterness had grown out
of the reality that she had connived in her own down-
fall…

For loving Tariq as she had a year ago, she had
wanted him at *any* price. The day he had asked her to

marry him, she might not have known about Percy's blackmail attempt, but she had suspected that Tariq might only have been proposing because Percy had surprised them in each other's arms in her bedroom. Nevertheless, she had *still* accepted that proposal, hadn't she? What did that say about her principles? In her own eyes, it sunk her beyond reclaim.

CHAPTER FIVE

FAYE shifted sleepily and turned over, wincing at the stiffness of her muscles.

It was reasonably cool which told her it was still early morning. She had only the haziest recollection of boarding a helicopter the night before and none at all of being removed from it again. Bone-deep exhaustion and stress had wiped out the last of her energy reserves. Perhaps the final straw had been hearing that the helicopter in which Tariq had flown to find her had been buried right up to the rotor blades by a collapsing dune during the storm. What would have happened to Tariq had he still been inside it? She suppressed a shudder. Why was it that her every mistake seemed to rebound on him?

Pushing her tumbled hair back from her troubled brow, she finally opened her eyes. Soft, billowing folds of heavily embroidered fabric met her astonished scrutiny. The whole bed was shrouded in curtains. No such bed had featured in the room she had briefly occupied in the Muraaba palace. Wondering where on earth she was, she sat up with a start.

'You are awake, my lady?' With a gentle hand, Shiran brushed back one of the curtains several inches. '*Sidi* Latif is waiting to speak to you—'

'But I'm in bed—'

'Please excuse the interruption.' Latif's quiet intervention sounded from somewhere close by but out of view. 'I am standing outside your bedroom and, with your agreement, may address you from here.'

Already engaged in gaping at what lay beyond her bed, Faye blinked. Latif said he was standing outside her bedroom but she was in a *tent*! It might be an incredibly opulent, large and well-furnished tent, but it was still a tent! Evidently, Tariq had decided to take her to his tribal gathering in the desert, rather than return her to the Muraaba palace as she had assumed he would.

'Yes…' Faye faltered, her attention resting on the exquisite tapestries screening all canvas from view, the Persian rug covering the floor and the beautiful suite of satinwood furniture inlaid with intricate mother-of-pearl scrolls.

Shiran backed out through a curtained exit and Latif spoke up again. 'Prince Tariq has gone without sleep for many hours. Throughout the night he visited those hurt during the sandstorm—'

'Were there many hurt?' Faye had paled at that news and the awareness that Tariq had been up all night.

'It pleases me that you should wish to know.' Latif's response exuded warmth and approval. 'The storm struck hardest in the desert but in the city some were injured by falling masonry and flying debris. There were also several traffic accidents. In all, only three deaths which was a much lower number than we had feared might result. However, for the sake of his good health,

His Royal Highness should now rest. I would be most grateful if you would make this suggestion.'

'If I see Prince Tariq, I'll do my best.'

'You will most assuredly see him.' Latif sounded slightly strained in his delivery.

She was to urge Tariq to go to bed? She was truly disconcerted that Latif should approach her with his concern. But, most of all, she was mortified by his clear acceptance that her relationship with Tariq was one of intimacy. Yet how *could* Tariq flaunt a woman as a lover without fear of censure? Surely standards of public propriety were too strict for such displays in Jumar? Surely even her presence in a tent at a tribal gathering was pretty reckless? Or was it a case of the old double standard? Her troubled face stiffened. Maybe people weren't too concerned about what their ruling prince did as long as the woman he did it with was a foreigner.

Not that they had yet done *anything*, Faye conceded ruefully, but that situation was unlikely to last. It was time she faced facts: she was stuck in Jumar for the foreseeable future. At the mercy of a male who knew exactly how weak she was in terms of physical self-restraint. No sooner had that reflection touched her cheeks with even warmer pink than she heard a rustle of movement and voices beyond the cloth partitions of her enclosed and private space, followed by Tariq's familiar dark, deep drawl speaking in a tone of command.

A split second later, the bed drapes were thrust back and Tariq himself appeared. 'Your maids are keen to keep you hidden from all male eyes…apparently even mine!'

'Yours?' Looking up, Faye collided with stunning tawny eyes that snarled the breath up in her throat and sent her nervous tension leaping.

'It has taken me ten minutes to find you.' Although Tariq looked exhausted, his bronzed skin ashen, strain etched in the taut line of his wide sensual mouth, his gaze was as brilliant as ever, the high-voltage energy that charged him still in the ascendant over the tiredness.

'You're not wearing traditional dress...' She stared at him, her heartbeat quickening and her mouth running dry. Sheathed in a dark formal business suit of superb fit, Tariq looked sensational.

'Robes were only worn for ceremonial occasions and often in the desert, for in truth they are more practical than Western clothing. Yesterday at the Haja, I was in *Majilis*, holding open court for my people to approach me as I do every week. They bring their disputes for me to settle, they come to seek redress for injustice. I stand in the place of a judge.'

Resting one lean hand on the canopy of the bed, he gazed down at her with smouldering eyes that skimmed over her hot face, glided across the smooth fair skin of slim shoulders crossed only by the straps of her nightdress, and then extended with flashing mockery to the sheet she still hugged beneath her arms. The atmosphere throbbed with the undertones of sensual threat he emanated.

'You said you couldn't find me but this is a tent...' Faye mumbled, desperate to break the build of that pulsing silence.

'A tent that covers several acres.' Thrusting a wayward curtain out of his path, Tariq came down with lithe elegance on the side of the bed in a movement that stopped her breathing altogether. 'A tent palace no less and often in use. We are a desert people and the need to escape the confinement of stone walls still burns in us. My father would often live out here with considerably less comfort for months at a time. He would send for a woman whenever he felt like one...'

'Send for a woman...?' Faye parroted shakily.

Tariq had curved long brown fingers into the folds of the sheet she was clutching and he was almost casually tugging it back towards him inch by inch. From below the black inky luxuriance of his lashes, he glanced at her with burning amusement. 'You look so shocked. Before he married my mother, my father had at least a hundred concubines. Sex was remarkably non-pc in those days, a fact of life to my people, unworthy of any comment or indeed particular interest...'

'But not now?' Horrendously conscious that the sheet was now under slight stress as he eased it back from her, Faye splayed a hand across her ribcage to hold it in place.

'I don't have to send for you. You are here waiting for me.' A wolfish smile played about the corners of his lips as he abandoned that idle play to loosen the sheet, the masculine gleam in his clear gaze telling her that he knew he would win any such bout with ease should he so desire. 'Some things do not change. But on this occasion, your presence here is as public as a press announcement.'

'And why is that?' At that statement, her embarrassment rose to an all-time high.

'Look to your own adventures yesterday. You can't walk the walls of the Muraaba like a trapeze artiste, borrow Omeir and force me to follow you into the teeth of a storm without rousing considerable public comment,' Tariq advised with taunting cool, watching her eyes drop and her mouth tighten and her colour rise as he spoke. 'I was angry but I am now calm. Tonight you will come to me as you should have come to me a year ago and I need practise no discretion.'

'*Come*...to you?'

'As a woman comes to a man. And *not* in a bath towel in a bedroom full of girlish fluffy toys...and *not* with a stepfather poised to interrupt with a vulgar pretence of shock and anger. Believe me, tonight there will be no interruptions from *any* source,' Tariq swore with silken satisfaction.

'But I—'

'What can you possibly find to argue about?' His golden eyes roamed over her with provocative satisfaction. 'Once you were far from shy in demonstrating your desire for me. What has changed?'

'I got older and wiser fast. I thought I loved you... you soon cured me of that—'

'And I thought I loved you too.' Releasing a derisive laugh to punctuate that startling declaration, Tariq skimmed her with a sardonic appraisal, his stubborn, passionate mouth compressed, his jawline at an aggressive slant. 'I too was cured when you lured me into your trap.'

Faye tried and failed to swallow, studying him in disbelief. *And I thought I loved you too.* No, no, a little voice screamed inside her head, no, she did not want to credit that admission for it had been so much more bearable to believe that he had never really cared about her and that she could hardly lose what, essentially, she had never had. 'You *didn't* love me—'

In a flurry of sudden movement, Tariq sprang upright, disconcerting her even more. He swung back to her and rested splintering dark eyes of condemnation on her disbelieving face. 'Do you know the moment you killed anything I still felt for you? It was when I proposed marriage the next day and you said yes without hesitation. That was what damned you…that was what convinced me that you *had* conspired with your stepfather to rip me off for whatever you could get!'

Beneath the onslaught of that blunt speech, every scrap of colour had drained from Faye's complexion. Had she been a target with a tender heart in the centre, Tariq would have hit a killing bullseye with his first dart. Furthermore he had not yet finished.

'When I asked you to marry me, you knew it was not right, you knew I was not myself, but you said nothing. By not acknowledging the true state of affairs, you let the whole sordid sham continue beneath a pretty pretence of normality…with your wedding gown and your wearing of something blue for luck. Oh, yes, I satisfied my curiosity as to the significance of the something blue in your culture. But what possible luck could you have hoped to attract when practising such blatant dishonesty?' Tariq's low-pitched drawl vibrated with his contemptuous distaste in the spreading silence.

'Tariq, please...' Faye muttered painfully, sick to the heart to have the one sin she could not lay at the door of naivete or stupidity exposed and known by him and thrown back in her face.

'No, you will hear me out. You were only nineteen but you knew enough to know that it was not normal for a man to come to you as grave as a judge to ask you for your hand in marriage without *ever* having spoken of love or commitment!' Tariq did not conceal his scorn. 'Yet only yesterday you dared to accuse me of destroying your wedding day. As I said that day and I say now...a marriage into which a man feels forced is a charade and no true bond to be respected.'

Faye's hands trembled and she laced them tightly together, tears closing up her throat in a convulsive surge.

'I looked at my beautiful bride...and you *did* look very, very lovely, but your calculated campaign to catch me made you as soiled in my eyes as any whore is by her trade! So do not talk to me of spoiling the happiest day of your life. I at least was honest in what I was feeling that day. Angry, bitter, disappointed in you. You were not worthy of loving...I was ashamed that I had been blinded by your beauty into imagining you as perfect on the inside as you were on the outside.'

Faye was frantically fighting back the sobs welling up in her throat. She was devastated by what her own bitter recriminations the day before had unleashed on her. Not once had she allowed herself to believe that Tariq might have guessed what was in her own heart and mind that day, what she had hidden even from herself in her shameless, selfish longing to be his wife.

'And that is what I said in Arabic when I was ranting and roaring. Forgive me for feeling so much more than you were capable of feeling that I forgot to speak in English,' Tariq completed grittily.

He strode out through the curtained exit like the proud desert warrior Percy had once labelled him. A great sob escaped Faye as she stumbled out of bed.

Shiran came running. 'My lady?'

'Is there a bathroom in this place?' Faye covered her eyes with one hand and turned away.

Mercifully there was and, in the mood that Faye was in, it was pure relief rather than a source of surprise to discover that the canopied passageway led to sanitary facilities sited behind a solid wooden door and enclosed within sturdy stone walls. Ushered into a giant marble bathroom, Faye took care of her most imminent needs and freshened up as best she could while she was still sobbing her heart out. At a sink anchored on the spread wings of a grandiose swan, she studied herself with swollen swimming eyes.

A 'calculated campaign to catch me...' She honestly thought her heart was either going to break right through or she was going to die of shame and humiliation right there and then. She did not think she would ever, ever look Tariq in the face again for there had been a dreadful mortifying truth in his every harsh word. Had she not slavishly followed her sister-in-law's every word of advice on how to keep Tariq interested? Lizzie had been so helpful on how she should behave, when to be available, when not to be, how to be a good listener, how to flatter with silence.

And although her entire relationship with Tariq had not been conducted on such superficial terms, it was horribly ironic that the one time she had strayed from Lizzie's rigid rules of dating she had wrecked everything. Lizzie had certainly *not* suggested that she invite Tariq to spend the night with her.

A frantic series of knocks was being rapped out on the door. But Faye was too distraught to open it. Sitting on the hard, cold floor, she wrapped her arms round herself and struggled to calm down. Tariq was clever and very quick off the mark. In the end, all illusions about her supposed perfection for ever buried, he had looked back and seen and recognised every single calculating move engaged to attract him. She was humiliated beyond belief and there was no hiding place.

Unlocking the door, Faye padded back to her tent room, uncaring of the massed rank of anxious female servants twittering in her wake. Slipping out of her nightdress, Faye made no demur when she was presented with a cool kaftan to don. Breakfast was brought to her in another airy section furnished with silk-upholstered low divans. Shiran watched with troubled eyes as Faye hiccuped through a piece of toast and sipped at a cup of tea both looking and feeling like tragedy personified.

'May we bring the children to see you?' the maid then enquired.

What children? Was Rafi one of them? Was she now a sight to be seen for entertainment purposes? But, not wishing to cause offence and scolding herself for doubting the courteous goodwill shown to her by everyone, Faye nodded assent. Indeed, she was surprised that there was not a distinct coolness in the air around her, for her escape attempt the day before had put Tariq in considerable danger.

Prince Rafi arrived first. Like a small adult he approached her with a stiff little face and for the first time she noted his resemblance to Tariq. 'I am sorry for upsetting you yesterday.'

'That's all right…as long as you don't do anything like that again.'

His brown eyes flooded with unexpected tears. 'I can't…they're all gone. Prince Tariq took them away.'

'They' being his retinue of slavish servants, Faye gathered, for Tariq had told her that that was what he would do. *Prince* Tariq? Was that how he had to refer to a brother old enough to be his father? Did such stifling formality in the ibn Zachir royal family exercise its rule even over little children? And, she thought sadly, yes, *yes*, it did for Tariq's hard self-discipline was the proof of it. Without even thinking about it, Faye scooped Rafi up and set him on her knee.

'I'm a big boy. Big boys don't get cuddled,' Rafi told her chokily.

'Shall I put you down again?' She wasn't teasing. She was afraid of embarrassing herself or him by doing something unacceptable.

Suddenly the little boy just pushed his head into her shoulder and sobbed out loud, clinging to her in considerable distress. She nursed him until the storm of tears was over, compassion stirred by the depth of the unhappiness he revealed. Even Tariq had called his little brother 'obnoxious', not an encouraging sign. So who did the poor child have to turn to? It was not his fault that he had been taught to behave like a little monster, but how hard it must be for Tariq, who had been raised far more strictly, to appreciate that fact.

'You like children.' Shiran wore a huge and relieved smile and she turned to address the servants waiting in the passageway.

Faye blinked in surprise as two middle-aged nursemaids hurried in with a pair of identically clad baby girls in their arms.

'Basma and Hayat,' Shiran announced.

'Twins? My goodness, what age are they?' Faye was enchanted.

'Nine months. You would like to see them closer?'

'They're only girls!' Rafi exclaimed fiercely.

Settling the little boy down on the seat beside her, Faye smiled at the twins. The little girls wore elaborate long pink satin frilly dresses with full net underskirts: so impractical and uncomfortable for babies she reflected with rueful sympathy. 'Basma and Hayat... those are pretty names—'

'I don't like them!' Rafi howled at the top of his voice.

'I don't like shouting, so please behave yourself—'

'I don't like you either!' Rafi threw himself off the divan and stormed away.

Ignoring him, Faye went on getting to know the little girls, who were easily told apart for they were not identical twins. Basma was full of confident mischief, her sister Hayat more anxious and shy.

Eventually, Rafi slunk back. 'You like them better than me.'

'Of course not,' Faye said gently. 'I like all of you.'

'Nobody likes me,' Rafi muttered fiercely and kicked at the divan base.

Faye looked down into his miserable little face and curved a wry arm round his rigid little body. 'I *do*...'

Toys were brought in then. Rafi was a pain, wanting all her attention, sulking when he couldn't have it but, between sulking and clinging, a kind of peace emerged. The morning hours passed and Faye was surprised when lunch was announced. The children were removed again to their own quarters. At the last minute, Rafi darted back. 'I see you soon...?'

'If you want.'

Some time after she had eaten, Shiran approached her to tell her that it was time for her bath. Faye frowned. 'Isn't it a little early?'

'It will take many hours to dress you for the ladies' reception tonight, my lady.'

'Oh...' Faye wasn't sure how she felt about making any form of public appearance. She still could not face the prospect of seeing Tariq again. The night he had promised her stretched before her like the worst of threats and the sweetest of dreams for the conflicting emotions dragging her first one way and then another would give her no peace.

She had only slipped into the water already drawn for her use when her maids hurried in loaded with baskets of lotions and she realised that privacy was not on offer. Rose petals were hastily scattered on the surface of the scented water and Shiran insisted on washing her hair. Such a production was made of the varying rinses that Faye sighed at the longevity of the experience.

There was washing and there was washing, but Faye felt as if she were being scrubbed within an inch of her life. Wrapped in a towel, she was urged into another room in the same block, a steam room full of billowing clouds which almost sent her to sleep, so lethargic did it leave her. Next she was persuaded to lie down on a special couch to be massaged. The rich perfume of the oil rubbed into her skin made her eyes even heavier but she enjoyed the stiffness being eased out of her muscles, the smooth feel of her own pampered skin. Tea was served in the aftermath, all the maids giggling and chattering with an informality that charmed her.

Her hair was dried and polished with a silk scarf. A manicure and a pedicure followed and a great debate opened over the shades of nail polish available. While that was going on and Faye lay back on her sofa feeling like a beauty queen, a slim leather box arrived and her companion became very excitable. With great ceremony the box was brought to Faye and opened. Within lay a note.

'Wear the anklet for me,' ran the note and it was signed by Tariq.

Anklet? Faye hooked a finger into an anklet studded with large dark blue sapphires.

'How His Royal Highness honours you!' Shiran proclaimed. 'This belonged to Prince Tariq's late mother.'

Faye wondered if a chain went with it. Since she rarely wore jewellery, it struck her as a very exotic item but she knew she was sentenced to wear it for, if she said no, she might then seem rude. A bouquet of white roses arrived an hour later. Again her companions were ravished by their admiration but Faye's heart turned as cold as the Ice Queen's. Too many memories that hurt were stirred by those pale perfect blooms.

When it was time to get dressed, she was taken aback by the fabulous outfit laid out for her perusal on the bed. But then she had nothing worthy in her case of *any* social occasion at which a sapphire anklet might be worn. Indifferent to her own appearance, she donned the gold silk strappy sheath which was worn as an underdress. Then with reverence she was inserted into an extraordinary violet-blue chiffon gown, every inch of which caught the light with exquisite gold embroidery overlaid with precious stones, and which dragged a fan-shaped train in its wake. The dress weighed a ton. Gold shoes with incredibly high heels were slipped onto her feet and she wondered how on earth she would move in so much heavy finery.

Another leather box was delivered. This time the maids whooped with unconcealed delight. Excitement was at a high. Faye undid the clasp to reveal a breathtaking diamond tiara, a pair of drop earrings and a bracelet. Why the heck was Tariq sending her such items? But the answer was writ large in the appreciative faces surrounding her. He was good as his own PR firm, she decided. His generosity in loaning her such hugely valuable articles to wear impressed everyone to death.

The tiara was slid into place, the earrings inserted, the bracelet attached to her wrist. A mirror was then carted over to her.

'You are *so* beautiful, my lady.' Shiran sighed happily.

In heels which elevated her a good few inches, Faye hardly recognised herself. Her hair had been transformed into a shining silken mane to support the tiara and fell smooth as a sheet of pale gold far below her shoulders. She glittered from head to toe like a fantastic jewellery display. In strong light, she would blind the unwary.

Led from the room, she had to walk with small shuffling steps. It was a long walk to the vast reception area thronged with women in outfits that soon gave her a different view of her own theatrical glamour. She still had the edge, but only just. Guided to a seat of honour and the cynosure of all eyes, she was introduced to one woman after another. Arabic phrases were murmured, no English was spoken. The amount of bowing and scraping she received increased her tension to the extent that she could almost have believed that she were dreaming the whole strange event.

And then the last woman approached, a flamboyant raven-haired beauty in her twenties. She was sheathed in an emerald-green gown, and her full pink mouth had a hard, sullen curve. The tension in the room was electric.

'I am Prince Tariq's first cousin, Majida. I offer you no compliments.' Her sultry eyes flared over Faye with derision. 'I say you are no virgin!'

The silence was ruptured by stricken gasps. Shocked faces were cast down, covered. An older woman rose heavily to her feet and wailed like a soul in torment. Faye's cheeks glowed red. How on earth was she supposed to meet such a very personal accusation flung at her in public? And why *should* that nasty brunette question whether she was or was not a virgin? How could such a thing be of interest to anyone?

At her feet, Shiran buried her face and moaned. 'This is a grievous insult, my lady. The woman crying is the lady Majida's mother. It is her way of expressing her shame at her daughter's behaviour.'

The wailing woman sank back down as if she had been disgraced. The food arriving was a very welcome diversion. Every dish was presented to Faye first but her appetite had died. As the lengthy meal ended, Majida approached her again and proffered a smooth apology. Feeling that the apology was as calculated as the insult, Faye responded with a tight smile of strain.

In that all female gathering, she was disconcerted when Tariq made an entrance to be greeted by a series of equally surprised but uniformly delighted cries of welcome. Looking at him, Faye drew in a sharp breath. Magnificent in silks as rich with gold decoration as her own, Tariq had never looked more exotic or more stunningly attractive. But, unable to forget the bitter anger he had shown her earlier, she stiffened and averted her attention from him to the other men filtering in behind him, some smiling, some looking a little awkward. Latif entered last, his wide smile suggesting that he was in the very best of good humour.

No fan of being ignored, Tariq took the seat beside Faye and leant towards her to murmur with the pronounced air of a male priding himself on his generosity, 'Let there be peace between us now.'

Faye compressed her generous mouth. 'I shouldn't think there's much chance of that breaking out tonight. According to you I'm so wicked, it's amazing a heavenly bolt of lightning hasn't struck me down—'

'In the name of Allah do not say such a thing even in amusement.'

'Not much amusement where I'm sitting,' Faye said stonily.

'We will exchange no more recriminations.'

'Well, you *would* be repeating yourself if you said anything more.'

'I am trying to mend bridges.'

'It's fences actually and you blew the bridges to kingdom come.' Having paraded into the centre of the room, musicians were beginning to play but it was very discordant stuff.

'It is not like western music but it is a traditional melody always played at such occasions,' Tariq volunteered, sounding just a little defensive.

A singer came on. She had a gorgeous husky voice but Faye took extreme exception to the suggestive way in which her lithe bodily undulations seemed to take place exclusively in front of Tariq. 'You're in with a good chance there,' she whispered, a poisonous, exhilarating edge to her tongue such as she had never before experienced and could not resist. 'There's a woman just gasping to get into your harem.'

'I do not have a harem,' Tariq gritted close to her ear.

'Too many women breaking out of it? Bad for the macho image?'

'One more word from you—'

'And you'll what? Have me delivered back to the airport? Well, I'll need to be carried because I'm literally weighed down by my fancy trappings. Tell me, do you only sleep with virgins?'

'What has got into you?' Tariq demanded in a shaken undertone.

'I'm coming to terms with being a concubine. Tell me, do I get sown into a sack and dropped into the Gulf when you get bored with me?'

'A sack would be very useful right now. You want me to apologise, don't you?'

'Oh, no, even you couldn't apologise for the embarrassment of a complete stranger stating that I'm *not* a virgin in front of so many people. Allow me to tell you that I found that weird and kinky and medieval—'

Both lean hands suddenly clenching on the arms of his chair, Tariq rounded on her like an erupting volcano. 'Who said that to you? Who *dared*?'

For the first time since his entrance, Faye focused on him in shock for he had not troubled to lower his voice. Outrage glittered in his flaring golden gaze, dark colour scoring his superb cheekbones. 'For goodness' sake, calm down—'

'After such offence is offered to you?' Tariq growled like a lion ready to spring. 'What man would be calm in the face of so great an affront?'

'You're making me nervous.'

'You will tell me the name of the offender.'

'Not the way you're carrying on, I won't. There's been enough drama for one evening.'

'This hurts my honour,' Tariq informed her doggedly.

Faye closed her eyes. It had been a day in which culture shock had made itself felt on several occasions. In fact she had been in almost continual shock from the day of her arrival in Jumar for absolutely nothing seemed comprehensible to her. Not the way she was treated, not the way Tariq behaved. He reached for her hand and gripped it in emphasis. 'My honour is *your* honour.'

'But I have no honour…you've said as much.'

At that far from generous reminder, Tariq sprang upright. He lifted an imperious hand. The music stopped with a mid-chord crash. He spoke a few words in Arabic. Then he swung round and swept Faye up out of her chair and into his arms to an astonished chorus of more gasps and strode from the reception area, leaving a screaming silence in their wake.

CHAPTER SIX

'WARS have broken out over lesser insults,' Tariq breathed with brooding darkness as he strode down canopied passageways. 'You do not appear to understand how high is the regard for a woman's virtue in my culture.'

Now, had Faye been his new bride, she would have understood his fury, but she was totally bewildered by his smouldering rage on such a score when she was not his wife. She was to be his mistress and there was nothing respectable about that, was there? Indeed, in her humble opinion, it was entirely *his* fault that she had been insulted in the first place! It was madness for her to have been treated as a guest of honour in the presence of women who had to believe she was a totally wanton hussy. True, with the exception of his cousin, Majida, she had received nothing but smiling courtesy, but no doubt that was the effect of Tariq's feudal power as a ruler. What else could it be? In fact, if his late father had once had a hundred concubines, it was quite possible his people thought having just *one* was the ultimate in self-denial and restraint on his part.

Regardless, here she was right now, being carted off very publicly to his bed, past innumerable guards saluting and standing to attention, past servants flattening themselves back out of his path. Faye was aghast. How *could* Tariq do this to her? Speeding up as he thrust his aggressive passage through a number of interconnecting tent rooms that convinced her that she would never in a million years find her way back to where she had slept the night before, Tariq finally came to a halt. He settled her down with immense and unexpected care. He smoothed down her dress where it was rumpled and stepped back from her.

'That you are *not* a virgin is my business alone,' Tariq announced, hard, stubborn jawline set like rock.

Faye reddened and attempted to walk away. It involved taking tiny, tiny steps and she wobbled on the unfamiliar heels. She was in a huge tent room, even more opulently furnished than her own and distinguished by a beautiful carved wooden bed large enough to sleep six. She studied it, butterflies suddenly flying loose in her tummy.

She flinched as about ten feet from her something metallic flew across the room and buried itself with a thud in the carved headboard of the bed. Her lips parting company, she gaped at the ornate dagger she had last noted attached to Tariq's sword belt. Now drawn from its jewel-studded sheath, the dagger was lodged halfway up to its hilt in solid wood.

'I will cut myself and smear blood on the sheet,' Tariq murmured in the most unnaturally calm tone she had ever heard. 'No more needs to be said.'

With difficulty, Faye dragged her attention from the dagger still twanging in the wood. She opened her mouth but no sound would emerge from her throat.

It was finally dawning on her that virginity appeared to be a major issue on all fronts as far as he was concerned. It was medieval but there was something terribly, strangely, crazily sweet about his equally barbaric solution to this lack he believed she had. Her desert warrior was prepared to shed his own blood and mount a cover-up on her behalf.

His tawny eyes rested on her with raw intensity as if he believed she must have been distressed by the same insult which had sent him up in volatile fireworks. Finally, Faye was recognising the pronounced change in him. The angry bitterness he had revealed at the outset of the day had vanished along with the icy forbidding distance he could assume at will.

'Tariq…' she said a little shakily because, although she was embarrassed, a hysterical giggle brought on by nerves was tugging at her throat and she was terrified it would escape and cause huge offence for she could see he was trying to be diplomatic and reassuring. 'I really can't believe we're having this crazy conversation.'

'When we first met, I made the mistake of assuming that you were as innocent as you appeared.' Tariq lifted a broad shoulder in a fluid dismissive shrug. 'But that was a boy's fantasy. Many Arab men cherish similar fantasies but I am now more contemporary in my outlook.'

Contemporary? His use of that particular word absorbed Faye the most. She focused on the dagger in the headboard and skimmed her gaze away again, suddenly extraordinarily reluctant to state an opinion on that score.

Powerful emotion was welling up inside her but she could not have put a name to what she was feeling. Tariq ibn Zachir was what he was, a feudal prince. His patina of cool sophistication had once grossly misled her. Not too far below that surface was the infinitely more conservative male whose existence she had not recognised until too late. The male with the reputation of a womaniser who had, nonetheless, been shattered when she'd asked him to stay overnight.

Why? Only now could she understand why. Prior to that fatal invite, Tariq had placed her on a lofty pedestal labelled 'pure as driven snow'. And then she had so shaken his faith in his image of her that he had decided he had never known her at all. She had made it that much easier for him to credit that she had been involved in her stepfather's strenuous efforts to make money out of their relationship.

Cheeks warm, Faye plucked an imaginary piece of lint from her sleeve. 'You seem very sure that I've had other lovers…'

'What else am I to believe after that invitation you gave me last year?'

So they were back to the catastrophic phone call during which she had virtually asked him to sleep with her and she could still only *cringe* at the mention of it. Barely twelve months had passed but the resulting fall-out had ensured that she had since grown up a lot for, while she had believed she was being daring and romantic, he had believed she was being crude and cheap. While she was willing to admit to herself that she had misjudged her man and made a mistake, she was not prepared to admit that to him.

Ignoring what she saw as a most ungallant reminder of her most humiliating moment, Faye said tightly, 'What if I told you…well…er…that there hadn't been other men?'

Tariq screened his stunning golden eyes. 'I would tell you that you don't need to lie on that score.'

'But I wouldn't *be* lying if I told you that…and if you have so much respect for a woman's virtue, you should be keeping your hands off me, shouldn't you be?'

His amusement broke through to the surface in a flashing smile that disconcerted her a great deal. 'No…'

'Why not?'

'Take it from me, you are a special case…so last-ditch efforts to change my mind are destined to fail. I cannot understand why you should even attempt to change my mind. With every look you give me you let me know how much you want to feel my hands on you. I saw that at our first meeting in the Haja.'

'Really?' Her face was hotter than hell-fire. She met molten golden eyes set between lush ebony lashes. She saw the kind of absolute confidence that shook her.

'Seeing that longing in you filled me with an unholy rush of triumph…I freely admit that as a fault.' With that frank admission, Tariq strolled up to her and lifted her back into his arms with complete cool. He settled her down on the edge of the bed and removed the tiara from her hair. Long, sure fingers detached the earrings, first one, then the other before dropping to her wrist to unclasp the bracelet. It was all achieved at a leisurely pace. 'But then I was not brought up to be a good loser. I was taught to be ruthless and competitive. I was made to be strong.'

Dumbfounded by his dexterity with jewellery and that sense of being in the power of an overwhelming force, Faye watched him set the exquisite diamond set down on a silver tray on a dresser and mumbled in dazed and belated repetition. 'A fault?'

'You have already noticed the temper—'

'Rafi has it too—'

Dispensing with his sword belt and *kaffiyeh*, Tariq sent her a dark look of reproof which let her know just how much he still felt the shame of his little brother's behaviour. 'Never have I raised my hand to anyone in anger!'

'He's four and all mixed-up…you're twenty-eight and…' A slight gasp escaped her parted lips as he bent down to tug off her shoes. His proud, dark head was within reach. She curled her fingers to stop herself from stretching out a hand to touch the enticing luxuriance of his black hair.

It was really going to happen, Faye thought, swallowing hard; they were definitely about to share the bed. No sandstorm, no Percy to keep them apart. But now that they were finally at the brink, Faye just could not imagine *being* in bed with Tariq, when to date she had never so much as seen him with his shirt off…

'I'm twenty-eight *and*?' Tariq prompted.

'I've forgotten what I was about to say. You're really planning on going through with this, aren't you?'

'What do you think?'

'I just…I just can't imagine it—'

'I have more than sufficient imagination for both of us.'

'Well, I've had enough of this!' Faye threw herself off the bed with the intention of stalking away. But she had forgotten the length of the gown she wore and the train wrapped round her ankles, tripping her up. As she teetered dangerously, Tariq caught her back into his arms to steady her.

'I think I have only had enough of you talking.' Running down the zip on the gown, he eased it off her taut shoulders. The sheer weight of the embroidered fabric sent the garment sliding straight down her arms and into a heap at her feet. In speedy succession, the underdress travelled the same way.

'Tariq!' Faye, left standing in her lacy bra and panties with little warning, was paralysed by dismay and mortification.

Scanning her hot face and the self-conscious arms she folded in front of her, his gaze narrowed. 'Ignore my last comment,' he advised softly. 'I do believe you should talk some more.'

'What about?'

A sudden smile curved his wide, passionate mouth. She saw the charm, the rueful amusement which had once reduced her to a mindless level of tongue-tied longing. It did so again. As he lifted her up and settled her on the bed again, she coiled back against the crisp white pillows, conscious only of a heartbeat that seemed to be thumping madly in her eardrums rather than where it ought to have been.

In the thrumming silence, Tariq reached up and plucked the dagger from the headboard. Sheathing the blade, he tossed it aside again. Smouldering golden eyes roamed over the full swell of her breasts, the feminine curve of her hip and the slim, shapely length of her legs and then whipped back to her strongly disconcerted face.

'So...' he murmured lazily '...perhaps you would care to explain *why* a virgin would make the kind of bold invitation you made to me last year?'

Her soft mouth compressed and she jerked a shoulder, eyes veiled, chin at a mutinous angle. 'Since you didn't take me up on it, I don't think you have the right to ask that—'

'When I saw you in that towel in your bedroom, I had every intention of taking advantage of the offer,' Tariq countered in level disagreement. 'However, it seems obvious to me now that your stepfather must've *forced* you into making that distasteful phone call...'

Her lovely face taut with flushed discomfiture, Faye muttered, 'No. I can't let Percy be blamed for that. That call was entirely my own idea—'

'So even now you will not tell me the truth!' Raising a highly expressive lean hand and dropping it again in scornful dismissal, Tariq strode away from the bed, soundless and graceful as a jungle cat on the prowl.

'No,' Faye said tensely. 'I just won't tell you any more lies...no matter what the cost.'

Tariq swung back, unimpressed brilliant eyes clashing with hers.

Faye sucked in a deep breath. 'I still don't know

how my stepfather found out that I had asked you to the house that night. Maybe it was just a horrible co-incidence…him turning up when he was supposed to be in London and walking in on a situation which he thought he could use to his own advantage. But there was no set-up as far as I was concerned. I *honestly* be-lieved we would be alone that night—'

'I do not believe in coincidences of that nature. And if you have not the courage to admit that you were in-volved right up to your pretty throat in your stepfather's intrigues, we have nothing more to discuss.'

'But—'

Tariq lifted his hands. 'I will not hear any more. I gave you the chance to tell me the truth and you wasted the opportunity. Your stepfather is a crook and he raised you without principles. Yet it is pointless for you to plead innocence in face of the facts as we both know them.'

Hurt resentment filled Faye. Here she was telling the truth but he would not accept it. He refused to be-lieve that she could have had nothing to do with Percy's sudden appearance at the worst possible moment that awful evening. She was willing to admit that the facts did make it hard for her to argue a convincing case in her own defence but, nevertheless, she *was* telling the truth. Her stepfather had always insisted that his arrival that night had been pure coincidence and how was she to prove otherwise? Only Percy knew the whole story and, Percy being Percy, he was unlikely to stage a con-fession.

Eyes strained, Faye lifted her head again and then

froze. While she had been lost in thought, Tariq had been discarding his clothes. How could she have forgotten for even *one* moment what was about to happen between them? Well, there was little chance of her forgetting a second time, she conceded in shock, violet-blue eyes now wide on the sight of Tariq shorn of his shirt.

Her shaken scrutiny roamed over his wide brown shoulders, strong arms and broad, muscular chest. A triangular haze of curling dark hair emphasised his powerful pectorals and then thinned into a silky line that arrowed down over his taut abdomen and disappeared beneath the low-slung waistband of his black briefs. Warmth prickled up from the very heart of her, making her shift on the bed and suddenly clasp her hands round her upraised knees. An enervating mix of fascination and embarrassment had her in its grip. She watched him stroll over to the dresser and discard his watch, every movement fluid with natural grace. He had the most extraordinary predatory sex appeal. Her breathing started to seize up at source at just the thought of him getting into bed with her.

Lowering her knees again, she grabbed at the sheet already turned back in readiness for them and pulled it up over herself. Her whole being was humming with raw tension. Wanting…but still seeing what a trap the wanting was, how it would ultimately smash her pride and hurt her. Yet when she focused on the stunning lure of those hawkish tawny eyes, she could hardly breathe, much less think.

He came down on the bed, all dominant male, steely

contours and hard muscle. He was very much aroused. Mouth dry, pulses racing, Faye's startled gaze skittered over him and off him again double quick. His virility was not in question. Panic and wicked excitement combined as he reached for her.

'We have all the time in the world,' Tariq asserted softly. 'I'm not a selfish lover.'

He captured her mouth with a passionate thoroughness that took her by storm, only to linger with the knowing eroticism of restraint and let his tongue delve into the tender interior and, with a smooth flicker, imitate a far more intimate penetration. She shivered with helpless anticipation, her heartbeat racing. He made her want more, with effortless ease he made her want *so* much more.

He lifted his head, his hair already tousled by her fingers. She stared up at him, wholly absorbed in the hard planes and angles of his lean, dark, devastating face. For a split second, nothing existed but the rising swell of her own unguarded emotions and her fingertips smoothed along a sculpted cheekbone, dropped to stroke in wonderment along his beautiful mouth.

'What?' Tariq husked.

'Nothing,' she framed, her voice the merest thread of sound, for in that moment she recognised the strength of her own feelings and felt terrifyingly vulnerable.

He tugged her up to him and kissed her again. Her eyes slid shut, all thought suspended for the potent hunger was more powerful. Heart hammering, her eyes flew wide as he drew back from her again, smouldering golden eyes pinned to her as he cast aside her bra.

She gazed down in abstracted surprise at the swell of her own bare breasts.

'You are even more beautiful than I imagined...' Tariq curved his hand to the pouting flesh he had revealed, catching a pert pink nipple between stroking fingers, sending such a shard of sensation through her that a muffled moan was wrenched from her.

Face burning but every skin cell alive and begging for his touch, she fell back on her elbows against the pillows, one feminine part of her glorying in his unconcealed appreciation of her body, some other tiny part of her standing back in shock at the growing completeness of her own surrender. 'Tariq...'

Her voice died in her throat as he bent his arrogant dark head and teased at a prominent peak with his lips and his tongue. Seductive pleasure stopped her breathing and tensed her every muscle. He laid her down again with sure hands. As he employed greater sensual force on the tender buds, exploring the firm contours of swollen flesh, her teeth gritted and her fingers clenched, tiny cries of response escaping her parted lips. Nothing mattered but that he continue that sweet torment which was so totally addictive.

'This was meant to be,' Tariq told her with husky satisfaction. 'This was meant to be the first day I saw you. *Inshallah*, we say...as God wills.'

She collided with the burning gold of his eyes, aware of him with every thrumming skin cell in her body. There was no room for pride or principle in what he could make her feel, what he already *knew* he could make her feel. He wound long brown fingers into her tumbled pale blonde hair.

'Fate...'

'But you like to tempt fate. Why else did you run into the desert?' Tariq let the tip of his tongue trace her reddened lips, part them, dip, tease, making love to her mouth, his breath fanning her cheekbone. 'Don't you know that had you got anywhere near the airport I would have closed it and grounded every flight...don't you know that, when I set my heart on anything, I will stop at nothing until I achieve it?'

'But I didn't want this...' Even in the grip of a desperate hunger that mounted higher with his every caress, she knew that. Even as she opened her mouth, turned it under his, driven by an instinct she could not resist, she knew that. But as he drove her lips apart with electrifying passion, she refused to think.

'You do now.' Glittering golden eyes rested on her as if daring disagreement.

'Yes...'

He swept her up to him and tugged off the panties clinging to her damp skin. She trembled. He ran his hands over her, toyed with the straining sensitivity of her nipples, traced the taut curve of her quivering stomach and parted her thighs to let his expert fingers trace the infinitely more tender and private place below the soft pale curls. Her heart slammed suffocatingly fast inside her, her excitement intense. His touch controlled her, made her writhe and moan and sob for breath. She twisted her head into his shoulder, drowning in the hot male scent of him, the power of every sense heightened.

Her fingers tangled with his hair, clutched restively over a brown shoulder, clenched there.

Tariq groaned something in Arabic.

'English,' she begged.

Fierce dark golden eyes held hers in an almost aggressive gaze. 'You excite me more than any woman I have ever known...'

The restive burning heat inside her was like a twisting, spiralling ache she could no longer withstand. 'Please...now.'

Without hesitation, his strong-boned face feverishly intent, he pulled her under him, pushed up her thighs and came down on her. As she felt the hard satin probe of his arousal against her softest flesh, she tensed. He smoothed her hair back from her damp brow. 'I'll try not to hurt you but you are very tight...'

And then he was there where she most ached for him to be. He eased himself just barely inside her, the sensation of his bold shaft stretching her, enthralling her, seeming to promise that nebulous fulfilment she so craved but had yet to experience. Then his hands lifted her and he tipped her back, shifting his lithe hips and thrusting deep. Sudden burning pain jolted her but almost as swiftly the hot, heady rush of pleasure returned and blanked out the memory of the first sensation.

'Assuredly paradise must be like this...' Tariq growled.

And she had no argument to make, indeed was so lost in the intoxicating world of scorching physical enjoyment, she could not have strung two sensible words together. She moved under him, skin flushed and damp, heart pounding, head thrown back, out of control and not caring as the wild surge of excitement built. She caught the age-old rhythm she had not known until he'd taught her it. She gloried in the raw dominion of his powerful body over and inside hers. She clung to him, reached a climax with a startled cry, soaring to a breathtaking peak and then writhing in the timeless ecstatic release of satiation.

Afterwards, Faye was just in shock. In shock at her own body's capacity for that much pleasure. In shock at her own hot, frenzied abandonment. In shock at the incredible sense of intimacy she felt still lying in the circle of his arms. His heart was still thumping at an accelerated rate against hers and he was struggling to catch his breath. She kept her arms wrapped round him, wanting the silence and the lack of eye contact to continue for ever, so that she could pretend that everything was bliss, everything normal…loving?

Loving? Faye stiffened at that impossibility, ironically provoking what she had wished to avoid. Tariq lifted his tousled dark head, lustrous golden eyes lingering on her as though magneticised. 'I am very pleased to be your first lover.'

Faye tensed even more and said nothing.

'But then that is justice.' With an appreciative hand, he touched the long silky streamers of her hair where it trailed across the pillow. 'Your hair is the same colour as the moonlight.'

'How romantic…' Something tight and painful knotted inside her, making her feel all kinds of a fool and she responded in a wooden tone, twisting her head away.

'Once you made me feel very romantic…'

Once. Bitterness threatened to rip Faye in two. She wanted to scream and shout. Justice that he should become her first lover? How was it justice? Wasn't it wonderful how he could seek to justify the most barbaric of bargains? His right to use her body in return for her brother's freedom. Or, as he himself had put it even more bluntly, sex in return for money, trade mark of the oldest profession in the world. She was a tramp now, she had even enjoyed being a tramp for him. She should have lain there indifferent, unresponsive, silent, maybe even smothering the occasional yawn. And what had she done? Humiliating recollections of her own begging, moaning and clinging engulfed her and she shuddered. No harem odalisque could have massaged a guy's ego more effectively than she just had!

Tariq caught her back to him so that she could no longer avoid his scrutiny. He smiled down at her with a charismatic warmth that made her feel as though he were crushing her tender heart between cruel, casual fingers and released her from his weight. 'I'm far too heavy for you…'

'As I dare say that's not the *only* drawback of being a concubine,' Faye stated in a tight little voice, face stiff as a frozen mask, 'I didn't like to complain.'

CHAPTER SEVEN

TARIQ sat up with a start. 'That joke has worn out its welcome. What is this stupid, trashy talk of being a concubine?'

'Forget it,' Faye said stonily, wrenching violently at the bedspread, hauling it round her and sliding off the bed in a series of fierce and jerky movements.

'Come back to bed,' Tariq ground out in a lethal tone of command, lean, strong face etched with cool exasperation.

Faye looked at him, all tawny and gorgeous and sexy as he was against the white bed linen, and her fury with herself, with him, with the whole wretched situation rose like a red mist in front of her. It was past time she reminded him that she was not one of his adoring subjects. 'Get stuffed!'

For the longest second of her life, Tariq simply stared at her in disbelief and then he was out of that bed faster than the jump jet her brother had once likened him to in his relations with her sex. 'Such abuse would infuriate me but for the fact that you sound like a truculent teenager...'

Shot down in flames, she conceded with infuriated acceptance, her colour rising.

'What is the matter with you?'

'The matter with *me*...?' she repeated on a rising note of volume.

Tariq stood there, naked and quite unconcerned by the fact, and focused censorious golden eyes on her. 'Tell me what is wrong.'

Wrapped in the iridescent spread, Faye flung her head high. 'Why should anything be wrong? Are you expecting me to fawn on you now like some harem slave thrilled to death by your attention?'

'Hardly,' Tariq said very drily, lean, strong features sardonic. 'Harems have been against the law in Jumar since the first year of my mother's marriage to my father.'

Confusion assailed her. 'But you *said*—'

'I was teasing you.' Taking advantage of her bemusement at that admission, Tariq lifted her up into his arms and strode, not back to the bed with her, but straight out of the room again.

'Where on earth are you taking me?' Faye gasped.

With a vibrantly amused smile at her disconcertion, Tariq strolled into a splendid green marble bathroom and shouldered shut the door. Lowering her, he extracted her from the cloaking folds of the bedspread. Before she could fully react to that new development, he had caught her up again and settled her down into the foaming waters of the Jacuzzi bath.

The water enveloped her overheated skin in an initially cooling surge that dragged a yelp from her. Then, becoming hugely conscious that she was as bare as a newborn baby and in full view of fiercely appreciative dark deep-set eyes, she sank her quivering body as far below the rippling water surface as she could.

Tariq joined her with all the cool and grace of a male to whom such inhibitions were unknown. He leant over her in a fluid arch, draping her hair over the pillowed rim so that it would stay mostly dry. Momentarily engulfed by his sheer male magneticism that close again, her instinctively raised hands accidentally brushed down over his hard male flanks as he stretched, her cheeks scorched and she dropped her hands again as if she had been burnt.

'Harems…' Tariq recalled lazily, sinking down like a lithe, tawny predator into the water to survey her highly embarrassed face. 'Although you were right in saying that I am above the law, there would be great unease in Jumar if I was to demonstrate *any* desire to veil my woman or lock her away from all male eyes. Harems now feature only in our history books in the chapter devoted to the emancipation of women.'

'Really…?' Even to Faye's own ears, her voice sounded slightly strangled, but she had never been in a Jacuzzi in her life and was already nervously wondering what might happen next.

'In the whole of our history, our women were never veiled. Berber women do not cover their faces. The harem was a foreign concept as well, imported into Jumar by my great-grandfather, a man whose appetite for your sex is a living legend.'

'Oh…?'

'But my own father simply knew no other way of life until he met my mother, Rasmira.' Reclining opposite her in complete relaxation, Tariq looked reflective and his expressive mouth quirked. 'She was the daughter of a Lebanese diplomat, highly educated and sophisticated. She would not agree to marry my father until the royal harem had been emptied and closed. It was a long and stormy courtship.'

Her interest fairly caught now, Faye said, 'But he must have been madly in love with her—'

'She was a special woman and my father chose wisely for she had a great impact on our culture. She opened up schools for girls. She drove a car. She flew a plane. It is thanks to her influence that our society became more liberal and just.'

Faye was even more intrigued. 'So when did your mother pass away?'

His lean-boned features shadowed, his sculpted mouth tightening. 'Ten years ago. She was bitten by a rare poisonous snake. She was given the wrong antidote and by the time the mistake was recognised it was too late to save her. My father went half mad with grief.'

'How awful...' she whispered with a shaken look of sympathy for, when it came to the loss of a loved one, accidents and mistakes which might possibly have been avoided had to leave the most bitter taste of all.

'Come here...you're too far away,' Tariq urged, matching the complaint to immediate action by leaning forward and reaching for her with both hands to tug her up and across into the circle of his arms.

Faye was totally taken aback to find herself first kneeling over him and then flipped over in a careful re-arrangement that left her lying on top of him and feeling very exposed. With her back turned to him, her bottom pinned between his hard thighs and her head resting back against his shoulder, she said with jerky stress in an effort to keep the conversation flowing, 'So...er... *how* many brothers and sisters do you have?'

'Only Rafi...'

'But...' She bit her lip uncertainly, concentration already challenged by the intimate contact of their bodies and the seemingly casual sweep of Tariq's hands sliding down over her smooth, taut ribcage, sending her treacherous heartbeat haywire. 'Your father...all those concubines...?'

'As a teenager, my father caught mumps. He believed he would never father a child. My arrival was greeted as being in the realms of a miracle and Rafi was conceived only with fertility assistance and my late stepmother's iron-willed determination,' Tariq admitted wryly.

'That doesn't...er...make Rafi less of a brother,' Faye said breathlessly as those lean brown hands came to rest just below the heaving swell of her breasts. She fought to keep oxygen in her lungs, sensual tension winging through her slender, trembling length like a storm warning she could not suppress. 'You should... er...think of your father when you look at him, not of your stepmother...whom I gather wasn't an awfully nice person.'

Above her head, Tariq loosed a grim laugh. 'Unhappily, Rafi is already labelled the length and the breadth of Jumar as being of a similar nature.'

'But he's still so young...how can that be?'

'His mother's unpleasant reputation went before him.

She was very unpopular.' Tariq loosed a rueful sigh and let his fingers rise to cover the rosy pink nipples involuntarily straining for his attention.

As an electrified shiver of helpless response ran through Faye and her eyes squeezed shut on the intensity of the sensation, Tariq continued talking in a slightly roughened undertone. 'Were anything to happen to me in the near future, my people might not accept Rafi as my successor. For that reason and others, I will soon have to take a second wife and father a son of my own.'

Emerging from the sensual haze provoked by his most minor foray over her shamelessly wanton flesh, Faye jerked rigid when that casual announcement finally sank in. Her shaken eyes opened very wide, pain biting into her very bones without warning. *A second* wife? Did that mean that, however briefly it had lasted, their marriage had been a true marriage a year ago? But what did that matter now when Tariq had long since divorced her?

'A second wife…?' Faye parroted, although she had waged a mighty battle with her impulsive tongue and tried very hard not to comment.

'I have had enough of the water…but *not* enough of you,' Tariq countered with a ragged edge to his sexy drawl, beginning to rise from the water and carrying her with him to lift her out of the Jacuzzi again.

Dazed and devastated by the unbelievably agonising idea of Tariq marrying another woman, Faye stood there streaming with water while she was wrapped in a huge fleecy towel like a small child. There was something extremely disorientating about the way Tariq just reacted with split-second timing and switched channel and subject, something decidedly terrifying about the totally offhand manner in which he had mentioned his plans to marry again.

Here she was naked within an hour of his becoming her first lover, her body still singing under even his most light and impersonal touch, and yet here *he* was treating her like a casual bed partner, a sex object who had no value beyond the fleeting physical pleasure she might give. An object without any apparent right to have vulnerable feelings of her own. Well, a little voice said inside her head, just what did you think becoming the mistress of an Arabian prince would entail?

'Another w—?' she began shakily again, gazing up into glittering lion-gold eyes, voice failing altogether as he released his hold on the towel and let it drop round her ankles instead.

'I want you all over again,' Tariq confided thickly. 'But then that is only to be expected when it has been so long since I have been with a woman—'

'So long?'

As if that was a rather stupid question, a slight frown-line furrowed his imperious brows as he drew her to him with purposeful hands. 'For the whole of the past year, I have naturally been in mourning for the tragic deaths in my family.'

His father, his stepmother, she assumed absently. Official mourning to show respect for the departed? What did she know about that? Yet she respected him for that self-denial. Or was it just that the knowledge that there had been no other woman for him since he had first met her gave her a much-needed sense of not being merely one more in a long line of available female bodies? For women, certainly in the West, would always be available to Tariq. When she had been seeing him, she had been painfully aware that he attracted her sex without even trying.

'Faye...so hungry am I for you, I could devour you where I stand,' Tariq admitted in a charged undertone.

Her lashes lifted, sensible thought snatched from her. She gazed up at him, jolted by the primal fire in his eyes, the hard male clenching of his superb bone structure. He knotted his fingers slowly into her hair, drawing her inexorably to him, anchoring her to his big, powerful frame. The hard, potent proof of his hunger brushed her quivering tummy and her legs turned hollow and her mind went blank and she could not drag her mesmerised eyes from the savage lure of his. The wanting was back with a vengeance, hotter and even less controllable than before. She could feel a damp, pulsing ache between her thighs, an ache that was becoming frighteningly familiar.

He swept her up and strode out of the bathroom. Like a doll without will or voice she didn't object but shame touched her deep for the fastest route back to the bed was all that mattered to her. Just that ragged note in his voice, just a touch, just a scorching look of raw hunger and something in her melted, reducing her to reckless, mindless surrender to his dominance, all defences forsaken. How could she fight herself?

'I meant to have you only once tonight.' Tariq

groaned. 'But the once was only the breaking of a fast, not sufficient...I could have taken you in the Jacuzzi, I could have taken you on that hard floor, against the wall...the dawn is far away but it threatens me for tomorrow I must spend all day in talks with the sheikhs—'

Enervated and intimidated by that series of earthly declarations of intent, Faye mumbled shakily, 'The wall?'

Tariq gave her a shimmering smile of pure blazing assurance. 'Anywhere you want, any way you want.'

'I only know one way...'

Tariq spread her across the bed. On some dim level of awareness her nostrils flared in vague surprise at the scent of freshly laundered sheets. Evidently even in the space of their brief absence the bed had been changed.

'That was basic,' Tariq husked. 'Think steep learning curve...'

Her feverish gaze welded to him, her face hot with embarrassment but her wanton body secretly burning. She couldn't take her eyes off him. The sexual heat he emanated filled her with helpless excitement. You're going to spend the rest of your days regretting this, her conscience warned. You're going to hate yourself...

'Think pleasure beyond your wildest fantasies...' Tariq lowered himself down over her inch by sexy inch, trapping the breath in her throat, charging her quivering length with the most intense anticipation. Well, maybe she could learn not to hate herself...fate, he had called it, no point fighting fate...no point denying that that wicked smile of sensual promise slashing his lean, dark, devastating face bereft her entirely of her wits.

'Thinking...' she conceded weakly.

'Feeling...' Tariq traded, sliding between her parted thighs with the slow carnal expertise of a male who liked to tempt and incite. 'Until you don't care what day it is or what time it is and hunger and need for me controls your every thought, your every action...'

A chill of foreboding touched her deep down inside. 'You want me to love you...'

'Yes...' Tariq studied her with dark, deep-set eyes of unutterable calm.

'So that you can throw me away again,' she framed unevenly.

'If you please me enough, I may only throw you as far as my villa in France,' Tariq breathed with lazy cool. 'Then I could visit you when I wanted to and the tables would be truly turned for you would be jumping every time the phone rang, praying it was me and you would never ever *dare* to be unavailable...'

'That's some agenda you've got,' Faye muttered with forced amusement. 'No harem but complete enslavement.'

'The only game player would be me...'

'Well, there wouldn't really be room for anyone else with that ego of yours.'

He threw back his proud dark head and laughed with rich appreciation and then he brought his mouth down on hers and kissed her breathless. Until all she was conscious of was the feel of him, the taste of him and her own deep, endless hunger...

FAYE SHIFTED IN THE DAWN LIGHT, waking slowly, conscious of a myriad sensations: Tariq holding her close, the weightless feel of her own limbs and a level of sweet contentment beyond anything she had ever imagined.

'Happy, *aziz*?' he murmured, easing her back into the hard heat and shelter of his lean, powerful frame, pressing his lips against a pale, slim shoulder, sending an evocative shiver winging through her awakening length.

'Blissful…' The hand he had splayed across her tummy melded her even closer and she felt his hair-roughened chest graze the skin of her back, the flex of his long, powerful thighs against her slender hips. A sheet of paper could not have squeezed between them and, at that instant, that was her definition of bliss.

Erotic images of the night they had shared assailed her mind, images that shook her but still filled her with an intoxicating heat she could not resist, any more than she could resist him. Now she understood what had once prompted her to make an utter fool of herself around him. Not just his devastating good looks or his powerful personality but the excitement, the sheer charge of physical excitement he evoked just walking into a room. That white-hot sexuality, that volatile charge of innate sensuality was as much a part of him as the cool self-discipline which cloaked it. So what was it like being an Arabian mistress? she asked herself, in a dizzy state of delight that had nothing to do with intellect. It was the passport to the sensual heaven of another world for she did not want the night to end, she did not want the light fingering through the tent room to rise to the strength of the full morning sun.

'Good…' Tariq let his hands glide up over her breasts

in the lightest of caresses and she arched her spine, instinctively pushing her swelling flesh into his palms, driven by the tingling demands of her own sensitised body.

'Everything's good,' she mumbled, jolted by her own instant response, shaken by the ever-ready heat he could ignite at will, wondering for a split second if she was insatiable, wondering anxiously if it was quite normal to want any male as much as she now seemed to want him. Constantly.

'Then I'm happy too…' He let his fingers encircle the swollen prominence of her nipples, stroking, tugging, teasing the tender tips.

She jackknifed back against him, a long sobbing breath escaping her throat, and just closed her eyes tight, letting the pleasure cascade through her like a drug she craved, for long, endless moments totally lost within its grasp.

'Although "happy" is something of an understatement,' Tariq husked above her head, the dark, smouldering rasp of his voice sending tiny shivers down her taut spine. 'You are very passionate.'

She was not capable of speech. There was no yesterday, no today, no tomorrow, she told herself feverishly, no reason why she had to think if she didn't want to, for to think might be to let go of the happiness singing through her veins like a heady intoxicant.

'Indeed you might have been fashioned at birth solely for me.' A faint bitter edge harshened his tone and then he buried his mouth with sensual force in the extended length of her throat. As he hit on a tiny pulse spot with devastating accuracy, she moaned in response.

No longer did she have to tell herself not to think as the slow burn of desire flooded her with mindless heat. He was moving against her, letting her feel his hard, potent arousal, and she lay back against him, quivering, waiting, anticipating, every skin cell alight. He rearranged her with a care that was as tender as it was teasing. He pushed up her knees, drew her back again, sought with deft fingers the damp, swollen centre of her and played there until tortured moans sobbed in her throat.

'Tariq—'

'Wait—'

'I don't want to wait…I can't!' But she knew why there was the need for that slight hiatus, knew he was ensuring that their lovemaking would not result in a pregnancy.

'Yes, you can…' Tariq pulled her back to him and entered her all too willing body with surging force.

The sensation was so delicious, she arched her back in helpless pleasure. But one thing he had already taught her: there was no end to the pleasure, no boundaries either. He caught her chin and tugged her face around so that he could possess her mouth in a hot, demanding kiss that branded her. As he took her with agonisingly slow, deep thrusts, she lost herself in the rising, burning excitement of her own hunger. It was as if he were all around her for she felt totally possessed by him and she moaned his name, driven by every invasive shift of his lean, hard body to a greater height. And then the roaring in her ears came like a great wave and she felt him shuddering against her in the grip of a hungry satisfaction as powerful and uncontrollable as her own... and that was even more of a joy to her than the aching, drowning flood of her own release.

In the aftermath, Tariq rolled her back against the pillows and stared down at her. He brushed the wildly tumbled pale blonde hair from her damp brow. She noticed his hand was unsteady. Hawkish golden eyes gazed down into hers, stubborn dark-stubbled jawline clenching hard. 'Surely you are sore now...I didn't mean to take you again. Your pleasure should not be less than mine.'

Faye reddened to the roots of her hair, turned her head away, for there was no denying that after a night of constant lovemaking she was tender, but she could no more resist him than she could have resisted water after a week in the hot sun. 'It wasn't,' she mumbled.

'I don't believe you.' Long brown fingers drew her discomfited face back to his keen scrutiny. 'No woman has ever wanted me as much as you. If I keep you here, I don't believe you'll be fit to rise from this bed and walk by tomorrow, *aziz*.'

With that mortifying and earthy assurance, Tariq released her and sprang out of bed.

'So you're not keeping me here?' Faye prompted before she could bite back that startled question.

'I think it would be best if you returned to the Muraaba.'

Slight effort at diplomacy in implying she had a choice when she so evidently did not have a choice if he did not want her around. After the night they had shared, she reeled in shock from that rejection.

'In any case, I'll be engaged in talks for the next few days and too busy to give you much attention,' Tariq completed.

Attention? Like a child or a pet might hope to receive? That particular word seemed to reduce her to a very low level of importance. Super-sensitivity to his every spoken word had now afflicted Faye. The harem might have been abolished but she could not help thinking of his father who had sent for a concubine whenever he'd felt like one. After only one night, she was to be dispatched back to the palace.

'I hope you won't mind travelling back by car, rather than by air. It will be a lengthy journey.'

'And why should you spare a helicopter for little insignificant me?' Faye flipped over onto her tummy and pushed her hot, mortified face into the pillow, cringing at how immature that response had made her sound.

'It is not like that,' Tariq responded with grave quietness. 'I do not believe in unnecessary flights being made merely to save time.'

No woman has ever wanted me as much as you. She shuddered with shame that he should have recognised that and confronted her with that reality. How attractive did men really find the women who found them irresistible? A too willing woman would not challenge or excite the essential hunter in any male. She had just spent the *whole* night being overwhelmed by how fantastic he was in bed.

'Faye…you're taking this too personally.'

'Maybe you'd like to tell me how *not* to take it personally,' she said jaggedly.

'Sex is a seductive force. I walked in paradise with you last night,' Tariq murmured coolly, 'but I have other responsibilities to meet.'

That cool reminder bit like a whip into her unprotected skin. But then she already felt that during the long, passionate hours of the night she had lost an entire layer of protective flesh and somehow turned into someone else, for she no longer knew the woman she had become. He was sending her away and she was arguing about it. She could not believe that she was letting herself down to such an extent. And Tariq had a wonderfully evocative turn of phrase and tone. He had made walking in paradise sound like a giant, hugely wicked taste of the forbidden, to be treated with extreme caution, possibly even *rationed*.

'If you stay here, you would be too great a distraction. I could turn a coffee break into an excuse for a private orgy,' he murmured darkly, undertones churning up the atmosphere around him.

A distraction? Her image of herself had already sunk lower than the soles of her own feet. Numbly, she lifted her head and focused on his lithe, powerful physique in profile. The hard, clean planes of his high cheekbones were fiercely taut, the set of his strong jawline decidedly aggressive. He was pulling on riding breeches. The long brown sweep of his once satin-smooth back bore scratch marks from her nails. He had a bruise from her teeth on one muscular shoulder—maybe more than one. Tariq looked as if he had had a run-in with a sex-starved woman, possibly even a whole bunch of them. But even unshaven and with his hair tousled by the all too frequent clutch of her greedy fingers, he was staggeringly beautiful to her stricken gaze. Her heart now felt as if it were in the palms of his lean hands, already crushed, soon to be dropped and maltreated in the worst of ways. And as she watched him dress with that easy, silent grace that was so much a part of him she could no longer pretend to herself, no longer hide from the truth of her own feelings or, even worse, her own wounding insight into his mood.

'You wish you had never set eyes on me again...' Faye said painfully.

'Do not presume to know what is in my mind,' Tariq urged with chilling immediacy, glancing up and transfixing her with brilliant golden eyes. 'Once you taught me regret but you will never do so again. Once you had the power to make me ignore common sense. *No more.*'

As a message for the immediate future it was not encouraging.

CHAPTER EIGHT

SILENCE and mute misery ruled the breakfast at which Faye shredded croissants and ate nothing for she had no appetite for food. The servants kept on bringing ever more tempting dishes to the table but she still could not eat. Soon she would be leaving the tent palace.

It was only two hours since she had woken up in Tariq's arms. Two hours since she had made the mistake of believing that she was more necessary to Tariq than she was. His seemingly insatiable hunger for her had somehow made her feel secure. But she had deceived herself into thinking what she wanted to think, she conceded strickenly. Tariq had set ruthless limits to their relationship and there was no longer any danger of her weaving fantasies. She was the light entertainment in the bedroom, nothing more.

Tears prickled at the back of her eyes. Strange how she had failed even to see that chilling single-minded ruthlessness in Tariq fourteen months ago when he had courted her with white roses and candlelit dinners. Yes, courted her, old-fashioned word that but very apt for those two months they had dated before Percy had wrecked everything. Of course, Tariq had thought he loved her back then and the officer-and-a-gentleman syndrome had ruled supreme. He hadn't tried to get her into bed, although he could have done so easily. He had not mentioned love or made any false promises.

No, even then Tariq had not asked her to love him or encouraged her to love him. But, regardless of common sense, she had fallen in love and had never stopped loving him, she now acknowledged painfully. It was impossible to continue denying the strength of her own feelings for Prince Tariq Shazad ibn Zachir. However, admitting that truth only made her feel more vulnerable than ever.

Loving Tariq put her more in his power. The guy she loved despised her yet continued to desire her. Only, now that he had slaked that hunger over and over again on her wanton and willing self, he just wanted her out of his sight. Banished to the Muraaba. How low could she sink that she should long to stay with him? Didn't she have any pride at all?

Her hands curled into tight, hurting fists. 'Sex is a seductive force,' he had said. Well, in her case, sex was a *destructive* force. With her body she had already given him eager consent to being his mistress. That was what she was…his mistress. She didn't even have the wedding ring any more. He had kept that. Yet he must have considered her as being his wife at some stage, possibly only momentarily, she reasoned, for why else would he have referred to his need to take *another* wife?

Yet even after he had told her that, she had still behaved like a lovelorn, stupid fool. She cringed, unable to credit the woman she had become during the hours of darkness. As she shifted her feet she felt the weight of the sapphire anklet which had some sort of trick lock on it that refused to be undone. She skimmed a trembling hand down her leg and wrenched at it for it suddenly seemed like a badge of servitude.

'Shiran, I want someone to speak to His Royal Highness and find out how to get this thing off me...'

The little maid departed. It was fifteen minutes before she reappeared. She got down on her knees and whispered, 'Prince Tariq says that it is his pleasure that you should wear his gift, my lady.'

His pleasure? Faye quivered with disbelief for it seemed to her that the entire country of Jumar revolved round Prince Tariq ibn Zachir's *pleasure*. So unassailable was his status with his devoted subjects that he could even parade his foreign mistress off to bed without offending anyone's sensibilities!

'His Royal Highness also said...' Shiran visibly swallowed.

'Yes, what did he say?' Faye's charged enquiry shook.

'Please not to bother him with trivial enquiries when he is engaged in matters of state.'

As Faye plunged to her feet as though jet-propelled by that arrogant jibe, Rafi provided a distraction by bursting in on them like a missile shot out of a cannon, servants in hot pursuit. Throwing himself at Faye, he clutched at the skirt of her summer dress with frantic hands. 'You can't go away...you take me with you...you take Rafi too!'

'What on earth...?' Faye lifted the little boy in an effort to calm him down.

'Prince Rafi knows you are returning to the Mu-raaba.' Shiran sighed.

Rafi wrapped his arms round Faye. 'I come too...I be good...I will be really good boy.'

'Will Prince Rafi accompany us and the babies too?' her maid asked her.

'I don't have the authority to make a decision like that—'

'There is only Prince Tariq but he will be too busy for the children while he is with the sheikhs.'

'Can I come...can I come?' Rafi demanded.

Nobody else? For even little Basma and Hayat, Faye wondered in surprise. 'Surely the twins have parents?'

Shiran gazed back at her in wide-eyed surprise. 'No, my lady. All their family were lost.'

'Lost?' Faye queried.

'People go away...they die,' the little boy in her arms told her woodenly. 'Bang bang... the plane fall out of the sky...all die.'

That explanation chilled the blood in Faye's veins and she paled.

'Terrible, terrible day...' Shiran said chokily, eyes swimming.

'Prince Tariq does not cry...Prince Rafi does not cry,' Rafi chimed in, but his strained little face was dripping tears.

Her arms tightening round the child, Faye hugged him to her, her own eyes stinging. She would never have opened the subject of the whereabouts of Basma and Hayat's parents had she been aware that they were dead. 'Well, if no one minds, you and I and the twins can all go back to the palace together,' she heard herself promising.

Rafi said that he would have to fetch his toys and took off at speed.

'Tell me about the plane crash,' Faye urged Shiran.

Rafi's mother, his cousin and his wife, who had been the parents of the twins, and even the twins' grandparents had all died in the same tragedy. On a flight between Jumar city and Kabeer on the Gulf coast, the plane had developed engine trouble and had attempted a crash landing which had failed. Basma and Hayat's father had entrusted his daughters to Tariq's care in his will. The poor man could never have dreamt that he might die so young and leave Tariq responsible for two babies still only months old.

In one appalling day, Tariq had lost a good number of his closest relatives. *I do not believe in unnecessary flights being made merely to save time.* Small wonder, Faye conceded sickly, sinking deep into shock.

It took four Toyota Landcruisers to transport so large a party back to the Muraaba and, during that lurching and often torturously slow drive over the desert sands, Faye had plenty of time to think over what she had learnt. She now fully understood why Tariq had spent an entire year in mourning and she felt terrible that she had not known for the tragedy must have been widely reported. However, she rarely watched television and the only newspaper she read at home was a local one which did not cover international events. Tariq, she finally grasped, had the responsibility of raising three orphaned children.

The entrance hall of the Muraaba was full of silent kneeling servants.

'Why are they doing that?' Faye whispered to Shiran in dismay. 'Who are they waiting for?'

'They are showing respect, my lady,' Shiran explained. 'Wave your hand and they will go about their duties again.'

Faye did so and passed on by. With Rafi tagging along, she was shown upstairs to a magnificent suite of rooms that rejoiced in balconies that overlooked the beautiful gardens. Signs of Tariq's occupancy were everywhere. Polo trophies, family photographs, the portrait of a gorgeous blonde woman with stunning dark eyes. His *mother*, Shiran told her with positive reverence. In another age, Tariq's late mother might have been a supermodel and no longer did Faye marvel at the surrendering of the hundred concubines.

Lunch was served to her in an imposing dining room but the presence of Rafi, Basma and Hayat made it a lively occasion. She spent the rest of the day with the children, relieved by their inability to sense the painful conflict of her warring emotions. For no sooner was she separated from Tariq than she felt empty, abandoned and miserable. She got very angry with herself and with the feelings she could not control. That evening when she had tucked the twins into their cots she read Rafi a story, but only after overcoming his temper tantrum at her refusal to allow him to share *her* bed.

By eleven, Faye was in bed reading the historical romance she had brought out to Jumar with her but hadn't got around to opening. It was a good book. Having lifted her head briefly at the noise of a helicopter landing on the palace heli-pad, she had returned her attention to her novel when the bedroom door opened.

Her head shot up. Tariq lounged in the doorway with a wolfish grin. 'I thought I would surprise you.'

Dry-mouthed, Faye stared at him. Clad in a crisp white short-sleeved shirt, open at his brown throat, and smoothly tailored cream chinos, he looked sensational. All sleek and sexy and sophisticated.

'Success…' Tariq murmured, indolently shouldering shut the door and strolling across the room. 'You look good in my bed.'

'I thought you had other responsibilities…' she said breathlessly.

'I will fly back to the talks at dawn.'

'I don't think you know what you want.'

'It is simple…*I want you.*'

Her violet-blue eyes dilated at the flashburn effect of his glittering golden gaze and the husky, intimate timbre of his dark, deep drawl. Beneath the fine cotton of her strappy nightdress, she was mortified to feel the languorous swell of her breasts and the tightening of her nipples as they pushed against the cloth.

Lean fingers twitched the book out of her nerveless grip. He studied the scantily clad Viking hero on the cover with very male amusement. 'Colourful.'

'Just something to pass the time—'

Stunning eyes glittering, Tariq studied the rising pink in her lovely face as she sat rigidly upright in the bed. 'But now I am here…'

'So?' Faye lifted her chin.

'I am much more accessible than the guy in the book…better taste in clothes too.' Sinking down on the side of the bed, Tariq closed his lean hands to her slim shoulders to tilt her forward into his arms.

I will freeze him out…I will not respond, she swore vehemently to herself.

'Ice is a challenge to those born in the desert,' Tariq breathed with audible amusement, the sun-warmed scent of him flaring her nostrils as he toyed with her tremulous lips in a provocative, darting foray. 'You know that you burn for me too.'

No more, she told herself feverishly. Ten ones are ten, she chanted inside her head as he pressed her lips apart and she quivered, suffering not only from temptation but also from the sheer weight of her anticipation. Ten twos are twenty, she continued, struggling not to lean into him, struggling not to moan as he let his tongue flick in a sexy intrusion between her parted lips. Parted lips? Close them! Think about something else, desperation urged.

Tariq laced one hand into her hair and kissed her slow and deep until the blood drumming in her veins hit fever pitch and her heart was hammering. *A second wife* hurtled up to grab her memory at the last moment, for during the afternoon she had wondered whether one of the reasons for remarrying that he had not declared was his responsibility for three young children. She jerked her head back from his, a sudden chill dousing her shameless heat and said jerkily, 'Last night, you used the expression "a second wife"…'

'Yes.'

'That suggested that you had *had* another wife...so I want to know if that was me you were sort of referring to?' Faye pressed awkwardly.

'Who else?' Tariq confirmed drily.

All of a sudden Faye had no need of multiplication tables to keep her brain focused. She drew back from him with a bewildered look. 'So you are saying that we were really married...properly married, even if it didn't last long?'

'What else?'

What else? *What else?* In complete shock as the reality that they had been truly married that day a year ago sank in, Faye snaked back from him, taut spine bracing to the banked-up pillows behind her. She studied him with huge, shaken eyes. 'But you told me that that wedding ceremony was a total sham!'

'No,' Tariq contradicted with extreme coolness. 'I told you that the essential meaning of a ceremony into which I felt forced was a sham but I never at *any* stage suggested that it was not a true marriage in the eyes of the law.'

Faye was transfixed as he made that outrageous nit-picking distinction. She just gaped at him. 'You mean I was *genuinely* your wife after that ceremony?'

'What else could you have been?' Tariq asked even more sardonically. 'You were my bride.'

'Your b-bride...?' she stammered, all wits having deserted her. 'Percy told me the ceremony could only have been some kind of Jumarian mumbo-jumbo when I told him that you had already divorced me again—'

'But I had not already divorced you and there is no

mumbo-jumbo in the law of Jumar,' Tariq ground out, his dark, deep-set eyes hard with disgust. 'But how typical that offensive suggestion was of the man who made it! How could your stepfather have made that judgement when I forbade him the right to attend? Naturally it was a legal marriage and, considering that we were first wed by a Christian man of the cloth, how could *you* pretend to believe otherwise? Unlike your stepfather, I am a man of honour.'

Faye was staring at him with a heart sinking further with every second that passed and every word he spoke. 'I'm not pretending, but the Christian minister didn't use a word of English either and I wasn't sure he was what I thought he was. I only believed it was all a sham because you *said* it was... And you knew I thought that—'

'I know you say you thought that *now*. When we talked at the Haja, that is certainly the excuse you attempted to employ for your behaviour in accepting that bank draft and fleeing the embassy last year,' Tariq outlined with daunting precision. 'I soon realised that.'

'The excuse?' No matter how hard Faye tried to master the stupor of shock settling over her, she failed. Only two days back, she was recalling that when they had sheltered from the storm Tariq had made comments that had struck her as utterly incomprehensible. 'In the cave, you said something about me not having followed you back to Jumar...you said a true wife would never have left the embassy. At the time, I didn't understand because your saying that made no sense—'

'I see no point in rerunning this drama so long after the event,' Tariq spelt out coolly.

Faye studied his lean, strong face fixedly. 'But I have a right to know. Are you telling me that a year ago you would have accepted me as your wife if I had stayed or later flown out to Jumar?'

'I have no crystal ball to tell me what I might have done in a set of circumstances that did not arise...so that is a foolish question.'

'A f-foolish question,' Faye parroted but inside her had sparked a flame ready to surge into a towering inferno of incredulous raging pain. 'I didn't notice *you* trying to haul me back from running away that day—'

'Naturally not—'

'Because you couldn't get rid of me fast enough! At least, be honest about that,' she urged him bitterly.

'Understandably I was still very angry with you but I was not responsible for the decisions that you made—'

'But I didn't know I was making any decision...I thought the decision had been *made* for me! For goodness' sake, I believed that you had divorced me within minutes of our wedding, so there wasn't the slightest chance that I would have hung around, was there?' she argued with feverish emotion.

Tariq dealt her a shimmering appraisal, his lip curling. 'Perhaps you would like to be my wife now that the money I gave you then is spent—'

'I won't even dignify that with an answer!' In receipt of that ultimate put-down, Faye felt a convulsive sob clog up her throat. 'You let me walk out on our marriage and you didn't come after me—'

'Why would I have done so?' Tariq countered with sardonic bite. 'You were in the wrong…I was *not*. You made no attempt to discuss our differences or defend yourself at the time. You simply took the money and ran.'

Faye trembled. All too late she was recognising Tariq's worst flaw. A level of stubborn, unyielding pride that appalled her. He had been so stubborn and so proud that he had let her walk away from their marriage for ever, never once allowing for the fact that she might have misunderstood the situation or that she might have been innocent.

'What else would I have done when I believed you had just divorced me and I had no idea there was a bank draft in that envelope for I never opened it? You misjudged me, yet I would have forgiven you for that…' An unsteady laugh empty of humour fell from her lips. 'But you can't believe that *you* could be wrong about anything. Aside of lying about my age which is something teenagers the world over do, my only sin was just accepting your marriage proposal—'

'Faye—'

She moved a shaking hand, too wounded to look at his lean, bronzed features. 'But you were offering me what I wanted more than anything in the world. I loved you… And, yes, guilty as charged, I desperately wanted to be your wife!'

Tariq closed a strong hand over hers but his own hand was not quite steady and she was able to detach her fingers with ease. 'No one of us may change the past.'

Faye turned her back on him, bitterness enclosing her

along with a mortification so deep it hurt. How could she talk as she had to him? How could she reveal so much? What was the point? He had never wanted to marry her in the first place, so naturally he was proofed against her every attempt to argue in her own defence.

'I've got only one more thing to say.' She breathed unsteadily. 'You know about as much about real love as I know about ruling Jumar so don't kid yourself that that was love you were feeling! Your horse has got more sensitivity. Percy tried to make a fool of you and that outraged you because I bet no one had ever dared to do that to you before. So you took it out on me and you're *still* taking your hurt pride out on me...'

The silence that followed seethed and sizzled.

'Are you quite finished?' Polar ice would have been warmer than that ground-out question.

She squeezed her eyes shut in misery. *Hurt pride.* Two words her macho desert warrior would never forgive her for. But then he was no good at forgiving anything, so why should she care? He thought she was a horrible little gold-digger, an inveterate liar and schemer, still set on trying to feather her own nest. But, worst of all, he had cared so little for her that he had let her leave him even though she had been his wife. *You were in the wrong...I was not.* She shuddered. No, that had not been love, not what she recognised as love, so she need not torment herself with the belief that she had lost his love, but tears still coursed silently down her cheeks.

'If I had taken my anger out on your stepfather... had I allowed myself within ten feet of him, I would have killed him with my bare hands. And not for the blackmail attempt but for turning *you* into something so much less than you might have been!'

The savage chill of sincerity in those words took her aback. In the rushing silence which followed, she listened to him undressing. She squirmed over to the far edge of her side of the bed and reached a determined resolve. From that very moment she swore she would not think again about their disastrous wedding day, their marriage which she had not even known existed in reality, or the fact that he might have divorced her since then. She had wasted a whole year of her life on endless regrets and now she had said sorry as well, so that was that. *Finito!*

The mattress gave beneath his weight. The lights went out.

A tiny betraying sniff escaped her as she opened her mouth to snatch in a ragged breath.

Tariq invaded her side of the bed without warning. 'Let me hold you—'

'No!' she snapped. 'Can't I even be miserable on my own?'

'Not when you are making me miserable too.' Tariq groaned, tugging her into his strong arms, tightening his hold on her when she made a squirming attempt to snake free. 'I will not touch you. We can be miserable together. Just lie still.'

The heat and solidarity of his big powerful frame crept into her stiffness like a sneak invasion. Slowly the tension leeched out of her. 'You know...the first I heard about that dreadful plane crash last year was today,' she heard herself whisper, for she felt that really she ought to say something on that subject.

Tariq tensed.

'I'm really sorry. Your father, your stepmother… The whole year must have been a nightmare for you to get through.'

'Surely the crash was mentioned on the British news?'

'I'm sure it was but six months ago my life was in total upheaval,' Faye confided ruefully. 'The house was being sold and I was seeing to all the packing and look-ing for somewhere to live. That's probably how I missed out on hearing about the crash. You mentioned your stepmother's death soon after I arrived here but I had no idea there were other relatives of yours involved—'

'Which house was being sold?' Tariq interrupted.

She frowned. 'What do you mean by *which*?'

'Your brother's home or yours?'

'Adrian lived in army quarters: he didn't own his house and when he quit the army he had to get out of it. I'm talking about the house where we grew up—'

'But why was it sold?'

Faye sighed. 'Adrian and I joint-owned it but it was too far out of London to suit Lizzie and him, so I agreed to the sale… I told you that he put the proceeds into starting up his business—'

'But I didn't realise that you had sacrificed your *own* home. How could you let your stupid brother sell the very roof over your head?' Tariq demanded rawly.

'Please don't call Adrian stupid, Tariq,' she muttered, very uncomfortably for it had occurred to her more than once over the years that her big brother, much as she loved him, was not the brightest spark on the block.

'But where have you been living since then?'

'I got a bedsit near where I work…although I don't suppose I'll have a job when I get back because I was only supposed to be away a few days—'

'What is a bedsit?'

'Are you serious?' She smiled in the darkness, thinking that there was no good reason why Tariq should understand what a bedsit was. She was probably the very first person he had met who lived at the poorest end of the rental market. She described her accommodation.

'You must share a bathroom with strangers?' Tariq demanded, aghast.

'Not all of us at the same time,' she pointed out, trying to suppress a giggle.

'I assumed you were living with your stepfather or your brother.'

'Adrian has his own family…and he came over here with them,' she reminded him. 'As for Percy, he only contacted me again when Adrian went into prison. You know it would break Percy's heart if he knew we had actually been married for real. You're lucky you divorced me…'

'Go to sleep…' A sliver of raw tension she could feel had entered Tariq's stillness but exhaustion was settling in on Faye and winding her down like a clock. Muffling a yawn, she surrendered to gravity and rested her head on his shoulder, marvelling that they were talking again and wondering if that was the result of her resolve to totally detach herself from their past.

Tariq was gone when she woke up at seven the next morning. As her seeking hand found nothing but emptiness beside her, she jerked in dismay at the sound of something moving about what sounded like *below* the bed. Sitting up with a start, she was just in time to see Rafi scramble out in his pyjamas, bounce up and shout, 'Boo! Did I scare you? Did I scare you?'

'*Yes*…what time is it?'

Rafi clambered up on the bed and landed himself on her lap. 'Can we have a picnic today?'

'Maybe.'

'I like you…'

'Please let me go back to sleep,' Faye begged.

Rafi climbed in below the sheet and snuggled up to her like a tadpole wriggling in itching powder, bony little knees and elbows jabbing in the small of her back. She swallowed a long-suffering groan. 'Did you see Tariq leaving?'

'I saw his helicopter.' Rafi imitated the noise at deafening pitch and sat up to start whirling his arms round and round at the same time. 'I won't go in a helicopter…it might fall out of the sky and go bang and die my brother—'

'Oh, Rafi…Tariq will be *fine*. Tariq is a wonderful pilot.' Faye groaned and, giving up on sleep, she flipped over and began tickling him until his giggles and hers rose to such a level that Shiran came running in to see what was happening.

She thought Tariq might come back that night but he did not. It was the afternoon of the following day before he reappeared. After enjoying a riotous couple of hours playing in the gorgeous terraced gardens that climbed the hillside, Rafi and the twins had been taken inside for a nap. Hot and sticky following such activity, Faye had taken advantage of the departure of the servants. Having kicked off her shoes, she was paddling in the wide shallow basin of a secluded fountain in a shaded arbour. The sensation of that cool water lapping her overheated skin felt like total bliss. Holding her dress up to her knees to prevent the hem from getting splashed, she kicked up water, watching the droplets sparkle in a shard of sunlight strong enough to pierce the hanging dark pink foliage of the spreading casuarina tree above her.

When she lifted her head, it was a considerable shock to see Tariq poised on the lush manicured grass only a dozen feet from her. His dark golden eyes flared over her comical look of dismay and glittered with rampant amusement. A devastatingly attractive smile flashed across his wide, sensual mouth and her heart hammered so hard in reaction to that charismatic charge, she felt dizzy and just kept on staring at him.

'You make a charming and refreshing picture,' he murmured huskily, moving forward and extending a lean hand to grasp hers and assist her back out of the basin.

'You were laughing—'

'Laughter has been painfully thin on the ground over the past thirty-six hours,' Tariq confided, retaining his hold on her slim fingers and gazing down at her with a mesmerising intensity that whipped colour into her already warm cheeks. 'I sat up half the night listening to two obstinate old men arguing about grazing rights that neither need. But now it seems worth it for I'm with you sooner than I had hoped.'

'My shoes…' Faye mumbled, her wide eyes stealing over him in greedy little bursts that she could not resist, taking in the exquisitely tailored pale beige suit that sheathed his very tall and powerful frame, lingering on the full spectacular effect of a colour that accentuated his black hair and sun-bronzed skin. It was no use. He still just took her breath away. Although she had sworn to be cooler than an ice cube, she could not shake the conviction that he was the most drop-dead gorgeous male alive.

'Never mind your shoes…although you are inconveniently small without them.' Banding both arms round her as he made that teasing comment, Tariq drew her close, lifting her up against him and draping her arms round his shoulders. 'Cling…'

'I don't cling,' she said tightly, shutting the allurement of him out with lowered eyelashes, fighting the urge to grab him and hold him tight and sink into the gloriously familiar scent and feel of him.

'Please…'

'You're wasting your time…'

He hoisted her higher with a strength that disconcerted her and bent his proud head to press his mouth against the tiny pulse beating out her tension just below her collar-bone. Jolted by that unexpected approach, she let her head fall back, felt a river of liquid heat forge a path through her thrumming body and loosed a choky little moan.

'Am I?' Tariq strode over to the stone bench below the tree and sank down, keeping her trapped in his arms. He gazed down at her, a wolfish grin forming on his beautiful mouth. 'I want to spend my time with you.'

'Well, I suppose I signed up for it,' Faye muttered grudgingly, maddeningly conscious of him with every wretched fibre of her being.

'What's that supposed to mean?'

'I'm your mistress. Spending time with you is hard to avoid.'

Tariq tensed and then breathed in slowly, lean, strong features taut. 'I have considered what you said the other night. It's possible that I have misjudged you to some extent—'

'It was Percy who made off with your half million—it serves you right too!' Faye told him squarely. 'You must've made the bank draft out to him—'

'Naturally. I believed you would still be living with him and he would be taking care of your needs—'

'Look, Percy never looked after me in his life and he hardly ever lived with us either, aside of the occasional weekend. He didn't *even* look after my mother. He just paid people to do it for him—'

'This is not the picture of the happy united family you gave me when I first met you—'

'Of course it's not,' Faye agreed ruefully. 'Who do you know who drags out all the dirty washing in their family if they can avoid it? And you've got to admit that Percy is a very *big* piece of dirty washing…you think I didn't see how you avoided him? You think I don't notice how much my stepfather offends people?'

'Why on earth did your mother marry such an unpleasant man?'

'Well, if she ever regretted it, she didn't show it.' Faye sighed. 'And, to be fair, he never spoke an unkind word to her that I heard, but somehow we mysteriously went from being well off to poor during their marriage.'

'Adrian once mentioned that your own father had made some very unwise investments. Your stepfather may not be responsible for the loss in family prosperity.'

'Adrian once mentioned…? Why didn't he *ever* mention that to me?' Faye demanded in exasperation.

'I can see that I've been remiss in my responsibility towards you,' Tariq breathed flatly.

Faye stiffened. 'No, you haven't been. As far as I'm concerned, I was never your wife. In fact I don't even want to *think* about all that nonsense any more.' And with that cool assurance, she broke from the loose circle of his arms and stood up in a hurry. Having forgotten that she had no shoes on, she felt the gravel below the seat bruise the soles of her bare feet, making her gasp and jump back onto the bench beside him where she hovered, stepping off one foot on to the other. 'That hurt!'

Tariq looked up at her with a slanting smile. 'A princess would have to be very dignified.'

Faye paled and then tossed her head. 'I wish you well of one…are you going to be a gentleman and fetch my shoes?'

Tariq sprang upright and reached for her hands, enclosing them tightly in his and startling her. He crushed her soft mouth under his with a devouring hunger that splintered through her in a shockwave. Then he lifted her and settled her down on the bench. Senses reeling in the aftermath of that stormy onslaught, she watched him retrieve her shoes and return with them.

'Just like Cinderella,' Tariq murmured playfully, sunlight gleaming over his luxuriant black hair as he crouched down to slide her sandals onto her small feet.

'No, she got the fairytale prince…I got the frog of little faith.'

'I beg your pardon?'

'You heard me.'

Tariq simply laughed and closed one lean hand back over hers, walking her back down the hill towards the palace.

'You only came out here to drag me back indoors again, didn't you?'

'I only came out here to find you, but you are right. I am now taking you back to my bedroom where I intend to remove every single garment you wear as fast as I possibly can and make passionate love to you,' he admitted without skipping a beat.

'Duty calls,' Faye quipped, but she could feel herself blushing, feel the spiralling ache of the exact same hunger twisting deep down inside her. And, in her opinion, that made her not one whit better than him. Moaning about being his mistress seemed a little hypocritical when she was as keen on him as she was.

He gave her a startled glance. 'You have changed.'

'Have I?'

'Now you are joking about sharing my bed.'

'Fancy that.' She shrugged. 'Bit of a problem for you, that, isn't it? Instead of feeling punished by your revenge, I'm enjoying myself.'

'I am no longer thinking of revenge—'

'It doesn't bother me. I'm only looking on this as an extended holiday.' Unfamiliar aggression was powering through Faye. If Tariq thought he was going to hear one more time about how he had broken her poor little heart, he was in for a surprise.

'Really? I suppose I'm the holiday romance?'

'No comment.'

Ten minutes of simmering silence later, Faye kicked off her shoes and lay down on the bed. 'Do you think you could remove this anklet now?'

Tariq nailed her with glittering golden eyes. 'I like to see you wear it.'

'All the time...everywhere? Even when I go paddling?'

He shed his jacket, jerked loose his tie in the manner of guy making a statement. Watching him, she stretched, conscious he could not take his eyes from her even though he was furious. She was thrilled by the discovery, a new sense of feminine power infiltrating her bloodstream like heady wine.

'You're fighting back...' he said softly.

'Did you expect me to stay in doormat mode for ever?'

Shedding his last garment, Tariq strolled over to the bed. Sunlight filtering in through the doors spread open on the balcony enveloped his bronzed magnificence and something caught in her throat. No today, no tomorrow, she told herself feverishly. She was living for the moment.

'You can't win.' Tariq came down on the bed one hundred per cent sexual predator. 'You are my woman, *aziz*.'

'While I still want you,' Faye heard herself point out.

His lean, sure fingers momentarily stilled on the buttons that ran down the front of her dress. Lush black lashes lifted on his stunning golden eyes and he gave her a slow-burning smile of pure sensual threat. 'I am not planning to bore you out of your mind in the near future.'

'Well, you're bound to think that...'

He spread the edges of the dress apart as thought he were unwrapping precious gold. She was not wearing a bra. 'I am not surprised that grazing rights failed to hold my attention last night,' he confided huskily, running an appreciative hand over one small pouting mound crowned by a prominent rosy peak. 'You are exquisite...'

She quivered at that glancing caress, forcing her spine back down to the bed. No need to wow him with overenthusiasm, she warned herself. 'You're bound to think that too after a year of celibacy—'

'And what would you know? Only days ago you were a virgin.' Tariq gazed down at her in exasperated challenge.

'I was only stating an opinion—'

'*Don't.*'

'Do you think other men would have the same opinion, then?' A little devil was dancing in Faye's head, priming her tongue.

Tariq ground out, 'Why would you ask me such an inappropriate question?'

'It's on a par with you having asked me that night how many other men I had invited to dinner and slept with.'

'I was *upset* by your behaviour—'

'Oh, were you? I thought you were just trying to make me feel cheap—'

'It was cheap.' Winding both hands into her tumbling hair as if he were imprisoning her, Tariq possessed her angrily parted lips with so much potent force, she lost her grip on her thoughts. She clutched at his shoulders, dizzy with pleasure.

But then he made the serious error of pausing to extract her from the dress. 'And you're not cheap—'

'No, indeed—to date, at my estimation, I have cost you upwards of a million pounds!'

Tariq froze at the reminder.

'Nobody could call that cheap,' Faye agreed sweetly.

Tariq glowered down at her, pale beneath his sun-darkened skin, superb cheekbones taut in his lean, strong face. 'You're worth it. Are you happy now?'

She wasn't but she nodded, wishing she had not mentioned the money: the bank draft Percy had purloined, the cost of her brother regaining his freedom.

Tariq traced her tremulous mouth with a soothing forefinger. She was blinking back tears but he didn't miss a trick and he smoothed them away. 'We are finally together. Think only of that.'

The instant he kissed her again, the hunger stormed back, intensified by her raw emotions. She loved him. She wanted him. She would not allow herself to think one step beyond those realities. A fever had got hold of her. Her hands roamed over him, adoring the flex of his hard muscles beneath his hair roughened skin. Trembling beneath her exploration, he pulled her over him, depriving her of that freedom and locking her into the hard heat of his aroused body while he plundered her lips.

'You drive me wild,' Tariq said raggedly while she struggled to catch her breath.

But even breathing was a challenge with his expert hands on her and his mouth tugging at her tender nipples. The excitement built so fast, she was lost in it, moving against him, parting her thighs with a sighing cry at his first touch. The wanting had never been so strong before, had never absorbed her so utterly. Her heart was racing, she couldn't breathe, couldn't wait, couldn't focus on anything *but...*

As Tariq sank into her in one forceful thrust, she rose against him with a driven moan of delight and what followed was the wildest pleasure she had ever known. Her heart pounding, she gave herself up to the raw excitement, wanting, needing, burning with greedy impatience and then surging so high she thought she might touch the sky in the grip of sweet ecstasy.

She surfaced back to the real world feeling glorious. Tariq was hugging her so tight, she didn't know where she began or he ended and that felt good. Even better was the way he was looking at her with tawny eyes that had a slightly dazed quality. She smiled.

'You are very special,' he murmured intently.

'So are you—'

'I might never let you go free…'

She smiled like the Sphinx, all woman and smug.

'WHERE DO YOU THINK I AM?' Tariq purred on the phone.

There was something so very sexy about Tariq on the phone, Faye reflected in a state of blissful abstraction, something so very sexy about Tariq even when he was saying the most ordinary things. He had given her the portable phone so that they could talk during the day when he had to be away from her and arrange meetings like secret lovers. It never left her side. It was her substitute for him, her instant hotline to reassurance that she was the most desirable woman in Jumar. Only two weeks ago, she had been calling him a frog, she recalled sunnily, but her frog had turned back into a prince.

'On the way home…?' she prompted eagerly.

'No.'

'How long are you going to be?' She sighed, face having fallen a mile.

'Where are you?'

'Outside…you'll have to look for me.'

'Could you doubt it?' he murmured in a husky tone of promise that sent a quiver of response down her spine.

Faye set down the phone, her attention returning to the children. It was just about nap time, she decided. Having enjoyed a long and leisurely picnic lunch, they were sitting on the carpets spread beneath the shade of the trees. Hayat clutched at Faye's arm to steady herself and planted a big soppy kiss on her cheek. Basma was already on her lap along with Rafi. When Tariq wasn't around, Faye was always with the children. She knew he spent time with them early mornings and evenings and, being painfully conscious that Basma, Hayat and Rafi were really none of her business, she never, ever intruded at those hours in the nursery section of the palace.

Indeed, she *had* wondered once or twice if Tariq had any idea just how many hours a day she passed in their company, but as he had not chosen to open the subject she was wary of doing so herself. She could not forget the way he had cut her off the couple of times she had tried talking about Rafi, but she was sure that Rafi must have mentioned her to his big brother on at least a few occasions.

In any case, when she and Tariq were together, nothing else in the world existed. They were locked into an affair of passionate, single-minded intensity and she just felt plain and simple happy. True, if she let her mind stray in the direction of the dark cloud of future foreboding threatening in the back corner of her mind, she got scared because she was more in love with Tariq than she had ever been. But all the rest of the time, she was content to let tomorrow take care of itself.

In the dreaming mood she was in, it was a shock when the two servants clearing up the picnic debris suddenly dropped down on their knees. She glanced up and was astonished to see Tariq poised about ten feet away. He had said he wasn't on his way home but he had been teasing her, she realised. What he had not said was that he had *already* arrived.

As he took in the tableau she made with the children gathered round her, Tariq could not conceal his astonishment. He dismissed the servants from his presence with a snap of his fingers. 'Exactly when did you all become this friendly?'

Without the smallest warning, Rafi leapt off her lap and shouted something in Arabic that made Tariq freeze.

'Stop it, Rafi,' Faye urged in dismay.

Rafi flung himself back at her sobbing as if his heart were breaking.

'It would appear that you have made yourself quite indispensable,' Tariq pronounced with sardonic bite, watching the twins burst into tears in concert and clutch at Faye for security. 'Accident or design?'

And with that cutting conclusion, Tariq swung on his heel and strode off.

'What did you say, Rafi?' Faye whispered shakily.

'You're my secret mama and if he takes you away, I'm going with you!' Rafi sobbed into her shoulder, turning her face to the colour of milk.

CHAPTER NINE

FAYE found Tariq in one of the ground-floor reception rooms.

'Tariq…?' she whispered apprehensively, stilling just inside the doorway.

Tariq swung round, lean, powerful face expressionless. 'Did you contrive to soothe the mass hysteria my appearance provoked?'

Faye flushed miserably. 'They're all down for a nap now. Tariq…I never dreamt that Rafi was keeping the time I've been spending with him and the twins a secret from you and certainly *not* that he's been thinking of me as his new mother.'

'I can't say I enjoyed being treated like the big bad wolf,' Tariq murmured wryly. 'Even by Basma and Hayat who usually greet me with smiles and giggles.'

'And so they would have done this afternoon if they hadn't been overtired and in the mood to be easily upset,' she assured him. 'This is all my fault.'

'That is not how I would describe the situation.' Tariq surprised her with a rueful laugh. 'I had naturally noticed the pronounced improvement in my little brother's behaviour but I had assumed it to be the result of the removal of his previous carers—'

'No, that just left him more unhappy and confused and I think that may have been why he turned to me—'

Tariq sighed. 'And then suddenly Rafi got happy and stopped his screaming tantrums and constant whinging practically overnight. To be frank, I was *so* deeply relieved by that development, I did not question the miracle. His behaviour had been a source of very real concern to me but I was hampered by the fact that he was brought up to fear me—'

'And you were always having to tell him off too…I know and I understand. But now I can see that I've been horribly thoughtless and selfish,' Faye muttered unevenly, her face taut with guilty regret. 'I've let the children become too attached to me and that wasn't fair to them.'

'It's quite amazing how well you have all bonded behind my back.' His expressive mouth quirked.

'If I've damaged your relationship with Rafi, I'm sorry.'

'No. Rafi has been much more relaxed with me since he got his hooks into his secret mama—'

'He's a very affectionate child.'

'And you're a very affectionate woman. It is just most ironic that I should have been the last to find out that you were so fond of children.'

Accident or design? he had demanded out in the gardens. But what design could she have had in befriending the children? And then her colour climbed. Did he suspect that she was angling to be considered as a wife yet again? By weaseling her sneaky way into the children's hearts and making it hard for him to end their relationship? She stiffened at that humiliating suspicion.

'Even more ironic that I would never have *dreamt* of wheeling out Rafi as he was a few weeks ago and expecting any woman to warm to him,' he commented, reaching for her curled tight hands and carefully smoothing her fingers straight to link them with his. 'In fact, most women would have run a mile at the threat of Rafi as he was then but you have great heart—'

'But not always a lot of sense...I didn't take a long-term view.'

'I don't believe you have ever taken a long-term view of anything.' Tariq stood there staring down at their linked hands as if they had become a source of deep and absorbing fascination to him. 'I, on the other hand, tend to be very decisive in most fields but most fortunately *not* when it came to divorcing you...'

'Divorcing me? When...when did you get around to it?' she muttered tightly.

Tariq breathed in very deep and then breathed out again without saying anything. She looked up at him with strained eyes, noting the line of dark colour scoring his proud cheekbones.

'Well...I actually didn't,' he finally stated curtly.

'Oh...' She was connecting with tawny eyes that could make stringing two sensible thoughts together the biggest challenge she had ever been called to meet.

'There seemed no point in telling you that three weeks ago when I still believed that I would eventually seek that divorce. At first, I thought I would be merely raising false hopes and then I thought it might distress you—'

'You actually *didn't* divorce me?' Faye was struggling a whole speech behind Tariq and a cold, clammy sensation was dampening her skin.

'You're still my wife...you have never been anything else.'

'I think I've had too much sun.' Her legs felt hollow and her tummy was churning.

Tariq urged her down onto the opulent sofa behind her. 'You've turned white.'

Word by word what he had burst upon her was sinking in, but only slowly.

'The day of the sandstorm, I agreed to a press announcement in which I claimed you as my wife. I really had very little choice. Once your presence in my life became a matter of public knowledge, I had to make a decision. Either I created a scandal that for ever soiled your reputation or I told the truth,' Tariq said, still retaining a noticeably tight hold on her now nerveless floppy fingers as he sank down beside her.

'The truth...you know, I thought you *always* told the truth,' Faye whispered, for shock was settling in on her hard.

'I have recently come to appreciate that the truth... once avoided...may be extremely hard to tell.'

Oh, how convenient, she almost said, thinking in a daze that, while her pathetic lies about her age had been held over her like the worst of sins, Tariq was now seeking to excuse himself for the same dishonesty. 'You lied to me—'

'No. I never once said that I had divorced you—'

'But you knew that I believed we were divorced—'

'Had you asked me direct, I would not have lied—'

'But you said, "Not then" when I questioned you in the cave,' she recalled shakily. 'How did you contrive to explain a mystery wife coming out of nowhere?'

'My family has never made our private lives a matter of public interest which is not to say that gossip, rumour and scandal do not abound,' he admitted tautly. 'However, I acknowledged that I made you my wife a year ago and it will be assumed, whether I like it or not, that I decided not to embark on our marriage while I was in mourning.'

'Should do wonders for your image with the *truly* pious.'

'That shames me.' Tariq breathed harshly. 'But it is not less than I deserve for setting in train a set of events which could only lead to disaster.'

Disaster? Of course, it was a disaster on his terms but not a disaster he would have to bear for long. Not with divorce being as easy as he had once informed her it was. All that she had not understood now became clear. 'Our marriage was being celebrated at that reception I attended in the desert…and you never uttered *one* word and neither did anyone else! How come I didn't guess?'

'My people, and that includes my relatives, would not open a conversation with you or I unless you or I did so first. That is simply etiquette. In addition, brides do not normally exchange conversation with anyone other than their husbands. But at the outset of that day, I believed you would inevitably appreciate what was happening—'

'And, my goodness, you were angry with me, furious at the position you had put yourself in,' Faye condemned, suddenly pulling free of him and plunging upright. 'That was our wedding night but you much preferred letting me think that I was your mistress being flaunted in front of everyone!'

'To some degree that is true but common sense should have told you that I could not have behaved in such a way with any woman in Jumar *other* than my wife,' Tariq pointed out.

'Oh, I know exactly what was on your mind. You would have cut out your tongue sooner than give me the presumed satisfaction of knowing that I was your wife!' Faye whispered bitterly. 'Please take note that I am not *feeling* satisfaction.'

'Faye?' Tariq rested his hands on her shoulders and attempted to turn her back to face him.

She whirled round and shook free of him in disgust. 'What an ego you have!'

Tariq reached out and hauled her back to him. 'Stop it,' he urged. 'I have made mistakes and so have you but if you do not appreciate how much has changed between us in the last couple of weeks, I certainly do. I *want* you as my wife. I will be honoured to call you my wife—'

'Since when?' A derisive laugh was wrenched from her. She was so angry, so hurt, so bewildered, she was trembling. 'All this time I've been your wife and I was the only person who didn't know it. Once again you have made an absolute fool of me and I will never forgive you for that!'

Tariq closed both arms even tighter around her. 'Only *I* know you didn't know you were still my wife—'

'You think that makes it any better…that I can't even trust the man I've been sleeping with…that you've been playing some kind of mind games with me for your own amusement? No, I am flat out fed up with you and finished! So let go of me!'

'No, not until I have made you see reason and you are in a calmer frame of mind—'

'Calmer?' Faye swung up her hand and dealt him a ringing slap across one high cheekbone. In the aftermath as his arms fell from her and he stepped back, she was as shaken as he was. Shocked by her own loss of control and that desire to physically attack a male who was protected by the laws of Jumar from such an offence.

In electric silence, he stared at her with fathomless tawny eyes.

'So now you can have me thrown into a prison cell and be finally rid of me *for ever*!' Faye launched at him in stricken conclusion before racing out of the room.

She didn't even know where she was running for there was no place far enough where she could hide from the enormous pain he had inflicted. Blinded by tears, conscious he was following her and wanting desperately to be alone, she headed for the nearest staircase: a spiral of stone steps generally used only by the servants.

'Faye!' Tariq called from somewhere close behind her.

She half turned, forgetting she was on a spiral staircase, and suddenly one of her feet was trying to find a resting place in mid-air. With a strangled cry of fear, she tried to right her mistake but it was too late for she was already falling. Her head crashed against the wall. She felt the momentary burst of pain but it was soon swallowed up in the deep, suffocating darkness that enclosed her.

'JUST A STUPID BUMP ON THE head, Rafi…I was really silly to run on those steps.' Faye patted his small hand where it gripped her nightdress until she gradually felt him relax beneath her soothing. 'I'm fine and glad to be out of hospital.'

'Can I stay?'

'Faye needs to rest for a while,' Tariq murmured, bending down to scoop his little brother up into his arms. 'You will see her later…that I promise.'

Faye would not look at Tariq. Having been knocked unconscious by her fall the day before, she had started coming round in the helicopter that had taken her to hospital in Jumar City. There she had been examined by three consultants in succession and had realised by Tariq's explanation that he had broken her fall and saved her from a more serious injury.

She had not looked at him when she had had to spend the whole of the previous night under observation by both the medical staff *and* Tariq. She had not even looked at him when he had reached for her hand at some stage of that endless night and begged her for her forgiveness. In fact, not looking at Tariq and just pretending with silence that he did not exist had become a rule set in stone for her survival.

As the door closed on Rafi's reluctant exit, Tariq released his breath audibly. 'Do you want me to leave?'

She squeezed her eyes tight shut and gave a jerky nod. The door opened with a quiet click and closed again. She couldn't cry. She lay staring up at the ceiling. What did she have left to say to him? What could he have left to say to her? All that time she had been his wife but he had ignored that reality for the simple reason that he had had *no* intention of keeping her as his wife. It felt even worse for her to think that, in one sense, he had been right to do that. For what would have been the point of her knowing that she was still married to him when the divorce was still to be got through? From her point of view, it just would have meant going through the same agonies twice over.

Why on earth had he started talking nonsense about wanting her to remain his wife? That had seemed the unkindest cut of all, that he should feel *so* guilty he decided he ought to make that offer. Well, you can forget that option, Tariq ibn Zachir, she thought painfully. There was only one way out of their current predicament: divorce. No more shilly-shallying! Why the heck had he let them stay married throughout the previous year? A great emptiness spread like a dam inside her and her headache got worse but at some stage she still drifted to sleep.

When she wakened a couple of hours later, her headache had receded and she examined the blue-black bruise on her right temple. Fortunately her hair concealed the worst of it. After a bath and a late light lunch, she rifled her wardrobe for something to wear.

Her wardrobe was now gigantic: it filled an entire room. Only a week earlier, Tariq had shipped in dozens of designer outfits from abroad from which she had made selections. Dazzling, fabulous clothing such as she had only previously seen in magazines. Initially she had been hugely embarrassed by his generosity but the terrible temptation of seeing herself in such exquisite garments had overcome her finer principles. Tariq was accustomed to fashionable women who wore haute couture. What woman who loved him would have chosen to keep on appearing in the same frugal and plain clothing contained in her single small suitcase?

Vanity and the desire for him to admire her had triumphed over conscience. Reddening at that awareness, Faye would have put on her own clothes had she still had them but unfortunately she had dumped the lot. The not-thinking-of-tomorrow rule she had observed in recent weeks had made her reckless. She selected an elegant skirt suit in a rich shade of old gold. When she told Tariq that she wanted a divorce, she wanted to look good—she wanted him to feel he was losing out even if it *was* only on a convenient bed partner.

Having eased on tights beneath the sapphire anklet and put on toning high heels, Faye went downstairs, only to discover that Tariq was not at home. He was at his office in the Haja. Discovering that only made her all the more determined to confront him and discuss what had to be discussed. After an exasperating long wait at her request for transport, a limo which flew two small Jumarian flags on the bonnet finally drew up.

She was taken aback when two police outriders on motorbikes took up position in front of the limo outside the palace gates, even more uneasy when she glanced out of the rear window and saw another two cars filtering out behind them. When the cavalcade she had naively not foreseen her outing might require reached the city, red stop lights were totally ignored and traffic was held up for their benefit on every approach road. For the first time, it began to truly dawn on Faye that being married to Tariq was not quite like being married to anyone else and that even the most minor thing she might choose to do could have consequences.

Latif awaited her at the side entrance of the giant building. He was full of concern about her fall, amazed she was already up and about, and assured her that every spiral staircase in the Muraaba was now to be renovated and hand-rails installed for greater safety.

As Faye was shown into Tariq's office, her heart began beating very fast. Sheathed in a light grey suit, immaculate as always, he was by the window, fabulous bone structure taut, stunning dark golden eyes slamming straight into hers in a look as compelling as his touch. 'I was astonished to hear you were on your way here. You're very pale. Sit down,' he urged. 'The doctors said you should take it easy for a few days.'

'I'd prefer to stand.' Meeting the sincere concern in his gaze, feeling the instant leap of her senses to the powerful magneticism of his presence, Faye reacted in self-defence, seeking hostility rather than pleasantries.

'Just as you let me stand sweltering out in that court-yard on my first visit here a few weeks back.'

'You should know me better. My lack of courtesy was not deliberate but an oversight. I too was under strain at that interview.'

She flushed at that hint of reproach. 'It didn't show—'

'It was quite a shock for me that day to discover that my wife did not appear to have the foggiest clue that she *was* my wife,' Tariq extended with gentle irony.

'Well, all that stuff doesn't matter now and I don't know why I mentioned boiling alive in that stupid court-yard—'

Tariq drew closer with fluid grace. 'Don't you? I have a good idea of what you're thinking and feeling right now, *aziz*. Do you imagine I am not aware that you are drawing up a great long list of my every past and present sin? So that you can impose them as a barrier be-tween us?'

Disconcerted, Faye breathed, 'I—'

'Once I went through the same process with you. Even *without* seeing you, I was able to stockpile more sins at your door. You did not even write me a letter of condolence when my father died,' Tariq pointed out. 'We were estranged but you were my wife and I was never not aware of that. I thought you were heartless—'

'I...I did *think* of writing,' muttered Faye in deep discomfiture, having turned pale as a ghost at that ref-erence to an omission which now seemed inexcusable. 'But I didn't know what to say so...so in the end I didn't bother.'

'You didn't appreciate that you were still my wife but I didn't know that,' Tariq reminded her. 'When that plane went down six months later and I lost my cousin, who was my closest friend from childhood…his wife and his parents, my aunt and uncle, who were all like a second family to me…what did you think I thought then of you when I *still* heard nothing?'

Feeling the tables had been turned on her with a vengeance, Faye squirmed and could no longer look at him direct, for her eyes were prickling with tears of sympathy. 'I didn't hear about the crash—'

'Yes, I am aware of that now and I am not trying to make you feel bad…'

Faye hung her head, wondering what he might achieve if he really *tried*, for she was feeling dreadful.

'I only want to illustrate how anger and hurt pride build on mistakes and misunderstandings. Don't do that to us now when we had already found our way through those barriers,' Tariq spelt out levelly.

Her tender pride took fire and she flung her head high, violet-blue eyes sparkling with angry resentment. 'Already? Where was I when this healing miracle was taking place?'

'Faye…if you love me, there *are* no true barriers and there is nothing that with time cannot be overcome.'

Rage was clawing at Faye. She had come to stage a confrontation with dignity. She had felt strong, committed to her purpose. But from the minute she had walked into his office, Tariq had been running verbal rings round her and making her cringe like an awkward schoolgirl in the presence of an adult. She could not bear to be reminded that she had gone on at such length about having been *crazy* about him only a year earlier.

'But the point is…I don't love you,' she snapped between gritted teeth. 'I discovered the joys of sex with you…that's all!'

Tariq studied her with unreadable cool but she could not help noticing that he had lost colour at that retaliation. 'It's good to know that I excelled somewhere.'

'I came here to discuss us getting a divorce,' Faye announced.

'You could not wait an hour for me to come home?'

Her colour heightened. 'Tariq—'

'I have no intention of continuing this conversation in my office,' he murmured levelly. 'Now go home.'

At that level command, Faye sucked in such a deep and charged breath she thought her lungs might burst.

Tariq stepped past her and cast wide the door. Her trembling hands closed into furious fists. 'I—'

'Her Royal Highness wishes to travel home before the rush hour begins, Latif.'

Faye was so dumbfounded to hear herself being referred to as 'Her Royal Highness' that she almost collided with Latif in the corridor.

The older man escorted her to a stone bench and hovered.

'Am I a princess?' The shaken enquiry just erupted from her and she went pink.

'From this moment on,' Latif informed her in a tone of great approval. 'The gift of that title is in the power of Prince Tariq alone. You are only the second princess in the history of our royal family—'

'Really?' she whispered dazedly.

Latif was now in full flood on a subject evidently close to his heart. 'Prince Tariq's lady mother first enjoyed the distinction but only on the birth of her son. However, I feel it is most appropriate that, in these more forward-thinking times, His Royal Highness should honour you early within your marriage.'

'Honour me...' Faye echoed weakly.

'It may be of interest to you to learn that you may now sit in His Royal Highness's presence in public and walk by his side as his equal without it being said that you are showing disrespect.' As Faye slowly raised her head, eyes very wide, Latif straightened his shoulders with immense satisfaction. 'Yes, we will be setting a precedent and an example in this part of the world.'

CHAPTER TEN

TARIQ did not actually return to the Muraaba until eight that evening. Having dined with the children and seen them off to bed through the usual baths, high jinks and bedside stories, Faye believed she had attained a much calmer frame of mind.

Tariq glanced into their sitting room where she was pacing the floor and flashed her a warm, appreciative smile as if everything was well between them. 'I'm going for a shower... I'll be with you soon.'

Her teeth gritted.

His brilliant golden eyes rested on her frozen face. 'You could always join me.'

Faye flew out of her seat and took the bait. 'How *dare* you suggest that?'

'Just testing the water,' Tariq murmured smooth as glass. 'No pun intended.'

She contained herself for all of ten minutes and then she headed into their bedroom. The bathroom door stood wide. Tariq was in the shower. She paced again, but the instant she heard the water switching off she lodged herself in the doorway.

'Why didn't you divorce me a year ago?' she demanded.

Tariq stepped from the shower, pushing his hair back

from his brow, all bronzed masculinity and easy grace. 'Obviously because I did not want to break that final link, regardless of how tenuous that link might have appeared. And I am very much afraid that, on the subject of divorce, I have no good news to share.'

'And what's that supposed to mean?' Watching him towel himself dry, Faye could feel familiar warmth stirring in her pelvis and she averted her eyes hurriedly.

'Some time ago, certain discreet enquiries cast that question open in a most revealing debate between the high court judges and, this evening, I learned much that I did not know. No ancestor of mine has ever applied for a divorce. There is therefore no facility for the ruler of Jumar to divorce…no case law, *no nothing*,' Tariq stated with flat emphasis.

Faye's lips parted company. 'But what about all that turning round three times and saying you divorce me stuff?'

'That must be done in a court before a high court judge and may obtain a divorce for any one of my subjects. But *not* for me. At the same time I threw those angry and foolish words at you on our wedding day, I was not aware of that. Indeed…I was so angry, I hardly knew what I was saying to you,' Tariq admitted between compressed lips.

'But you've *got* to be able to get a divorce—'

'Presumably the law would eventually work out how to allow me to divorce when I stand outside the laws of our country *but*…' Tariq rested shimmering golden eyes on her '…I don't want a divorce.'

Faye trembled. 'Yes, you do…well, you *did* when

those discreet enquiries were casting open questions to some legal debate between judges!'

'No, it was my father who had those enquiries made some months before his death—'

'Your...*father*?'

'I had no idea he was considering divorcing Rafi's mother but, evidently, he was. It was Latif who enlightened me on that news this evening.' The towel draped round his lean hips, Tariq crossed the floor and rested his hands on her shoulders to stop her from spinning away out of reach. 'I will say again. I don't want a divorce...do you think you could *listen*?'

'Well, we can't stay together, so obviously I just go home and...the legal stuff can be sorted out some time later, some time never! I really don't care how or when.'

'Faye...' Tariq breathed tautly. 'Until yesterday, you were happy. There is no reason why that happiness should not be recaptured—'

'Maybe you'd like me to go on acting like your mistress!'

'Considering that believing yourself to *be* my mistress appeared to give you quite a thrill on several recent occasions, only you can answer that question.'

Her cheeks flamed at that rejoinder for there was truth in it. Pulling away, she stalked back into the bedroom.

'I care about you and I don't want to lose you but my patience is running out—'

'Just like my patience did when you were content to misjudge me for the supposed blackmail that caused all the trouble between us in the first place!'

'But I stopped judging you,' Tariq shot back at her with icy force. 'You said you wanted more than anything else in the world to be my wife because you *loved* me and, in the space of hours, I have forgiven everything and let go of every piece of my bitterness. Do you think I have no heart? Do you think I did not *feel* your sincerity?'

Faye did not want to be reminded of the more embarrassing things she had uttered in the grip of her overtaxed emotions. 'You forgave me for the blackmail…'

'As I was planning to marry you in any case before your stepfather intervened,' Tariq delivered in a velvety smooth tone, 'It was not a major problem.'

And Faye picked up on that admission and reeled in shock inwardly as he no doubt intended her to reel. Fighting Tariq was a constant debilitating struggle, she recognised in furious frustration. He was fast on his feet and kept on throwing the unexpected back at her. But Tariq had been planning to marry her even *before* Percy tried to blackmail him? Never in her life had Faye been so desperate to snatch at the carrot offered to her as a distraction. But she would not allow herself to snatch.

'But you still didn't trust my word.' She flung that promising branch on the fire with satisfaction. 'I have every right to leave you—'

'What is right? Strive to recall Rafi, whose love you have also won and who is a great deal less able than I am to cope with another major loss in his life!' Tariq ground out fiercely. 'Before you pack, you go and you tell him why you are leaving him after teaching him to love you for I will have no part of that dialogue!'

And at the exact same moment as he strode off in evident disgust with her into the room he used as a dressing room, the anger and the ferocious need to hit back every way she could fell away from Faye. She slumped back against the foot of the bed, her legs suddenly shaking beneath her.

As if she were someone waking from a dream, the previous twenty-four hours replayed within her memory and she squirmed. She recalled ignoring him all through the night while he'd sat by her bed in the private hospital room. She had acted like a huffy, ill-mannered child but he had not uttered a word of reproof. He had behaved as though her accident had been his fault. He had bowed that proud head and begged her to forgive him. And she had lain there in that bed, relishing her power like a real shrew and stoking up her resentments to new heights. Confronting him at the Haja had been even less forgivable.

She loved him. But it was as if her love had got lost for twenty-four hours, yet it was her pride Tariq had hurt more than anything else. She was his wife when all was said and done. A wife by default, though. He had not known that divorce might be a real challenge to achieve and he no longer wanted a divorce. Indeed, according to him he had *never* wanted a divorce enough to even find out how to go about getting one, even when he had believed she was heartless and mercenary. But then he also had the needs of three children to consider, children whom she had encouraged to care about her, children she had been threatening to walk out on.

'Tariq...?' she muttered unevenly.

'*What?*' he demanded, obviously thinking she was starting on round three and ready for her now with gloves off.

'Nothing…'

'Surely you have not run out of steam yet?' he growled.

'Pretty much. I would never hurt Rafi or Basma or Hayat,' Faye told him very quietly.

'If you are set on leaving, you should go now for, the longer you stay, the harder it will be on the children.' Tariq expelled his breath in a hiss. 'I have nothing more to say. I have said it all.'

The silence weighted Faye down with its electrifying tension. A current of fear new to her experience was infiltrating her. 'I got carried away,' she said, drymouthed. 'I'm sorry.'

Tariq said nothing. She watched him zip up faded denim jeans that accentuated his lithe muscular physique and pull on a dark green shirt, more casual clothing that she had ever seen him wear. He was *not* watching her any more. Indeed, he might have been on his own. All of a sudden it was as if she had become invisible. His bold profile grim, he was not ignoring her as she had ignored him; he simply seemed buried in his own thoughts.

'I'm sorry for…everything.' At that moment everything seemed to encompass so much Faye did not know where to begin.

'I'm sorry…you're sorry…the children will be sorry

too.' Darkly handsome features taut and spectacular eyes cloaked, Tariq headed straight for the bedroom door.

Wide shoulders straight, he walked tall. He had magnificent carriage, she reflected numbly, and he was walking *out* on her without another word. But then she had been screaming at him like a banshee wailer. Yet he had kept his temper and explained all that he could with irreproachable honesty. Only it hadn't got him anywhere and now he appeared to have decided that her leaving was possibly for the best in the long run.

'Tariq...?' Her voice emerged all squeaky.

'I wish I could say something profound...' his lean brown hand clenched on the door knob '...but our whole relationship has been a black comedy of errors and I am out of words. *Inshallah.*'

Her throat was convulsing. Her mind was an appalling blank. She could only wish she had run out of words sooner.

He opened the door and then paused. 'What will I do with the mare?'

'What mare?'

He turned back with a frown. 'It was to be a surprise...Delilah, your mare that you had to sell last year. I had her traced and purchased from the riding school but she is in transit and, until you have stables again... Don't worry, I will deal with it.'

Faye was so shaken by that unexpected revelation and conclusion, she stood there with a dropped jaw, and by the time she unfroze and decided to chase after him he was gone. Really *gone*, for absolutely nobody seemed to have the slightest idea *where* he had gone, which dismayed her.

She phoned Latif and, after a lot of circling round the subject but somehow never actually answering her anxious questions, Latif said he would call at the Muraaba.

'There is no need for concern. Prince Tariq is quite safe,' he informed her on his arrival.

'I only want to know where he is…that's all.'

Latif sighed. 'His Royal Highness has places where he goes when he wishes to be alone. It is a great luxury for him to be alone. He might be on the beach. He might be in the desert. He might be driving himself around the city, perhaps even walking down a street somewhere as if he is an ordinary person.'

'How can he be safe if you don't even know where he is? It *can't* be safe for him to do that!'

Latif lowered his wise eyes to the exquisite Aubusson rug in silence.

'He's not alone at all…*ever*, is he?' Faye realised with initial relief and then a surge of the most powerful and guilty sympathy for Tariq. 'You still have him under security surveillance.'

'There is no reason for concern.' Latif lifted his head again. 'We understand that Prince Tariq carries huge responsibilities and endures many exasperating restrictions without complaint. Yet he is still a young man. He has never known the freedom that his father enjoyed and, sadly, he never will for the world has changed too much. But if you ask to know his whereabouts, it is, of course, my duty to tell you, Your Royal Highness.'

Faye was very pale by the end of that speech. 'No, that's all right, I no longer wish to know and, as far as I'm concerned, we never had this conversation.'

With a strained smile, Faye walked with Latif to the very doors of the palace, a courtesy which he definitely deserved for she could see she had put him in a very awkward position, not to mention dragging him out late at night.

'Last year…it was a period of almost intolerable strain,' the older man mused with his usual tact, 'but over the past weeks, the strain seemed absent.'

'It will be absent again,' Faye promised tightly.

She went to bed and lay awake. She was grateful to Latif for his advice. He had not embarrassed her but he had added a whole new and unsettling dimension to her understanding of the male she had married. Tariq only took time out when he was really at the end of his tether. Tears burned in her eyes as she remembered him admitting that he had had to acknowledge her as being his wife, just as he had once felt forced to marry her. *A black comedy of errors?* But hadn't he also said that he had been thinking of marrying her even before everything had gone wrong? So, a year ago, he had loved her and wanted her, and two days ago he had still been making mad, passionate love to her. She was not going to give up on him.

Tariq moved like a silent predator through the bedroom when he came home in the early hours. She lay still as a stone, hardly breathing. He went for a shower and she wondered if he had even noticed her presence in the bed. The curtains were not drawn and moonlight filtered over his lean bronzed length as he approached the bed and she stole a glance.

'When you're asleep, you breathe more heavily,' Tariq imparted as he slid between the sheets. 'I knew you were awake the instant I entered the room.'

'Oh…'

His hand brushed her fingertips. It might well have been accidental for he could simply have been stretching. But Faye was in no mood for subtlety and she practically threw herself across the space that separated them into his arms. Without hesitation he curved her to him.

She listened to the solid thump of his heart and slowly dared to breathe again. 'I don't need any more words.'

'We might say the wrong ones.' His strong arms tightened round her and it was more than enough. 'But curiosity is killing me. What did Latif tell you?'

She tensed. 'You *know* he was here?'

Tariq uttered a husky laugh. 'I have my own ways and means.'

'I was worried about you…stupid, really.'

'Caring,' Tariq contradicted, driving the tension back out of her again with his pronounced calm. 'I would have liked to go to the beach for a swim. But then they have to get the divers out and I am always worried that one of them will have an accident in the dark through trying so very hard not to be seen.'

'So you know you've got company?'

'I've got so much company I sometimes feel like

throwing a party but it is a matter of great pride to my surveillance teams to believe they are invisible to me.'

'Only not much fun for you,' she whispered ruefully.

'But they enjoy the challenge so much.' Brushing her tumbled hair back from her cheekbones, he stared down at her, his eyes glittering like jet in the moonlight. 'I drove around half the night thinking—'

'Don't think,' she urged.

'You are staying.' It was not a question but a declaration.

'Yes.'

'A generous man would give you a choice but I can't pretend a generosity I do not feel.'

'That's OK…'

He rested back and eased her over him, shaping his hands to the feminine swell of her hips, acquainting her with the urgency of his arousal. She quivered, answering heat racing through her as if he had switched on an electric current.

'It would be cruel to sentence me to any more cold showers.'

'Agreed.'

'All of a sudden you are very amenable. But then there is true equality in the joys of sex,' Tariq commented softly.

But as her head lifted and her lips parted in dismay, he took her mouth in a hungry, seeking kiss that was quite irresistible.

CHAPTER ELEVEN

THREE days later, Faye attended her first public engagement with Tariq. A new centre for children with learning disabilities had been built and Tariq had been invited to preside over the official opening.

'But no one will be expecting me,' Faye had pointed out nervously.

'Since our marriage was announced, you have been included in all my invitations. My schedule is arranged months ahead but the organisers of every event have contacted the palace to declare that your presence would be most welcome. Indeed, extra secretarial help has had to be brought in,' Tariq revealed with some amusement.

Faye was disconcerted by that information.

'Everyone will be hoping you will make an appearance. There is great curiosity about you. However, if you prefer to keep a low profile, that is not a problem either.'

'No?'

'Your predecessor, Rafi's mother, made no public appearances. She went veiled and demanded the strictest seclusion—'

Faye grimaced. 'I'm not going to go that far—'

His vibrant smile tipped her heart over. 'She was very unpopular. Our women felt threatened by the old ways suddenly reappearing in the heart of their ruling family. In any case, I wish to show you off, not hide you away.'

In receipt of those quiet supportive words, Faye glowed and overcame her apprehension. In truth, her nerves vanished once she found that it was merely a matter of talking to people, chatting to the children present and doing a lot of smiling when the language barrier made itself felt. Photographs were taken but only after Tariq had given his permission. Only when refreshments were being served did Faye recognise Tariq's cousin, Majida, who had caused her such embarrassment at the reception held in the desert.

Her beautiful face arranged in a cloying smile, her shapely figure displayed in a cerise-pink brocade suit, Majida approached Faye while Tariq was chatting with another man several feet away.

Now very conscious that she had to lead the conversation, Faye said with a determined smile, 'How are you? I didn't see you earlier but obviously you must be involved with the learning centre.'

'I organised the fund-raising. I am well known in Jumar for my charitable endeavours.' Her dark eyes hard as nails, Majida threw her head high and, as the brunette was much taller, Faye had to resist an urge to stretch her own neck. 'May I congratulate you on your wonderfully deft touch with small children, Your Royal Highness?'

Suspecting sarcasm, Faye tensed. 'Thank you.'

'But then with three children to raise already and a pressing need for one of his own, Prince Tariq knew exactly what nursery qualities to seek in his wife,' Majida murmured sweetly. 'Rather you than me.'

As Majida dipped her head and went into instant retreat, Faye was left waxen pale. The brunette's barbs had hit a tender target. Nursery qualities? In the space of ten seconds, Faye's buoyant inner happiness just imploded into a tight little knot of hurt and pain.

For, of course, there was no arguing with what Tariq's venomous cousin had said. How might Tariq have felt about their marriage had she *not* been a success with Rafi, Basma and Hayat? Tariq had been very much taken aback by that development but had soon decided to be pleased instead. He was very anxious to do right by the children. He took his obligations seriously and might well put their needs ahead of more personal inclinations.

In addition, Tariq might have a pressing need for a child of his own to ensure the succession, but he protected Faye from pregnancy with scrupulous care. Suddenly, even though they had only been together a few weeks, that reality made her feel even more insecure. Perhaps he didn't trust her enough yet, she decided painfully. Naturally her stridently stated apparent willingness to *leave* the children would leave its mark on his opinion of her. She had been dreadfully immature, throwing angry threats more for effect than anything else. But how was he to know that when she had not yet admitted that lowering truth? Perhaps he wanted to be sure that their marriage was going to last before discussing the matter of them having a child together.

Across the room, Faye's gaze was drawn by Tariq's

proud dark head bent down to Majida's. She stiffened, uneasy at seeing him in the other woman's company. What clever remarks aimed at undermining Faye might the brunette plant without Tariq even realising it? Weren't men supposed to be vulnerable to such manipulation? By the time she got the chance to look in the same direction again, all she caught was a brief glimpse of Majida slipping out the door, her profile oddly pinched and pale.

In the limo on the drive back to the Muraaba, Tariq shook her by carrying her hand to his lips and kissing her fingers in a gesture that was both teasing and sincere. 'You were wonderful. I was very proud of you.'

She smiled, some of her tension ebbing. 'As long as people don't look to me to try and follow in your mother's footsteps. Then I'd be sure to be a disappointment.'

'Is that what made you so apprehensive?' At her reluctant nod of confirmation, Tariq released a rueful laugh. 'My mother was a very fine woman, but no saint. She was too aggressive in her support of the causes she took up and quite often offended people with her frank speech. It was her natural warmth which won her forgiveness…and you have that same special quality without the desire to change the whole world overnight.'

Touched by his honesty on her behalf and by that compliment, Faye felt her spirits rise again.

'My cousin, Majida, won't be bothering you again,' Tariq imparted with awesome casualness. 'I was very annoyed when I heard her speak to you in the manner that she did—'

Faye reddened. 'You *heard*?'

'I was listening and not by accident. I was already well aware that it could only have been Majida who insulted you on our wedding night.' His gaze gleamed with wry amusement at her look of surprise. 'I know my relatives through and through. Only Majida was likely to be unhappy with me for producing a young and beautiful wife, for the rest of my family were keen to see me married.'

'I expect she thought she would have been a better candidate.' Faye sighed.

'Marriages between first cousins are frequent in Arab countries but it was a practice always frowned on within my own family circle.'

Faye stiffened. 'So even if you had wanted to marry her, you couldn't have done—'

'No, I always had freedom of choice in that field. Majida has a great opinion of herself and she was jealous. But from now on she will be careful to treat you with proper respect.'

'You really didn't need to interfere—'

'Oh, yes, I did. When I saw you standing there like a little girl with big hurt eyes refusing to fight your own corner, I thought to myself...isn't that *just* like a woman?'

'Meaning?' Faye was stung on the raw by that description.

'You see what I mean? You're ready to shout at me already! You have tremendous spirit yet you didn't put Majida in her place.'

Faye bristled. 'I was *trying* to be dignified.'

Tariq curved a long arm round her and pulled her

close. 'I know but I was outraged to see you swallow that speech of hers. At the very least, you should have snubbed her and walked away, although I very much doubt that you will meet with such behaviour ever again. I apologise for my cousin's rudeness.'

'Not your problem,' Relaxing, Faye curved round him, tucking her head under his chin, drinking in the warm, familiar scent of him with pleasure. He might not love her but he definitely did care about her. She wondered what he had said to Majida, though, and noticed that he did not offer that information.

The car phoned buzzed. With an impatient sigh, Tariq reached for it. Faye was immediately aware of the tension that flared through his big, powerful frame and anxiety made her sit up straight.

'What's happened?' she prompted when he had set the phone down again. 'It's nothing to do with the children, is it?'

'No,' he reassured her instantly. 'But gather your inner strength and hold tight to your dignity for you will need it. It seems that this must be the chosen day for our mutual families to embarrass us.'

'Sorry, I—'

'Your stepfather awaits us at the Muraaba and Latif, who is at home with the crowned heads of Europe, sounds like he is very much in need of rescue,' Tariq told her gently.

'Percy is here in Jumar...*again*?' Faye gasped in dismay.

'What shall I do with him?' Tariq asked lazily. 'Shall I be corrupt and have him thrown into a prison cell on some trumped-up charge such as taking up too much space on the pavement? It is only what he expects of a primitive people such as he believes us to be. It seems a real shame to disappoint him.'

Faye was not soothed by his dark humour for the mere threat of Tariq being forced to have any dealings whatsoever with Percy Smythe affronted her. 'You don't need to worry. I'll get rid of him—'

'I am not worried. I am even looking forward to the encounter.' Tariq dealt her incredulous face a mocking smile. 'No, I am not planning to kill him with my bare hands. Unlike Majida, who is not a laughing matter, Percy can be richly entertaining in his own peculiar way.'

Faye was thinking that only Percy would have the neck to enter the home of a man he had once tried to blackmail. 'But what on earth does he want?'

'Perhaps your loyal and caring brother has with immense effort recalled the existence of his kid sister and has finally noted that she has gone missing.'

'That's not very kind, Tariq—'

'I don't enjoy hearing you always ask if there have been any letters or phone calls for you,' he countered. 'Your family do not deserve you.'

Faye was discomfited by the way Tariq noticed everything even if he might not choose to comment on it at the time. It had worried her that she had not heard a word from Adrian. Assuming that Adrian and his family were staying with Percy, she had phoned her stepfather's home on several occasions but, in spite of leaving messages on the answering machine, she had not been contacted. Her letter had not brought a response either.

'Adrian's never been great at keeping in touch. Men aren't,' she said defensively.

'But he owes his freedom to you—'

'Adrian doesn't know about the bargain you and I made—'

'Even the dimmest of men must have made an association by now between his own miraculous release from prison and his sister's vanishing act.'

'I'll see Percy on my own!' Outside the Muraaba, Faye tried to dive out of the limo ahead of Tariq. 'But I can't think why Latif should've brought him here to our home.'

'Only think of Percy let loose in the Haja loudly giving forth on his views of Jumar,' Tariq suggested lethally. 'He could cause a riot.'

Faye flushed and Tariq took advantage of her chagrin to close his hand over hers and walk her indoors. Latif awaited them in the entrance hall and, with a polite word of greeting and apology to Faye, turned to address Tariq in a low-pitched flood of explanatory Arabic.

An unexpected smile skimming his darkly handsome features, Tariq turned back to Faye. 'Latif tells me that Percy has come into a large amount of money.'

'Where from?'

'The British lottery had bestowed its largesse on a most undeserving man.'

Faye was shaken but she did not agree with Tariq. Percy *with* money was surely less dangerous than Percy *without* money. Her fear that her stepfather now knew that she and Tariq were husband and wife and had arrived to ask for a loan receded.

When they entered the grand drawing room, Percy was holding a very fine Minton vase upside down to peer at its base. He set it down again, quite untouched by embarrassment. 'I suppose I'm looking at the rich rewards of four hundred years of looting and plunder. No wonder your lot were always raiding each other,' Percy commented enviously.

Faye just wanted to sink through the floor at that opening speech.

'Welcome to the Muraaba, Percy,' Tariq drawled with a slow smile. 'You are quite right. My ancestors were ruthless to the extreme. They slaughtered their way to supremacy.'

Percy gave him an appreciative appraisal. 'I knew you wouldn't hold a grudge, Tariq. You're a businessman just like myself.' His small eyes flicked in his stepdaughter's direction. 'You're looking a treat, Faye. But run along, there's a good girl. I've got some private business to discuss with His Royal Highness.'

Faye folded her arms. 'I'm not going anywhere.'

Percy rolled his eyes. 'Before the day's out, you might be surprised.'

Ignoring that forecast, Faye asked, 'How is Adrian and why haven't I heard from him?'

'I sent him and Lizzie off to Spain for a fortnight with the kiddies. He still hasn't a clue you're out here. Well, I'll not beat about the bush,' her stepfather announced with the aspect of a man about to make a weighty announcement and pausing for effect. 'I'm here to fetch Faye home, Tariq.'

'I beg your pardon?' Faye whispered shakily.

Without further ado, Percy slapped down a cheque on the table beside him. 'I'm sure old Latif has brought you up to speed on my good luck in the lottery. So there you are, everything that's owed to you, including accrued interest.'

Tariq elevated a level dark brow. 'You are here to repay me for the settlement of Adrian's debts?'

'As well as the five hundred grand you shelled out to keep Faye quiet last year after that clever stunt you pulled in your London embassy.' Percy gave him an outrageous wink.

Faye could feel the cringe factor growing by the second.

'You refer, I believe, to our wedding,' Tariq said quietly.

'Whatever you want to call it, but I'll tell you one thing—I couldn't have done better myself! It's not often anyone puts one over on me but I have to confess you did all right.'

'You tried to blackmail me,' Tariq reminded the older man.

'No, I didn't try to do that, now be fair,' Percy urged with unblemished good humour. 'I only took you to one side and asked you how it would look if it got out into the newspapers that a man in your privileged position had been carrying on with a kid, Faye's age!'

'I was nineteen,' Faye gritted in disgust.

Blithely ignoring her, Percy continued, 'It was my job to look out for Faye and you can't say it wasn't.'

'You do have a point.' Faye was stunned to hear Tariq concede.

Percy beamed. 'I don't mind admitting I was gobsmacked when I lifted the phone extension and heard her offering you dinner with bed thrown in. To look at her, you'd think butter wouldn't melt in her mouth and there she was talking like a *right* little raver—'

'I appreciate your frankness,' Tariq slotted in at speed.

Face red as fire, Faye was staring into the middle distance, mortification looming so large that it did not immediately occur to her that Percy had just carelessly confirmed her own version of events that awful night a year back. But then what did he have to lose by lying now? And what on earth did he mean by slapping down a cheque and saying he was here to fetch her home like an old umbrella that had been left behind?

'I mean, I *knew* you were leading her down the old garden path—'

'How very astute,' Tariq remarked.

'You think so? It was dead simple as I saw it. In the long run, I'd be doing Faye a favour if I saw you off—'

'And you certainly achieved that,' Faye enunciated with pronounced care, the old bitterness clawing at her for the first time in weeks.

'By the way, I invested that five hundred grand for Faye in a *family* business. So if Faye has been suggesting I ripped her off, it's just sour grapes,' Percy contended with a decided touch of aggression. 'Right,

Faye...I'm sure His Royal Highness here is a busy man...isn't it time you were getting your stuff together?'

'Faye is not a commodity you may buy back,' Tariq murmured icily.

'Why would you even *want* to take me home? You don't give two hoots what happens to me,' Faye contended tightly.

'I wouldn't leave my worst enemy in this neck of the woods!' Percy declared in full self-righteous mode. 'I got robbed of my bottles of whisky just coming through the airport!'

'Our customs officials are not thieves. Visitors are not allowed to bring alcohol into Jumar but it is available in most hotels,' Tariq said drily.

'Look, Faye...I may not always have been a great stepfather,' Percy conceded with growing impatience. 'But, let's face it, you never liked me much either and there's no point you hanging on here hoping you're going to hook a wedding ring—'

'None whatsoever,' Tariq interposed in a smooth agreement that sent Faye's startled eyes flying to him in bemusement. 'My great-grandfather gave his favourite concubine a sapphire anklet which has been worn by the wife of almost every ruling prince since then in place of a ring.'

'You see what I mean?' Percy rolled his eyes in speaking appeal at Faye. 'There's nothing normal about that, is there?'

Faye tilted her head over to one side and stared down at the beautiful anklet with very wide eyes. Knowing that Tariq found the very sight of it adorning her slim ankle incredibly sexy, she had become rather attached to the anklet once he had shown her how to undo it.

'What's that on your leg?' Percy suddenly demanded of his stepdaughter.

'Faye is my wife,' Tariq breathed wearily.

'Bloody hell…how did you manage that, Faye?' Percy studied her with beady eyes practically out on stalks.

'We've been married for over a year,' Tariq said.

'You mean—?'

'Our wedding was perfectly legal,' Faye informed her stepfather thinly.

'Well, fancy that…' In an apparent daze Percy gaped at Tariq, thunderstruck by their revelation. 'And there I was thinking you were a real sharp operator! You could have had her for nothing but you actually went and *married* her?'

Faye saw Tariq stiffen with outrage but as he took a sudden threatening step forward she grabbed the hand he had curled into a clenched fist. But Percy had already taken fright at what he had seen in Tariq's lean, strong face and he went into retreat so fast he went backwards into the table and hit the floor with a tremendous crash. Soaked by the vase of flowers he had sent flying, he lay there like a felled log, before sitting up with a groan.

'If you value your own safety, you will not attempt to enter Jumar again,' Tariq delivered stonily.

'Goodbye, Percy,' Faye said without regret.

Tariq led her back out to the hall. 'Clean out the drawing room, Latif. Have him conveyed straight to the airport and escorted onto his flight.'

'I wanted to hit him,' Tariq growled, curving a protective arm round her taut shoulders as they went upstairs together. 'My one chance and you interfered. Why?'

'He said one thing that made me feel bad. He said I never liked him either.' Faye sighed that reminder. 'He was right and that's probably why he never took to me.'

'Even at five years old, you were a lady with good taste. He is a very crude man.'

'Never mind, he won't be back. I wonder if I will ever see Adrian again—'

'Of course you will. If necessary, I will extract your brother and his family from your stepfather's clutches,' Tariq told her soothingly.

'Percy is much more embarrassing than Majida,' she groaned.

'He asked Latif what the going rate was for a woman in Jumar,' Tariq said not quite steadily.

'He did...*what*?'

'Latif believed he was referring to either slaves or prostitutes and was offended to the extent that he could not bear to remain in the same room, but it was *you* that Percy was talking about!' Beneath her arrested gaze, Tariq threw back his head and laughed with helpless appreciation. 'You whom I would not surrender at any price!'

'I think you could have mentioned before now that the anklet was more than just a piece of jewellery,' Faye remarked.

'Ah, but I was playing it cool and there is no cool way of telling a contemporary woman that every possessive bone in your body thrills to seeing a chain round her ankle,' Tariq pointed out with a slight grimace.

She smiled. 'A chain with special family significance.'

'I must give you your ring back. It belonged to my mother.'

That he had still given her that wedding ring on that long-ago day when so much strife and misunderstanding had lain between them touched her.

'The anklet was also supposed to provide the luck of the something blue on our wedding night,' Tariq admitted.

Her eyes widened. 'You know, you're much more thoughtful than I ever give you credit for.'

'I owe you a profound apology for ever doubting your word on the score of Percy's blackmail attempt.'

Faye flushed. 'I did give you the wrong impression with that phone call I made and I suppose I ought to explain that now. You see, I hadn't the faintest idea that you were serious about me and I knew your father was dying...and I thought you were just going to vanish out of my life—'

'There was never any chance of that until my stubborn pride undermined my intelligence,' Tariq informed her darkly.

'It was a mad impulse and I thought I was being incredibly romantic and mature—'

'Well, you were certainly a lot more romantic than I was that night. I was in a rage with you because I was...*gutted* by the idea that you seemed to regard sex as something casual,' Tariq admitted, poised in the centre of their bedroom, lean, powerful face taut. 'That you might not, after all, be feeling the same special bond that I was feeling for you. That you were probably thinking of me as just another boyfriend when I was head over heels in love with you.'

'Were you really?' Faye whispered unevenly. 'Honestly?'

'And I have never been in love before. Lust, yes, but not love and it was not a grounding experience for me,' Tariq revealed with rueful dark eyes. 'Every other Western woman I had been with was only interested in fun, sex and what I could buy. But then, before I met you, fun and sex was all I wanted too, so no doubt I was only attracted to that type of woman.'

'Probably.' Faye did not really want to hear about his past.

As if he knew he had erred in being that frank, Tariq closed the distance between them and reached for her hands. 'What I am trying to explain is that, having had affairs that were nothing to be proud of...I then went on to idealise you as if you were an angel—'

'I'm not that—'

'I shouldn't have liked living with one anyway.' His breathtaking smile of innate self-mocking charm banished her tension and warmed her like the sunlight. 'I wanted to get to know you really well before I mentioned love or marriage.'

'I can understand that—'

'My father's appalling second marriage had a powerful effect on me. He was not a foolish man but he *was* fooled into making a big mistake.'

'That must have made you feel very wary—'

Dropping her hands, he raised his own to frame her cheekbones with spread fingers and a look of deep regret in his tawny eyes. 'Faye...I made an even bigger mistake. I married you still wanting you, still loving you, but my terrible pride, my even worse temper and my sheer obstinacy drove you away. I did not know a *single* moment of happiness last year but an army tank could not have dragged me back to you...'

'Percy did a lot of damage. It's not your fault—'

'It *was*,' Tariq contradicted heavily. 'Never dreaming that you believed our marriage was not a real marriage, I waited for twenty-four hours at the embassy for you to return—'

'Oh, no,' Faye mumbled tearfully.

'And then I flew home in an absolute fury and I told nobody that I had married for I *had* no wife to produce! Stop crying...I don't deserve your tears.' He groaned. 'I believed that to make the smallest approach to you would be an act of shocking weakness. Then my father died and I thought you might use his death as an excuse to contact me—'

'And I didn't do that either,' Faye muttered guiltily.

'And, for the first time, it struck me that you might really be gone, quite content to have only that money to live on—'

'I was so miserable—'

'You were left on your own without even my financial support and that shames me. I made it possible for your family to take advantage of your good nature. But I did initially believe that you cared for me and then I had to face that you did not care in any way,' Tariq related. 'When there was not even a word from you after the plane crash, I became very bitter.'

Faye rested her brow against his shirtfront and linked her arms round him. 'And then you started wanting revenge.'

'What I wanted was any excuse to get you back *without* having to admit I wanted you back. That day at the Haja, I was astonished when you informed me that you believed either that I had already divorced you or that our marriage was a sham, but it was welcome news—'

'I can't credit now that I was stupid enough to just accept that—'

'You are excused. After all, I was stupid enough to persuade myself that I could somehow have you without ever letting on to you that you were in truth my wife...and you can't get much stupider than that!' Tariq pointed out without hesitation. 'Poor Latif had to stand back aghast as I sunk deeper into this madness to have you at any cost.'

Faye spread appreciative fingers against his taut spine beneath the jacket of his suit and turned up her face. 'It's the kind of madness I like—'

'And then you frightened me out of my wits by taking off with Omeir and sanity began to return. I was so afraid that I wouldn't find you before the storm closed in that I finally admitted to myself that I was still in love with you—'

'Still in love with me...?' Relief and joy washed over her.

'Yet you only value me for my athletic performance

in bed.' Tariq gazed down at her with adoring eyes full of playful reproach and swept her off her feet into his arms. 'My mistress-wife, who can insult with a compliment.'

'I'm mad about you and you know it—'

'So I had hoped, until you found out you might be tied to me for life and threw a fit.' He set her down on the bed and eased her out of her jacket.

'I was awful—'

'No, I was worse. I did not foresee how much hurt my reckless games would cause. Nor am I very good at being shouted at...I expect I'll improve with practice. I really thought you were planning to leave—'

'So you just took off and left me to it?' she complained.

'Not before ensuring that your passport was in my safe. I could not have stood by and allowed you to walk out on what we had found together...I am so incredibly happy with you.'

In receipt of that charged confession, Faye arranged herself on the bed like a very willing woman. Tariq gave her a highly appreciative perusal. 'You were made for me—'

'You were made for me first. Tell me...' Faye leant up on one elbow with newly found confidence '...when are we going to try for a baby?'

'Perhaps in a few years,' Tariq suggested. 'I am painfully conscious that I have already landed you with three children at the age of twenty.'

'I love them and I wouldn't mind having a baby—'

'But I care most about what is best for *you*.' Tariq

leant over her and kissed her breathless. 'We have Rafi in reserve and no need to think further on the subject at present. I am selfish. Those first weeks when we lived only for each other and I had no idea you were seeing the children, I just didn't want to share you—'

'Is that why you never mentioned them?' Faye grinned.

'I was also afraid you would take total fright if I rolled them all out as an unavoidable extra to living with me,' Tariq admitted ruefully. 'While I am very grateful that you have room in your heart for them, that could not have made me love you or made me want to stay married to you. The night I flew home from the tribal talks because I couldn't *stand* to be separated from you, I knew I never wanted to let you go.'

'I love you so much,' she whispered dreamily, letting her fingers slide possessively into his silky hair and mess it up.

'"A frog of little faith?"' Tariq teased, sliding her out of her dress with the most deft of manoeuvres and folding her back into his arms.

'Very occasionally frogs turn into princes. I'll be sure to let you know if it ever happens.'

EIGHTEEN MONTHS LATER, Faye settled her baby son into his pram in the shade of the trees.

Little Prince Asif had been something of a surprise package to his parents. They honestly had planned to wait another year but a Caribbean cruise on a private yacht the previous year had resulted in a certain reck-lessness. Asif stretched sleepily, big dark blue eyes flickering and then slowly sinking shut. He was a very laid-back baby.

Basma and Hayat, clad in shorts and T-shirts, were paddling in the basin of the fountain and giggling. Lifting them out at the same time as she listened to Rafi chatter about his day at school, Faye could only think how contented she was. With so many willing hands to help and acres of space, parenting four children was not the burden which Tariq had feared.

Adrian and Lizzie and their children had stayed with them for a week only the previous month. Her brother now worked for Tariq in London in a job which had literally been tailormade for him. According to Adrian, Percy was doing very well in the field of property speculation.

Leaving the staff to preside over the nursery evening meal, Faye went for a shower. When she emerged from the bathroom, wrapped in a fleecy towel, Tariq was in the bedroom.

'You've got perfect timing.' Faye studied her tall, dark and sensationally attractive husband with bright eyes.

His tawny gaze whipped over her slim figure with molten appreciation. 'You think *this* is coincidence?'

Her cheeks warmed. 'Not when it happens for the third time in a week.'

As Tariq drew her close, he murmured huskily, 'Are you complaining?'

'What do you think?' Faye said breathlessly.

'I think, as always, we are of one mind.' He tasted her mouth with smouldering hunger and as she pushed into his hard, muscular frame he scooped her up into his arms. 'Happy?'

'Totally,' she whispered blissfully.

'You know, you never did mention when I made it out of frogdom—'

'Oh, you went from frog to prince faster than the speed of light!'

Coming down on the bed, Tariq leant over her with pure sensual threat. 'Say that again…'

'Probably when my mare, Delilah, arrived and she was the most ugly-looking horse you thought you'd ever seen but you lied to save my feelings.'

'You realised that?' Tariq was dismayed.

'Or when you fixed up that job for Adrian and he got it without realising it *had* been fixed…or when you pretended I was the sexiest woman alive when I was pregnant with Asif…or when you put in the swimming pool so that we could have fun without divers around.'

'Anything else?' Tariq surveyed her with helplessly amused dark eyes.

Faye reckoned that she had possibly about a hundred other good reasons why she loved him more with every passing day, but she did not want to give him them all at once.

'Is it my turn? OK. You learning Arabic,' he told her.

'You not laughing at my mistakes—'

'You just being you. A wonderful wife…a terrific princess…a fabulous mother…and the mistress of my heart, *aziz*.' As every phrase was punctuated by kisses, the dialogue faltered to a halt and it was a long time until it started up again.

* * * * *

THE CONTAXIS BABY

CHAPTER ONE

WHEN Sebasten Contaxis strode to Ingrid Morgan's side to offer his condolences on the death of her only son, she fell on his chest and just sobbed as though her heart had broken right through.

A ripple of curiosity ran through the remaining guests in the drawing room of the Brighton town house. The tall, powerfully built male, every angle of his bronzed features stamped with strength and authority, looked remarkably like...but surely not? After all, what could be the connection? Why would the Greek electronics tycoon come to pay his respects *after* Connor's funeral? But keen eyes picked out the long, opulent limousine double-parked across the street and then judged the two large men waiting on the pavement as the bodyguards that they were. Heads turned, moved closer together and the whispers started.

Stunning dark eyes veiled, Sebasten waited until Ingrid had got a grip on that first outburst of grief before murmuring, 'Is there anywhere that we can talk?'

'Still looking after my good name?' Ingrid lifted her blonde head and he tensed at the sight of the raw suffering etched in her once beautiful features. Then he knew that even her love for his late father had in the end been surpassed by her devotion to her son. 'It doesn't really

matter now, does it? Connor's gone where he can never
be embarrassed by my past...'

She took him into an elegant little study and poured
drinks for them both. Always slim, right now she looked
emaciated and every day of her fifty-odd years. She had
been his father's mistress for a long time and some of
the few happy childhood memories Sebasten had related to her and Connor, who had been five years his
junior. For all too short a spell, Connor had been the
kid brother he had never had, tagging after Sebasten on
the beach, a little blond boy, cheerfully and totally fear-
less. As an adult, he had become a brilliant polo player,
adored by women, in fact very popular with both sexes.
Not the brightest spark on the block but a very likeable
guy. Yet it had been well over a year since Sebasten had
last seen the younger man.

'It was murder, you know...' Ingrid condemned half
under her breath.

Sebasten's winged dark brows drew together but he
remained silent, for he had heard the rumour that Connor's car crash had been no accident, indeed, a deliberate act of self-destruction, and he knew that there was
no more painful way to lose a loved one. She needed to
talk and he knew that listening was the kindest thing
he could do for her.

'I liked Liza Denton...when I met that evil little
shrew, I actually *liked* her!' Ingrid proclaimed with
bone-deep bitterness.

The silence lay before Ingrid continued in a tremulous tone. 'I knew Connor was in love when he stopped
confiding in me. That hurt but he was twenty-four...
that's why I didn't pry.'

'Liza Denton?' Sebasten was keen to deflect her from that unfortunate angle.

Her stricken blue eyes hardened. 'A spoilt little rich brat. Gets her kicks out of encouraging men to make an ass of themselves over her! It's only three months since Connor met her but I could tell he'd fallen like a ton of bricks.' The older woman swallowed with visible difficulty. 'Then without any warning, *she* got bored. She cut him dead at a party two weeks ago...made an exhibition of herself with another man, laughed in his face...his friends told me *everything*!'

Sebasten waited while Ingrid gathered her shredded composure back together again.

'He begged but she wouldn't even take a phone call from him. He'd done nothing. He couldn't handle it,' Ingrid sobbed brokenly. 'He wasn't sleeping, so he went for a drive in his car in the middle of the night and drove it into a wall!'

Sebasten curved an arm round her in a consoling embrace and seethed with angry distaste at the ugly picture she had drawn up. Connor would have been soft as butter in the hands of a manipulative little bitch like that.

'You're going to hate me for what I t-tell you now...' Ingrid whispered shakily.

'Nonsense,' Sebasten soothed.

'Connor was your half-brother...'

Sebasten released his breath in a sudden startled hiss and collided with Ingrid's both defiant and guilty gaze.

'No...that's not possible,' he breathed in total shock, not wanting it to be true when it was too late for him to do anything about it.

Ingrid sank down in a distraught heap and sobbed out a storm of self-justification while Sebasten stared at her as though he had never seen her before. She had never told his father, Andros, because she had known how ruthless Andros would be at protecting the good name of the Contaxis family from scandal.

'If Andros had known, he would've bullied me into having a termination. So I left him, came back eighteen months later, confessed to a rebound relationship, *grovelled*...eventually he took me back!' For a frozen instant in time, Ingrid's face shone with the remembered triumph of having fooled her powerful lover and then her eyes fell, the flash of energy draining away again.

'How could you not tell me before this?' Sebasten bit out in an electrifying undertone, lean, strong face rigid with the force of his appalled incredulity. In the space of seconds, Connor's death had gone from a matter of sincere and sad regret to a tragedy which gutted Sebasten. But he knew why, knew all too well why she had kept quiet. Fear of the consequences would have kept her quiet throughout all the years she had loved his father without adequate return.

'I'm only telling you now because I want you to make Liza Denton sorry she was ever born...' Ingrid confided with harsh clarity as his brilliant gaze locked to her set features and the hatred she could not hide. 'You're one of the richest men on this planet and I don't care how you do it. There have got to be strings you could pull, pressure you could put on somewhere with someone to *punish* her for what she did to Connor...'

'No,' Sebasten murmured without inflection, a big, dark, powerful Greek male, over six feet four in height and with shimmering dark golden eyes as steady as rock. 'I am a Contaxis and I have honour.'

Minutes later, Sebasten swept out of Ingrid's home, impervious to the lingering mourners keen to get a second look at him. In the privacy of his limo, he sank a double whiskey. His lean, dark, handsome face was hard and taut and ashen pale. He had no doubt that Ingrid had told him the truth. Connor...the little brother he had only run into twice at polo matches in recent years. He might have protected him from his own weakness but he hadn't been given the chance. Certainly, he could have taught him how to handle *that* kind of woman. Had Liza Denton found out that, in spite of his popularity and his wealthy friends, Connor was essentially penniless but for his winnings on the polo field? Or had Connor's puppy-dog adoration simply turned her off big time? His wide, sensual mouth curled. Was she a drop-dead babe who treated men like trophies?

He pitied Ingrid for the bitterness that consumed her. Yet even after all those years in Greece, she *still* hadn't learned that one essential truth: a man never discussed family honour with a woman or involved her in certain personal matters...

MAURICE DENTON STARED out of his library window and then turned round to face his daughter, his thin, handsome face set with rigid disapproval.

'I can't excuse *anything* you've done,' he asserted.

Lizzie was so white that her reddish-blonde hair seemed to burn like a brand above her forehead. 'I didn't ask you to,' she murmured unevenly. 'I just said...we all make mistakes...and dating Connor was mine.'

'There are standards of decent behaviour and you've broken them,' the older man delivered as harshly as if she hadn't spoken. 'I'm ashamed of you.'

'I'm sorry.' Her voice wobbled in spite of all her efforts to control it but that last assurance had burned deep. 'I'm really...*sorry*.'

'It's too late, isn't it? What I can't forgive is the public embarrassment and distress that you've caused your stepmother. Last night, Felicity and I should have been dining with the Jurgens but it was cancelled with a flimsy excuse. As word gets around that your cruelty literally *drove* the Morgan boy to his death, we're becoming as socially unacceptable as you have made yourself—'

'Dad—'

'Hannah Jurgen was very fond of Connor. A lot of people were. Felicity was extremely upset by that cancellation. Indeed, from the minute the details of this hideous business began leaking into the tabloids Felicity has scarcely slept a night through!' Maurice condemned fiercely.

Pale as milk, Lizzie turned her head away, her throat tight and aching. She might have told him that his young and beautiful wife, the woman who was the very centre of his universe, couldn't sleep for fear of exposure. But what right did she have to play God with his marriage? She asked herself painfully. What right did she have to speak and destroy that marriage when the future security of her own little unborn brother or sister was also involved in the equation?

'Do you think it's healthy for a pregnant woman to live in this atmosphere and tolerate being cold-shouldered by those she counted as friends just because you've made yourself a pariah?' her father demanded in driven continuance.

'I broke off my relationship with Connor. I didn't do anything else.' Even as Lizzie struggled to maintain her brittle composure she was trembling, for she was not accustomed to hearing that cold, accusing tone from her father, and in her hurt and bewilderment she could not find the right words to try and defend her own actions. 'I'm not to blame for his death,' she swore in a feverish protest. 'He had problems that had nothing to do with me!'

'This morning, Felicity went down to the cottage to rest,' the older man revealed with speaking condemnation. 'I want my wife home by my side where she ought to be. Right now, she needs looking after and my first loyalty lies with her and our unborn child. For that reason, I've reached a decision, one I probably should have made a long time ago. I'm cutting off your allowance and I want you to move out.'

Shock shrilled through Lizzie, rocking what remained of her once protected world on its axis: she was to be thrown to the wolves for her stepmother's benefit. She stared in sick disbelief at the father whom she had adored from childhood, the father whom she had fought to protect from pain and humiliation even while her own life disintegrated around her.

Maurice had always been a loving parent. But then the death of Lizzie's mother when she was five and the fifteen years that had passed before the older man remarried had ensured that father and daughter had a specially close bond. But from the day he had met Felicity, brick by brick that loving closeness had been disassembled. Felicity had ensured that she received top billing in every corner of her husband's life and his home.

'Believe me, I don't mean this as a punishment. I hope I'm not that foolish,' the older man framed heavily. 'But it's obvious that I've indulged and spoilt you to a degree where you care nothing for the feelings of other people—'

'That's not true…' Lizzie was devastated by that tough assessment.

'I'm afraid it is. Making you go out into the world and stand on your own feet may well be the kindest thing I can do for you. There'll be no more swanning about at charity functions in the latest fashions, kidding yourself on that that's real work—'

'But I—'

'—and after the manner of Connor's death, who is likely to invite you to talk about generosity towards those less fortunate?' Maurice enquired with withering bite. 'Your very presence at a charity event would make most right-thinking people feel nauseous!'

As the phone on the desk rang, Lizzie flinched. Her father reached for it and gave her a brusque nod of finality, spelling out the message that their meeting was at an end. The distaste he could barely hide from her, the angry shame in his gaze cut her to the bone. She stumbled out into the hall and made her way back to the sanctuary of her apartment, which lay behind the main house in what had once been the stable block.

For a while, Lizzie was just numb with shock. Over the past ten days, shock had piled on shock until it almost sent her screaming mad. Yet only a fortnight ago, she had been about to break the news of the fabulous surprise holiday in Bali she had booked for Connor's birthday. She had not even managed to cancel that booking, she acknowledged dimly, must have lost every penny of its considerable cost. But then when had she ever had to worry about money? Or running up bills on her credit card because she had overrun her monthly allowance? Now, all those bills would have to be paid…

But what did that matter when she had lost the man she had loved to her own stepmother? Sweet, gushy little Felicity, who was so wet she made a pond look dry. Yet Felicity, it seemed, had also been the love of Connor's life and, finally rejected by her, he had gone off the rails.

'I didn't mean it to happen…I couldn't help myself!' Connor had proclaimed, seemingly impervious to the consequences of the appalling betrayal he had inflicted on Lizzie. The guy she had believed was her best friend ever, maybe even her future husband, and all the time he'd just been using her as a convenient cover for his rampant affair with her stepmother—the whiny, weepy Felicity! A great, gulping sob racked Lizzie's tall, slender frame and she clamped a hand to her wobbling mouth. She caught an unwelcome glimpse of herself in the mirror and her bright green eyes widened as she scanned her own physical flaws. Too tall, too thin with not a shadow of Felicity's feminine, sexy curves. No wonder Connor had not once been tempted all those weeks…

And Connor? Her tummy twisted in sick response. What a ghastly price he had paid for his affair with a married woman! Connor…dead? How could she truly hate him when he was gone? And how could she still be so petty that she was feeling grateful that she had never got as far as offering her skinny body to Connor in some ludicrous romantic setting in Bali? He would have run a mile!

Mrs Baines, the housekeeper, appeared in the doorway looking the very picture of discomfiture. 'I'm afraid that your father has asked me to pack for you.'

'Oh…' In the unkind mirror, Lizzie watched all her freckles stand out in stark contrast to her pallor before striving to pin an unconcerned expression to her face to lessen the older woman's unease. 'Don't worry about it. I'm all grown now and I'll survive.'

'But putting you out of your home is *wrong*,' Mrs Baines stated with a sharp conviction that startled Lizzie, for, although the housekeeper had worked for the Dentons for years, she rarely engaged in conversation that did not relate to her work and had certainly never before criticised her employer.

'This is just a family squabble.' Lizzie gave an awkward shrug, touched to be in receipt of such unexpected support but embarrassed by it as well. 'I…I'm going for a shower.'

Closeted in the bathroom, she frowned momentarily at the thought of that surprising exchange with Mrs Baines before she stabbed buttons on her mobile and called Jen, her closest remaining female friend. 'Jen?' she asked with forced brightness when the vivacious blonde answered. 'Could you stand a lodger for a couple of days? Dad's throwing me out!'

'Are you jossing me?'

'No, talking straight. Right at this very moment, our housekeeper is packing for me—'

'With your wardrobe…I mean, you *are* the original shop-till-you-drop girl…she'll still be packing at dawn!' Jen giggled. 'Come on over. We can go out and drown your sorrows together tonight.'

At that suggestion, Lizzie grimaced. 'I'm not in a party mood—'

'Take it from me, you *need* to party. Stick your nose in the air and face down the cameras and the pious types. There, but for the grace of God, go I!' Jen exclaimed with warming heat only to spoil it by continuing with graphic tactlessness, 'You ditched the guy… you were only with him a few months, like how does that make *you* responsible for him getting drunk and smashing himself up in his car?'

Lizzie flinched and reflected that Jen's easy hospitality would come with a price tag attached. But then, where else could she go in the short term? People had stopped calling her once the supposed truth of Connor's 'accident' had been leaked by his friends. She just needed a little space to sort out her life and, with the current state of her finances, checking into a hotel would not be a good idea. Maybe Jen, whose shallowness was legendary, would cheer her up. Maybe a night out on the town would lift her out of her growing sense of shellshocked despair.

'WORK?' JEN SAID IT AS IF it was a dirty word and surveyed Lizzie with rounded eyes of disbelief as she led the way into a bedroom mercifully large enough to hold seven suitcases and still leave space to walk around the bed. '*You...work?* What at? Stay with me until your father calms down. Just like me, you were raised to be useless and decorative and eventually become a wife, so let's face it, it's hardly your fault.'

'I'm going to stand on my own feet...just as Dad said,' Lizzie pronounced with a stubborn lift of her chin. 'I want to prove that I'm not spoilt and indulged—'

'But you *are*. You've never done a proper day's work in your life!' A small, voluptuous blonde, Jen was never seen with less than four layers of mascara enhancing her sherry-brown eyes. 'If you take a job, when would you find the time to have your hair and nails done? Or meet up with your friends for three-hour lunches or even take off at a moment's notice for a week on a tropical beach? I mean, it would be *gruesome* for you.'

Faced with those realities, it truly did sound a gruesome prospect to Lizzie too, although she was somewhat resentful of her companion's assertion that she had *never* worked. She had done a lot of unpaid PR work for charities and had proved brilliant at parting the seriously wealthy from their bundles of cash with stories of suffering that touched the hardest hearts. She had sat on several committees to organise events and, well, *sat* there, the ultimate authority on how to make a campaign look cool for the benefit of those to whom such matters loomed large. But nine-to-five work hours, following orders given by other people for some pocket-change wage, no, she hadn't ever done that. However, that didn't mean that she *couldn't*...

Four hours later, Lizzie was no longer feeling quite so feisty. Whisked off to the latest 'in' club, Lizzie found herself seated only two tables from a large party of former friends set on shooting her filthy looks. She was wearing an outfit that had been an impulse buy and a mistake and, in addition, Jen had been quite short with her when she had had only two alcoholic drinks before trying to order her usual orange juice. Reluctant to offend the blonde, who felt just then like her only friend in the world, Lizzie was now drinking more vodka.

'When my girlfriends won't drink with me, I feel like they're acting superior,' Jen confessed with a forgiving grin and then threw back a Tequila Sunrise much faster than it could have been poured.

When Jen went off to speak to someone, Lizzie went to the cloakroom. Standing at the mirrors, she regretted having allowed Jen to persuade her to wear the white halter top and short skirt. She felt too exposed yet she often bought daring outfits even though she never actually wore them. While she was wondering why that was so, she overheard the chatter of familiar female voices.

'I just can't *believe* Lizzie had the nerve to show herself here tonight!'

'But it does prove what a heartless, self-centred little—'

'Tom's warning Jen that if she stays friendly with Lizzie, she's likely to find herself out on her own with *only* Lizzie!'

'How could she have treated Connor that way? He was so much fun, so kind...'

Lizzie fled with hot, prickling tears standing out in her shaken eyes. Returning to her table, she drained her glass without even tasting the contents. Those female voices had belonged to her friends. One of them had even gone to school with her. *Ex-friends.* All of a sudden everybody hated her, yet only weeks ago she had had so many invitations out she would have needed a clone of herself to attend every event. Now she wanted to bolt for the exit and go home. But she wasn't welcome at home any more and Jen would be furious if she tried to end the evening early.

Yes, Connor had seemed kind. At least, she had thought so too until she went down to the Denton country cottage and found Connor in bed with Felicity. Her skin turned cold and clammy at that tormenting memory.

She had been thinking about inviting a bunch of friends to the cottage for the weekend. Believing that the property had been little used in recent times, she had decided to check out that there would be sufficient bedding. Connor must have come down from London in her stepmother's car and it had been parked out of sight behind the garage, so Lizzie had had no warning that the cottage was occupied. She had been in a lovely, bubbly mood, picturing how amazed Connor would be when she told him that he would be spending his twenty-fifth birthday in Bali.

Lizzie had been on the stairs when she heard the funny noises: a sort of rustling and moaning that had sent a momentary chill down her spine. But even at that stage she had not, in her ignorance, suspected that what she was hearing was a man and a woman making love. Blithely assuming that it was only the wind getting in through a window that had been left open, she had gone right on up. From the landing, she had got a full Technicolor view of her boyfriend and her stepmother rolling about the pine four-poster bed in the main bedroom.

Felicity had been in the throes of what had looked more like agony than ecstasy. Connor had been gasping for breath in between telling Felicity how much he loved her and how he couldn't bear to think that it would be another week before he could see her again. Throughout that exchange, Lizzie had been frozen to the spot like a paralysed peeping Tom. When Felicity had seen her, her aghast baby-blue eyes had flooded with tears, making her look more than ever like a victim in the guise of a fairytale princess.

But then crying was an art form and a way of life for her stepmother, Lizzie reflected, striving valiantly to suppress the wounding images she had allowed to surge up from her subconscious. Felicity wept if dinner was less than perfect... 'It's my fault...it's my fault,' she would fuss until Maurice Denton was on his knees and promising her a week in Paris to recover from the trauma of it. In much the same way and with just as much sincere feeling she had wept when Lizzie found her in bed with Connor Morgan. Tears had dripped from her like rain but her nose hadn't turned red and her eyes hadn't swelled up pink.

When Lizzie cried, it was noisy and messy and her skin turned blotchy. That afternoon, Connor and Felicity had enjoyed a full performance to that effect, before Lizzie's pride came to the rescue and she told them to get out of the cottage. After they had departed, she had made a bonfire of their bedding in the back garden. Recalling that rather pointless exercise, she forced herself

upright with an equally forced smile when Jen urged
her up to dance.

Up on the overhanging wrought-iron gallery above,
Sebasten was scanning the crowds below while the club
manager gushed by his side, 'I recognised the Denton
girl when she arrived. She looks a right little goer...'

Derisive distaste lit Sebasten's brooding gaze. The
very fact that Liza Denton was out clubbing only forty-
eight hours after the funeral told him *all* he needed to
know about the woman who had trashed Connor's life.

'Although *little* wouldn't be the operative word,' the
older man chuckled. 'She's a big girl...not even that
pretty; wouldn't be my style anyway.'

His companion's inappropriate tone of prurience gritted Sebasten's even white teeth. Beyond the fact that
he had a very definite need to put a face to the name,
he had no other immediate motive for seeking out Liza
Denton. She would pay for what she had done to Connor but Sebasten never acted in reckless haste and invariably employed the most subtle means of retribution
against those who injured him.

At that point, his attention was ensnared by the slender woman spinning below the lights on the dance floor
below, long hair the colour of marmalade splaying in a
sea of amber luxuriance around her bare shoulders. She
flung her head back with the kind of suggestive abandonment that fired a leap of pure adrenalin in Sebasten. Every muscle in his big, powerful length snapped
taut when he saw her face: the exotic slant of her cheekbones below big, faraway eyes and a lush, full-lipped
pink mouth. Her beauty was distinctive, unusual. Her
white halter-neck top glittered above a sleek, smooth

midriff and she sported a skirt the tantalising width of a belt above lithe, shapely legs that were at least three feet long. Bloody gorgeous, Sebasten decided, sticking out an expectant hand for the drink he had ordered and receiving it while contemplating that face and those legs and every visible inch that lay between with unashamed lust and wholly dishonourable intentions. Tonight, he would *not* be sleeping alone...

'That's *her*...the blonde...'

Recalled to the thorny question of Liza Denton by his companion's pointing hand, Sebasten looked to one side of *his* racy lady with the marmalade hair and, seeing a small blonde with the apparent cleavage of the Grand Canyon, understood why the manager had referred to his quarry as a big girl. So *that* was the nasty little piece of work whom Connor had lost his head over. Sebasten was not impressed but then he hadn't wanted or expected to be.

On the dance floor below, Jen touched Lizzie's shoulder to attract her attention. Only then did Sebasten appreciate that the two women knew each other and he frowned, for such a close connection could prove to be a complication. It was predictable that within the space of ten seconds Sebasten had worked out how that acquaintance might even benefit his purpose.

Jen reached the table she had been seated at with Lizzie first and then turned with compressed lips. 'I've been thinking that...well, perhaps it's not such a good idea for you to stay with me...'

Remembering the dialogue that she had overheard in the cloakroom, Lizzie felt her heart sink. 'Has someone been getting at you?'

'Let's be cool about this,' Jen urged with a brittle smile. 'I have every sympathy for the situation you're in right now but I have to think of myself too and I don't want to—'

'Get the same treatment?' Lizzie slotted in.

Jen nodded, grateful that Lizzie had grasped the point so fast. 'You should just go to a hotel and keep your head down for a while. You can pick up your things tomorrow. By this time next week, everybody will have found something other than Connor to get wound up about.'

And with that unlikely forecast, Jen walked without hesitation into the enemy camp two tables away and sat down with the crowd, who had been ignoring Lizzie all evening. For an awful instant, Lizzie was terrified that she was going to break down and sob like a little baby in front of them all. Whirling round, she pushed her way back onto the crowded dance floor, where at least she was out of view.

It was an effort to think straight and then she stopped trying, just sank into the music and gave herself up to the pounding beat. Her troubled, tearful gaze strayed to the male poised on the wrought-iron stairs that led down from the upper gallery and for no reason that she could fathom she fell still again. He was tall, black-haired and possessed of so striking a degree of sleek, dark good looks that the unattached women near by were focusing their every provocative move on him and even the attached ones were stealing cunning glances past their partners and weighing their chances.

He looked like a child in a toy shop: spoilt for choice while he accepted all those admiring female stares as his due. He was also the kind of guy who never looked twice at Lizzie except to lech over her legs and then wince at her flat chest and her freckles when he finally dragged his Neanderthal, over-sexed gaze up that high. Story of my life, Lizzie conceded. An over-emotional sob tugged at her throat as self-pity demolished a momentarily entrancing fantasy of said guy making a bee-line for her and thoroughly sickening Jen and her cohort of non-wellwishers.

Ashamed of her own emotional weakness, Lizzie headed for the bar, for want of anything better to do.

A hand suddenly closed over hers, startling her. 'Let me…' a dark, deep, sinfully rich drawl murmured in her ear.

Let him…*what*? Flipping round, Lizzie had the rare experience of having to tilt her head back to look up at a man. She encountered stunning dark golden eyes and stopped breathing, frozen in her tracks by shock. It was the guy from the stairs and close to he was even more spectacular than he had looked at a distance, not to mention being very much taller than she had imagined. Male too, very, *very* male, was the only other description she could come up with as she simply stared up at him.

Beneath her astonished scrutiny, he snapped long brown fingers, tilted his arrogant dark head back to address someone out of view and then began to walk her away from the crush at the bar again.

'I've got freckles…' Lizzie mumbled in case he hadn't noticed.

'I shall look forward to counting them.' He flashed her the kind of smile that carried a thousand megawatts of sheer masculine charisma and her heart, her *dead* and battered heart, leapt in her chest as though she had been kicked by an electrical charge.

'You *like* freckles?'

'Ask me tomorrow,' Sebasten purred with husky amusement.

CHAPTER TWO

As SEBASTEN approached the table where Lizzie had been seated, his bodyguards, who Lizzie assumed were bouncers, shifted the people about to take it over with scant ceremony. Two waiters then appeared at speed to clear the empty glasses.

Watching that ruthless little display of power being played out before her, Lizzie blinked in surprise. Was he the manager or the owner of the club? Who else could he be? The bar was heaving with a crush of bodies but the bouncer types only had to signal to receive a tray of drinks while others less influential fumed.

Looking across the table as her companion folded down with athletic grace into a seat, Lizzie still found herself staring: he was just *so* breathtaking. His lean, bronzed features were framed with high cheekbones, a narrow-bridged classic nose and a stubborn jawline. He had the kind of striking bone structure that would impress even when he was old. Luxuriant black hair curled back from his forehead above strong, well-marked brows, his brilliant, deep-set dark eyes framed by thick black lashes. Her heart hammered when he smiled at her again but she could not shake the lowering sensation that his choice of her with her less obvious attractions was a startling and inexplicable event.

'I'm Sebasten,' Sebasten drawled, cool as glass. 'Sebasten Contaxis.'

His name meant nothing to Lizzie but, as what she had already seen suggested that she *ought* to recognise the name, she nodded as if she had already recognised him and, having finally picked up on the sexy, rasping timbre of his accent, said, 'I'm Lizzie…you're not from London—er—originally, are you?'

Taking that as a case of stating the obvious with irony, Sebasten laughed. 'Hardly, but I'm very fond of this city, Lizzie? Short for? The obvious?'

'Yes, after my mother…it's what my family and closest friends call me.' As Lizzie met the concentrated effect of those spectacular dark golden eyes, a *frisson* of feverish tension not unlaced with alarm seized her: he was not the sort of straightforward, safe male she was usually drawn to. There was danger in the aura of arrogant expectation he emanated, in the tough strength of purpose etched in that lean, dark, handsome face. But perhaps the greatest threat of all lay in the undeniable sizzle of the sexual signals in that smouldering gaze of his.

'I take it that you saw at one glance that we were likely to be close,' he said in a teasing undertone that sent a potent little shiver down her taut spine.

Her breath snarled up in her throat. Caution urged her to slap him down but she didn't want him to walk away, could not, at that instant, think of clever enough words with which to gracefully spell out the reality that she was not into casual intimacy on short acquaintance. But for the first time in her life, Lizzie realised that she was seriously *tempted* and that shook her.

In surprise, Sebasten watched the hot colour climb in her cheeks so that the freckles all merged, the sudden downward dip of her eyes as she tilted her head to one side in an evasive move that was more awkward than elegant. For a moment, in spite of her sophisticated, provocative appearance, she looked young, *very* young and vulnerable.

'Smile…' he commanded, suddenly wondering what age she was.

And her generous mouth curved up as if she couldn't help herself in an entirely natural but rather embarrassed grin that had so much genuine appeal that Sebasten was entrapped by the surprise of it. 'I'm not the best company tonight,' she told him in a tone of earnest apology.

Sebasten rose in one fluid movement to his full height and extended a hand. 'Let's dance…'

As Lizzie got up she caught a glimpse of the staring faces at that table of ex-friends that she had been avoiding all evening and she threw her head back, squaring her taut bare shoulders. It felt good to be seen with a presentable male, rather than being alone and an object of scornful pity.

Just as it had once felt good to be with Connor? Lizzie snatched in a sharp gasp of air, painfully aware that Connor had smashed her confidence to pieces. She had thought that he was as straight and honest as she was herself. When he had made no attempt to go beyond the occasional kiss, she had believed his plea that he *respected* her and wanted to get to know her better. In retrospect that made her feel such an utter and naïve fool, for his restraint had encouraged her to make all

sorts of foolish assumptions, not least the belief that
he was really serious about her. When she was forced
to face the awful truth that Connor had instead been
sleeping with her much more beautiful stepmother, she
had been devastated by her own trusting stupidity.

A strong arm curved round Lizzie and tugged her
close in a smooth move that brought her into glancing collision with Sebasten's lean, muscular length.
A shockwave of heated response slivered through her
quivering body.

'What age are you?' Sebasten demanded, an aggressive edge to his deep, dark drawl, for he had seen the
distant look in her eyes and he was unaccustomed to a
woman focusing on anything other than him.

Putting that tone down to the challenge of compet-
ing against the backdrop of the pounding music, Lizzie
told him, 'Twenty-two...'

'Taken?' Sebasten prompted, a primal possessiveness
scything up through him at the sudden thought that she
might well be involved with some other man and that
that was the most likely explanation for her total lack
of flirtatiousness.

He was holding her close on a floor packed with
people all dancing apart but as Lizzie looked up into
his burnished lion-gold eyes she was only aware of the
mad racing of her own heartbeat and the quite unfamiliar curl of heat surging up inside her.

'Taken?' she queried, forced to curve her hands
round his wide shoulders to rise on tiptoe so that he
could hear her above the music.

Indifferent to the watchers around them, Sebasten linked his other arm round her slender, trembling

length as well, fierce satisfaction firming his expressive mouth as he felt the tiny little responsive quivers of her body against his. 'It doesn't matter. You're going to be mine...'

And with that far-reaching assurance, retaining an arm at the base of her spine, Sebasten turned her round and headed her up the wrought-iron staircase.

You're going to be mine. Men didn't as a rule address such comments to Lizzie and normally such an arrogant assumption would simply have made her giggle. She got on well with men but few seemed to see her as a likely object of desire and her male friends often treated her like a big sister. Perhaps it was because she towered over most of them, was usually more blunt than subtle and never coy and was invariably the first to offer a shoulder to cry on. Until Connor, her relationships had been low-key, more friendly than anything else, drifting to a halt without any great grief on either side. Until Connor, she had not known what it was to feel ripped apart with inadequacy, pain and humiliation. Sebasten—and she had already forgotten his surname—was just what her squashed ego needed most, Lizzie told herself fiercely.

He took her up to the VIP room, the privilege of only a chosen few, and her conviction that he owned the club increased as she spread a bemused glance over the opulence of the luxurious leather sofas, the soft, expensive carpet and the private bar in the corner.

'We can hear ourselves think up here,' Sebasten pointed out with perfect truth.

Lizzie stared at him, for the first time appreciating that his more formal mode of dress had picked him out as much as his looks and height. His superb grey suit had the subtle sheen of silk and the tailored perfection of designer-cut elegance.

'Do you own this place?' she asked.

'No.' Sebasten glanced at her in surprise.

'Then who are you that you get so much attention here?' Lizzie enquired helplessly.

'You don't know?' Amusement slashed Sebasten's lean, bronzed features, for not being recognised and known for who and what he was a novel experience for him. 'I'm a businessman.'

'I don't read the business sections of the newspapers,' Lizzie confided with palpable discomfiture.

'Why should you?'

Lizzie coloured. 'I don't want you thinking I'm an airhead.'

A tough, self-made man, her father had refused to let her take any interest in the family construction firm. As a teenager she had told him that she wanted to study for a business degree so that she could come and work for him and Maurice Denton had hurt her by laughing out loud at the idea. But then, that he had done well enough in the world to maintain his daughter as a lady of leisure had *once* been a source of considerable pride to him.

'I think you're beautiful…especially when you blush and all your freckles merge,' Sebasten mocked.

'Stop it…' Lizzie groaned, covering her hot face with spread hands in reproach.

He lifted a glass from the bar counter and she lowered one hand to grasp it, green eyes wide with fascination on his lean, strong face. Did he *really* think she was beautiful? She so much wanted to believe he was sincere, for she was more used to being told she was great fun and a good sport. Her fingers tightened round the tumbler and she drank even though her head was already swimming.

'Very beautiful and *very* quiet,' Sebasten pronounced.

'Guys like talking about themselves…I'm a good listener,' Lizzie quipped. 'So what was the most exciting event of your week?'

Sleek black lashes lowered to partially screen his shimmering dark eyes. 'Something someone said to me after a funeral.'

Lizzie's soft lips parted in surprise and then sealed again.

'Connor Morgan's funeral…' Sebasten let the announcement hang there and watched her tense and lose her warm colour with quiet approval. He was no fan of cold-hearted women and her obvious sensitivity pleased him. 'Did you know him?'

Lizzie's tummy muscles were tight as a drum but she kept her head high and muttered unevenly. 'I'm afraid that I never got to know him very well…'

It *was* true: she had barely scratched the surface of Connor's true nature, had been content to accept the surface show of the younger man's extrovert personality, had never once dreamt that he might lie to her and cheat on her without an ounce of remorse.

'Neither did I…' Sebasten's dark, deep drawl sent an odd chill down her spine.

'Let's not talk about it…' Taut with guilty anxiety over the near-lie she had told, Lizzie wondered if he was aware of the rumours and if he would have approached her had he known of her previous connection with Connor.

Aware he ought to be probing for some first-hand information on the voluptuous little blonde who had ditched his half-brother, Sebasten studied Lizzie's taut profile. However, his attention roamed of its own seeming volition down over her long, elegant neck to the tiny pulse beating out her tension beneath her collarbone and from there to the delicate curve of her breasts. By that point, his concentration had been engulfed by more libidinous promptings. Below the fine fabric, her nipples were taut and prominent as ripe berries and the dull, heavy ache at Sebasten's groin intensified with sudden savage force. Without hesitation, he swept the glass from her grasp and reached for her.

As she was sprung with a vengeance from her introspection, Lizzie's bemused gaze clashed with his and the scorching heat of his appraisal. She trembled, her body racing without warning to a breathless high of tension. Excitement, naked excitement flared through her, filling her with surprise and confusion. Dry-mouthed, pulses jumping, knees shaking, she felt his hand slide from her spine to the fuller curve of her behind and splay there to pull her close. She shivered in contact with the lean, tight hardness of his muscular thighs, every inch of her own flesh suddenly so sensitive she was bewildered, embarrassed, *shocked*.

'This feels good…' Sebasten husked, revelling in the way she couldn't hide her response to him. He could feel every little quiver assailing her, recognise the hoarseness of the breath she snatched in, read the bright luminosity of her dilated pupils and the full enticement of her parted lips.

'I hardly know you.' Lizzie was talking to herself more than she was talking to him. But that attempt to reinstate her usual caution didn't work. Being that close to him felt like perching at the very top of a rollercoaster a nanosecond before the breathtaking thrill of sudden descent and she was incapable of denying herself the seductive promise of that experience.

'I'll teach you to know me...' Sebasten framed with thickened emphasis, the smouldering glitter of his pagan golden eyes fixed to her with laser force. 'I'll teach you everything you need to know.'

'I like to go slow...'

'I like to go fast,' Sebasten imparted without hesitation, letting a lean brown hand rise to stroke through a long silken strand of her amber-coloured hair before moving to trace the tremulous line of her mouth with a confident fingertip. 'So fast I'll leave you breathless and hungry for more.'

Mesmerised, her very lips tingling from his light touch, Lizzie couldn't think straight. He might have been talking a foreign language, for right at that instant her leaping hormones were doing all of her thinking for her. She just wanted him to kiss her. In fact, she was so desperate to have that wide, sensual mouth on hers that she had to clench her hands to prevent herself from reaching for him first and, since she had never felt anything quite like that shameless craving before, it felt as unreal as a dream.

But when his mouth found hers, teased at her tender lips with a series of sensual little nips and tantalising expertise, no dream had ever lit such a powder-keg of response in Lizzie. Suddenly she was pushing forward into the hard, muscular contours of his powerful frame, hands flying up to link round his neck to steady her wobbling knees and from deep in her own throat a tiny moaning, pleading sound emerged as frustration at his teasing built to an unbearable degree.

He reacted then with a hungry, satisfying urgency that pierced her quivering length with the efficacy of a burning arrow thudding into a willing target. Suddenly he gave her exactly what she had wanted without even knowing it. As he drove her lips apart in a devastating assault of erotic intensity, her very skin-cell seemed to spontaneously combust in the whoosh of passion that shockwaved through her. Her own excitement was as intoxicating as a drug and all the more dangerous because raw excitement in a man's arms was new to her.

'Theos mou,' Sebasten groaned as he lifted his arrogant dark head. 'You're blowing me away...'

Bereft of his mouth on hers, Lizzie blinked in confusion. Only then conscious of the urgent tightness of her nipples and the pulsing ache between her thighs, she was surprised by the painful effect of both sensations. Her body didn't feel like her own any more. Her body was sending out frantic signals that the only place it was happy was up against *him*.

Sebasten flipped her round, curved her back to him again and let his hands glance over the pointed invitation of her sweet breasts, feeling her jerk and shiver and gasp as though she was in the eye of a storm. He eyed the nearest sofa. He didn't want to wait. He wanted her here, now, fast and hard to ease the nagging throb of his aroused sex. Sleazy, his mind told him while his defiant and fertile imagination threw up various explicit scenarios that threatened that conviction. No, he preferred to take her home to his own bed, where he could take his time, and he already knew once wouldn't be enough.

On fire from sensation, Lizzie broke free of him and dragged in a great gulp of oxygen. It was an effort to walk in a straight line to the table where he had set her drink. Lifting it with a shaking hand, she tipped it to her swollen lips, needing to occupy herself while she came to terms with the amazing feelings gripping her. She wanted to know everything about him from the minute he was born. She wanted to know him as nobody else had ever known him and a crazy singing happiness filled her when she looked back at him over the rim of her glass.

'I've never felt like this before,' she whispered with an edgy laugh that screened her discomfiture.

'I don't want to hear about how it felt with anyone else.' Burning golden eyes slammed into hers and he extended a commanding hand. 'Let's go…'

Lizzie moved and let him engulf her fingers in his. 'Are you always this bossy?'

'Where did you get that idea?' Sebasten purred like a very large and amused jungle cat because she had just leapt to do as he asked without even thinking about it. But then women always did. In his entire adult life, Sebasten had never met a woman who was *not* eager to please him.

He swept her back down the stairs, past a welter of curious eyes and on towards the exit. Her nerves were jumping like electrified beans. She relived the bold caress of his sure hands over her breasts and her cheeks flooded with hot self-conscious colour. Not the sort of familiarity she normally allowed. What was she doing with him? Where on earth was he taking her? *He* thought she was beautiful. *He* wanted to be with her, she reminded herself with feverish determination. Nobody else did, not her father, who had cut her out of his life, not a single one of her friends.

On the wet pavement outside, a uniformed chauffeur extended an umbrella for their protection and hurried to open the door of a long, opulent silver limousine. Lizzie was impressed and she got in, refused to think about what she was doing and turned to look at Sebasten again. The dizzy sense of rightness that had engulfed her only minutes earlier returned. 'Where were you born?' she heard herself ask.

In the act of tugging her close, Sebasten grinned at what struck him as an essentially feminine and pointless question. 'On an island the size of a postage stamp in the Aegean Sea…and you?'

'In Devon,' she confided, heart skipping a beat over that incredible smile of his. 'My parents moved to London when I was a baby.'

'How fascinating,' Sebasten teased, lacing his fingers into her hair and kissing her. She drowned in the scent and the taste of him, head falling back on her shoulders as his tongue darted in an erotic sweep between her lips and made her gasp with helpless pleasure.

At some point, they left the limo, climbed steps, traversed a low-lit echoing hall, but true awareness only returned to Lizzie when she swayed giddily on the sweeping staircase she found herself on. His hands shot out to steady her. 'Are you OK?'

'These stupid shoes…' Lizzie condemned in mortification and she kicked off her spike-heeled sandals where she stood as though her unsteady gait had been caused by them.

'How much have you had to drink?' Sebasten enquired with lethal timing, a dark frown-line forming between his ebony brows.

'Hardly anything,' Lizzie told him breathlessly while making a conscious effort not to slur her words. She was taut as a bowstring, suddenly terrified of receiving yet another rejection to add to the many she had already withstood.

As he received that assurance Sebasten's tension evaporated and he swept her on into a massive, opulent room rejoicing in a very large and imposing bed. She was jolted by the sight of the bed and a rather belated stab of dismay made her question her own behaviour. She barely knew Sebasten and she was still a virgin. But then she had never been tempted until she met Connor and she had expected *him* to become her first lover. As the degrading memory of finding her boyfriend and her stepmother in bed together engulfed Lizzie afresh, she rebelled against her own moral conditioning. After all, hadn't her old-fashioned principles let her down badly when it came to men? A more experienced woman would have been suspicious of Connor's lack of lusty intent.

Eyes flaring like emerald-green stars on that bitter acknowledgement, Lizzie spun round and feasted her attention on Sebasten. He was gorgeous and tonight he was hers, *all* hers, absolutely nobody else's. She had never met anyone like him before. He was so focused, so sure of himself that he drew her like a magnet and the heat of his appreciative appraisal warmed her like the sun after weeks of endless rain.

Lizzie tilted her head back, glossy marmalade hair tumbling back from her slanted cheekbones. 'You can kiss me again,' she informed him.

With an appreciative laugh, Sebasten claimed her parted lips in a long, drugging kiss that rocked her on her feet. Lifting her up into his arms with easy strength, he brought her down onto his bed. What was it about her that made her seem so different to other women? One minute she was quiet and mysterious, the next tossing an open challenge, glorious green eyes telegraphing pure invitation.

Lizzie surfaced from the mindless spell of her own response and stared up at him. 'Are you as good at everything else as you are at kissing?'

Sebasten tossed his jacket on a chair, enjoying the wide, wondering look in her face as she watched him. 'What do you think?'

That she could barely breathe when those shimmering dark golden eyes rested on her and her mouth ran dry as a bone when he unbuttoned his shirt. From his broad shoulders to his powerful, hair-roughened pectorals and flat, taut abdomen, he was all sleek, bronzed skin and rippling muscles.

'That you're very sexy,' Lizzie confided helplessly.

'We match...' Sebasten strolled lithe as a hunting animal and barefoot towards the bed.

'Do we?' Her heart hammered behind her ribs. She

felt like an infatuated teenager confronted without warning by her idol: butterflies in her tummy, brain empty, teeth almost chattering with nerves. Every lingering strand of caution was urging her to acknowledge her mistake and take flight but those prudent promptings fell into abeyance at the same instant as Sebasten rested shimmering dark golden eyes of appreciation on her.

'Ne...'

'No?' Lizzie was confused.

'Ne...is Greek for yes.' Sebasten came down on the side of the bed with a smile that lit up his lean, strong face and melted her.

'You're Greek?'

'Ten out of ten,' Sebasten gathered her close and threaded lazy hands through her tumbling mane. 'I *love* the colour of your hair...but I still don't know your surname.'

In the expectant silence, Lizzie tensed. Fearful of his reaction were he to recognise the name of Denton, she heard herself quote her late mother's maiden name. 'Bewford.'

'Now I can't lose you again,' Sebasten asserted.

'Would it matter if you did?' Heart racing so fast now that she could barely speak and keep her voice level, Lizzie curved an uncertain hand round his arm.

'Absolutely, *pethi mou*.' Sebasten reflected that he might even make it to the three-month mark with her, a milestone he had yet to share with any woman. Unsettled by that uninvited and odd thought, he kissed her again.

He made love to her mouth with devastating virtuosity, plundering the tender interior she opened to him. Lizzie pressed forward, unsteady hands linking round his neck, fingers uncoiling to rise and sink into the depths of his luxuriant black hair. It was sweeter and wilder and more intense than anything she had ever known. He bent her back over his arm so that her bright hair trailed across the pillows and let his lips seek out the tiny pulse going crazy beneath her collarbone.

Lizzie quivered in surprise and what little grip she had left on reality vanished. When he then located the tender pulse spot below her ear, her body thrummed into a burst of life so that not one part of her was capable of staying still. She was not even conscious of the deft unsnapping of the clasps on her halter top, only of the air grazing her distended nipples and cooling the swollen sensitivity of her flesh. He eased off her stretchy skirt to leave her clad in only a pair of white lace panties.

'You're perfect,' Sebasten groaned, cupping the ivory-pale rose-tipped mounds he had unveiled with possessive hands, easing her back against the pillows to direct his attention to the tender tips straining for his attention.

Capturing a throbbing peak between his lips, he flicked it with his tongue and she moaned out loud at the surge of tormenting sensation that made her tense and tremble and jerk beneath his ministrations. Nothing before had ever felt so good that it almost hurt and she was lost in the shocking intensity of her own response. She was breathing in fast little pants, aware of her body as she had never been before, feeling the charged readiness of wild anticipation, the crazed race of her own pounding heartbeat, the damp heat pulsing between her thighs.

'Talk to me...' Sebasten urged.

'I...can't find...my voice,' Lizzie tried to say after a bemused hesitation in which she had to struggle just to force her brain to think again. Even to her own ears, the words emerged sounding indistinguishable and slurred.

Sebasten stilled and, scanning her dismayed face, he removed his hands from her. 'You're drunk...'

As that harsh judgement came out of nowhere at her, Lizzie flinched. Bracing herself on one awkward hand, she sat up. His lean, powerful face was taut, stunning golden eyes betraying angry distaste.

'I'm—'

'Out of your skull on booze...*not* my style!' Sebasten incised, springing upright to his full intimidating height.

Dragged with little warning from the breathtaking hold of unbelievable passion, Lizzie found herself in need of a ready tongue. But there was nothing ready about her tongue when her brain was in a haze of confusion. 'Not your style?' she echoed.

It was a terrible strain for her to try to enunciate each word with clarity. She reeled off the bed in an abrupt movement, suddenly feeling horribly naked and under attack.

As he watched her stagger as she attempted to stay vertical Sebasten's wide, sensual mouth clenched even harder, his whole body in the fierce grip of painful frustration while he questioned how he could possibly have failed to register the state she was in. 'The consent issue,' he breathed with icy restraint. 'No way would I even consider bedding a woman too inebriated to know what she is doing!'

Her toes catching in her discarded skirt where it lay, Lizzie tipped forward and only just managed to throw out her hands to break her own fall. As she went down with a crash, punctuated by a startled expletive from Sebasten, she just slumped on the soft, deep carpet.

With a mighty effort of will, Lizzie lifted her swimming head again and focused on Sebasten's bare brown feet. Even his toes were beautiful, she thought dimly as she tried to come up with something to say in a situation that had already gone far beyond embarrassment. 'Do you think...do you think you could sober me up before we continue?' she muttered hopefully.

CHAPTER THREE

SEBASTEN surveyed Lizzie with thunderous incredulity and then he wondered what he *was* going to do with her.

After all, he was responsible for her, wasn't he? He had pressed more alcohol on her when she must already have had enough and he had brought her into his home. In the condition she was in, he could hardly stuff her into a taxi or ask his chauffeur to cope with her and, since he too had had several drinks, he could not drive her anywhere.

In the tense silence which would have agonised Lizzie had she been sober, she surveyed his carpet fibres and then looked up. Sebasten was down on one knee, contemplating her with an expression of fierce frustration.

'I could just sleep here on the floor,' Lizzie proffered, striving to be helpful.

Sebasten collided with huge green eyes.

The beginnings of an irreverent grin pulled at her full, reddened mouth because she was suffering from a dreadful urge to succumb to uncontrollable giggles. 'You see...I don't think I can get up...can't feel my legs.'

Sebasten experienced a sudden near-overwhelming desire to shake her until he could force some sense back into her head. Had she no idea how much at risk she could be in a stranger's house? Or of how dangerous it was for a woman to drink so much that she could neither exercise caution nor defend herself? The very idea of her behaving in such a way with another man filled him with dark, deep anger.

'Do you make a habit of this kind of behaviour?' he demanded rawly.

As she was assailed by that gritty tone, all desire to giggle was squashed at the source. 'No...you're the first...sorry,' Lizzie slurred, sinking back to the carpet again.

Vaulting to his feet, Sebasten strode over to the phone by the bed and lifted it to order a large pot of black coffee and sandwiches to be brought upstairs. Then he contemplated his victim with brooding intensity and his long, powerful legs carried him over to the windows. Depressing the locks, he thrust the French windows back to let in the cold night air.

As that chilly breeze touched her slender bare back, Lizzie gave a convulsive shiver. Sebasten surveyed her without remorse. He would sober her up and *then* have her conveyed home. Wrenching the top sheet from the bed, he flung it over her prone body and gathered her up with determination to carry her into the adjoining bathroom.

'Sleepy...' Lizzie mumbled.

'You need to wake up,' Sebasten informed her, settling her with some difficulty onto the seat in the spacious shower cubicle and hitting the buttons to switch on the water. Only as the water cascaded down did he appreciate that he hadn't removed the sheet. Then he no longer felt quite so comfortable with her semi-clad state.

As the water hit her, Lizzie opened bewildered and shaken eyes. 'No...don't want to be wet,' she framed weakly.

'Tough,' Sebasten told her, barring the exit in case she made a sudden leap for freedom.

Far from making a dive for it, in slow motion and wearing an only vaguely surprised expression, Lizzie slithered off the seat like a boneless doll into a heap on the floor of the cubicle.

'Up!' Sebasten urged in exasperation.

Lizzie curled up and closed her eyes, soothed now by the warm flooding flow of water. 'Sleepy,' she mumbled again. 'Night...night.'

Teeth gritted, Sebasten stepped into the shower to hit the controls and turn the water cold. She uttered a satisfying yelp of surprise as the water went from warm and soothing to icy and tingling. However, Sebasten got so wet in his efforts to haul Lizzie's uncooperative body back up onto the seat, he ended up squatting down to hold her up and suffering beneath the same cold gush.

'C-cold!' Lizzie stammered.

'I'm freezing too!' Sebasten launched, shirt and trousers plastered to his big, powerful body as the same chill invaded him. He withstood the onslaught with masochistic acceptance. Served him bloody well right, he thought grimly. She was way too young and immature for him. What had got into him? Bringing her home had been a mistake and he had never sunk low enough to take advantage of a stupid woman.

'Very...cold,' Lizzie moaned.

'And you said you weren't an airhead,' Sebasten recalled out loud with a deep sense of injustice, watching her wet hair trail in the water, looking down at her miserable face which was now—aside of the odd streak of mascara—innocent of all cosmetic enhancement. She still had perfect skin and amazing eyes, he noted. But he could not credit that he was trapped in his own shower with a drunk woman. He didn't get into awkward situations like that.

'Not,' Lizzie pronounced with unexpected aggression, her chin tilting up.

A loud knock sounded on the door in the bedroom beyond. With a groan, Sebasten put her down but she slumped without his support. A vision of having to explain a drowned woman in his shower overtaking him, he switched off the water.

'Don't move...' he instructed Lizzie as he strode back to the bedroom, dripping every step of the way.

A faint flush over his hard cheekbones as the member of staff presenting the laden tray of coffee and sandwiches stared in open stupefaction at his drenched appearance, Sebasten kicked the door shut again and set down the tray beside the bed.

When he returned to the bathroom, Lizzie was striving to crawl out of the shower on her hands and knees and being severely hampered by the trailing sopping sheet.

'Feeling a little livelier?' Sebasten quipped with dark satire.

'Feel...*a-awful*!' Lizzie stuttered through teeth chattering like castanets and she laid her head down and just sobbed in weakened rage. 'Hate you!'

She looked pathetic. Sebasten snatched up a big bath towel, crouched down to disentangle her from the sheet and wrapped her with care into the towel. Hauled up into a standing position, she fell against him like a skater on ice for the first time and he lifted her up and carried her through to the bedroom to settle her back on the bed. Keeping a cautious eye on her in case she fell off the bed too, he backed away to strip off his own wet clothing and pitch the sodden garments onto the bathroom floor.

It was like babysitting, he decided, his even white teeth gritting. Not that he had ever *done* any babysitting, for Sebasten was not in the habit of putting himself out for other people. But the comparison between his own erotic expectations earlier in the evening and reality was galling to a male who was accustomed to a life than ran with the smooth, controlled efficiency of an oiled machine.

'Close the windows...' Lizzie begged, deciding there and then as cold dragged her mind from its former fog that she had fallen live into the hands of a complete sadist.

'Yes, you're definitely waking up now.' Sheathed only in a pair of black designer jeans, Sebasten crossed the room to pull the French windows shut.

Lizzie blinked and then contrived to stare. The jeans fitted him as well as his own bronzed skin, accentuating his flat, muscular stomach, his narrow hips and long, hard thighs. Colouring, she looked away, sobered up enough already by the shock of that cold shower to cringe with mortification. Sebasten tugged her forward, tossed pillows behind her to prop her up and proceeded to pour the coffee.

'Don't feel like coffee—'

'You're drinking it,' Sebasten told her and he laid the tray of sandwiches down beside her. *'Eat.'*

'I'm not hungry,' she dared in an undertone.

'You need food to soak up the booze in your system,' Sebasten delivered with cutting emphasis.

Squirming with shame and embarrassment, Lizzie reached for a sandwich. 'I don't get drunk…I'm not like that…I just had a hideous day—'

'So you decided to give me a hideous evening,' Sebasten slotted in with ungenerous bite. 'Count your blessings—'

'What blessings?' Lizzie was fighting hard to hold back the surge of weak tears that that crack had spawned.

'You're safe and you're still all in one piece. If you'd picked the wrong guy to spring this stunt on, you might not have been,' Sebasten pointed out.

Chilled by what she recgonised as a fair assessment, Lizzie swallowed shakily and made herself bite into the sandwich. It was delicious. Indeed, she had not realised just how hungry she was until that moment. In silence, she sipped at the black coffee, wincing with every mouthful, for she liked milk in her coffee, and worked her way through the sandwiches.

Sebasten watched the sandwiches melt away and noted that for all her slenderness she had a very healthy appetite. 'When did you last eat?' he finally asked drily.

'Breakfast,' Lizzie worked out with a slight frown and that had just been a slice of toast. Lunch she hadn't touched because just beforehand her father had phoned to say that he was coming home specially to talk to her and her appetite had vanished. As for supper, well, Jen hadn't offered her anything but her first alcoholic drink of the evening.

'No wonder you ended up flat on your face on my carpet,' Sebasten delivered as he topped up the cup she had emptied.

Lizzie paled. 'Not the world's most forgiving person, are you?'

'No.' Sebasten made no bones about the fact. 'What did your "hideous" day encompass?'

Lizzie looped unsteady fingers through her fast-drying hair to push it back from her brow and muttered tightly. 'My father told me to move out and get a job. I was *very* upset—'

'**At** twenty-two years of age, you were still living at home and dependent on your family?' Sebasten demanded in surprise. 'Are you a student?'

Lizzie reddened. 'No. I left school at eighteen. My father didn't *want* me to work. He said he wanted me to have a good time!'

Sebasten scanned the delicate diamond pendant and bracelet she wore, conceding that they might well be real rather than the imitations he had assumed. Yet she didn't speak with those strangulated vowel sounds that he associated with the true English upper classes, which meant that she was most probably from a family with money but no social pedigree. He was wryly amused that Ingrid, who was obsessed by a need to pigeon-hole people by their birth and their bank balance, had taught him to distinguish the old moneyed élite from the *nouveau riche* in London society.

'And, *no*...having a good time did not cover my behaviour tonight!' Lizzie advanced in defensive completion. 'That was a one-off!'

'So you were *very* upset at the prospect of having to keep yourself,' Sebasten recapped with soft derision and innate suspicion that her apparent ignorance of who he was had been an act calculated to bring his guard down. 'Is that why you came home with me?'

Startled by that offensive question, Lizzie sucked in a sudden sharp breath. As the fog of alcohol released her brain, she had already absorbed enough of her surroundings to recognise that she was in the home of a male who inhabited a very much wealthier and more rarefied world than her own. She lifted her chin. 'No, to tell you the truth, now that I'm recovering my wits, I haven't the foggiest idea *why* I came home with you because I don't like you one little bit.'

A disconcerting smile flashed across Sebasten's dark, brooding features. Angry green eyes the colour of precious emeralds were hurling defiance at him and her spine was as rigid as that of a queen in a medieval portrait. Unfortunately for her, though, her tangled hair and the bath towel supplied a ridiculous frame for that attempt to put him in his place.

The instant that incredible smile lit up his lean, strong features, Lizzie's heartbeat went haywire and her mouth ran dry and she knew exactly why she had come home with him. If he kept his smart mouth closed, he was just about irresistible.

'You're angry that you made a fool of yourself,' Sebasten retaliated without hesitation. 'But I may have done you a big favour—'

Hot colour burned in Lizzie's cheeks. 'You call throwing the windows wide and torturing me in a cold shower doing me a *favour*?'

'Yes…if the memory of that treatment stops you drinking that much again in the wrong company.'

Unused to a woman fighting with him, Sebasten savoured the sheer frustrated rage in her expressive face and his body hardened again in sudden urgent response. He wanted to flatten her back onto his bed and remind her of how irrelevant liking or anything else was when he touched her. His own reawakened desire startled him. Then her tangled torrent of hair was drying to gleam with rich gold and copper lights and that exotic and passionate face of hers still kept drawing him back. The intimate recollection of her lush little breasts and that lithe, slender body of hers shaking with hunger beneath his own was all the additional stimuli required to increase Sebasten's level of arousal to one of supreme discomfort.

In the midst of swallowing the sting of that further comment destined to humble her, Lizzie felt the burn of Sebasten's stunning dark golden eyes on her and what she had been about to say in an effort to save face died on her tongue. Stiffening, she shifted forward onto the edge of the bed. Suddenly aware of the high-voltage tension that had entered the atmosphere, she felt too jittery to handle her discomfiture and she settled her feet down onto the carpet.

'It's time I went home,' she announced but she hesitated, afraid that the awful dizziness might return the instant she tried to stand up.

'Where is home?'

'No place right now,' Lizzie admitted after a dismayed pause to appreciate the threatening reality. 'I still have to find somewhere to live. Right now my luggage is parked at a friend's place but I can't stay there.'

Sebasten watched her stand up like a newborn baby animal afraid to test her long slim legs and then breathe in slow and deep. She plotted a passage to the bathroom and vanished from view. Closing the door, she caught her own reflection in a mirror and groaned out loud, lifting a trembling hand to her messy hair. Any pretence towards presentability was long gone, she reflected painfully. It was little wonder Sebasten had been sprawled in an armchair at a distance, talking down to her as if he were a very superior being.

And she guessed he *was*, she conceded, snatching up a comb from the counter of a built-in unit to begin disentangling her hair. He could have thrown her back out on the street. He could have taken advantage of her... well, not really, she decided, reckoning that Sebasten would prefer a live, moving woman to one showing all the animation of a corpse. And he *had* prevented her from making a very big mistake! Why didn't she just admit that to herself? Her life was in a terrible mess and she shouldn't even have been looking at Sebasten, never mind behaving like a tramp and coming home with him. She ought to be really grateful that nothing much had happened between them...

Only she *wasn't*. Tears stung the back of Lizzie's eyes and she blinked them back with stubborn determination. The ghastly truth was that she still found Sebasten incredibly attractive and she had blown it. Really blown her chances with him. There was nothing fanciable or appealing about a woman who had to be dumped in a shower to be brought out of a drunken collapse, naturally he was disgusted with her. But she was much angrier with herself than he could possibly have been. She had never been so attracted to any guy and she was convinced that alcohol had had very little to do with her extraordinary reaction to him. Why had she had to meet the most gorgeous guy of her life on the one night that she made a total, inexcusable ass of herself?

Wishing that she had thought to reclaim her clothing before she entered the bathroom and embarrassed to death as stray memories of her wanton behaviour broke free of her subconscious to torment her, Lizzie crept back into the bedroom.

Dawn was beginning to finger light through the heavy curtains. She had hoped that Sebasten would have fallen asleep or taken himself tactfully off somewhere else to allow her a fast and silent exit but no such luck was hers.

Sebasten was watching the television business news but the instant the door opened he vaulted upright and studied her. Still wrapped in the towel, hair brushed back from her scrubbed-clean face, she looked even more beautiful to Sebasten than she had looked earlier. Even pale, she had a fresh, natural appeal that pulled him against his own volition.

'You might as well sleep in one of my guest rooms

for what's left of the night,' Sebasten surprised himself by suggesting.

'Thanks…but I'd better be going.' Strained eyes centred on him in a look so brief he would have missed it had he not been watching her like a hawk. 'I've taken up enough of your time.'

His mouth quirked. She sounded like a little girl who had attended a very bad party but was determined to leave saying all that was polite. He watched her stoop in harried movements to snatch up her clothes and shoes, mortification merging her freckles with a hot pink overlay of colour. Her inability to conceal her embarrassment was oddly touching.

'How sober are you?' Sebasten prompted lazily, eyes flaring to smouldering gold as her lush mouth opened and the tip of her tongue snaked out in a nervous flicker to moisten her full lower lip. Hunger, fierce and primitive as a knife at his groin, burned through him.

'Totally wised up…' Lizzie tried hard to smile, acknowledging her own foolishness.

'Then *stay* with me…' Sebasten murmured thickly.

Thrown by that renewed invitation, Lizzie gazed across the room, green eyes full of surprise and confusion. 'But—'

'Of course there *are* conditions,' Sebasten warned, smooth as silk. 'With your eyes closed, you have to be able to touch the tip of your nose with one finger and you only get one chance.'

An involuntary laugh escaped Lizzie as she looked back at him. Still clad only in the jeans, he was dropdead gorgeous: all sleek, bronzed, hair-roughened skin, lean muscle and masculinity. Even the five o'clock shadow now roughening his strong jawline only added to his sheer impact. Feeling just then that it would be more sensible to close her eyes and deny herself the pleasure of staring at him as though he had just dropped down from heaven for a visit, Lizzie strove to play the game and performed the exercise even though at that point she had every intention of leaving.

'Then you have to open your eyes again and walk in a straight line to the door,' Sebasten instructed.

Growing amusement gripping her, Lizzie set out for the door.

'Full marks,' Sebasten quipped.

Lizzie spun round. 'You've got to do it *too*.'

Disconcerted, Sebasten raised a brow in scornful dismissal of that challenge.

'You take yourself very seriously.' Lizzie watched him with keen intensity because it was one of the most important things she had learnt about him. 'You don't even like me to suggest that you might be anything less than totally in control.'

'I'm a man. That's normal,' Sebasten drawled.

Not to Lizzie, it wasn't. She was used to younger men who were more relaxed about their image and the differences between the sexes but she could see that Sebasten inhabited another category altogether. The strong, brooding, macho type unlikely to spill his guts no matter how tough the going got. Not her type at all, she told herself in urgent consolation.

Sebasten strode in a direct line to the door but only because where she was was where he wanted to be at that instant. 'Satisfied?'

'Yes…we are two sober people…and I need to go and

get dressed.' Breathless at finding herself that close to him again, Lizzie coloured, heartbeat thumping at what felt like the base of her throat.

'I'll only take it all off again,' Sebasten threatened in a dark, deep undertone of warning that sent a tingle of delicious threat down her taut spine.

'Walking in a straight line to the door when you asked was just my effort to lighten the atmosphere,' Lizzie shared awkwardly.

'While every lingering look you give me tells me how much you still want me,' Sebasten delivered without an instant of hesitation.

'You've got some ego!' Lizzie condemned in disconcertion.

'*Earned*…like my reputation,' Sebasten slotted in, closing his lean, sure hands to her slender waist to tilt her forward. 'We'll conduct an experiment—'

'No…*no* experiments,' Lizzie cut in on a higher pitch of nervous stress. 'I don't *do* stuff like this, Sebasten. I don't have one-night stands. I don't sleep with guys I've only just met…in fact, I haven't got much experience at all and you'd probably find the business news more riveting—'

Sebasten recognised one of the qualities that had drawn him to her but which he had failed to identify: a certain degree of innocence. Fired by the rare event of being challenged to persuade a woman into his bed, he focused his legendary negotiating skills on Lizzie. 'I'm riveted by *you*,' Sebasten incised with decisive conviction. 'Right from the first moment I saw you at the club.'

'Stop kidding me…' Skin warming, Lizzie connected

with his stunning golden eyes and trembled, wanting to believe, her battered self-esteem hungry for that reassurance. That close to him, it was difficult to breathe and the warm, clean male scent of his skin flared her nostrils with a familiarity that tugged at her every sense. She wanted to lean into him, crush the tender tips of her swollen breasts into the hard wall of his chest, feel that wide, sexy mouth ravish her own again.

'I'm not kidding. One look and I was hooked.' Sebasten gazed down at her from below the dense fringe of his black lashes and just smiled and that was the moment she was lost, that was the moment when any pretence of self-control ran aground on the sheer strength of her response to him. Her pulses racing, Lizzie felt the megawatt burn of that smile blaze through her and she angled into him in a helpless movement. When his mouth came down on hers again, the heat of that sensual assault was pure, addictive temptation.

In the midst of that kiss, Sebasten carried her back to the bed and peeled away the towel. He cupped her breasts, bent his arrogant dark head over the pale pink distended peaks and used his knowing mouth and his even more knowing hands to give her pleasure.

'Are you protected?' he asked.

'Yes…' She had started taking contraceptive pills a month after she had begun dating Connor but she crushed that unwelcome association back out of her mind again, the bitterness that had haunted her in recent weeks set behind her. A fresh start, a new and more productive life, Sebasten. She was more than ready for those challenges when Sebasten was giving her the impression that *he* felt much the same way that *she* did.

As he slid off the bed in one fluid movement to dispense with his jeans, her cheeks reddened and she turned her head away while wicked but self-conscious anticipation licked along her every nerve-ending.

He came down beside her again and she let her hands rise up over his powerful torso. She had never really wanted to explore a man before but she could not resist her need to touch him. Her fingers roved from the satin-smooth hardness of his shoulders to graze through the short black whorls of hair hazing his pectorals to the warm tautness of his stomach, feeling his muscles flex in response.

'Don't stop there, *pethi mou*,' Sebasten husked.

Lizzie got more daring, let her fingers follow the in-triguing furrow of silky black hair over his stomach and discovered the male power of him with a jolt of mingled dismay and curiosity. He was smooth and hard but there was definitely too much of him.

'*This way*,' Sebasten murmured with concealed amusement, initially startled by her clumsiness and then adapting to teach her what he liked. It was a les-son he had never had cause to give before but it sent his desire for her surging even higher.

That intimate exploration made Lizzie feel all hot and quivery and she pressed her thighs together on the disturbing ache stirring at the very heart of her. When he teased at her swollen lower lip before letting his tongue delve into the tender interior of her mouth in a darting foray that imitated a far more elemental pos-session she trembled against his lean, strong body, fe-verish hot craving gripping her.

His breathing fractured, Sebasten dragged his mouth

from hers to gaze down at her with fiery golden eyes. 'I don't think I've ever been so hot for a woman as I am for you.'

He pulled her to him and his expert hands traced the beaded sensitivity of her breasts. She couldn't stay still any more. Tiny little tremors were racking her. Her breath was rasping into her dry throat, pulses thrumming, heart pounding. At the apex of her legs he traced the moist, needy secret of her femininity and she moaned out loud, couldn't help herself. The pleasure was dark and deep and terrifyingly intense. He controlled her and she didn't care; she just didn't want him to stop. The bitter-sweet torment of sensation sizzled through every fibre of her writhing body with increasing intensity until she was on the edge of a desperation as new to her as intimacy.

'I need you...*now*,' Sebasten growled.

Rising over her, he tipped her up with strong hands and came down over her. She barely had time to learn the feeling of his urgent demand for entrance before he plunged his throbbing shaft into her slick heat and groaned with an earthy pleasure at the tightness of his welcome.

The momentary stab of unexpected pain made Lizzie jerk and cry out but the passionate urgency controlling her allowed no competition. Too much in the grip of the feverish need he had induced, she gave him a blank look when he stilled in questioning acknowledgement of that cry. Her whole body craved him with a force of hungry excitement that nothing could have haltered and she arched up to him in frantic encouragement until he succumbed to that invitation and ground his body into hers again, sheathing himself fully and sending another shockwave of incredible desire through her. His pagan rhythm drove her to the edge of ecstasy and then flung her over the wild, breathtaking peak before the glorious, peaceful aftermath of fulfilment claimed her. As he reached his own shuddering release, she wrapped her arms round him tight.

'Sublime,' Sebasten muttered hoarsely in Greek and then he rolled back and hauled her over him to study her flushed and shaken face, the unguarded softness and warmth in her green eyes as she looked back at him. He pushed his fingers into her tumbling hair and tugged her back down to him so that he could kiss her again. 'I think we're going to do this again and again... and again.'

'Hmm...' Lizzie was more mesmerised by him than ever now. She scanned his lean, strong face and let her fingertips roam from his shoulder to curl into his tousled black hair instead. His features were *so* masculine: all taut angles from the clean slant of his high cheekbones to the proud jut of his nose and the blue-shadowed roughness of his hard jawline. His stunning gaze gleamed lazy gold beneath the semi-screening sweep of his spiky lashes. She just wanted to smile and smile and smile like an idiot.

She had been a virgin, he was *sure* of it, Sebasten thought, but he wasn't quite sure enough to broach the issue. He recalled her clueless approach to making love to him and amusement filled him. A split-second later the renewed ache of desire prompted him to kiss her again and it was the last even semi-serious thought he had for some hours.

LIZZIE WAKENED WITH A START, feeling horribly queasy.

Sebasten was asleep. Sliding as quietly as she could from the bed, she fled to the bathroom, where nature took its course with punishing efficiency. Humbly grateful that Sebasten had not witnessed the final reward for her own foolishness, Lizzie got into the shower and used his shampoo to wash her hair. Even the already familiar smell of his shampoo turned her inside-out with intense longing. She felt weak, frighteningly vulnerable and yet crazily happy too. Yet hadn't she honestly believed that she was in love with Connor? What did that say about her? Connor had never lowered her to the level of sniffing shampoo bottles. Connor had never turned her brain to mush with one smile, never made her feel *scared*...

Yes, she *was* scared, Lizzie acknowledged as she made use of the hair-dryer and surveyed her own hot, guilty face in the mirror. She was in wholly uncharted territory and she was scared that Sebasten would just think of her as a one-night stand and would not want to see her again. Wouldn't that be just what she deserved? After all, how much respect could he have for a woman who just fell into his arms the very first night she met him? A woman, moreover, whom he had had to sober up first from the most disgusting state of inebriation. Shame and confusion enveloped Lizzie as she recalled how she had behaved *and* how he had reacted: angry and sardonic but essentially decent in that he had looked after her.

In the bedroom next door, Sebasten asked himself if he ought to be sympathetic towards her being ill and decided that support or sympathy might only encourage her to repeat the offence in the future. No, he definitely didn't want to risk that. He might be almost convinced that she was not an habitual drunk but it was his nature to be cautious with women. So they had a future? He could not remember ever thinking that with a woman before and it really spooked him.

Springing out of bed, Sebasten lifted the phone and ordered breakfast and might well have made it into the bathroom to join her in the shower had he not stood on her tiny handbag where it had been abandoned on the floor the night before.

With a muttered curse as he wondered whether he had broken anything inside it, he swept it up and the contents fell out because the zipper hadn't been closed. Reaching for the items, he thrust them back into the bag and in that rather impatient handling her driver's licence slipped out of her purse. He studied her photograph with a smile and was in the act of putting it back when he saw the name.

Liza Denton.

What the hell was Lizzie doing with another woman's driving licence in her possession? Sebasten stilled with a dark frown until he looked back at the photograph and the truth exploded on him with all the efficacy of an earthquake beneath his feet. Lizzie was usually short for Elizabeth but mightn't it also be a diminutive for Liza? In thunderous disbelief, he recalled the club manager pointing out the small blonde on the dance floor the night before. It dawned on him then that the man might well have been pointing at Lizzie instead, for the two women had been standing together.

In a rare state of shock, Sebasten stared back down

at the photo. Lizzie was Liza Denton, the vindictive, man-hungry tramp who had driven his own kid brother to self-destruction. Sebasten shuddered. Not only had Lizzie pretended to have only the most tenuous acquaintance with Connor, but she had also outright *lied* by giving him a false surname! Her awareness of the notoriety of her own name and her deliberate concealment of her true identity was, in his opinion, absolute proof of her guilt.

Lizzie Denton was a class act too, Sebasten acknowledged as he threw on clothes at speed, ferocious rage rising in direct proportion to the raw distaste now slicing through him. That he should have *slept* with the woman whom poor Connor had loved to distraction! That he himself should then have been taken in to the extent of believing her to be a virgin! Sebasten snatched in a harsh breath.

On top of that first shattering discovery the conviction that the judgement and intelligence that he prided himself on should have fallen victim to a clever act was even more galling. Of course, it had been an act calculated to impress! So calculating a woman would be well aware that, for a male as cynical and bone-deep Greek as he was, a pretence of sexual innocence had immense pulling power. For he *had* liked that idea, hadn't he? The idea that he was the *first* to make her feel like that? The first to stamp that look of shellshocked admiration on her lovely face?

And why had she done it? Well, hadn't she told him that herself? And very prettily too with tears glistening in her big green eyes. Her adoring daddy had pulled the plug on her credit line and she had to be desperate to find a rich and generous boyfriend to keep her in the style to which she was accustomed, sooner than accept the hard grind of the daily employment that others less fortunate took for granted as their lot in life. Then Lizzie Denton had not bargained on dealing with Connor's big brother, had she?

In the fiery space of a moment, Sebasten knew exactly what he was about to do and little of his usual caution was in evidence. He would play her silly games until she was wholly in his power and then when she least expected it he would dump her as publicly as she had dumped Connor. He would repay lies with lies, hurt with hurt and pain with pain. It might not be the towering revenge he had quite envisaged but then why should her entire family suffer for her sins when it was evident that her father had already repudiated his daughter in disgust? It would be a much more *personal* act of vengeance…

With a chilling smile hardening his handsome mouth, Sebasten knocked on the bathroom door, cast it open only a few inches, for he did not yet trust himself to look her in the eye without betraying the sheer rage still powering him. 'I'll see you for breakfast downstairs…'

CHAPTER FOUR

HAVING stolen one of Sebasten's shirts from a unit in the dressing room to cover her halter top, Lizzie descended the stairs in hopeful search of a dining room. She was a bag of nerves, her heart banging against her ribs.

Sebasten had not even waited for her to emerge from the bathroom and he had sounded so cold and distant when he had said that he would see her downstairs. After the night they had shared, it was not the way she had naïvely expected him to greet her and now she was wondering in stricken embarrassment if he was eager just to get her out of his house. Perhaps only some refined form of good breeding had urged him to offer breakfast at noon.

*One look and I was hooked…*wasn't that what Sebasten had told her the night before? For an instant, she hugged that recollection to her and straightened her taut shoulders. But then maybe that had only been the sort of thing the average male said when things got as far as the bedroom. When she had no other man to compare him with, how would she know? Furthermore, he *wasn't* the average male, was he? Lizzie stole an uneasy glance at the oil paintings and the magnificent antique collector's cabinet in the huge hall. Everywhere she looked, she was seeing further signs of the kind of stratospheric wealth that could be rather intimidating.

A manservant appeared from the rear of the hall and opened a door into a formal dining-room, where Sebasten was seated at the end of a long polished dining-table. Colliding unwarily with veiled dark golden eyes as he rose upright with the kind of exquisite manners that she was unused to meeting with, she felt a tide of colour warm her pale complexion, and broke straight into nervous speech. 'I pinched one of your shirts. I hope you don't mind.'

'I should have sent out for some clothes for you,' Sebasten countered, throwing her into a bewildered loop with that assurance and then the unsettling suspicion that he brought a different woman home at least three times a week. 'My apologies.'

As the unfamiliar intimate ache at the heart of her tense body reminded her of just how passionate and demanding a lover Sebasten was, Lizzie dragged her tense gaze from his in awful embarrassment and sank down fast into a seat.

Sebasten was very tempted to give her a round of applause for her performance. The blushing show of discomfiture was presumably aimed at convincing him that she had never before spent a night with a man and faced him the next morning.

'I have an apartment you can use,' he murmured evenly.

Startled by that sudden offer of accommodation, Lizzie glanced up. 'Oh...I wouldn't dream of it.'

'I can't bear to think of you being homeless,' Sebasten quipped.

'Well, I won't be after I've found somewhere of my own, which I intend to do today,' Lizzie hastened to add, grateful for the distraction of the food being presented to her by the manservant.

'It's not that easy to find decent accommodation in London,' Sebasten countered.

'I'll manage. Thousands do and so will I. In fact, I'm looking forward to proving to my father that I can look after myself,' Lizzie admitted. 'I did offer to leave home after Dad remarried but he wouldn't hear of it. He had a self-contained flat built in the stable block at the back of the house for me.'

Settling back in his antique rosewood carver chair, Sebasten cradled his black coffee in one lean brown hand and surveyed her with a frown-line dividing his level ebony brows. 'I can't understand why the indulgent father you describe should suddenly go to the other extreme and practically *throw* you out of your home.'

Visibly, Lizzie lost colour and after some hesitation said, 'Dad thinks he's spoilt me rotten—'

'Did he?'

'Yes,' Lizzie confided ruefully. 'And I have to be honest and admit that I *loved* being spoilt.'

'Any man would feel privileged to offer you the same treatment,' Sebasten drawled, smooth as glass.

Lizzie laughed out loud. 'Stop sending me up!' she urged.

Grudging appreciation flared in Sebasten's veiled gaze. She was clever, he conceded. She had not snatched at the apartment he had mentioned and was determined to demonstrate an appealing acceptance of her reduced circumstances. 'So what *are* your plans?'

Lizzie thought of the number of bills she had to settle and almost flinched. Before leaving home she had trotted up the sum total of her liabilities, and she was well aware that without her father's generous allowance only the sale of her jewellery and her car would enable her to keep her head above water on a much smaller budget. However, she had no intention of startling him with those uncomfortable realities.

'Somewhere to live is my first priority and then a job.'

It was evident that he had made use of another bathroom while she hogged his own. His black hair was still damp, his strong jawline clean shaven and she couldn't stop staring at him. Inherent strength and command were etched in his devastatingly attractive features and, regardless of the little sleep he had enjoyed, no shadows marked the clarity of his dark golden eyes. Even in his mood of cool reserve that increased her own apprehension as to how he now saw her, she was fascinated by him.

'On the career front, try the Select Recruitment agency.' Sebasten not only had a controlling interest in the business but also used it to recruit all his own personal staff. 'I've heard that they're good.'

'They would need to be,' Lizzie remarked with a wry twist of her lush mouth. 'I have no references, only basic qualifications and very little work experience to offer.'

'I'm sure you'll manage to package your classy appearance and lively personality as the ultimate in saleable commodities. It all comes down to presentation. Concentrate on what you can do and *not* what you can't,' Sebasten advised.

Grateful for his advice and the indirect compliment, Lizzie nibbled at a delicious calorie-laden croissant spread with honey and sipped at her tea. Did he want to see her again? She thought *not*. As her hand trembled, the cup she held shook and she set it back on the saucer in haste. Don't be such a baby, she urged herself furiously, willing back the stinging moisture at the backs of her eyes. Indeed she might console herself with the reflection that what had been so special for her had probably been *equally* special for him in that she could not credit that he made a regular habit of sharing cold showers with a drunk.

As the grandfather clock in the corner struck the hour, Sebasten rose to his feet again with a sigh. 'I'm afraid I have a lunch engagement I can't break at my club but my chauffeur will drive you back to wherever you're staying. Please don't feel that you have to hurry your meal.'

'It's OK...I've finished anyway.' With a fixed and valiant smile, Lizzie extracted herself from behind the table with uncool speed and walked back out to the hall ahead of him, her hand so tight on her bag that her knuckles showed white. No, she wasn't very good at this morning-after-the-night-before lark and possibly it was a lesson she had needed. Never, ever again would she drink like that, never, ever again would she let a squashed ego persuade her to jump into bed with a guy she had just met.

Possibly being awkward and gauche came naturally to her, Sebasten reflected in surprise, raising a brow at her headlong surge from his dining room. She was behaving like one of his dogs did when he uttered a verbal rebuke: as though he had taken a stick to her. He was pretty certain that Connor had not exercised similar power over her and grim amusement lit his keen gaze.

'I might as well give you a lift,' he proffered equably, determined to drag out her discomfiture for as long as he could. 'What's the address?'

Ensconced in the opulent limousine while Sebasten made a phone call and talked in Greek, Lizzie was just counting the minutes until she could escape his company. She watched him spread the long, shapely fingers of one lean, bronzed hand to stress some point that he was making and her tummy flipped at the helpless recollection of how he had made her feel in his bed: driven, possessed, wild, ecstatic. All unfamiliar emotions on her terms and mortifying and painful to acknowledge in the aftermath of an intimacy that was not to be repeated.

Having made arrangements to have her followed every place she went, Sebasten flipped open a business magazine out of sheer badness until the limo drew up outside the smart block of flats where she was staying. Only as she leapt onto the pavement like a chicken fleeing the fox did he lean forward and say, 'I'll call you...'

Lizzie blinked and her long, naturally dark lashes swept up on her surprised eyes as she nodded, staring back at him while his chauffeur hovered. 'You don't have my number,' she suddenly pointed out and before he could be put to the trouble of asking for it, she gave him the number of her mobile phone.

When Lizzie finally sped from view, slim shoulders now thrown back, marmalade hair blowing back like a banner in the breeze and long, perfect legs flashing beneath her short skirt, Sebasten was recovering from the new experience of being told that *nobody* had a photographic memory for numbers and then directed to punch hers straight into his phone so that he didn't forget it because she wouldn't be at her current address much longer.

Without a doubt, he was now recognising what might have drawn Connor in so deep, Connor, who had had strong protective instincts for the vulnerable: that jolly-schoolgirlish bluntness she practised, that complete seeming lack of a cool front, that seductive, what-you-see-is-what-you-get attitude she specialised in. And it was novel, different, but it *was* indisputably a pose de-signed to charm and mislead, Sebasten decided in con-temptuous and angry dismissal.

Did I really make him put my number straight into his phone? Lizzie asked herself in shock as she stepped into the lift. Oh, well, he already knew how keen she was and at least that way she deprived herself of the time-wasting comfort of wondering if he had just for-gotten her number when he didn't call. And he wouldn't call, she was convinced he wouldn't call, because he had been polite but essentially aloof.

At no stage had he made the smallest move to touch her in any way and yet he was a very hot-blooded guy, the sort of male who expressed intimacy with contact. Indeed, looking back to the instant of their first meet-ing the night before, she was challenged to recall a mo-ment when he had not automatically maintained some kind of actual physical contact with her. Yet in spite of that, when she joined him for breakfast he had been as remote as the Andes around her. Then why had he offered her the use of an apartment? Maybe such a proposition was no big deal to a male who might well deal in property, maybe it had even been his way of saying thanks for a sexually uninhibited night with a total tart. After all, weren't all single men supposed to secretly crave a tart in the bedroom?

As Jen answered the doorbell, Lizzie was pale as death from the effects of that last humiliating thought.

'You have a visitor,' Jen informed her in a disgruntled tone, her pretty face stiff with annoyance. 'Your stepmother has been plonked in my sitting room since twelve, waiting for you to put in an appearance.'

At that announcement and the tone of it, Lizzie stiffened in dismay. What on earth was Felicity playing at? All that needed to be said had been said and it was still a punishment for her to even look at her stepmother. And did Jen, who had invited her to stay in the first place, really have to be so sour?

'Look, I'll get changed and get rid of her and then I'll be out of here just as fast as I can get my cases back into my car,' Lizzie promised, hurrying down to the bedroom, refusing to subject herself to the further embarrassment of greeting Felicity in an outfit that spelt out the demeaning truth that she had not slept anywhere near her own wardrobe the night before.

Clad in tailored cream cotton chinos and a pink cashmere cardigan, Lizzie walked into Jen's sitting room ten minutes later. Felicity spun round from the window, a tiny brunette, barely five feet one inch tall with a gorgeous figure and a tiny waist that Lizzie noted in surprise was still not showing the slightest hint that she had to be almost four months pregnant. Her classic, beautiful face was dominated by enormous violet-blue eyes. Predictably, those eyes were already welling with tears and Lizzie's teeth gritted.

'When your father told me what he had done, I was devastated for you!' Felicity gushed with a shake in her breathless little-girl voice. 'I felt *so* guilty that I had to come straight over here and—'

'Check out that I would continue to keep quiet about you and my former boyfriend?' Lizzie slotted in with distaste, for the brunette's shallow insincerity grated on her. 'I gave you my word that I wouldn't talk but it's not something I want to keep on discussing with you.'

'But how on earth will you cope without your allowance?' Felicity demanded. 'I've been thinking...*I* could help you out. Maurice is very generous and I'm sure he wouldn't notice.'

Hush money, Lizzie found herself thinking in total revulsion. 'I'll manage.'

Felicity gave her a veiled assessing look that was a poor match for her tremulous mouth and glistening eyes. 'You've never been out there on your own and you don't know how hard it can be. If only I didn't have our baby's future to think of, I *swear* I would have told your father the truth.'

The truth? And which version would that be? Lizzie thought back to the conflicting stories that Felicity and Connor had both hurled at her in the aftermath of her inopportune visit to the cottage which had become their secret love-nest. Her stepmother's priorities had been brutally obvious. Felicity had had no intention of surrendering her comfortable lifestyle and adoring older husband to set up home with an impecunious lover. As he had listened to the brunette lie in her teeth about their affair and accuse him of trying to wreck her *happy* marriage, Connor's jaw had dropped, his disbelief palpable. When her stepmother had followed up that with the announcement that she was pregnant, Lizzie's shock had been equal to Connor's devastated response.

Dredging herself back from her disturbing recollections of that day, Lizzie was so uncomfortable that she could no longer stand to look at the other woman. 'Dad will come round in his own good time. And with Connor gone, you have nothing to worry about.'

'That's a wicked thing to say...' Felicity condemned tearfully.

But deserved, Lizzie reflected. It would be a very long time before she forgot the flash of relief that she had seen in the brunette's face when she had first learnt that Connor had died in a car crash. But then what was the point of striving to awaken a conscience that Felicity did not have? The brunette had few deep emotions that did not relate to herself.

As soon as Felicity had gone, Lizzie got stuck into repacking her luggage. Jen appeared in the bedroom doorway and remarked. 'If it's any consolation, we were all eaten alive with raging envy when you landed Sebasten Contaxis last night...'

Encountering the sizzling curiosity in the pert blonde's gaze, Lizzie coloured and concentrated on gathering up the cosmetics she had left out on the dressing-table.

'Mind you,' Jen continued, 'I hear he's a real bastard with women...lifts them, *lays* them, then forgets about them. But then who could blame him? He's a young, drop-dead gorgeous billionaire. Women are just arm candy to a guy like that and of course he's happy to overdose on the treats.'

Even as a chill of dismay ran over Lizzie that Sebasten's reputation should be that bad with her sex, she angled up her chin. 'So?'

'When you get dumped, everyone will crow because you weren't entitled to get him in the first place. He dates supermodels...and let's face it, you're hardly in that category. It's my bet that, once he gets wind of all the nasty rumours there have been about you and Connor, you'll never hear from him again!'

'Thank you for the warning.' In one move, Lizzie carted two cases out to the hall in her eagerness to vacate the blonde's apartment. 'But I wasn't actually planning on *dating* Sebasten. I was just using him for a one-night stand.'

Twenty minutes later, Lizzie climbed into her Mercedes four-wheel-drive and the startled look on Jen's spiteful face travelled with her. It had been a cheap, tasteless response but it had made Lizzie feel just a little better. So where did she go now that she was truly homeless and friendless? Well, she had better try to sell her little horde of jewellery first to get some cash so that she could pay upfront for accommodation.

ONE WEEK LATER, LIZZIE dealt her new home a somewhat shaken appraisal. Six nights in an overpriced bed and breakfast joint and then *this*...

Her bedsit was a dump and, as far as she could see, a dump with no secret pretensions to be transformed into a miraculous palace. But then neither her car nor her jewellery had sold for anything like the amount that she had naïvely hoped, and until she had actually trudged round the rental agencies and checked the newspapers she had had no idea just how much it actually cost to rent an apartment. Any solo apartment, even the *tiniest* was way beyond her budget and, since she had been reluctant to share with total strangers, a bedsit had been her only immediate option.

But on the bright side, she had an interview the next day. When she got a job she would make new friends and then possibly find somewhere more inspiring to live, and in the meantime life was what you made of it, Lizzie told herself sternly. She would buy herself a bucket of cheap paint and obliterate the dingy drabness of the walls rather than sit around drowning in self-pity!

Sebasten had *not* called. Well, had she really expected him to? An aching wave of regret flooded Lizzie. It was so hard for her to forget the sense of connection that she had felt with him, that crazy feeling that something magical was in the air. Indeed she had slept with her mobile phone right beside her every night. However, the something magical had only been her own stupid fantasy, she conceded, angry that she still hadn't managed to get him out of her mind. After all, if what Jen had said about Sebasten's reputation was true, she had had a narrow escape from getting her heart broken and stomped on. In any case, how could she possibly have explained why she had lied and given him a false surname?

READING HIS SECURITY CHIEF'S efficient daily bulletins on Lizzie's fast-disintegrating life of ease and afflu-

ence had supplied the major part of Sebasten's entertainment throughout the past week.

Lizzie had been conned into flogging her six-month-
old-low mileage Mercedes for half of its worth and then
ripped off in much the same way when it came to parting with her diamonds. Having run a credit check on
her, Sebasten had appreciated the necessity for such immediate financial retrenchments and could only admire
her cunning refusal to snatch at his offer of an apartment. Evidently, Lizzie was set on impressing on him
the belief that she was not a gold-digger or a free-loader.
Now in possession of both her Merc and her jewellery
and having paid very much more for both than she had
received for either, Sebasten was ready to make his next
move.

When her mobile phone sang out its musical call,
Lizzie was standing on top of three suitcases, striving to
get the paint roller to do what it was supposed to do as
easily as it did in the diagram on the back of the pack. It
had been so long since her phone rang that it took her a
second or two to recognise the sound for what it was. With
a strangled yelp, she made a sudden leap off the precari-
ous mound of cases, the roller spattering daffodil-yellow
paint in all directions as she snatched up her phone with
all the desperation of a drowning woman.

'Sebasten…' Sebasten murmured.

Lizzie pulled a face, suddenly wishing she knew at
least three Sebastens and could ask which he was. At
the same time, she rolled her eyes heavenward, closed
them and uttered a silent heartfelt prayer of thanks. He
had called…he had called…he had *called*!

'Hi…' she answered, low-key, watching paint drip

down from the ceiling, knowing that she had overloaded the roller and now wrecked her only set of sheets into the bargain and not caring, truly not caring. Her brain was in a blissful fog. She couldn't think straight.

'You'd better start by giving me your address,' Sebasten told her before he could forget that he wasn't supposed to know it already.

Lizzie rattled it off at speed.

'Dinner tonight?' Sebasten enquired.

Her brain peeped out from behind the romantic fog and winced at that last-minute invitation. Breathing in deep and slow, she dragged her pride out of the hiding place where it was eager to stay. 'Sorry I can't make it tonight.'

'Try...' Sebasten suggested, a wave of instant irritation gripping him. 'I'll be abroad next week.'

Lizzie paled at that additional information and then surveyed the devastation of the room which she had only begun to paint. 'I really *can't*. I'm in the middle of trying to decorate my bedsit—'

'I've had some novel excuses in my time but—'

'If I leave it now, I'll never finish it...are you any good at decorating?' Lizzie asked off the top of her head, so keen was she to break into that far from reassuring response of his.

'Never wielded a paintbrush in my life and no ambition to either,' Sebasten drawled in a derisive tone of incredulity, thinking that she was taking the I'm-so-poor façade way too far for good taste. Decorating? *Him?* She just had to be joking!

Wishing she had kept her mouth shut, Lizzie felt her cheeks burning. Of course, a male of his meteoric wealth wasn't about to rush over and help out. But it was hardly her fault that she wasn't available at such very short notice, and for all she knew he had only called because some other woman was otherwise engaged. 'Oh, well, looks like I'm on my own. To be frank, it's not a lot of fun. I'd better go…I've got paint dripping everywhere but where it should be. Maybe see you around… thanks for calling. Bye!'

Before she could weaken and betray her anguished regret, she finished the call. Maybe see you around? Lizzie flinched. Some chance! Her fashionable nights out on the town in the top clubs and restaurants were at an end.

In outraged disbelief, Sebasten registered that she had cut him off. Who the bloody hell did Lizzie Denton think she was? When the shock of that unfamiliar treatment had receded, a hard smile began to curve his wide, sensual mouth. She was trying to play hard to get to wind him up and increase his interest. He phoned his secretary and told her to find him a decorator willing to work that night.

By six that evening, Lizzie was whacked and on the brink of tears of frustration. Practically everything she possessed including herself was covered with paint and the first layer on the ceiling and two of the walls had dried all streaky and horrible. When a knock sounded on the door, she thrust paint-spattered fingers through her tumbled hair and tugged open the door.

Sebasten stood there like a glorious vision lifted straight from some glossy society-magazine page. His casual dark blue designer suit screamed class and expense and accentuated his height and well-built, muscular frame. A flock of butterflies broke loose in her tummy and her heartbeat hit the Richter scale while she hovered, staring at him in surprise.

'What are you wearing?' Sebasten enquired, brilliant golden eyes raking over what looked very like a leotard but his true concentration absorbed by the lithe perfection of the female body delineated by the thin, tight fabric. Instantaneous lust ripped through him and smouldering fury at his lack of control over his own libido followed in its wake.

'Exercise gear...I didn't have anything else suitable.' She was unsurprised that he was staring: she knew she had to look a total fright with no make-up on. 'I'd have been better doing it naked!' she quipped tautly, her mind a total blank while she tried to work out what he was doing on her doorstep.

Naked; now there was an idea... Sebasten stopped that forbidden thought dead in its tracks but lust had a more tenacious hold still on his taut length.

'I've brought a decorating crew...and we're going out to dinner,' he informed her, scanning the chaos of the room and the horrendous state of the walls with elevated brows of wonderment, certain that should he have taken the notion he could have done a far more efficient job. 'Grab some clothes. We'll stop off at my place and you can get changed there, leaving the crew to get stuck in.'

'You've brought...*decorators*?' Lizzie was still staring at him with very wide green eyes, striving to absorb his announcement that he had drummed up decorators to finish her room for her. She was stunned but even more stunned by the manner in which he just *dropped* that astonishing announcement on her. As if it was the most natural thing in the world that he should hire decorators so that she could be free to join him for dinner. This, she registered, was a male who never took no for an answer, who put his own wishes first, who was willing to move proverbial mountains if it got him what he wanted.

'Why not?' Sebasten turned his devastating smile on her and, in spite of her discomfiture at what he had done and what it revealed about his character, her heart sat up and begged and sang at that smile. 'You did say painting wasn't a lot of fun.'

'And I'm not exactly brilliant at it,' Lizzie muttered, head in a whirl while she reminded herself that it was also a compliment that he should go to such extravagant lengths just to spend time with her. He might not be willing to wield a paintbrush for her benefit but he was certainly no sleeper in the practicality stakes.

'So?'

Aware of his impatience and even while telling herself that she ought not to let herself react to that or be influenced by his macho methods into giving instant agreement, Lizzie found herself digging into the wardrobe and drawing out a raincoat to pull on over her leotard. 'I'm a complete mess,' she pointed out anxiously, grabbing up a bag and banging back into the wardrobe and several drawers to remove garments.

'You'll clean up to perfection,' Sebasten asserted, planting a lean hand to her spine to hustle her out of the room.

'Are you always this ruthless about getting your own way?' Lizzie asked breathlessly after she had passed her keys over to the businesslike-looking decorators waiting by their van on the street below and had warned them that she had bought rubbish paint.

'Always,' Sebasten confirmed without hesitation, lean, powerful face serious. 'I work hard. I play hard. And I didn't want to wait another week before I saw you again, *pethi mou*.'

Clutching her raincoat round her, Lizzie tried to keep her feet mentally on the ground but her imagination was already soaring to dizzy heights. Presumably he had been really, really busy all week but couldn't he at least have called to chat even if he hadn't had the time to see her sooner? Squashing that unwelcome reflection, she discovered that she couldn't wait to tell him about the highlight of her week.

'I've got an interview for a job tomorrow afternoon,' she told him with considerable pride.

'Where?'

'CI...it's a big City Company,' Lizzie advanced with a grin.

Sebasten veiled his amused gaze with dense black lashes. Select Recruitment had come up trumps on his request and even faster than they had promised, for the agency had not yet come back to him to confirm that she had paid them a visit. CI was *his* company and the fact that she hadn't even registered yet that CI stood for Contaxis International did not say a lot about the amount of homework she had done in advance of the interview. Or was she just pretending and did she know darned well that it was his company?

'Of course, it's only a temporary position where I fill in for other people on holiday and stuff but I gather that if I do OK it *could* become permanent,' Lizzie continued.

'You sound as if you're just gasping to work,' Sebasten mocked, knowing that there was no possibility on earth that the position would become permanent as it had been dreamt up at his bidding and styled to deliver the maximum pain for the minimum gain. He couldn't wait to see her application form and discover how many lies she had put in print.

'Of course I am…I'm skint!' Lizzie exclaimed before she could think better of it.

As she encountered Sebasten's enquiring frown, a wave of colour ran up from her throat to mantle her cheekbones. 'Well, don't tell me you're surprised,' she said ruefully. 'I'm not living in a lousy bedsit so far out of the city centre so I'll need to rise at dawn to get into work just for the good of my health!'

'I can't understand why you didn't accept the apartment I mentioned…but then the offer remains open,' Sebasten delivered.

'Thanks…but I've got to learn to look after myself. I was so annoyed when I screwed up the painting project,' Lizzie confided truthfully. 'I didn't appreciate that it wasn't as easy as it looked and I *hate* giving up on anything! I should have stayed and watched those guys work and learned how to do it for myself.'

'Let's not go overboard.' Sebasten reckoned that the number of fresh challenges awaiting her at CI would prove quite sufficient to occupy her in the coming weeks.

An hour and a half later, Lizzie scanned her appearance in the mirror in the opulent guest room she had been shown into in Sebasten's beautiful town house. She had enjoyed freshening up in a power shower, for it was slowly sinking in on her that a thousand things that she had once taken for granted were luxuries she might never get to experience again. Her dress was leaf-green with a cut-away back and a favourite, but in the rush to leave her bedsit she had forgotten all her cosmetics.

As she descended the stairs she thought about how much she had appreciated not being shown into *his* bedroom as if how the evening might end was already accepted fact. It wasn't. She had her interview tomorrow and she wanted to be wide awake for it and, furthermore, she suspected that it might be unwise to fall into Sebasten's arms too soon, at least not before she had got to know him better.

When Sebasten watched her descend his magnificent staircase, he stilled.

Feeling self-conscious, Lizzie pulled a comic face. 'Want to change your mind about being seen out with me? I forgot my make-up.'

'You have fabulous skin and I like the natural look.'

'All men say that because they think anything artificial is somehow a deception being practised on them but very few of them are actually *wowed* by the natural look if they get it!' Lizzie laughed.

Their arrival at the latest fashionable eaterie caused a perceptible stir of turning heads and inquisitive eyes. Afraid of seeing any familiar faces and meeting with an antagonistic look which would take all the gloss off her evening, Lizzie looked neither to her right nor her left and stared into stricken space on the couple of occasions that Sebasten broke his stride to acknowledge someone, for she was terrified that he might try to introduce her using the false name she had given him. Mercifully he did not but she saw that there was no escaping the unpleasant fact that she would *have* to admit to lying and give him an acceptable explanation for her behaviour.

As soon as the first course was ordered, Lizzie breathed in deep and dived straight in before she could lose her nerve. 'I have a confession to make,' she asserted, biting at her lower lip, green eyes discomfited. 'And I don't think you're going to like me very much after I've told you. My surname isn't Bewford, it's—'

'Denton,' Sebasten filled in, congratulating her mentally on her timing, for few men would contemplate causing a scene or staging a confrontation in a restaurant where, whether she had noticed it or not, they were the cynosure of all eyes. Yes, he had definitely found a foe worthy of his mettle.

Taken aback, Lizzie stared at him. 'You already *know* who I really am?'

Never one to tell an untruth without good reason, Sebasten explained that he had seen her driving licence that morning a week ago.

Lizzie paled. 'Oh, my goodness, what must you have thought of me?' she gasped in shamed embarrassment, recalling his failure to await her emergence from his bathroom and his subsequent coolness on parting from her and now seeing both events in a much more presentable light. 'I'm really sorry...and I'm just *amazed* that you wanted to see me again after I'd told a stupid lie like that!'

'As to what I thought...I assumed you would explain

when the time was right and that you must have a very good reason for giving me a false name. As to not seeing you again…' Brilliant dark golden eyes rested with keen appreciation on her lovely, flushed face, absorbing the anxiety stamped into every line of it with satisfaction. 'I'm not sure that was ever an option. We shared an incredible night of passion and I want to be with you.'

Relief and shy pleasure mingled in Lizzie's strained appraisal and she decided that she owed him the fullest possible explanation in return for his forebearance. 'I was—er—sort of *involved*,' she stressed with reluctance, 'with Connor Morgan up until a few days before he died. I don't know whether you're aware of the rumours—'

Sort of involved? Sebasten wanted to laugh out loud in derision at that grotesque understatement. The troubled plea for understanding in her beautiful eyes was an even more effective ploy. Lounging back in his seat as the head waiter appeared to refresh their wine glasses, Sebasten endeavoured to ape the role of a sympathetic audience. 'I had heard the suicide story but I also understand that he never made any such threat and that he left no note either.'

Relieved to hear him acknowledge those facts, Lizzie clutched her wine glass like a life belt and then put it down again, her hands too restless to stay still. 'If I tell you the whole truth, will you promise me that you won't repeat it to anybody?'

His contempt climbing at that evident request not to carry the lies she was about to tell to any other source, who might fast disprove her story, Sebasten nodded in confirmation but then murmured. 'Connor called you Liz, not Lizzie…didn't he?'

'That was typical Connor,' Lizzie sighed. 'He had an ex called Lizzie and he always insisted on calling me Liza.'

'So tell me about him…' Sebasten encouraged.

'I first met Connor just over three months ago. I liked him; well, we all did. He was the life and soul of every event.' Lizzie frowned as she strove to pick her words, for inexperienced she might be, but she knew that discussing her previous relationship with the new man in her life might not be the wisest idea. 'I suppose I developed quite a crush on him but I never expected anything to come of it. When he grabbed me one night at a party and kissed me and then asked me out, I was surprised because I didn't think I was his type…and as it turned out, I *wasn't*.'

'Meaning?'

'That four days before he died, I discovered that Connor had been using me as cover for his steamy affair with a married woman.' Lizzie winced as Sebasten's intent appraisal narrowed in disbelief. 'I know it doesn't sound very credible because Connor always seemed to be such an upfront guy but it's the truth. I found them together and nobody could have been more shocked than I was.'

'Who was she?' Sebasten enquired, impressed by her creativeness in a tight spot, for her tale was a positive masterpiece of ingenuity. In one fell swoop, she sought to turn herself from a heartless little shrew into a cruelly deceived victim and Connor into a cheat and a liar.

His anger on his late half-brother's behalf smouldered beneath the deceptive calm of his appraisal.

'I can't tell you that. It wouldn't be fair because I gave my word to the woman involved that I wouldn't. She was very distressed and she regretted the whole thing and she broke off with him. All I can tell you is that he believed he was crazy about her but I think that for *her* it was just a little fling because she was bored with her marriage.'

'I'm curious. Tell me her name,' Sebasten prompted afresh, ready to put her through hoops for daring to tell him such nonsensical lies.

Her persistence made her squirm with obvious discomfiture. 'I'm sorry, I can't. Anyway, now it's all over and behind me, I can see that Connor really just treated me like a casual girlfriend he saw a couple of times a week…we didn't sleep together or anything like that,' she muttered, her voice dwindling in volume, but she had wanted to let him know that last fact. 'But it was still a very hurtful experience for me and I didn't like him very much for making such an ass of me.'

'How could you?' Sebasten encouraged, smoother than silk.

'It wasn't until I drove down to Brighton to try and pay my respects to his mother that I realised that *I* was getting the blame for his death. People just assumed that he'd got drunk and crashed his car because I had ditched him,' Lizzie shared heavily.

Ingrid had not admitted that Lizzie had made a personal visit to her home, Sebasten recalled, hating the way women always told you what they wanted you to hear rather than simply dispensing all the facts. 'What happened?'

'Mrs Morgan said some awful things to me…I can forgive that,' Lizzie stated but she still paled at the recollection of Ingrid Morgan's vicious verbal attack on her. 'I mean, she was just beside herself with grief and naturally Connor hadn't admitted to his own mother that he was carrying on with someone else's wife. She said that if I tried to go to the funeral she'd have me thrown out of the church!'

'So you've been getting the blame for events that had nothing to do with you. That's *appalling*,' Sebasten commented with harsh emphasis.

'It's also why all my friends have dropped me and my father showed me the front door,' Lizzie confided, grateful for the anger she recognised in both the taut set of his hard bone-structure and the rough edge to his dark, deep drawl, for she believed it was on her behalf.

'Surely you could have confided in your own father?'

Lizzie tensed, averted her gaze and thought fast. 'No—er—he knows the woman concerned and I don't think I could rely on him to keep it quiet.'

'I'm astonished *and* impressed by your generosity towards a woman who doesn't deserve your protection at the cost of your own good name,' Sebasten drawled softly.

'Wrecking her marriage wouldn't bring Connor back and I'm sure she's learned her lesson.' Lizzie studied her main course without appetite, certain that she had just put paid to any sparkle in the evening with her long-winded and awkward explanation.

Sebasten reached across the table and covered her

clenched fingers where they rested with his own. 'Relax…I understand why you lied to me. You were seriously *scared* that after one extraordinary night with you I might make a real nuisance of myself.'

After a bemused pause at that teasing and laughable assertion, Lizzie glanced up, amusement having driven the apprehension from her green eyes, and she grinned in helpless appreciation, for with one mocking comment he had dissolved her tension and concluded the subject. He was clever, subtle, always focused. Meeting his dark golden gorgeous eyes, she felt dizzy even though she was sitting down.

They had a slight dispute outside the restaurant when Sebasten assumed she was coming home with him.

'Where else are you going to go?' he demanded with stark impatience. 'The decorators aren't finished yet!'

'How do you know that? By mental telepathy?'

'I only needed to take one look at the havoc you wreaked with a paintbrush. They'll be lucky to finish by dawn!' Sebasten forecast.

'Call them and check.' Lizzie smothered a large yawn with a hurried hand, for she was becoming very sleepy.

'I can't…don't know how to reach them. Even if they had finished you couldn't sleep in a room full of paint fumes,' Sebasten spelt out, getting angrier by the second because the very last thing he had expected from her was an exaggerated pretence of *not* wanting to share his bed again, most particularly when *he* was determined not to repeat that intimacy. 'The bed I'm offering you for the night doesn't include me!'

'Oh…' Lizzie computed that surprising turn of events and gave him full marks for not acting on the supposition that her body was now his for the asking. 'That's fine, then. Thank you...thank you very much.'

Never had Sebasten snubbed a woman with so little satisfying effect. With an apologetic smile, Lizzie climbed into his limo, made not the smallest feline attempt to dissuade him from the rigours of a celibate night and then compounded her sins by falling asleep on him. He shook her awake outside his town house.

'Gosh, have I been asleep? How very boring for you,' she mumbled, stumbling out of the car and up the steps, heading for the stairs with blind determination but pausing to remove her shoes, which were pinching her toes. 'I'm almost asleep standing up. I shouldn't even have had *one* glass of wine over dinner.'

But for all her apparent sleepiness, Lizzie was thinking hard. She might have been pleased that he had no expectations of her, but when it dawned on her that she was heading for his guest room and that he had still not even attempted to kiss her she was no longer quite so content. Telling him about Connor, it seemed, had been a horrible mistake. It had turned him right off her.

On the landing her stockinged feet went skidding out from under her on the polished floor and she fell with a wallop and hit her knee a painful bash. 'What is it about your wretched house?' she demanded, the pain hitting her at a vulnerable moment and bringing a flood of tears to her eyes. 'It's like...booby-trapped for my benefit!'

In instinctive concern, Sebasten crouched down beside her. Tears were running down her face in rivulets and he assumed she had really hurt herself. 'I'd better get an ambulance—'

'Don't be stupid…I only bumped it…I'm just being a baby!' Lizzie wailed in mortification. 'I'm tired and it's been a tough week, that's all.'

And when she cried, she really cried, Sebasten noted. There were no delicate, ladylike sniffs, no limpid, brimming looks calculated to induce male guilt. She just put her head down and sobbed like a child. She was miserable. He *should* be happy about that. Lean, powerful face taut, he snatched her up off the floor and into his arms. Reasoning that sticking her in a guest room alone with her distress would not only seem odd but also suspicious behaviour for a male supposed to be interested in her, he carried her into his room, where he deposited her on the bed and backed off.

With a tremendous effort of will, Lizzie gulped into silence and squeezed open her swollen eyes. It was true that she was very tired but it was her over-taxed emotions which had brought on the crying jag. In the frame she was in, she didn't think that she was capable of having a relationship with anybody. She missed her home, she missed her father.

'I'm sorry you met me last week,' Lizzie confided abruptly. 'You're never going to believe that I'm not normally like this.'

From the shadows outside the pool of light shed by the bedside lamps, Sebasten strolled forward. 'Have a bath. Get some sleep. You're exhausted.'

'Not very sexy… Exhaustion, I mean,' she muttered, plucking at the sheet with a nervous hand, peering out from under her extravagant torrent of hair, which shone with copper and gold lights.

'I'll be up later…I've got a couple of calls to make.'

'Kiss me goodnight,' Lizzie whispered on a breathless impulse before he reached the door.

Sebasten stopped dead and swung round, emanating tension. 'Surely, feeling so tired, you're not up for anything tonight?'

'So if there's no—er, sex, you don't kiss either,' Lizzie gathered and nodded, although she was cut to the bone at his rejection.

'Don't be ridiculous!'

'You don't fancy me any more?' Lizzie was determined to get an answer.

Sebasten strode across the room, closed firm hands over her arms and hauled her up onto her knees on the mattress. She could have drowned in the pagan glitter of his splintering golden eyes. He brought his mouth plunging down on hers and it was like being pitched into a stormy sea without warning. Excitement shivered and pulsed through her in answer, heat and craving uniting at the thrumming heart of her body until she went limp in his hold, all woman, all invitation.

'I hope that answers that question,' Sebasten breathed thickly, dark colour accentuating his fabulous cheekbones as he let her sink back from him in sensual disarray.

Lizzie had a soak in his sunken bath, let the water go cold while she waited for him to join her. Then, ashamed of her own wanton longing, she took advantage of another one of his couple of hundred shirts and climbed into bed. That fiery, demanding kiss had soothed her though and she drifted off to sleep with a dreamy smile on her face…

CHAPTER FIVE

L IZZIE opened her eyes just when morning light was spilling through the bedroom and found Sebasten wide awake and staring down at her.

She didn't feel shy or awkward; she just felt happy that he was there. Indeed, so right and natural did it feel that she might have been waking up beside him for absolute years. But then had she been, she might have been just a little more cool at the effect of that all lean, bronzed, hair-roughened masculinity of his poised within inches of her. With a languorous stretch, she gazed up into the dark golden eyes subjecting her to an intense scrutiny and her heart fluttered like a frantic trapped bird inside her.

'Good morning,' she whispered with her irrepressible smile. 'You shouldn't stare. It wakes people up.'

Three brandies and a cold shower had failed to cool Sebasten's ravenous arousal and he had never been into celibacy. It was just sex, he reasoned, thought and integrity had nothing to do with it and denying himself was a pointless sacrifice when he had already enjoyed her.

He threaded caressing fingers through a shining strand of her amber hair and then knotted it round his fist to hold her fast, his stunning eyes semi-screened by his lush black lashes to feverish gold. 'Lust is keeping *me* awake, *pethi mou*.'

'Oh...' Breathing had already become a challenge for Lizzie.

'*And* you've been nicking my shirts again...there's a price to pay.' Long brown fingers flicked loose the topmost button and she quivered, melting like honey on a hot plate and mesmerised by his dark male beauty.

'Will I want to pay it?'

'I *know* you will,' Sebasten husked, releasing another button with tantalising slowness, watching her spine arch and push her pert little breasts up tight against the silk, delineating the straining pink buds already eager for his attention.

'How do you know?' Lizzie prompted unevenly, mortified by his absolute certainty of his welcome.

'Your exquisite body is screaming the message at me...' Sebasten parted the edges of the shirt with the care of a connoisseur and bent his arrogant dark head to graze his teeth over a pale pink swollen nipple.

Her entire body jackknifed up towards his, a low, moaning cry breaking from her lips.

With a groan, Sebasten lifted his head again. 'Different rules this time. You lie still...if you move or cry out, I stop.'

'S-sorry?' she stammered.

'You get too excited too fast.'

'That's wrong?' Lizzie had turned scarlet.

A shimmering smile flashed across Sebasten's lean, bronzed features. 'I want an excuse to torture you with sensual pleasure...*give* me it.'

A quiver of wild, wanton anticipation sizzled through

Lizzie. 'I'll just lie back and—er—think of painting then—'

'It's going to be a lot more exciting than watching paint dry,' Sebasten promised with a husky laugh of amusement, scanning her expressive face.

And she found out that it *was* within minutes. The tension of struggling to stay still and silent no matter what he did electrified her with heat and desperate craving. He shaped her tender breasts, toyed with the throbbing peaks until every muscle in her shivering length was whip-taut and then switched his attentions to other places that she had never dreamt had even the tiniest erotic capability. But she soon found out otherwise. Sebasten ran his mouth down her spine and she was reduced to a jelly. He sucked her fingers and she was ready to flare up in flames, wild, helpless, terrified he might stop as he had threatened, turn off that wholly seductive, enslaving flow of endless exciting pleasure.

'You're doing really good,' Sebasten groaned and it was an effort to find the words in English as a telling shudder racked his big, powerful frame. The challenge he had set her from the pinnacle of his own bedroom supremacy was gnawing with increasing savagery and ego-zapping speed at his own self-control.

Lizzie gave him a smile old as Eve, leant up and ran the tip of her tongue in provocation and encouragement along his sensual lower lip and he growled and pushed her back against the pillows and drove his mouth down on hers with raw, hungry demand. Literal fireworks went off inside her. She was with him every step of the way, ecstatic at the change of pace that matched her own fevered longing and impatience.

'I want you…*now*!' Sebasten ground out hoarsely, hauling her under him with an incredible lack of cool when she had not the smallest intention of arguing.

And then he was there where she had *so* needed him to be, coursing into her and burying himself deep. Her climax was instant, shattering. Shorn of all control, she was thrown to a fierce peak and then she splintered into a million shellshocked pieces in an experience so intense she was left in a daze.

'You're a lost cause,' Sebasten bit out with a sudden laugh and then he kissed her, slow and tender, and her heart gave a wild spin as though it were a globe on a hanger.

'Sorry,' she muttered but that was the exact moment that she realised that she was in love, head over heels, fathoms-deep in love as she had never been before.

'Don't be…you're incredible in bed,' Sebasten assured her, reminding himself that tomorrow was another day to reinstate restraint before he took her to heaven and back again.

EXACTLY A FORTNIGHT LATER, Lizzie experienced her first day at work.

Her concentration was not all that might have been: Sebasten was due back that afternoon from his *second* trip abroad since she had met him. In the intervening weeks, he had only managed to see her twice, once meeting her for dinner when he was actually *en route* to the airport, and on the second occasion taking her to the races to help him entertain a group of foreign businessmen in his private box. As neither event had entailed anything in the way of privacy, Lizzie was counting the hours until she could see him again and could indeed think of nothing else *but* Sebasten.

True love, she recognised ruefully, had taken a long time to hit her. What she had felt for Connor had just been a practice run for the main event. Connor had damaged her pride, her self-confidence and her blind faith in others more than her heart. With Sebasten, she had discovered an entire new layer of more tender feelings. She worried about the incredible hours he seemed to work. She cherished every tiny thing she found out about him but Sebasten could be stingier than Scrooge when it came to talking about himself. His different moods fascinated her, for the cool front he wore concealed a volatile temperament controlled by rigid self-discipline. He was full of contradictions and complexities and every minute she spent with him, even on the phone, plunged her deeper into her obsession with him.

Even so, the poor start she contrived to make at CI on her first day annoyed and frustrated her.

'A couple of little points,' Milly Sharpe, the office manager on the sixth floor, a whip-thin redhead in a navy business suit, advanced with compressed lips. 'Getting off at the wrong tube station is not an acceptable excuse for being late. Please ensure that you arrive at the correct time tomorrow. Did you receive a copy of the CI dress code?'

Lizzie almost winced. 'Yes.'

'The code favours the darker colours, suits—longer skirts or trousers—and sensible shoes. The key word is *formal*, not casual.'

There was a pause while a speaking appraisal was angled over Lizzie's fashionable green skirt worn with a matching fitted top that sported *faux* fur at cuff and neckline and the very high sandals on her slender feet. Lizzie reddened and wondered if the woman honestly believed that she had the wherewithal to rush out and buy a complete new wardrobe. She had never bought dark colours, had never owned sensible shoes that were not of the walking-boot variety and her trouser collection consisted of jeans, chinos and pure silk beach wear.

'I would suggest that you also do something with your hair. It's a little too long to be left *safely* loose when you're working with office equipment.'

It was worse than being back at school, Lizzie thought in horror, waiting to be told to take off her earrings and removed her nail polish as well.

By the time Lizzie was shown to the switchboard and taken through a bewildering number of operations while various messages flashed up lightning-fast on the screen in front of her, sheer nervous tension had killed her ability to concentrate on the directions she was being given or remember them.

The hours that followed were a nightmare for her. She learnt that if she pressed the wrong button, she created havoc. She put calls through to lines that were engaged, cut people off in the middle of conversations, connected calls to the wrong extensions, lost others in an endless loop which saw them routed round the building and back to her again. The amount of abuse she got was a colossal shock to her system. Furious callers raged down the line at her and several staff appeared in person to remonstrate with her.

'A switchboard operator must remain calm,' Milly Sharpe reproved when Lizzie was as wrung out as a rag, jumping and flinching at the mere sight of an incoming call and ducking behind the screen if anybody walked past in case they were about to direct a volley of complaints at her.

She was weak with relief when she was switched to photocopying duties after lunch. Although the machine's sensors gave her a real fright by buzzing into sudden life the instant she approached, she felt better able to cope. In addition, something more than mere nerves was afflicting her: the longer she stood, the more light-headed she felt and her queasy tummy had put her off eating any lunch. She prayed that she was not developing summer flu.

Having access to a computer that was linked to the colour photocopier, while she waited for the copier to finish printing she succumbed to the temptation of doing an online search for information on Sebasten. But the very site she found brought up a to-die-for portrait photo of Sebasten and she never got any further. Her heartrate quickening at first glimpse of that lean, strong face, she drank in his image with intense appreciation. The stress of her difficult day seemed to evaporate as she hit the print button to get a copy of that photo to take home.

When *more* than one photo began to pile up in the copier, she did not initially panic. In fact she just thought she would have a photo for every handbag, would indeed not need to go an hour without a frequent fix of studying Sebasten. However, as the pile began to mount beyond the number of bags that even *she* possessed she tried to cancel the print run. But nothing she did would persuade the wretched machine to cease the operation. As luck would have it, Milly Sharpe arrived at that point.

Scooping up the first picture of Sebasten, she held it up like an exhibit at a murder trial, icy condemnation in her challenging gaze. 'Where did you get this from?'

'I only meant to print one—'

'You mean…there's *more* than one?' the redhead demanded and swooped on the fat pile in disbelief, checking the print run with brows that vanished below her fringe. 'You have printed four *hundred* copies of this photo?'

Lizzie reddened to her hairline, feeling like a kid caught languishing over a secret pin-up. 'I'm really very sorry—'

'Have you any idea how much this special photographic paper costs per *single* sheet?'

Lizzie was shattered to be informed that she had wasted a couple of hundred pounds of very expensive stationery.

'*And* on company time!' The other woman's voice shook with outrage. 'I would also add that I consider it the height of impertinence to print photos of Mr Contaxis. I think it would be best if you spent the rest of the afternoon tidying up the stationery store room across the corridor.'

Just when Lizzie was wondering why it should be 'impertinent' to print images of Sebasten, a wave of such overpowering nausea assailed her that she was forced to bolt for the cloakroom. After a nasty bout of sickness she felt so dizzy that she had to hang on to the vanity counter before she felt steady enough on her feet to freshen up. While she was doing that, a slight, youthful blonde came in.

'I'm Rosemary. I'm to check up on you and show you to the sick room,' she explained with a friendlier smile than Lizzie had so far received from any of the female staff.

'I'm fine now,' Lizzie asserted in haste, thinking that if she ended up in the sick room on top of such a disastrous work performance, her first day would definitely be her *last* day of employment in the building.

'You're still very pale. Don't let Milly Sharpe get to you,' the chatty blonde advised. 'If you ask me, she's just got a chip on her shoulder about how you got your job.'

Lizzie frowned. '*How*...I got my job?'

Rosemary shrugged a carefully noncommittal shoulder. 'There's this mad rumour flying round that you didn't come in by the usual selection process but got strings pulled for you by someone influential on the executive floor—'

Lizzie coloured in dismay. 'That's not true—'

'The average temp doesn't wear delectable designer suits either and we're all killing ourselves over what you did with the photocopier,' Rosemary confided with an appreciative giggle as they left the cloakroom. 'Four hundred copies of our hunky pin-up boss, Sebasten. I bet Milly takes them home and papers her bedroom walls with them! Glad you're feeling better.'

'*Boss?*' Lizzie queried that astonishing label several seconds too late, for the blonde had already disappeared into one of the offices and Lizzie was left alone, fizzing with alarm and confusion.

She hastened into the stationery store room and yanked her mobile phone from her bag to punch out Sebasten's personal number. When he answered, she broke straight into harried speech. '*Am* I working for you?'

'Yes...did you finally get to read a letterhead?' Sebasten murmured with silken mockery. 'CI stands for Contaxis International.'

'Did you *fix* this job for me?' Lizzie demanded with a sinking heart, devastated by that first confirmation.

'You wouldn't have got it on your own merits,' Sebasten traded, crushing her with that candid assessment. 'Personnel don't take risks when they hire junior employees even on a temporary basis.'

'Thanks...' Lizzie framed shakily and then with angry stress continued. '*Thanks* for treating me like an idiot and not telling me that this was your company! *Thanks* for embarrassing me to death by doing it in such a way that the staff here know that I got preferential treatment!'

'Anything else you want to thank me for?' Sebasten enquired in an encouraging tone that was not calculated to soothe.

'I needed a job but you should have told me what you were doing!' Lizzie condemned furiously. 'I don't need your pity—'

'Trust me,' Sebasten drawled, velvety soft and smooth. 'The one emotion I do not experience in your radius is...pity. I'll pick you up at eight for the dinner party...OK?'

Lizzie thrust trembling fingers through the hair flopping over her damp brow. 'Has one thing I've said got through to you?'

'I'm not into phone aggro,' Sebasten murmured drily.

'I don't want to see you tonight—'

'I didn't hear that—'

'I…don't…want…to…see…you…tonight,' Lizzie repeated between clenched teeth, rage and pain gripping her in a vice that refused to yield. 'If you don't care about my feelings, I shouldn't *be* with you!'

'Your choice,' Sebasten breathed and cut the call.

After work, Lizzie returned to her bedsit in a daze. She stared at her fresh, daffodil-yellow walls, completed to perfection by the decorators he had hired. It was over, finished…just like that? Without ever seeing him again? Had she been unfair? Even downright rude and ungrateful? How long would it have taken her to find a job *without* his preferential treatment? She had no references, no office skills, no qualification beyond good A-level exam results gained when she was eighteen. In the following four years she had achieved nothing likely to impress a potential employer, although she had gone to great creative endeavours to try and conceal that fact on her application form.

When her father phoned her on her mobile phone out of the blue at seven that evening and asked her if she would like to meet him for dinner she was really pleased, for they had not spoken since she had left home. Over that meal, she made a real effort to seem cheerful. Felicity, Maurice Denton then confided wearily, had demanded that he dismiss their housekeeper, Mrs Baines, and he didn't want to do it. The older woman had worked for the Dentons for over ten years and was very efficient, if somewhat dour in nature.

'I thought possibly you could have a quiet word with Felicity on the subject,' her parent completed hopefully.

'No, thanks. It's none of my business.' But, even so, Lizzie was curious as to what the housekeeper could have done to annoy Felicity and she asked.

'Nothing that I can see...' Maurice muttered with barely concealed irritation. 'To tell you the truth, sometimes I feel like I don't know my own wife any more!'

Sebasten went to the dinner party alone, smouldered in a corner for an hour with a group of men, listening to sexist jokes that set his teeth on edge, snubbed every woman who dared to so much as smile at him and left early. On the drive home, he decided he wanted to confront Lizzie.

When he pulled up in the street he was just in time to see Lizzie, sheathed in a little violet-blue dress that would have wowed a dead man, in the act of clambering out of a Porsche. Smiling as if she had won the lottery, she sped up onto the pavement to embrace the tall, well-built driver.

Maurice Denton returned his daughter's hug and sighed. 'Let's not leave it so long the next time. I'm really proud that you're managing on your own. I can't have got it as wrong as I thought with you.'

Lizzie was so busy keeping up her happy smile as her father drove off again that her jaw ached from the effort. In truth it had been an evening that provoked conflicting reactions inside her. Her father had let her see that his marriage was under strain. Once she would have been selfishly overjoyed by the news, but now she was worried, wondering if she had been a mean, judgemental little cat when it came to her stepmother. Felicity was pregnant and stressed out and surely *had* to be labouring under a burden of guilt and unhappiness?

'Busy night?' a familiar accented drawl murmured, breaking into Lizzie's uneasy thoughts with sizzling effect.

In bemusement, Lizzie spun round and just feet away saw Sebasten lounging back against the polished bonnet of a fire-engine-red Lamborghini Diablo. Instantly, she went into melt-down with relief: *he* had come to see *her*. Shimmering dark golden eyes lanced into hers.

'Sebasten…?' Lizzie tensed at the taut angularity of his hard features.

Like a jungle cat uncoiling prior to springing, Sebasten straightened in one fluid movement and strode forward. '*Theos mou*…you staged a deliberate fight with me today, didn't you?'

Her brow furrowed in confusion. 'Sorry?'

'You had *other* plans for tonight,' Sebasten grated, ready to ignite into blistering rage and only holding on to his temper while his intellect continued to remind him that he was in the street with a car-load of his own bodyguards sitting parked only yards away.

'I really don't know what you're talking about.' And Lizzie didn't, for she had already forgotten her father's brief presence while her brain strove to comprehend what Sebasten was so very angry about.

'You slut!' Sebasten bit out, lean hands coiled into powerful fists. 'I should've been waiting for this!'

Acknowledging that the volatile side of Sebasten that she had once considered so very appealing was in the ascendant, Lizzie sucked in a sustaining breath and murmured with determined calm. 'Could you lower your voice and say whatever it is you just said in—er—English?'

When Sebasten appreciated that he had spoken in Greek, incandescent rage lit up in his simmering gaze. He gave her the translation at sizzling speed.

So taken aback was Lizzie by that offensive charge that she just stared at him for a count of ten incredulous seconds.

'And you're coming home with me so that we can have this out in *private*!' Sebasten launched at her between even white gritted teeth.

A shaken little laugh with a shrill edge fell from Lizzie's parted lips. Even as pain that he should attack her out of the blue with such an unreasonable accusation assailed her, she could not credit that he should imagine that she would now go *any* place with him.

Without warning, Sebasten closed a purposeful hand to her elbow.

Temper finally igniting, for caveman tactics had never had even the smallest appeal to her, Lizzie slapped his hand away and backed off a pointed step. 'Are you crazy? What's got into you? I have a stupid argument with you and you come out of nowhere at me and call me a name like that?'

'I saw you smarming over the jerk in the Porsche! How long has *he* been around?' Sebasten raked at her, all awareness of surroundings now obliterated by a fury stronger than any he had ever experienced.

At that point, clarification was shed on the inexplicable for Lizzie: he was talking about her father. Green eyes sparkling, she tilted her chin. 'Since before I was born. My father looks well for his age, doesn't he? But then he keeps himself very fit.'

'Since before you were *born*...your father?' Sebasten slung before the proverbial penny dropped, as it were, from a very great height on him.

'Goodnight, Sebasten,' Lizzie completed and she swanned into the terraced building behind him with all the panache and dignity of a queen.

Out on the pavement, Sebasten turned the air blue with bad language and then powered off in immediate pursuit.

When a knock that made the wood panels shake sounded on the door of her bedsit, Lizzie opened it on the security chain and peered out. 'Go away,' she said fiercely. 'How dare you insult me like that? And how dare you call my father a jerk?'

Before Sebasten had the opportunity to answer either furious demand, the door closed again in his face. Her father. What he had witnessed was the innocent family affection of a father and daughter. The mists of rage were dimming only to be replaced by a seething awareness that he had got it wrong. And she had *laughed*. Lean, whipcord muscles snapping to rigidity as he recalled that shrill little laugh, Sebasten went home and collected a speeding ticket on the way.

In the bath that Lizzie took to wind down, she ended up humming happily to herself. True, she had been furious with Sebasten, but Sebasten had been beside himself with rage only because he was *jealous*. No man had ever thrown a jealous scene over Lizzie before and she could not help but be impressed by the amount of emo-

tion Sebasten had put into that challenge. For the first
time in her life, she felt like an irresistible and dangerous woman. Just imagine Sebasten getting that worked
up over the belief that she was two-timing him! Lizzie
smiled and smiled. But he just had to learn what was
acceptable and what wasn't. He wasn't very trusting
either, was he? However, he did seem pretty keen. He
would phone her, wouldn't he? Should she just have let
him come in?

The following morning, Lizzie wakened feeling out
of sorts again and groaned with all the exasperation of
someone rarely ill. Perhaps she had picked up some bug
that her system couldn't shake off. About that point,
she registered that, although she had finished taking
her contraceptive pills for that month, her period had
still not arrived and she tensed. No, she couldn't possibly be pregnant! Why was she even thinking such a
crazy thing? All the same, accidents did happen, she
reasoned anxiously and she decided to buy a testing kit
at lunchtime just to *prove* to herself that she had nothing to worry about.

When she arrived at Contaxis International, she was
taken down to the basement file-storage rooms with an
entire trolley-load of documents to be filed away. As
Milly Sharpe smiled after showing her the procedure
with her own personal hands, Lizzie had the sneak-
ing suspicion that the subterranean eerie depths of the
building were where she was destined to stay for the
remainder of her three-month contract.

Footsteps made a creepy hollow sound in the long,
quiet corridors and Lizzie had a rich imagination. She
peered out of the room she was in: there was a security

guard patrolling. As she worked, she heard occasional distant noises and indistinct echoes. With the exception of the older man parked at a desk with a newspaper at the far end of the floor, there seemed to be nobody on permanent duty in the basement. It was boring and lonely and she hated it but she knew she had to stick it out. Not having made a good start the day before, she reckoned she was still lucky to be employed.

When she heard brisk footsteps ringing down the corridor just before lunchtime, she assumed it was the security guard again until she heard her own name called loud and clear and setting up a train of echoes. 'Lizzie!'

It was Sebasten's voice and he was in no need of a public-address system, for, having done an initially discreet but fruitless search of half a dozen rooms for her, he was out of patience. He had ensured that a magnificent bouquet of flowers had been delivered to her early that morning and he had expected her to phone him.

Lizzie ducked her head round the door. 'What are you *doing* down here?'

'This is my building—'

'Show-off,' she muttered, colour rising into her cheeks as she allowed herself to succumb to the temptation of looking at him.

'Isn't this a great place for a rendezvous?' Sebasten leant back against the door to shut it, sealing them into privacy.

'I don't think you should come looking for me when I'm at work,' Lizzie said with something less than conviction, for in truth she was pleased that he had made the effort.

From the crown of his proud dark head to the soles of his no doubt handmade shoes, he looked utterly fantastic, Lizzie acknowledged, the flare of her own senses in response to his vibrant, bronzed virility leaving her weak. His charcoal-grey business suit exuded designer style and tailoring. His shadow-striped grey and white shirt would have an exclusive monogram on the pocket: she ought to know, after all; she had two of them in her possession and had no intention of returning them.

As Sebasten began at her slender feet and worked his bold visual path up over her glorious legs to the purple silk skirt and aqua tie top she wore, sexy, smouldering intent emanated from every lithe, muscular inch of his big, powerful body.

'Miss me…?' he enquired lazily.

'After the way you behaved last night? You've got to be joking!' Lizzie dared.

'How was I to know the guy with the Porsche was your father?' Sebasten demanded, annoyed that she was digging up a matter that he believed should be closed and forgotten.

'You could have given me the benefit of the doubt and just come over and spoken to us.' With unusual tact, Lizzie swallowed the 'like anybody normal would have done' phrase she had almost fired in addition.

Sebasten dealt her a level look golden eyes now dark, hard and unapologetic. 'I don't give women the benefit of the doubt.'

Lizzie stiffened. 'Then you must've known some very unreliable women but that's still not an excuse for throwing a word like "slut" at me!'

'What I saw looked *bad*,' Sebasten growled, evading the issue.

'Did you have a really nasty experience with someone?' Lizzie was dismayed by his stubborn refusal to apologise but far more disturbed by that initial statement of distrust in her sex.

'Oh, just a mother and three stepmothers,' Sebasten imparted with acid derision, dark eyes burning back to gold in warning.

'Three?' Her lush mouth rounded into a soundless circle and slowly closed again, for she was so disconcerted she could think of nothing to say.

'One gold-digger, two sluts and one pill-popper,' Sebasten specified with raw scorn, for he loathed any reference to his family background. 'I suppose you now think you understand me.'

No, what she understood was how deep ran his distrust and his cynicism and she was shaken by what he had kept hidden behind the sophisticated façade. Well, you admired the complexity and now you've got it in spades, a dry little voice said inside her head. This is the guy you love: running in the opposite direction is not a realistic option. What was in her own heart and the reality that she already ached at the thought of the damage done to him would pull her back.

'No, I think you'll do just about anything, even spill the beans about the family from hell...*anything* rather than apologise,' Lizzie quipped, making her tense mouth curve into a rueful grin.

Thrown by that unexpected sally, Sebasten stared down into her dancing green eyes, the worst of his aggressive tension evaporating. 'The flowers were the apology—'

'What flowers?'

'You should've got them this morning—'

'I leave for work at the crack of dawn.' Lizzie tossed her head back. 'Was there a card with a written apology included?'

'Just a signature,' Sebasten admitted, sudden raw amusement sending a slashing smile across his lean dark face. 'You're very persistent, aren't you?'

The megawatt charm of that smile made Lizzie's knees wobble. Her body was held fast by a delicious tension that made her skin prickle, her breasts swell and her nipples tighten with sudden urgent and embarrassing sensitivity. 'Don't try to change the subject,' she warned him shakily.

'Or persuade you into silence?' Sebasten questioned, closing his hands to her narrow waist and lifting her up to bring her down on the table at which she had been sitting sorting documents just minutes earlier.

'Sebasten…' she gasped, disconcerted by that sudden shift into lover mode but secretly thrilled by it too. 'Suppose someone comes in?'

'The door's locked—'

'That was sneaky—'

'Sensible…' Sebasten contradicted, bracing long fingers either side of her and leaning forward to claim a teasing kiss. But the instant his mouth touched the lush softness of hers, he remembered how he had felt the night before when he had seen her in another man's arms and a sudden primitive need that was overwhelming swept him in stormy reaction. Instead of teasing, he forced her willing lips apart with the hungry driving pressure of his own.

Her heart banging in both surprise and excitement at his passion, Lizzie only worked up the will-power to tear free when her lungs were near to bursting. 'We have serious stuff to talk about—'

'This is *very* serious, *pethi mou*,' Sebasten broke in with fierce intensity, brilliant eyes locked to her as he let his lean hands travel with possessive appreciation up over her slender thighs. 'It was two weeks since we'd made love…two weeks of indescribable frustration…I think that must be why I lost my head last night.'

With a mighty effort of will Lizzie planted her hands in a staying motion over his, even though every weak, sinful skin-cell she possessed was thrumming like a car engine being revved. 'We haven't even discussed you fixing up this job for me—'

'But I'm so bloody grateful I did…it keeps you within reach,' Sebasten groaned, escaping her attempt at restraint with single-minded purpose and sinking his hands beneath her hips instead to tug her to the edge of the table and lock her into contact with him.

Brought into tantalising connection with the virile thrust of his potent masculine arousal, Lizzie uttered a sudden moan and plunged both hands into his luxuriant black hair and kissed him with all the wild hunger she had suppressed during his absence unleashed. Sebasten sounded a raw, appreciative groan low in his throat. Throwing back his broad shoulders to remove his jacket, he jerked loose his silk tie with a distinct air of purpose and cast both away.

Her mouth ran dry even as shock gripped her that he intended to take their lovemaking further.

'I'm so hot for you, I *ache*,' Sebasten spelt out hoarsely, golden eyes smouldering over her with burning intent, any hope of restraint wrested from him by the sheer charge of shaken anticipation he could see in her feverishly flushed face.

'Yes…me too,' Lizzie muttered, instinctively ashamed of the intensity of her own hunger for him but unable to deny it.

With deft fingers Sebasten undid the tie on her aqua top, spread it wide and then tipped her back over one strong arm to claim a plundering kiss of raw, sensual urgency while he unclipped the front fastening on her white bra. 'I'm not used to frustration…I've never felt this *desperate*,' he grated truthfully.

That same seething desperation had Lizzie in an iron hold. She was trembling, already breathing in short, shallow little spurts. The bra cups fell from her tender breasts and a lean brown hand captured an erect pink nipple to toy with first one throbbing peak and then the other. The pleasure was hot, heady and so immediate that all the breath was forced from her in a long, driven gasp. The maddening twist of craving low in her belly was a growing torment.

Sebasten sat her up, sank impatient hands beneath her and peeled off her panties. She was helpless in the grip of her own abandonment. An earthy sound of approbation was wrenched from him when he discovered the slick satin heat already awaiting him, and from that point control no longer existed for him either.

'Please...' Lizzie heard herself plead in helpless thrall to the pleasure and to him.

Sebasten straightened, hauled her back to him at the point where she had all the resistance of a rag doll and sank into her silken sheath in one forceful thrust. She clung to him on a wave of such powerful excitement, she thought she might pass out with the sheer over-load of sensation. It was wild, wilder than she had ever dreamt it could be even with him. When she finally convulsed in almost agonised ecstasy, he silenced her cry of release with the hot demand of his mouth, stilled the writhing of her hips and ground deep into her one last time.

In the wake of the most explosive climax of his life, Sebasten was stunned. He took in his surroundings, his attention lodging in disbelief on the bland office walls, and he was even more stunned. Feeling as though he had just come out of a blackout, he raised Lizzie, smoothed her silky, tumbled hair back from her brow with a hand he couldn't keep steady and began to re-store her clothing to order at speed.

The loud staccato burst of knocking on the door froze him into stillness.

Dragged from the dazed aftermath of their intimacy, Lizzie opened shattered eyes wide on the aghast aware-ness of how impossible it would be to hide a male of six feet four inches in a room full of wall-to-wall filing cabinets. 'Oh, no...there's someone wanting t-to get in here—'

'Ignore it.'

'We can't!' she whispered frantically.

'We *can*—'

'I'm calling Security if this door is not unlocked immediately!' a furious female voice threatened from the corridor.

CHAPTER SIX

SEBASTEN swore under his breath, swept up his jacket and dug his arms into it while Lizzie leapt off the table, smoothed down her mussed skirt and retrieved the one item of her clothing which Sebasten had removed with a face that burned hotter than any fire.

'This is Sebasten Contaxis…the lock's jammed and I'm stuck in here! Call Maintenance!" Sebasten called back, all ice-cool authority.

Five seconds later, high-heeled shoes were to be heard scurrying down the corridor. As soon as the racket of the woman's retreat receded, Sebasten stepped back and aimed a powerful kick at the lock. The door sprang open all on its own but the lock now looked damaged enough to support his story. Lizzie was still paralysed to the spot, transfixed by his speed and inventiveness in reacting to what had threatened to be the most humiliating encounter of her entire life.

'After you…' Sebasten invited with the shimmering golden eyes of a male who enjoyed a healthy challenge and enjoyed even more turning in a gold-medal performance for the benefit of an impressed-to-death woman. 'Grab a few files and lose yourself at the other end of the floor. I'll pick you up at half-six. We're entertaining

tonight at Pomeroy Place, my country house, so pack
a bag.'

'Sounds great,' she mumbled, revelling in the cou-
pley togetherness of that 'we' he had employed.

'I forgot about the blasted party,' Sebasten admitted with a frown over that same slip of the tongue as
he swung away.

'Sebasten…?' In a sudden surge of emotion that
Lizzie could no more have restrained than she could
have held back floodwater, she flung herself at him as
he turned back with an enquiring ebony brow raised.
Green eyes shining, she linked her arms round his neck
and gave him a hug. 'That's for just b-being you,' she
told him, her voice faltering as he tensed in surprise.

'Thanks.' Sebasten set her back from him, his keen
dark gaze veiling as he read the soft, vulnerable look
in her expectant face. 'I should get going,' he pointed
out.

Lizzie gathered up some loose papers and found another room in which to work. From there she could hear
the rise and fall of speculative voices as maintenance
staff attended to the damage door further down the corridor but she was incapable of listening. She pressed
clammy hands to her pale, stricken face, unable to combat the deep inner chill spreading through her. Even
after the incredible passion they had shared, even while
her wretched body still ached from the penetration of
his, her affectionate hug and declaration had been received like a step too far. He might have attempted to
conceal that reality but his lack of any true response
had spoken for him.

But why? For a split-second, Sebasten had looked

down into her eyes and what had he seen there? *Love?*
She felt humiliated, foolish and scared all at once.
Whatever he had seen, he had not wanted to see. It
was as though she had crossed some invisible bound-
ary line and, instead of moving to meet her, he had
turned his back. But then what had she been thinking
of when she threw herself at him like that? The wildness of their lovemaking had shattered her and perhaps
she had wanted reassurance…emotional reassurance.

At that awful moment of truth, Lizzie regretted her
first night in Sebasten's bed with an angry self-loathing
of her own weakness that nothing could have quenched.
She had been reckless and now she was paying the price
for not resisting temptation until she knew him better. Even more did she suffer at the recollection of her
own wanton response to him only thirty minutes earlier. What Sebasten wanted it seemed Sebasten got. He
touched her and she demonstrated all the self-will of a
clockwork toy. For the first time, she understood with
painful clarity just how cruelly deceptive sexual intimacy could be. Was she at heart the slut he had called
her? She winced, her throat aching, because she was
just so much in love with him. But did Sebasten see her
as anything more than a casual sexual affair?

In the mood Lizzie was in, the prospect of devoting
her lunch hour to buying a pregnancy test had scant appeal. Where had the insane fear that she might have conceived come from in the first place? It wasn't as though
she had felt sick or even dizzy since she had come into
work. She was just being silly, working herself up into
a panic because she was involved in her very first inti-

mate relationship. All the same, oughtn't she to check just to be on the safe side?

She bought the test kit, buried it in her bag, tried to forget it was there and discovered she could not. Then that afternoon, when she sprang up in a sudden movement after leafing through a bottom file drawer, her head swam and she swayed. As soon as she got home she knew she would use the test because a creeping sense of apprehension was growing at a steady rate at the back of her mind.

On the top floor of the CI building, Sebasten stared out at the city skyline with a brooding distance etched in his grim gaze. He was in a state of angry conflict that was foreign to him. *What was he playing at with Lizzie Denton?* When had his own motivations become as indistinct to him as a fog? Since the morning he learned her true identity, he had not once stopped to think through what he was doing in getting involved with her. That reality shook him at an instant when he was still striving without success to come up with an adequate explanation for what he had already labelled the 'basement episode'. He felt out of control and he didn't like it.

How could he keep on somehow neglecting to recall how cruelly Lizzie had treated his half-brother, Connor? Or the number of sweet studied lies that had tripped off her ready tongue on that same subject? What was he suffering from? Selective-memory syndrome? Did that glorious body of hers mean more to him than his own honour? Or even basic decency? From start to finish, his intimacy with her had defied every tenet he lived by.

He could no more easily explain why he had bought her diamonds and her car back for her. Did Lizzie deserve a reward for demonstrating that buckets of winsome pseudo-innocent charm could conceal a shallow nature? After all, most women made a special effort to impress and hide their worst side around a male of his wealth. Furthermore, he was very fond of Ingrid Morgan but he was bitterly aware that on the day of Connor's funeral he had made the rare mistake of letting emotions cloud his judgement. It was past time he ended what should *never* have begun...

While Sebasten was coming to terms with what he saw as an inevitable event, Lizzie was seated on her bed in shock, just staring at the little wand that had turned a certain colour ten minutes earlier. She picked up the test kit instructions and read the section on false results for the third time. Maybe the kit had been old stock. She checked the sell-by date on the packaging but there was no comfort to be found there.

Although it seemed incredible to her, she *was* going to have a baby...Sebasten's baby. If he reacted to a hug as if it were a marriage proposal, how would he react to a baby? She paled and shivered and wrapped her arms round herself. That first night she had told him that she was protected, had fully, confidently believed that she was, but hadn't she also known that no form of contraception yet existed that was a hundred per-cent effective?

The concept of having a child in her life transfixed Lizzie. As yet none of her former friends had children and discussing babies had always been considered deeply uncool. Lizzie had always kept quiet about the fact that she adored babies, had had to restrain herself from commenting in public about how seriously attractive some of them were and how insidious was the appeal of the shops that sold tiny garments. She stood up and studied her stomach in the mirror, sucked what little of it there was in…was there just the very faintest hint of it not going in quite as far as it once had? Registering what she was doing, she frowned in dismay at her inability to think sensible thoughts.

She wasn't married, she wasn't solvent, she didn't even have a proper job, and on being told the father of her baby would most probably demonstrate *why* he had such a bad reputation. He might try to deny that he was the father or he might assume that she would agree to a termination that would free him from the responsibility for her child. In fact, it would be extremely naïve of her to expect anything but a shocked and angry reaction from Sebasten. This was a guy who had told her that he *never* gave women the benefit of the doubt. In her situation that was not good news.

Here she was, living in a crummy bedsit, having come down in the world the exact same day she met a very rich man, and lo and behold…a few weeks later she would be telling him that she had fallen pregnant by him. Even to her that scenario did not look good. The least suspicious of men might have doubts about conception having been accidental in such circumstances, so the odds were that Sebasten would immediately think that he had been deliberately entrapped. An anguished groan escaped Lizzie.

She might really love Sebasten but she was getting acquainted with his flaws and her pride baulked at the

prospect of putting herself in such a demeaning position. There was no good reason why she should make an
immediate announcement though, was there? Wouldn't
it make more sense to wait until she had at least seen
a doctor? Furthermore, that would give her more time
to work out how best to broach the subject with Sebasten…

AS SEBASTEN DROVE OVER to collect Lizzie, he cursed the
necessity of their having to spend the night under the
same roof at Pomeroy.

He was about to break off their relationship, so where
had his wits been when he had made an inconvenient
arrangement like that? But then he had since worked
out exactly where his wits had been over the past three
weeks: *Lost in lust*. Indeed, recalling his own extraordinary behaviour that same morning, his strong jawline
took on an aggressive cast. Unbelievably, he had staged
a clandestine sexual encounter at Contaxis International
in the middle of his working day. All decent restraint
had vanished the same instant he laid eyes on Lizzie's
lithe, leggy perfection: he had had that door shut and
locked within seconds.

So, in common with most single males with a
healthy sex drive, Sebasten reasoned, he had proved to
be a pushover when it came to the lure of a forbidden
thrill. But that angle was cold consolation to a Greek
who prided himself on the strength of his own self-
discipline. Yet in that file room he had behaved like a
sex-starved teenager who took advantage of every opportunity, no matter how inappropriate it might be. That
demeaning image rankled even more.

It just went to show that a guy should never, *ever* relax his guard round a woman, Sebasten conceded in grim conclusion. Lizzie was an absolute powder-keg of sexual dynamite. Why else could he not keep his hands off her? Why else had he dragged her home with him only hours after meeting her?

After all, he had never been into casual encounters. Had anyone ever told him that he would some day sink to the level of sobering up a drunk woman and then falling victim to her supposed charms afresh, he would have laughed out loud in derision. Only now he wasn't laughing. After all, he had only got through the previous couple of weeks of self-denial by virtually staying out of the country and seeing her only in public places, he acknowledged with seething self-contempt.

When he picked up Lizzie he would be really cool with her and she would register that the end was nigh for herself. Exactly *why*, he asked himself then, was he agonising about something that had cost him only the most fleeting pang with other women?

Relationships broke up every day. She had ditched Connor without an ounce of concern, he reminded himself. But then how did he judge her for that when he had done pretty much the same thing himself? The rejected lover was hurt and what could anybody do about that? He recalled Lizzie's shining, trusting green eyes clinging to him and something in his gut twisted. He didn't want to hurt her.

Lizzie was still getting ready when Sebasten arrived.

'Are you always this punctual?' she groaned, hot, self-conscious colour burning her cheekbones as she evaded his gaze, for all she could think about at that instant was the pregnancy test that had come up positive.

'Always,' Sebasten confirmed, shrugging back a cuff to check his Rolex for good measure, determined to be difficult.

He looked grim, Lizzie registered, her heart skipping a beat as she noted the tautness of his fabulous bone-structure.

'I'll wait in the car,' Sebasten said drily, striving not to notice the way her yellow silk wrap defined her slender, shapely figure. For a dangerous split-second he thought of her as a gaily-wrapped present he couldn't wait to unwrap and the damage was done: his body reminded him with ferocious and infuriating immediacy that their stolen encounter earlier had only blunted the edge of his frustration.

'Don't be daft...I'll only be a minute.' Lizzie watched the faintest hint of dark colour score his chiselled cheek-bones and wondered in dismay what on earth was the matter with him.

Desperate for any form of distraction that might lessen his awareness of the ache in his groin, Sebasten studied the open suitcase festooned with an enormous heap of garments as yet unpacked. He frowned. She was very disorganised and he was quite the opposite, so why was there something vaguely endearing about the harried, covert way she was now trying to squash everything into the case without regard for any form of folding whatsoever? He hated untidiness, he hated unpunctuality. Tell her it's over *now*, his intelligence urged him just as Lizzie looked up at him.

'You've had a lousy day, haven't you?' she guessed

in a warm and sympathetic tone that snaked out and wrapped round Sebasten like a silken man-trap. 'Why don't you just sit down and chill out and I'll make you a cup of coffee?'

Disconcerted, Sebasten parted his lips. 'I—'

'I bet the traffic was appalling too.' Lizzie treated him to the kind of appreciative appraisal that implied he had crossed at least an ocean and a swamp just to reach her door and disappeared behind the battered wooden screen that semi-concealed the tiny kitchen area in one corner.

'Lizzie…' Sebasten felt like the biggest bastard in creation but what hit him with even more striking effect was the sudden acknowledgment that he did not *want* to dump Lizzie. Shattered by that belated moment of truth with himself, he snatched in a deep, shuddering breath.

'Yes?' She reappeared, her wide, friendly smile flashing out at him as she handed him a cup of coffee. 'What's your favourite colour?'

'Turquoise,' Sebasten muttered, struggling to come to terms with what he had refused to admit to himself all afternoon. It was as if she had put a spell on him the first night: he and his hormones had been haywire ever since. Yet there was no way on earth that he could add to Ingrid's grief by keeping the woman she blamed for Connor's death in his own life. And did he not owe more respect to his late brother's memory? Lizzie's only hold on him was sex, he reminded himself angrily. She was also an appalling liar and he ought to tell her that before they parted company.

Lizzie rustled through the wardrobe, grateful for the

opportunity to occupy her trembling hands. She just had a bad feeling about the mood Sebasten was in. She could only equate his presence with having a big black thundercloud hanging overhead. Clutching a turquoise dress, she went behind the screen to change.

Never had the audible rustle and silky slither of feminine garments had such a provocative effect on Sebasten's libido. Out of all patience with himself, infuriated by the threatening volcano of opposing thoughts, urges and emotions seething inside him, he paced the restricted confines of the room until she was ready and said little after they had driven off in the Lamborghini.

'Do you like—children?' Lizzie shot at him then right out of the blue.

Already on red alert, Sebasten's defensive antenna lit up like the Greek sky at dawn. The most curious dark satisfaction assailed him as his very worst expectations were fulfilled. After just weeks, it seemed, she was dreaming of wedding bells. But that satisfaction was short-lived as it occurred to him that, possibly, he had given her grounds to believe she had him hooked like a fish on a line.

Hadn't he made a huge prat of himself when he saw her hugging her father? And what about all those phone calls he had made to her when he was abroad? Why had he felt a need to phone her every damn day he was away from her? And sometimes *more* than once. Not to mention activities that were the total opposite of cool and sophistication in the CI basement. She might well believe that he was infatuated with her.

'Children are all right...at a distance,' Sebasten pronounced, cool as ice.

Lizzie lost every scrap of her natural colour and caution might have warned her to keep quiet but she was quite incapable of listening to such promptings. 'What sort of answer is that?'

'They *can* look quite charming in paintings,' Sebasten conceded, studying the traffic lights with brooding concentration. 'But they're noisy, demanding and an enormous responsibility. I'm much too selfish to want that kind of hassle in my life.'

'I hope your future wife feels the same way,' was all that Lizzie in her shattered state could think to mutter to cover herself in the hideous silence that stretched.

'I'm not planning to acquire one of those either,' Sebasten confessed in an aggressive tone. 'If even my father couldn't strike gold *once* in four marriages, what hope have I?'

'None whatsoever, I should think, with your outlook,' Lizzie answered in a tight, driven reply. 'Of course, some women would marry you simply because you're loaded—'

'Surprise…surprise,' Sebasten slotted in with satiric bite.

'But personally speaking…' Lizzie's low-pitched response quivered with the force of her disturbed emotions and she was determined to have her own say on the subject…'not all the money in the world would compensate me for being deprived of children. I also think there's something very suspect about a man who dislikes children—'

'*Suspect?* In what way?' Sebasten demanded with wrathful incredulity, exploded from his already unsettled state of mind with a vengeance.

'But then, as you said, you're very selfish, but to my way of thinking…a *truly* masculine man would have a more mature outlook and he would appreciate that a life partner and the children they would share would be as rewarding as they were restricting.'

Sebasten was so incensed, he almost launched a volley of enraged Greek at her. Who was she calling immature? And when had he said that he *disliked* children? A truly masculine man? His lean brown hands flexed and tightened round the steering wheel as he sought to contain his ire at her daring to question what every Greek male considered the literal essence of being.

'Your mind is narrow indeed,' he gritted, shooting the Lamborghini down the motorway at above the speed limit.

'You're entitled to your opinion.' Lizzie was wondering in a daze of shock how she could have been so offensive but not really caring, for what he had told her had appalled her. Dreams she had not even known she cherished had been hauled out into the unkind light of day and crucified. 'But please watch your speed.'

Deprived of even that minor outlet for his rage, Sebasten slowed down, lean, bronzed features set like stone. 'The minute my father, Andros, suffered a setback in business and her jetset lifestyle looked to be under threat, my mother demanded a divorce. She traded custody of me for a bigger settlement,' he bit out rawly. 'Although she had access rights, she never utilised them. I was only six years old.'

In an altogether new kind of shock, Lizzie focused her entire attention on his taut, hard profile. 'You never saw her again?'

'No, and she died a few years later. A *truly* feminine, maternal woman,' Sebasten framed with vicious intent. 'My first stepmother slept with the teenager who cleaned our swimming pool. She liked very young men.'

'Oh…dear,' Lizzie mumbled, bereft of a ready word of comfort to offer.

'Andros divorced her. His next wife spent most of their marriage in a series of drug rehabilitation clinics but still contrived to die of an overdose. The fourth wife was much younger and livelier and she was addicted to sex but *not* with an ageing husband,' Sebasten delivered with sizzling contempt. 'The night that my father suffered the humiliation of overhearing her strenuous efforts to persuade *me* into bed, he had his first heart attack.'

After that daunting recitation of matrimonial disaster, Lizzie shook her head in sincere dismay. 'Your poor father. Obviously he didn't have any judgement at all when it came to women.'

Not having been faced with that less than tactful response before, Sebasten gritted his even white teeth harder until it crossed his mind that there was a most annoying amount of truth in that comment. Throughout those same years, Ingrid, who would have made an excellent wife, had hovered in the background, at first hopeful, then slowly losing heart when she was never once even considered as a suitable bridal candidate by the man who had been her lover on and off for years. Why not? She had been born poor, had had to work for a living and had made the very great strategic error of sharing his father's bed between wives.

But how the hell had he got on to such a very personal subject with Lizzie? What was it about her? When had he ever before dumped the embarrassing gritty details of his background on a woman? He was furious with himself.

Given plenty of food for thought, Lizzie blinked back tears at the mere idea of what Sebasten must have suffered after his greedy mother's rejection was followed by the ordeal of three horribly inadequate stepmothers. Was it any wonder that he should be so anti-marriage and children? Her heart just went out to him and she was ashamed of her own face-saving condemnation of his views earlier. After all, what did she know about what *his* life must have been like? Only now, having been given the bare bones, she was just dying to flesh them out.

However, Sebasten's monosyllabic responses soon squashed that aspiration flat and silence fell until the Lamborghini accelerated up a long, winding drive beneath a leafy tunnel of huge weeping lime trees. Pomeroy Place was a Georgian jewel of architectural elegance, set off to perfection by a beautiful setting.

Before the housekeeper could take Lizzie upstairs, Lizzie glanced back across the large, elegant hall and focused with anxious eyes on Sebasten's grim profile before following the older woman up the superb marble staircase. Shown into a gorgeous guest room, she freshened up, a frown indenting her brow. In the mood Sebasten was in, he felt like an intimidating stranger. But then, it was evident that she had roused bad memories, but did he have to shut her out to such an extent? Could he not appreciate that she had feelings too?

Downstairs, receiving the first of his guests, Sebasten was discovering that a bad day could only get much worse when the vivacious gossip columnist Patsy Hewitt arrived on the arm of one of his recently divorced friends. Aware that Lizzie had been attacked by one of the tabloid newspapers for not attending Connor's funeral, the very last person he wanted seated at his dining-table was a journalist with a legendary talent for venom against her own sex. He did not want his relationship with Lizzie exposed in print just when he was about to end it. In fact, he was determined to protect Lizzie from that final embarrassment.

Quite how he could hope to achieve that end he had no clear idea, and then even the option seemed to vanish when Lizzie walked into the drawing room. He watched Patsy look at Lizzie and then turn back to the other couple she had been chatting to and he realised with relief that the journalist had no idea who Lizzie was.

'And this is Lizzie,' he murmured with a skimming glance in her general direction, drawing her to the attention of his other guests in a very impersonal manner.

'Do you work for Sebasten?' a woman in her thirties asked Lizzie some minutes later, evidently having no suspicion that Lizzie might be present in any other capacity.

'Yes.' The way Sebasten was behaving, Lizzie was happy to make that confirmation but an angry, discomfited spark flared in her clear green eyes.

Another four people arrived and soon afterwards they crossed the hall to the dining room. Pride helped Lizzie to keep up her end of the general conversation but she did not look at Sebasten unless she was forced to do so. What she ate or even whether she *did* eat during that meal she was never later to recall. She started out angry but sank deeper into shock as the evening progressed. Had she really expected to act as his hostess? Certainly, she had not expected to be treated like someone merely invited to keep the numbers at the table even.

'So...which luscious lady are you romancing right now?' the older brunette, who had entertained them all with her sharp sense of humour, asked Sebasten in a coy tone over the coffee-cups.

Lizzie froze and watched Sebasten screen his dark eyes with his spiky black lashes before he murmured lazily. 'I'm still looking.'

With a trembling hand, Lizzie reached for her glass of water. Feeling sick, betrayed and outraged, she backed out of her chair without any perceptible awareness of what she was about to do, walked down the length of the table and slung the contents of her glass in Sebasten's face. 'When I find a real man, I'll let you know!' she spelt out.

Sebasten vaulted upright and thrust driven fingers through his dripping hair.

The silence that had fallen had a depth that was claustrophobic.

And then, as Lizzie went into retreat at the shimmering incredulity in Sebasten's stunned golden eyes, one of the guests laughed out loud and she spun to see who it was that could find humour in such a scene.

'Bravo, Lizzie!' Patsy Hewitt told her with an amused appreciation that bewildered Lizzie. 'I don't think I've *ever* enjoyed a more entertaining evening.'

'I'm glad someone had a good time,' Lizzie quipped

before she walked out of the room and sped upstairs with tears of furious, shaken reaction blinding her.

Had that guy talking been the guy she thought she loved? The male whose baby she carried? Denying her very existence? He was *ashamed* of her. What else was she to believe but that he was ashamed to own up to being involved with Connor Morgan's ex-girlfriend? He needn't think she had not eventually read the significance of his having neglected to speak her surname even once or his determination not to distinguish her with one atom of personal attention. So why the heck had he invited her? And how did she ditch him when she was expecting his baby?

But such concerns for a future that seemed distant were beyond Lizzie at a moment when all that was on her mind was leaving Sebasten's house just as fast as she could manage it. So it was unfortunate that while she had been downstairs dining her case had been unpacked.

She was in shock after the evening she had endured and the shattering discovery that Sebasten could turn into a male she really didn't want to know. Why? *Why* had he suddenly changed towards her?

In a flash, she recalled his cool parting from her that morning at Contaxis International and stilled, comprehension finding a path through her bewilderment. Nothing had been right since then. He had been in a distant mood when he came to pick her up and then in the car she had asked that stupid question about whether or not he liked children and the atmosphere had gone from strained to freezing point. He wanted *out*. Why had she not seen that sooner?

With nerveless hands, she dragged out her case and plonked it down on the bed. She remembered the way he had made love to her earlier in the day and she shivered, almost torn in two by the agony that threatened to take hold of her.

When Sebasten strode in, she was gathering up the items she had left out on the dressing-table earlier and in the act of slinging them willy-nilly into her case.

'What do you want?' Lizzie asked, refusing to look higher than his snazzy dark blue silk tie.

'Perhaps I don't like having water thrown in my face in front of an audience,' Sebasten heard himself bite out, although that had not been the tack he had planned to take. 'And the audience didn't much enjoy the fall-out either…it's barely midnight and they've all gone home.'

'If I had had anything bigger and heavier within reach, the damage would have been a lot worse!' Lizzie's soft mouth was sealed so tight it showed white round the edges.

'Do you even realise who the woman who last spoke to you *was*?'

'I don't know and I don't care. There is just no excuse for the way you treated me tonight!' Lizzie was fighting to retain a grip on her disturbed emotions and walk out on him with dignity. Deep down inside she knew that if she allowed herself to think about what she was doing or what was happening between then she might come apart at the seams in front of him.

'Patsy Hewitt is the *Sunday Globe*'s gossip columnist. No prizes for guessing which couple will star in her next lead story!'

The journalist's name had a vague familiarity for

Lizzie but so intense was her emotional conflict that she could not grasp why he should waste his breath on something that struck her as an irrelevant detail.

'I didn't flaunt our relationship tonight because I wanted to protect you from that kind of unpleasant media exposure,' Sebasten completed angrily.

That *he* should dare to be angry with *her* after the way he had behaved added salt to the wounds he had already inflicted. In the back of her mind, she discovered, had lurked a very different expectation: that he might grovel for embarrassing her in such a way, for denying her like a Judas before witnesses. And nothing short of grovelling apologies would have eased the colossal pain of angry, bewildered loss growing inside her.

'Why the heck should a guy with *your* reputation care about media exposure?' Lizzie demanded and looked at him for the first time since he had entered the room.

And it hurt, it hurt so much to study those lean, devastatingly attractive features, note the fierce tension etched in his fabulous bone-structure and recognise the hard condemnation in his scorching golden eyes.

'And why the heck would I care anyway?' she added in sudden haste, determined to get in first with what she knew was coming her way. 'We're finished and I want to go home. You can call a taxi for me!'

'You can stay the night here. It would be crazy for you to leave this late at night.' Instead of being relieved that the deed he had been in no hurry to do had been done for him, a jagged shot of instant igniting fury leapt through Sebasten.

'The very idea of staying under the same roof as

you is offensive to me. You're an absolute toad and I hope Patsy whatever-her-name-is shows you up in print for what you are!' Lizzie slung back not quite levelly, for a tiny secret part of her, a part that she despised, had hoped that he might argue with her announcement, might even this late in the day magically contrive to excuse his own behaviour and redress the damage he had done.

'Perhaps had you considered telling me the truth about Connor *this* might not be happening,' Sebasten heard himself declare, his jawline clenching hard. 'Instead you lied your head off to me!'

'I beg your pardon…?' Settling perplexed green eyes on him, Lizzie stared back at him, her heart beginning to beat so fast at that startling reference to Connor that it felt as if it was thumping inside her very throat. Why was he dragging Connor in?

'Connor's mother, Ingrid, is a close family friend.'

Her gaze widened in astonishment at that unexpected revelation, pallor driving away the feverish flush in her cheeks, an eerie chill tingling down her spine. 'You didn't tell me that before…you *said* you hardly knew him—'

'I knew Connor better as a child than as an adult.' On surer ground now, Sebasten let true anger rise and never had he needed anger more than when he saw the shattered look of incomprehension stamped to Lizzie's oval face. She was so pale that all seven freckles on her nose stood out in sharp relief. 'You also said you didn't know him well and then told repeated lies about your relationship with him.'

'I *didn't* lie,' Lizzie countered in angry bewilderment, her tall, slender body rigid as she attempted to challenge the accusation that she was a liar while at the same time come to terms with the shocking reality that Sebasten had close ties that he cherished with the Morgan family but that he had not been prepared to reveal that fact to her. 'I actually told you a truth that nobody other than myself, Connor and the woman involved knew!'

'*Theos mou*...the *truth*?' Sebasten slammed back with raw derision, infuriated that he had noticed her freckles in the middle of such a confrontation and outraged by the unfamiliar stress of having to fight to maintain his concentration. 'Your most ingenious story of Connor's secret affair with a married woman that would be impossible to disprove when you declined to name the lady involved. That nonsense was a base and inexcusable betrayal of Connor's memory!'

'You *didn't* believe me,' Lizzie registered in a belated surge of realisation and she shook her bright head in a numbed movement. 'And yet you never said so, never even mentioned that Ingrid Morgan was a friend of yours. Why did you conceal those facts? If you believed I was lying, why didn't you just confront me?'

'Maybe I thought it was time that someone taught you a lesson.' No sooner had Sebasten made that admission than he regretted it. 'That was *before* I understood that what I was doing to you was as reprehensible as what you did to Connor.'

Lizzie only heard that first statement and her blood ran cold in her veins. *Maybe I thought it was time that someone taught you a lesson.* That confession rocked her already shaken world and threatened to blow it away altogether. He had gone after her, singled her out, and it had *all* been part of some desire to punish her for what she had supposedly done to Connor? She was shattered by that final revelation.

'What sort of a man are you?' Lizzie demanded in palpable disbelief.

Anger nowhere within reach, Sebasten lost colour beneath his bronzed skin and fought an insane urge to pull her into his arms and hold her tight. 'The night I met you, the first night, I didn't *know* who you were. I didn't find out until the following morning when I saw your driving licence.'

Lizzie dismissed that plea without hesitation. 'I don't believe in coincidences like that…you went on the hunt for me.'

'Had I known who you were I would never have gone to bed with you,' Sebasten swore half under his breath.

A wave of dizziness assailed Lizzie. She could not bear to think of what he had just said. Blocking him from her mind and her view, she sank down on the foot of the bed and reached for her mobile phone. Desperate to leave his house, she punched out the number of a national cab firm to request a taxi.

'Hell…*I'll* take you back to London!' Sebasten broke in.

Having made the call, Lizzie ignored him and breathed in slow and deep to ward off the swimming sensation in her head. The guy she had fallen in love with had embarked on their relationship with the sole and deliberate intent of hurting and humiliating her. She could not believe that he could have been so cruel, and why? Over the head of Connor, who had already cost her so much!

Sick to the heart, she stood up like an automaton and headed for the dressing room, where she assumed her clothes had been stowed away. She dragged garments from hangers and drawers, dimly amazed at the amount of stuff she had contrived to pack for a single night. But then she had been in love, hadn't she been? Unable to make up her mind what she might need, what would look best, what *he* might admire most on her. A laugh that was no laugh at all bubbled and died again inside her. Her throat was raw and aching but, in the midst of what she believed to be the worst torture she would ever have to get through, her eyes were dry.

Sebasten hovered, lean, powerful hands clenching and unclenching. 'I should never have slept with you,' he admitted with suppressed savagery. 'If I could go back and change that I *would*—'

'Try staying out of basements too.' Her tone one of ringing disgust, Lizzie quivered with a combustible mix of self-loathing and shame that he could have been so ruthless and wicked as to take advantage of her weakness. 'There could never have been an excuse for what you've done. That you should have set out to cause me harm is unforgivable.'

'Yes,' Sebasten conceded in Greek, snatching in a deep-driven breath and switching back to English to state. 'I *do* accept that two wrongs do not make a right, but in the heat of the moment when I was confronted with the depth of Ingrid's despair my mind was not so clear. I was appalled that first morning when I discovered your true identity and what took place today was indefensible. But from the outset I was very much attracted to you.'

Heaping clothes into the case, Lizzie made herself look at him, hatred in her heart, hatred built on a hurt that went so deep it felt like a physical pain. 'Is that supposed to make me feel better? I met you when my whole life had crashed around me. I was very unhappy and you must have seen that…yet you waded in and made it worse,' she condemned. 'How could you be such a bastard?'

'I lost the plot…isn't that obvious?' Sebasten threw back at her with a savage edge to his accented drawl as he swept up the couple of garments she had dropped on her passage from the dressing room but held on to them because he did not want to hasten her departure. 'I got in deeper than I ever dreamt and I'm paying a price for that now too.'

Lizzie thought in a daze of the child she carried and a spasm of bitter regret tightened her facial muscles. She was no longer listening to him. 'Connor cheated on me and he didn't spare my feelings a single thought. I lost my friends and my father's respect. I paid way over the odds for being the fall guy in that affair. But this is something else again…I *loved* you…' Her voice faltered to a halt and she blinked, shocked that she had admitted that and then, beyond caring, she snapped her case closed with trembling hands and swung it down off the bed.

'I don't want you to leave in this frame of mind…' Sebasten declared as much to her as to himself.

'I hate you. I will never forgive you…so stop saying really *stupid* things!' Lizzie slung at him with a wildness that mushroomed up from within her without any warning and made her feel almost violent. 'What did you expect from me? That I was going to shake hands and thank you for wrecking my life again!'

Sebasten had no answer, but then he had never thought that far ahead and just then cool, rational thought evaded him. 'If you want to go back to London tonight, let me drive you,' he urged, taking refuge in male practicality.

'You're wired to the moon,' Lizzie accused shakily, hauling her case past him.

His hand came down over hers and forced her fingers into retreat from the handle. She just let him have the case. She walked to the door, threw it wide and started down the stairs while she willed the taxi to come faster than the speed of light.

Sebasten reached the hall only seconds in her wake. As a manservant hurried from the rear of the hall to relieve him of the case, only to be sent into retreat by the ferocious look of warning he received from his employer, Lizzie wrenched open the front door on her own.'

'Give me my case!' she demanded, fired up like an Amazon warrior.

With pronounced reluctance, Sebasten set the case down. 'Lizzie...Connor was my half-brother...'

Lizzie spun back to him in astonishment and an image of Connor surged up in her mind's eye: the very dark brown eyes that had been so unexpected with her ex-boyfriend's blond hair, the classic bone-structure, his height and build. She did not question Sebasten's ultimate revelation. Indeed, for her it was as though the whole appalling picture was finally complete.

'*Two* of you...' she muttered sickly as she turned away again to focus with relief on the car headlights approaching the front of the house. 'And *both* of you arrogant, selfish, lying rats who use and abuse women! Now, why doesn't that surprise me?'

Sebasten froze at that response. The cab driver got out to take her case. Within the space of a minute, Lizzie was gone. Sebasten looked down at the flimsy white bra and red silk shirt he was still grasping in one hand and he knew that he was about to get so drunk that he didn't know what day it was.

CHAPTER SEVEN

LIZZIE didn't cry that night: she was reeling with so much shock and reaction she was exhausted and she lay down on her bed still clothed and fell asleep.

After only a few hours, she wakened to a bleak sense of emptiness and terrible pain. She had fallen in love with a sadist. Sebasten had got under her skin when she was weak and vulnerable and hurt her beyond relief. Yet he was also the father of her baby. Her mind shied away from that daunting fact and her thoughts refused to stay in one place.

If Sebasten was Connor's half-brother that meant that the still attractive Ingrid must have had an affair with Sebasten's father. A very secret affair it must have been, for Connor himself when she asked had told Lizzie a different story about the circumstances of his birth.

'Ingrid met up with an old flame and the relationship had fizzled out again before she even knew I was on the way,' he had confided casually. 'He was an army officer. She did plan to tell him when he came back from his posting abroad but he was killed in a military helicopter crash shortly before I was born.'

Had that tale been a lie? Her brow indented as she dragged herself out of bed to look into her empty fridge. What was the point of thinking about Connor and the blood tie that Sebasten had claimed? She needed to keep busy, she told herself dully. She also had to eat to stay healthy, which meant that she had to shop even when the very thought of food made her feel queasy. In addition, she reminded herself, she had to make an appointment with the doctor.

Without ever acknowledging that she was still so deep in shock from the events of the previous twenty-four hours that she could barely function, Lizzie drove herself through that day. She got a cancellation appointment at the doctor's surgery. She learned that she was indeed pregnant and when she asked how that might have happened when she had been taking contraceptive pills was asked if she missed taking any or had been sick. Instantly she recalled that first night with Sebasten when she had been ill, stilling a shiver at the wounding memories threatening her self-discipline, she fell silent. Concentration was impossible. Behind every thought lurked the spectre of her own grief.

From the medical centre she trekked to the supermarket, where she wandered in an aimless fashion, selecting odd items that had more appeal than others, but she returned to her bedsit and discovered that she had chosen nothing that would make a proper meal. She grilled some toast, forced herself to nibble two corners of it before having to flee for the bathroom and be ill.

Sebasten rose on Sunday with a hangover unlike any he had ever suffered. He had virtually no memory of Saturday. Any thought of Lizzie was the equivalent of receiving a punch to the solar plexus but he couldn't get her haunting image out of his mind. Was it guilt? What else could it be? When had any Contaxis ever sunk low enough to contemplate taking revenge on a woman? What the hell had got into him that he had even considered such a course of action? And now, when he was genuinely worried about Lizzie's state of mind, how could he check up on her?

Over breakfast, he flipped open the gossip page of the *Sunday Globe* and any desire to eat receded as he read the startling headline: 'CONTAXIS 0, DENTON 10.'

For all of his adult life, Sebasten had been adored and fêted and flattered by the gossip-column fraternity but Patsy Hewitt's gleeful account of events at his dinner party was very much of the poison-pen variety and directed at *him*. She made him sound like a total arrogant bastard and recommended that Lizzie keep looking until she found a man worthy of her, a piece of advice which sent Sebasten straight into an irrational rage.

Of course Lizzie wasn't about to race off on the hunt for another man! She was in love with him, wasn't she? But since their affair was over, ought he not to be keen for her to find a replacement for him? Just thinking about Lizzie in another man's bed drove Sebasten, who ate a healthy breakfast every morning without fail, from the breakfast table before he had had anything more than a single cup of black coffee.

He went out for a ride, returned filthy and soaked after a sudden downpour and got into the shower. After that, he tried to work but he could not concentrate. Why shouldn't he be concerned about Lizzie? He asked himself defensively then. Wasn't he human? And why shouldn't he give her the Mercedes and the diamonds

back? After all, what was he to do with them? She was
having a hard time and possibly getting back the pos-
sessions which she had been forced to sell would cheer
her up a little.

As for her father, Maurice Denton, *well*, Sebasten
was starting to cherish a very low opinion of a man he
had never met. Family were supposed to stick together
through thick and thin and forgive mistakes. Instead the
wretched man had deprived his daughter of all means
of support when it was entirely *his* fault that she was
quite unequal to the task of supporting herself in the
style to which her shortsighted parent had encouraged
her to become accustomed.

Inflamed on Lizzie's behalf by that reflection, Sebasten snatched up his car keys and arranged for the
Mercedes to be driven back to London to be delivered.
He could not wait long enough for his own car to be
driven round to the front of the house and he startled
his staff by striding through the rear entrance to the
garages and extracting his Lamborghini for himself.

After attending church, guiltily aware that it was her
first visit since she had left home, Lizzie wondered why
her father and Felicity were absent from their usual pew
and realised that they must be spending the weekend at
the cottage. Buying a newspaper before she went back
to the bedsit, Lizzie read what Patsy Hewitt had written about that evening at Pomeroy Place and assumed
that the journalist had decided to take a feminist stance
for a change. She frowned when she perused the final
cliff-hanging comment that advised readers to watch
that space for a bigger story soon to break and then as-

sumed that it could be nothing to do with either her or Sebasten.

Studying Sebasten's lean, dark, devastating face in the photo beside the article, her eyes stung like mad. Angry with herself, she crushed the newspaper up in a convulsive gesture and rammed it in the bin. Then she opened the post that she had ignored the day before and paled at the sight of a payment request from an exclusive boutique where she had a monthly account. She had barely had enough cash left in her bank account to cover travel expenses and eat until the end of the month, when she would receive her first pay cheque. She would have to ask for a little more time to clear the bill. Furthermore, she would have to exert bone and sinew to try and find part-time evening or weekend employment so that she could keep up her financial commitments.

The first Lizzie knew of the mysterious reappearance of the Mercedes she had sold was the arrival of a chauffeur at her door. 'Miss Denton...your car keys,' he said, handing them to her.

'Sorry?' Lizzie stared at him in bewilderment. 'I don't own a car.'

'Compliments of Mr Contaxis. The Merc is parked outside.'

Before Lizzie even got her breath back, the man had clattered back down the stairs again.

Compliments of Mr Contaxis? What on earth was going on? In a daze, Lizzie left her room and went outside. There sat the same black glossy Mercedes four-wheel-drive which her father had bought her for her twenty-second birthday. She couldn't credit the evidence of her own eyes and she walked round it in slow motion, her mind in a feverish whirl of incomprehension.

Where had Sebasten got her car from and why would he give it back to her? Why would a guy who had dumped her only thirty-six hours earlier suddenly present her with a car worth thousands of pounds? Oh, yes, she knew that—technically speaking—she had dumped him first but in her heart she accepted that she had only got the courage to do that because she had known that he intended to do it to her if she did not.

Having reclaimed the diamonds from the safe in his town house, Sebasten arrived on Lizzie's doorstep, feeling much better than he had felt earlier in the day, indeed, feeling very much that he was doing the right thing.

Lizzie opened the door. The sheer vibrant, gorgeous appeal of Sebasten in sleek designer garments that exuded class and expense exploded on her with predictable effect. Just seeing him hurt. Seeing him dare to *almost* smile was also the cruel equivalent of a knife plunging beneath her tender skin. Even an almost smile was an insult, a symptom of his ruthless, cruel, nasty character and his essential detachment from the rest of humanity.

Lizzie dealt him a seething glance. 'You get that car taken away right now!' she told him. 'I don't know what you think you're playing at but I don't want it.'

Engaged in looking Lizzie over in a head-to-toe careful appraisal that left not an inch of her tall, shapely figure unchecked and thinking that he might like the way turquoise set off her beautiful hair but that she did something remarkable for the colour red as well, Sebasten froze like a fox cornered in a chicken coop and attempted to regroup.

'I don't want your car either…it's no use to me,' he pointed out in fast recovery, closing the door and, without even thinking about what he was doing, leaning his big, powerful length back against that door so that she couldn't open it again.

'Exactly what are you doing with a car that I sold?' Lizzie demanded shakily, temper flashing through her in direct proportion to her disturbed emotions.

'I bought it back for you weeks ago…as well as these.' Sebasten set down the little pile of jewellery boxes on the table. 'I had you watched the first week by one of my bodyguards and I knew everything that you did.'

'You had me watched?' Lizzie echoed in even deeper shock and recoil as she flipped open a couple of lids to confirm the contents and the sparkle of diamonds greeted her. 'You bought my jewellery as well? *Why?*'

Sebasten had been hoping to evade that question. 'At the time I planned to win your trust and impress you with my generosity.'

'You utter bastard,' Lizzie framed with an agony of reproach in her clear green gaze. 'So that's why you offered me the use of an apartment! You thought you could tempt me with your rotten money. Well, you were way off beam then and you're even more out of line *now*—'

'I just want you to take back what's yours,' Sebasten slotted in with fierce determination.

'Why? So that you can feel better? So that you can *buy* your way out of having a conscience about what you did to me?' Lizzie condemned in a shaking undertone. 'Don't you even have the sensitivity to see that you're insulting me?'

'How…am I insulting you?' Sebasten queried between gritted teeth, for he was in no way receiving the response he had expected and he wondered why women always had to make simple matters complicated. He was trying to make her life easier. What was wrong with that?

'By making the assumption that I'm the kind of woman who would accept expensive gifts from a guy like you! How dare you do that? Do you think I was your mistress or something that you have to pay me off?' Lizzie was so worked up with hurt and anger that her voice rose to a shrill crescendo.

'No, but I never bought you a single thing during the whole time we were together,' Sebasten pointed out, one half of his brain urging him to take her in his arms and soothe her, the other half fully engaged in stamping out that dangerous temptation to touch her again.

'I suppose that's how you get so many women…you pay them with gifts for putting up with you!' Lizzie slung fiercely, fighting back the tears prickling at the backs of her eyes.

Determined not to react to that base accusation, Sebasten was staring down at the bill from the boutique that lay on the table and then studying the little column of figures added up on the sheet of paper beside it. Was she *that* broke?

'I could give you a loan. You would repay it when you could,' he heard himself say.

Lizzie wrenched open the door and said unsteadily. 'Go away…'

'It doesn't have to be like this.' Sebasten hovered, full of angry conflict and growing frustration. 'I came here with good motivations and no intention of upsetting you.'

Lizzie scooped up the jewel boxes and planted them in his hands along with the car keys. 'And don't you dare leave that car outside. I can't feed a parking meter for it on my income.'

'Lizzie—?'

'You *stay* away from me!'

'All I wanted to know was that you were OK!' Sebasten growled.

'Of course I'm OK. A visit from you is as good as a cure!' Lizzie hurled, her quivering voice breaking on that last assurance.

Sebasten departed. He should have thought about her not being able to afford to run a car, he reflected, choosing to focus on that rather than anything else she had said. However, the disturbing image of her distraught face and the shadows that lay like bruises beneath her eyes travelled with him. She didn't look well. Was he responsible for that? For the first time since childhood Sebasten felt helpless, and it was terrifying. He could not believe how stubborn and proud she was. He saw Lizzie in terms of warmth and sunlight, softness and affection, and then he tried to equate that belated acknowledgement with the character that Ingrid had endowed her with.

Lizzie threw herself face down on the bed and sobbed into the pillow until she was empty of tears. What must her distress be doing to her baby? Guilt cut deep into her. She rested a hand against her tummy and offered the tiny being inside her a silent apology for her lack of control and told herself that she would do better in the future.

As for Sebasten, did she seem so pitiful that he even had to take her pride away from her by offering her a loan as well as the car and the diamonds? Why had she ever told him that she loved him? And why was he acting the way he was when all that she had ever known about him suggested that a declaration of love ought to drive him fast in the opposite direction? How dared he come and see her and make her feel all over again what she had lost when he wasn't worth having in the first place?

When was she planning to tell him about the baby? She drifted off to weary sleep on the admission that she was not yet strong enough to face another confrontational scene.

CHAPTER EIGHT

ON MONDAY morning, Sebasten thought his personal staff were all very quiet in his radius and he assumed that the *Sunday Globe* gossip column had done the rounds of the office.

He swore that he would not think about Lizzie. At eleven he found himself accessing her personnel file. When he discovered that she had been reprimanded for the printing of four hundred copies of a photo of himself, all hope of concentration was vanquished. He was annoyed that he liked the idea of those photos.

Sebasten did not believe in love. He was crazy about Lizzie's body...and her smile...and her hair. He had enjoyed the way she chattered too. She talked a lot, which in the past was a trait which had irritated him in other women, but Lizzie's chatter was unusually interesting. He had also liked the easy way she would reach out and touch him; nothing wrong with that either, was there? It didn't mean he was infatuated or anything of that nature, merely that he could still appreciate her good points.

On the other side of the equation, she was a rampant liar and she *must* have slept with his half-brother and he could not work out how he had managed to block that awareness out for so long. At the same time, he could no longer credit the dramatic contention that Lizzie had driven Connor to his death. Ingrid had needed someone to blame. But Connor had got behind the wheel of his car, drunk. That car crash had been the tragic result of his half-brother's recklessness and love of high speed.

At that point, without any prior thought on the subject that he was aware of, Sebasten decided to settle that outstanding bill he had seen in Lizzie's bedsit. She couldn't prevent him from doing that, could she?

That same day, Lizzie went into work and found herself the target of covert stares and embarrassing whispers. Only then did she recall the article that had been in the newspaper the previous day. In a saccharine-sweet enquiry, Milly Sharpe asked her where she would like to work and Lizzie reddened to her hairline.

'Any place,' Lizzie answered tautly and ended up at a desk in a corner where she was given nothing like enough to keep her occupied.

She saw then that continuing employment in Sebasten's company could well be less than comfortable for her. During her lunch break, she called into the employment agency across the road from the CI building and enjoyed a far more productive chat with one of the recruitment consultants there than she had received at the establishment which Sebasten had recommended a month earlier.

'You have a great deal of insider knowledge and experience in the PR field,' the consultant commented. 'I'm sure we can place you in a PR firm. It would be a junior position to begin with, and of course you're entitled to basic maternity leave, but if you prove yourself you could gain quite rapid advancement.'

On Tuesday, Sebasten took sudden note of how very long it had been since he had staged a meeting with the accounts team on the sixth floor and he instructed his secretary to make good that oversight. That Lizzie worked on that floor was not a fact he allowed to enter his mind once. On Wednesday, he was infuriated by the announcement that the accounts meeting could not be staged until Friday, as key personnel were away on a training course.

On Thursday, Ingrid phoned Sebasten and demanded to know if it was true that he had been seeing Liza Denton. Sebasten said it was but that it was a private matter not open to discussion, and if Ingrid's shock at that snub was perceptible Sebasten was equally disconcerted by the very real anger that leapt through him when the older woman then made an adverse comment about Lizzie. On Friday, Sebasten arrived at the office even earlier than was his norm, cleared his desk by nine, strode about the top floor unsettling his entire staff and checked his watch on average of once every ten minutes.

On the sixth floor, Lizzie's week had felt endless to her. She was craving Sebasten as though he were a life-saving drug and hating herself for being so weak. She knew she had to tell him that she was pregnant, but while she still felt so vulnerable she was reluctant to deal with that issue. Mid-week, during the extended lunch break she hastily arranged, she had an interview for a position with a PR firm but had no idea whether or not she was in with a chance. On Friday morning, Milly Sharpe greeted her arrival at work with a strange little smile and put her on the reception desk.

When Sebasten strode out of the lift, the first person he saw was Lizzie. Lizzie, clad in a yellow dress as bright as sunshine. He collided with her startled green eyes and walked right past the senior accounts executive waiting to greet him without even noticing the man.

'Lizzie…' Sebasten said.

Taken aback by his sudden appearance, Lizzie nodded in slow motion as though to confirm her identity while her gaze welded to him with electrified intensity. His sheer physical impact on her drove out all else. She drank him in, heart racing at the sudden buzz in the atmosphere and there was not a thought in her head that was worthy of an angry, bitter woman. His luxuriant black hair gleamed below the lights and her fingers tingled with longing. His brilliant golden eyes, semi-screened by his spiky lashes, set up a chain reaction deep down inside her, awakening the wicked hunger that melted her in secret places and made her tremble.

'So…' His mind a wasteland, his hormones reacting with a dangerous enthusiasm that made lingering an impossibility, Sebasten snatched in a deep, sharp breath. 'How are you?'

'OK…' Lizzie managed to frame after considerable effort to come up with that single word.

'I have a meeting…' Sebasten swung away, her image refreshed to vibrance in his memory.

As he strode down the corridor, Lizzie blinked and emerged from the spell he had cast. A slow, deep, painful tide of colour washed over her fair complexion. A burst of stifled giggles sounded from the direction of Milly Sharpe's office, which overlooked Reception, and her heart sank. Had she somehow shown herself up? Well, what else could she have done when she had just sat staring at Sebasten like a lovesick schoolgirl? Squirming in an agony of self-loathing and shame, Lizzie decided she would not be around when Sebasten emerged from his meeting again.

That afternoon the recruitment agency called and informed her that Robbins, the PR firm, were keen for her to start work with them the following week. Deep relief filled Lizzie to overflowing and she accepted the offer. Away from Contaxis International, she would be better able to put her life together again and possibly it would be easier to face telling Sebasten what he would eventually *have* to be told.

On Friday evening, for the sixth night in a row, Sebasten stayed home and brooded. He didn't want to go out and he didn't want company.

Lizzie called her father for a chat. He seemed very preoccupied and apologised several times for losing the thread of the conversation. She asked what he had decided to do about Mrs Baines, the housekeeper, whom Felicity had wanted dismissed.

Maurice Denton released a heavy sigh. 'I offered Mrs Baines a generous settlement in recognition of the number of years she'd worked for us. She accepted it but she was very bitter and walked out the same day. Felicity was delighted but I must confess that the whole business left a nasty taste in my mouth.'

'How is Felicity?'

'Very edgy...' the older man admitted with palpable concern. 'She bursts into tears if I even *mention* the baby and when I suggested that *I* ought to have a word with the gynaecologist she's been attending, she became hysterical!'

Lizzie raised her brows and winced in dismay. Was her stepmother heading for a nervous breakdown? All over again, she felt the guilty burden of the secret knowledge she was withholding from her father. Then she wondered how Maurice Denton, never the most liberal of men and very set in his traditional values, would react to a daughter giving birth to an illegitimate child and paled. Such an event might well sever her relationship with her father forever...

On Sunday morning, Sebasten again lifted the *Sunday Globe*, which he had always regarded as a rubbish newspaper aimed at intellectually-challenged readers. However, he only wanted to check out that Patsy Hewitt had not picked up any other information relating either to himself or Lizzie. The front page was adorned with the usual lurid headline offering the unsavoury details of some sleazy affair, he noted, and only at that point did he recognise that the article was adorned with a photo of Connor.

And Sebasten was gripped to that double-page spread inside the paper with a spellbound intensity that would have delighted Patsy Hewitt, who had found ample opportunity to employ her trademark venom after doing her homework on Lizzie's stepmother, Felicity Denton. Mrs Baines, the Denton housekeeper, had sold her insider story of Felicity's affair for a handsome price and Connor, even departed, still had sufficient news value to make the front page with his once tangled lovelife.

Lizzie was still in bed asleep when her mobile phone began ringing. Getting out of bed to answer it, she was bemused to realise that it was a former friend calling to express profuse apologies for misjudging her over Connor.

'What are you talking about?' she mumbled.

'Haven't you seen this morning's *Sunday Globe* yet?'

Learning that Mrs Baines had sold her story of Felicity's affair with Connor shook Lizzie rigid. No longer did she need to wonder why her stepmother had been so eager to get rid of the family housekeeper: Felicity had been justifiably afraid that Mrs Baines knew too much. Had Connor visited the Denton home as well? Lizzie wrinkled her nose with distaste. The housekeeper had probably known about that affair long before she herself did.

Over an hour later, Lizzie arrived at her family home to find it besieged by the Press. A half-dozen cameras flashed in her direction and she had to fight her way past to get indoors. Her father was sitting behind closed curtains in a state of severe shock.

CHAPTER NINE

'FELICITY walked out late last night. A friend in the media phoned to warn her about the story appearing in the *Sunday Globe*,' Maurice Denton shared in a shattered tone as Lizzie paced the room, too restive to stay still. 'Felicity isn't coming back. She made it clear that she wants a divorce.'

'But…but what about the baby?' Lizzie pressed, disconcerted by the speed and dexterity of her stepmother's departure from the marital home.

The older man regarded her with hollow eyes. In the space of days, he seemed to have aged. 'There *is* no baby…'

Lizzie's mouth fell wide. 'You mean, Felicity's lost it…oh, *no*!'

'There never *was* a baby. She wasn't pregnant. It was a crazy lie aimed at persuading you not to tell me about her affair with Connor.' Her parent shook his greying head with a dulled wonderment that he could not conceal. 'Felicity thought that if she *tried*, she could get pregnant easily and then pretend she'd mixed up her dates. But it didn't happen: she didn't conceive. As time went on and she was forced to pretend to go to pre-natal appointments she decided that she would have to fake a miscarriage...thank heaven, I was spared that melo-drama!'

'Do you think...er...Felicity's having a breakdown?' Lizzie suggested worriedly. 'I mean, maybe it was one of those false pregnancies that come from *genuine* long-ing for a baby—'

'No.' Maurice Denton's rebuttal was flat, bitter. 'Last night, she informed me that she didn't even like children and that she was fed up not only with the whole insane pretence that she had foisted on us all but also sick and tired of living with a man old enough to be her father! She wasn't even sorry for the damage she did to you, never mind me!'

Lizzie flinched. 'I'm so sorry...'

'Perhaps when a man of fifty-five marries a woman more than thirty years younger he deserves what he gets. Why didn't you come to me about her and the Morgan boy?'

'I...I told myself I couldn't tell you for the baby's sake...but possibly, I just couldn't *face* the responsibil-ity.' Listening to the mayhem of raised voices outside the front door, Lizzie said gently, 'Look, maybe the re-porters will go away if I make a statement to them... what do you think?'

'Do as you think best,' Maurice Denton advised heavily. 'Felicity is gone and it can only be Felicity or you that those vultures are interested in. I've never had much of a public profile.'

Lizzie went outside to address the assembled jour-nalist and parry some horrendous questions of the low-est possible taste. 'Was Morgan sleeping with both you and your stepmother?'

'Connor and I were only ever friends,' Lizzie declared with complete calm.

'What about you and Sebasten Contaxis?' she was asked.

'Oh, I'm *not* friends with him!' Lizzie asserted without hesitation and there was a burst of appreciative laughter at that response.

It was only later while she was making a snack for her father that she truly appreciated that her own name had been cleared. Would Sebasten find out? Sooner or later, he would discover that he had targeted the wrong woman. How would he react? But why should she care? What he had confessed to doing was beyond all forgiveness. She looked into the fridge, where a jar of sun-dried tomatoes sat, and her tastebuds watered. Sun-dried tomatoes followed by ice-cream. She shut the fridge again in haste, unnerved by recent food cravings that struck her as bizarre.

An hour later, Sebasten sprang out of his Lamborghini outside the Morgan household in the leafy suburbs. A lingering solitary cameraman took a picture of him. Waving back the bodyguards ready to leap into action and prevent that photo being taken, Sebasten smiled. Sebasten had been smiling ever since he read Patsy Hewitt's hatchet job on Lizzie's stepmother. The wicked stepmother, a typecast figure and a perfect match to Sebasten's own prejudices. He could not imagine how he had contrived not to register that Lizzie's father had a very much younger wife who bore more than a passing resemblance to the evil queen in *Snow White*. He could not imagine how it had not once crossed his mind that Lizzie might be engaged in protecting a member of her own family.

'Lizzie's not friends with you, mate,' the cameraman warned Sebasten.

'Watch this space,' Sebasten advised with all the sizzling, lethal confidence that lay at the heart of his forceful character. He just felt happy, crazy happy, and all he could think about was reclaiming Lizzie.

'She's a gutsy girl…I wouldn't count my chickens.'

Sebasten just laughed and leant on the doorbell and rattled the door knocker for good measure.

CHAPTER TEN

IT WAS very unfortunate for Sebasten that Lizzie had watched his arrival from the safe, shadowy depths of the dining room.

Even at a distance, the slashing brilliance of his smile rocked Lizzie where she stood. He was so gorgeous but that he should *dare* to smile, sure of his welcome, it seemed, before he even saw her, lacerated her pride, fired her resentment and drove home the suspicion that he lacked any sense of remorse. He was tough, ruthless and hard and no relationship with Sebasten would ever go any place where she wanted it to go, she acknowledged with agonised regret. He had already spelt that out in terms no sane woman could ignore.

Hadn't she already got through the first week of being without him? She would get over him eventually, wouldn't she? It dawned on her that on some strange inner level she had not the slightest doubt that Sebasten was about to suggest a reconciliation and that shook her. But once she announced that she had already conceived his child and in addition had every intention of raising that child, Sebasten would surrender any such notion fast. So really, what was she worrying about?

Sebasten had killed his smile by the time Lizzie opened the door. 'Come in…'

'I suggest we go out, so that we can talk,' Sebasten murmured levelly. 'I imagine your family aren't in the mood for visitors today.'

'Only my father is here and he's having a nap in the library.' A quiver assailing her at his proximity, Lizzie pushed wide the door into the drawing room.

'Where's the...' Sebasten bit back the blunt five-letter word brimming on his lips in the very nick of time and substituted, 'your stepmother?'

'Already gone,' Lizzie admitted, tight-mouthed with tension. 'They'll be getting a divorce.'

'Your father's got his head screwed on,' Sebasten asserted with an outstanding absence of sensitivity. 'Booting her straight out the door was the right thing to do.'

'Actually Felicity left under her own steam,' Lizzie declared, making the humiliating connection that she had once been booted out of Sebasten's life with the same efficiency that he was so keen to commend.

'Even better...she won't collect half so much in the divorce settlement,' Sebasten imparted with authority.

'Right at this moment, my father has more to think about than his bank balance!' Lizzie hissed in outrage. 'He's devastated.'

'I was thinking of you, *not* your father. Not very pleasant for you, having to put up with a woman like that in the family,' Sebasten contended, allowing himself to study her taut, pale face, the strain in her unhappy eyes, and then removing his attention again before he was tempted into making the cardinal error of a premature assumption that forgiveness was on the table and dragging her into his arms. 'Why the blazes didn't you spill the beans on your stepmother weeks ago?'

'I believed she was pregnant with my little brother or sister…only it turns out now that she was lying about that to protect herself and keep me quiet.' A tight little laugh fell from Lizzie's lips as she thought of the baby that she carried. It seemed so ironic that the conception which Felicity must initially have been desperate to achieve should have come Lizzie's way instead.

'It sounds like she was off the wall. If it's any consolation, Ingrid Morgan is shattered too and feeling very guilty about the way she treated you,' Sebasten revealed. 'She called me this morning.'

'I don't hold any spite against Connor's mother.' Taut as a bowstring, Lizzie hovered by the window.

'I don't understand why you couldn't tell me the *whole* truth. If you had named your father's wife, I would never have disbelieved your explanation and I could have been trusted with that information.'

Lizzie noted without great surprise that Sebasten was playing hardball and landing her with a share of the blame for *his* refusal to have the smallest faith in her. 'I'm not so sure of that. You and your old friend Ingrid wanted your pound of flesh, regardless of who got hurt in the process!'

Sebasten did not like the morbid tone of that response at all. 'I misjudged you and I'll make it up to you.'

'Was that an apology?'

'*Theo mou*…give me time to get there on my own!' Sebasten urged in a sudden volatile surge that disconcerted her and let her appreciate that he was not quite as cool, calm and collected as he appeared. 'I am sorry, truly, deeply sorry.'

'I can't be,' Lizzie confided shakily.

'I'm not asking *you* to be sorry,' Sebasten pointed out in some bewilderment, wondering whether the shine of tears in her eyes was a promising sign that the very first humble apology he had made to a woman in his entire life had had the right effect.

'You see, I *can't* be sorry that you misjudged me because if I hadn't found that out, I would never have discovered what a ruthless, conscience-free louse you are,' Lizzie completed in a wobbly but driven voice.

Sebasten spread lean brown hands in a natural expression of appeal. 'But I'll never be like that with you again,' he protested. 'I want you back in my life.'

'Oh, I'm sure you'll find another dumb woman to take my place,' Lizzie snapped out brittly and turned her back on him altogether while she fought to rein back the tears threatening her.

'Yes, I could if I wanted to but there's one small problem...I only want *you*.'

In his bed, that was all, Lizzie reflected painfully, her throat thick with tears. She forced herself back round to face him again and tilted her chin. 'I think you'll give up on that ambition when I tell you what I have to tell you.'

'Nothing could make me give up on you,' Sebasten swore, moving forward and reaching for her without warning to tug her forward into his arms.

Lizzie only meant to stay there a second but Sebasten had come to the conclusion that action was likely to be much more effective than words that appeared to be getting him precisely nowhere. He framed her flushed face with two lean hands and gazed down into her distraught green eyes. 'Why are you looking at me like that?' he was moved to demand in reproach. 'I will never hurt you again.'

Trembling all over, Lizzie parted dry lips and muttered, 'I'm pregnant…'

Pregnant? That announcement fell on a male quite unprepared for that kind of news. Sebasten tensed, not even sure he had heard her say what she had just said. 'Pregnant?' he echoed, his hands dropping from her.

'Yes,' Lizzie confirmed chokily.

'Pregnant…' Sebasten said again as though it was a word that had never come his way before and innate caution was already telling him to shut up and not say another single sentence. But he was so shattered by the concept of Lizzie being pregnant that not all the caution in the world could keep him quiet. 'Is it Connor's?' he shot at her rawly, savage jealousy gripping him in an instant vice.

Watching the flare of volatile gold in his stunning eyes, the fierce cast of his superb bone-structure, Lizzie was backing away from him and she only stilled when her shoulders met the china cabinet behind her. 'No, it is not your half-brother's child. Even Connor was not low enough to try to get me into bed while he was making mad, passionate love to my stepmother behind my back. I never slept with Connor,' Lizzie spelt out shakily.

Sebasten recalled his own belief in her inexperience the first night he had shared with her but Sebasten was always stubborn and not quite ready in the state of numb shock he was in to move straight in and embrace the possibility of a child he had never expected to have. 'How do I know that for sure?'

Temper leapt with startling abruptness from the sheer height of Lizzie's tension. 'You're the only lover I've ever had…is it *my* fault you were too busy taking advantage of me to even notice that I was a virgin?'

'I didn't take advantage of you and if you're telling me the truth you're the only virgin I've ever slept with,' Sebasten launched back, playing for time while he mulled over what she had said but all his anger ebbing at miraculous speed. Even so, that did not prevent him from finding another issue. 'You said you were protected.'

'I was sick the next morning…it might have been that or it might just be that I fall into the tiny failure-rate percentage…but the point *is*,' Lizzie framed afresh, 'I am pregnant and it's yours.'

'Mine…' Sebasten was now unusually pale at the very thought of what he saw as the enormous responsibility of a baby. All he had to do was think about his own nightmare childhood, the misery inflicted on him by self-preoccupied adults who left him to the care of unsupervised staff when it suited them and isolated him in boarding schools, where he had also been forgotten with ease. Nobody knew better than he that even great wealth was no protection when it came to a child's needs.

'I appreciate that this is a shock for you,' Lizzie conceded when she could hear that ghastly silence no longer. 'But I should also add that I'm going to *have* this baby—'

Emerging from his unpleasant recollections. Sebasten frowned at her in complete innocence of her meaning. 'What else would you do?'

Silenced by that demand, Lizzie blinked.

'I suppose we'll have to make the best of it,' Sebasten breathed, squaring his broad shoulders in the face of his inner conviction that life as he knew it had just been slaughtered. But much of his gloom lifted on the sudden realisation that, of course, Lizzie would come in tow with the baby. With Lizzie back in his life and him ensuring in a discreet way that the baby was never, ever neglected for even a moment, he could surely rise to the challenge?

'And what would making the best of it...entail?' Lizzie prompted thinly.

'Sebasten expelled his pent-up breath in an impatient hiss. 'Obviously, I'll have to marry you. It's my own fault. I should've taken precautions too that night but we're stuck with the consequences and I'm a Contaxis...not the sort of bastard who tries to shirk his responsibilities!'

During that telling speech, Lizzie almost burst into a rage as big as a bonfire. She went lurching from total shock at the speed with which he mentioned marriage when she had never dreamt he might even whisper that fatal word. Then she truly listened and what she heard inflamed her beyond belief.

'I don't want to marry you—'

'You've got no choice—'

'Watch my lips—I do not *want* to marry you!'

Sebasten dealt her a grim appraisal in which his powerful personality loomed large. 'Of course you do. Right now, we've got a bigger problem than me being a ruth-less, conscience-free louse!' he countered with sardonic bite. 'Can we please focus on the baby issue?'

'You don't want to marry me…you don't want the baby either!' Lizzie flung at him in condemnation, feel-ing as though her heart was breaking inside her and hat-ing him for not being able to feel what she felt.

'I want you and I'll get used to the idea of the baby,' Sebasten declared.

Intending to show him out the front door, Lizzie yanked the drawing-room door wide and then froze. Her father was standing in the hall, his face a stiff mask of disbelief. It was obvious that he had heard enough to appreciate that she was carrying Sebasten's child. He looked at her with all his disappointment written in his eyes and it was too much to her after the day she had already endured. With a stifled sob, Lizzie fled for the sanctuary of her old apartment in the stable block.

Sebasten could see 'potential ally' writ large in his future father-in-law's horror at the revelation that his unmarried daughter was expecting a baby. 'I'm sorry you had to hear the news like that. Naturally, Lizzie's upset by the circumstances but I'm just keen to get the wedding organised.'

Maurice Denton was relieved by that forthright dec-laration. Unfreezing, almost grateful for a distraction from his own personal crisis, he offered Sebasten a drink. Sebasten accepted the offer.

He had never been more on edge: he felt as if Lizzie was playing games with him and that was not what he expected from her. It took time to concede that he might have been a little too frank about his reactions and that perhaps lying in his teeth would have gone down better. After a third drink to Sebasten's one, Maurice informed Sebasten that should be himself live until he was ninety-nine he had no hope of ever hearing a marriage proposal couched in less attractive terms. He then asked his son-in-law-to-be if he was shy about being romantic.

Sebasten tried not to cringe at the question but he was honest in his response: he had never made a romantic gesture in his entire life.

'I think you'd better get on that learning curve fast,' Lizzie's father advised before going on to entertain Sebasten with stories of how devoted a mother Lizzie had been to her dolls and how much she had always adored fussing round babies.

While the older man began to find some solace not only in those happier memories of the past but also in the prospect of a grandchild after the humiliation of his own disappointed hopes of another child, Sebasten began to imagine the baby as a miniature version of Lizzie tending to her dolls and relax and even warm to the prospect.

A copy of Lizzie's birth certificate having been supplied helpfully by her parent, Sebasten drove off to apply for a special licence that would enable him to marry Lizzie within the week. Mindful of that galling advice about romance, he went on to pay a visit to a world-famous jewellery store. He chose the most beautiful rare diamond on offer and a matching wedding ring.

Late that evening, Sebasten returned to the Denton household as confident as he had been of his reception earlier in the day, only on this second occasion convinced he was infinitely better prepared to deliver exactly what was expected of him. Lizzie could hardly doubt the strength of his commitment to marrying her when he had already made *all* the arrangements for the wedding on his own.

That afternoon, Lizzie had had a good cry about Sebasten's crass and wounding insensitivity. She had tried hard to respect his honesty but in point of fact it had hurt too much for her to do that. She might love him but there were times when furious frustration and pain totally swallowed up that love. With the best will in the world, how could she marry a guy who didn't want a wife and could only stick children at a distance or inanimate on a painted canvas? No crystal ball was required to foresee the disaster that would result from Sebasten making himself do what he had always sworn he would not do.

Sebasten took the steps up to Lizzie's apartment three at a time. The door wasn't shut and he frowned. It was dangerous to be so careless of personal safety in a big city. She really *did* need him around. He let himself in. Lizzie was curled up on a big, squashy sofa, fast asleep. She was wearing a pale pink silk wrap, another colour to add to the already wide spectrum of shades which Sebasten considered framed Lizzie to perfection. He crouched down by her side.

Lifting up her limp hand, he threaded the engagement ring onto her finger. Now she was labelled *his* for every other man to see. As that awareness dawned on him, Sebasten finally saw the point of engagements. She got the little ring, he got to post the much more important hands-off-she's-mine giant ring of steel. He liked that. This romantic stuff? Easy as falling off a log, Sebasten decided.

With a sleepy sigh, Lizzie opened her eyes and focused on Sebasten and thought she was back in bed with him again, which she very often *was* in her most secret dreams. Enchanted by the pagan gold glitter of his intense gaze, she let appreciative fingers drift up to trace a high, angular cheekbone. He caught her hand in his and captured her lips in a sensual, searching exploration that was an erotic wake-up call to every sense she possessed. She leant up the better to taste him, breathe in the achingly familiar scent that was uniquely his, close her arms round his neck so that she could sink greedy fingers into the depths of his luxuriant black hair.

Sebasten made a low, sexy sound of encouragement deep in his throat. Scooping her up, he sank back with her cradled in his arms and let his tongue dip in a provocative slide between her lips. Lizzie jerked and strained up to him, wanting, needing, possessed by helpless excitement and hunger for more.

'You still want me, *pethi mou*,' Sebasten husked, pausing to trail his mouth in a tantalising caress down the line of her long, elegant neck. 'But I can't stay long. Your father has been very understanding and tolerant but I won't risk causing offence.'

Emerging for the first time since she had wakened to proper awareness, Lizzie snatched in a quivering gasp of shame and embarrassment: she had fallen like an overripe plum into Sebasten's ready hands. 'This shouldn't be happening,' she bit out shakily and flew upright to smooth down her wrap.

Only then did she register the weight of the ring now

adorning her hand. In disbelief, she raised her fingers to stare at the fabulous solitaire diamond sparkling in the lamplight.

'Like it?' Sebasten lounged back on the sofa with the indolent, expectant air of a male bracing himself to withstand fawning feminine approbation.

'What is it?'

'You really need to be told?'

Lizzie jerked her chin in an affirmative nod, for she could not credit that the male she had flatly refused to marry could have bought her an engagement ring and what was more put in on her finger without her knowledge or agreement.

'It matches the wedding ring. I got it too.' Well-aware of her shaken silence and proud of that seeming achievement, Sebasten rose to his full height so that she could fling herself at him and hug him.

'You...*did*!' Lizzie parroted, a swelling forming in her tight chest that she did not immediately recognise as rage.

'In fact, I've been extremely busy,' Sebasten extended in his rich dark drawl. 'I've got a special licence. I've got the church booked and a top-flight wedding-planners outfit burning the midnight oil on the finer details even as we speak. You have nothing to do but show up looking gorgeous on Saturday—'

'You mean...I get to pick my own dress?'

'I contacted an Italian designer...they're flying over a team on Wednesday with a selection for you.'

'Oh...*this* Saturday?' Momentarily Lizzie's rage took a back seat to shock at the sheer level of organisation that had taken place behind her back and the news that her own wedding was to be staged in just six days' time.

'Your father agreed that we shouldn't hang around.'

'Did he really?' Lizzie queried in a rather high-pitched tone. 'Sebasten…cast your mind back to my answer to your declaration that we should marry.'

'You said no but I knew you didn't mean it,' Sebasten informed her.

'D-did you?' Lizzie's response shook with the force of her feelings but she looked again at the ring on her engagement finger. Her eyes stung and she spun away, remembering the guy who had hired decorators to leave her free to dine with him. He did what *he* thought best and if that meant refusing to credit her refusal, using her own father as back-up and going ahead and arranging a wedding all on his own, he was more than equal to the challenge.

And more than anything else in the world she would have loved to have faith in that blazing confidence he wore like an aura and rise to that same challenge. But he didn't love her, was only offering to marry her because she was pregnant and he had *never* wanted a child. Where would they be in a few months' time when she was more in love and more dependent on him than she was even now and he discovered that good intentions were not enough? He wouldn't find her so attractive once her slender figure vanished. He might even be downright repulsed by her fecund shape. He might get bored, he might even stray and she would be destroyed…absolutely, utterly destroyed by such a rejection.

'I can't do it,' Lizzie whispered.

Sebasten linked strong arms round her and slowly turned her round. 'Bridal nerves,' he told her with a determined smile.

'I can't do it,' Lizzie whispered again, white as milk. 'I *can't* marry you.'

Sebasten freed her and took a step back. He was making a real effort to control the stark anger threatening his control but he could not understand what was the matter with her. He had done every single thing he could think of to please her and she had not voiced one word of appreciation. She had not even appeared to register his enthusiasm for something he had never, ever thought he would do.

'The baby *must* have the Contaxis name and my protection,' he spelt out. Eyes dark as the night sky pinned to her taut, trouble face. 'That's not negotiable.'

'Commands don't cut it with me,' Lizzie snapped, feeling the full onslaught of his powerful personality focused on her and rebelling.

'Then tell me what *does* because I sure as hell have no idea!' Sebasten raked back at her in sudden dark fury.

Trembling, Lizzie whirled away again. Although she loved him, she had a deep instinctive need to keep herself safe from further hurt and disillusionment. He had too much power over her, and how could she trust him when only his sense of responsibility had persuaded him to offer marriage? She saw the sense in his insistence that they marry to give their baby his name, for the law as it stood did not recognise less formal relationships. Yet to marry him and live with him as a wife felt like a giant step too far for her at that moment.

If *only* there was something in between, a halfway house that could answer her needs and the baby's without trapping Sebasten into immediate domesticity and commitment before he could judge whether or not he could meet those demands in the long term. A halfway house, she thought in desperation, and then the solution came to her in a positive brainstorm.

'I want an answer,' Sebasten told her fiercely.

A flush on her cheeks, excitement in her eyes, for Lizzie was eager to come up with a blueprint that would allow her to marry him. 'I have it. We don't live together…you buy me a house of my own!'

'Say that again…no, *don't*.' Sebasten warned, studying her with laser-like intensity, shimmering golden eyes locked to her in disbelief.

'But don't you see it? It would be perfect!' Lizzie told him with an enthusiasm that could only inflame. 'You could visit whenever you liked.'

'Really?' Sebasten's bitten-out response was not quite level while he wondered if she was feeling all right, but he was reluctant to risk asking that question in case she took it as an insult.

'We would each hold on to more of our own separate lives than married couples usually do. You'd have your business and I'd have my new PR job—'

'What new PR job?' Sebasten interrupted faster than the speed of light.

'I'm starting tomorrow—'

'But you're pregnant—'

'Pregnant women work in PR too—'

'You were working for *me*, Sebasten remind her, taking a new tack as his raging frustration rose to almost ungovernable heights. He didn't want her working any place and certainly not in some freewheeling PR firm where she would be engaged in constant interaction with other men and a frantic social life.

'Not any more and it wasn't a good idea, was it? Other people don't feel comfortable working around a woman who may be involved with the boss. So, as I was saying…if we lived in separate houses we wouldn't crowd each other.'

Dark colour now scored Sebasten's rigid cheekbones. 'Maybe I fancied being crowded.'

Lizzie breathed in deep. 'And I think…the first couple of months anyway…you shouldn't stay overnight.'

'I can tell you right now upfront that I won't buy a separate house and either you take me overnight or you take me not at all!' Sebasten launched at her with savage incredulity.

Lizzie swallowed the thickness of tears clogging her throat. 'You can't blame me for trying to protect myself. I don't want to be hurt again and it's going to take time for me to be able to trust you.'

Sebasten spread rigid hands and clenched them into tight, angry fists in silence. So it was payback time. Oh, yes, he understood that. She wanted to put him through hell to punish him and it would be a cold day in hell before he accepted humiliation from any woman!

'You're taking this the wrong way,' Lizzie said anxiously.

'I don't like being taken for a ride—'

'I just want us both to have the space and the freedom to see whether or not we want to live together—'

'I know that now…what is the matter with *you*?' Sebasten demanded rawly.

'I won't agree to any other arrangement before Saturday,' Lizzie countered shakily, crossing two sets of fingers superstitiously behind her back and offering up a silent prayer.

A sexless, endless probation period during which she made him jump through hoops like a wild animal being trained? Sebasten could barely repress a shudder.

'Forget it…' he advised between clenched teeth, outraged, stormy dark eyes unyielding.

The silence lay thick and heavy and full of rampant undertones of aggression.

'Is it…well, is it the lack of sex that makes this idea of mine so unacceptable?' Lizzie finally prompted awkwardly.

'Where would you get a weird idea like that?'

'OK…sex is included,' Lizzie conceded, reddening to her hairline at her own dreadful weakness in failing to stand firm.

So he would buy her a house which she would never, never live in, Sebasten reflected, sudden amusement racing through him at the speed with which she had removed the ban on intimacy.

'I suppose it might be rather like keeping a mistress,' Sebasten mused, watching her squirm at that lowering concept with immense satisfaction. 'OK…it's a deal. I'll go for it.'

But when Sebasten climbed into his car minutes later, neither satisfaction nor amusement coloured his brooding thoughts. She didn't love him. If she had ever loved him, he had killed that love. She would accept the security of marriage but she was set on having a separate life. Yet he had always been separated from other people, initially by wealth and being an only child, later by personal choice, when keeping his relationships at an undemanding superficial level had become a habit.

Yet somewhere deep down inside him Sebasten registered that he had had a dream of living a very different life with Lizzie, Lizzie *and* the baby. A life where everything was shared. He did not know when that had started or even how it had developed and that such a dream even existed shook and embarrassed him. Especially after his bride-to-be had spelt out *her* dream of two separate households, talked about space and freedom and only included her body as a last-resort sop to his apparent weak masculine inability to get by without sex.

Intellect told him that he would be insane to accept such terms.

Only a guy who was plain stupid would accept such terms.

Or a guy who was…desperate?

At supersonic speed, Sebasten reminded himself that their main objective was taking care of their future child's needs and that it was better not to dwell on inconsequentials.

CHAPTER ELEVEN

LIZZIE discovered the hard way that embarking on her first career job the same week she planned to get married was a very great challenge.

On the balance side, she thrived in a more informal working environment where a designer-clad appearance was a decided advantage and she was earning almost twice the salary she had earned at CI. She got on great with her new colleagues, was immediately given sole responsibility for organising a celebrity party for the opening of a new nightclub and spent the entire week wishing there were more hours in the day.

Having to slot in choosing her entire bridal trousseau in the space of one extended lunch hour, however, annoyed her. Spending two evenings drumming up interest in the new club by frantic socialising with acquaintances now all too keen to be seen in the company of the future wife of Sebasten Contaxis was even worse. Being pregnant also seemed to mean that she tired much more easily and she just paled when she thought of how difficult it would be to fit ante-natal appointments into such action-packed extended work hours.

She thought about Sebasten with a constant nagging anxiety that kept her awake at night when she most needed to sleep. He spent the first half of the week away on a business trip, and although he called her he seemed rather distant. She asked herself what more she had expected from him. What had seemed in the heat of the moment to be the perfect solution to her concerns about marrying him now seemed more and more like a mistake.

What real chance was she giving their marriage or Sebasten by insisting on separate accommodation? What true closeness could they hope to achieve if they lived apart? It was also much more likely that, shorn of any perceptible change in his life, Sebasten would continue to think of himself as single. That was hardly a conviction she wanted to encourage. And, in telling him upfront that she didn't trust him and yammering about space and freedom, wasn't she giving him the impression that he would be wasting his time even *trying* to adapt to the concept of a normal marriage?

In the light of those unsettling second thoughts on the issue, Lizzie's heart just sank when Sebasten phoned her forty-eight hours before their wedding to announce that he had found the perfect house for her requirements.

'Gosh, that was quick!' was all she could think to say in an effort to conceal her dismay at the news.

Lizzie had not seen Sebasten since the night they agreed to marry. Yet when he picked her up that evening to take her to view the house, he proved resistant to her every subtle indication that she was just dying to be grabbed and held and kissed senseless. After a week in which she had missed him every hour of every day, one glimpse of his lean, devastatingly handsome features and lithe, powerful frame and she was reduced to a positive pushover of melting appreciation.

'I really love my ring,' she told him encouragingly. 'And the wedding planners you hired are just fantastic.'

'I didn't want you overdoing things when you were pregnant. How's the PR world shaping up?'

'It's demanding but a lot of fun,' she said with rather forced cheer, not adding that after only four days she had reached the conclusion that it was the perfect career for a single woman without either a husband or children.

'You'll be able to rest round the clock on our honeymoon,' Sebasten informed her drily.

'*What* honeymoon?' Lizzie gasped. 'A week into the job, I can't ask for time off!'

'Then it's just as well I asked for you. Your boss was very accommodating—'

'He was…?'

'Naturally. You're an enormous asset to the firm. As my wife, you will have unparalleled access to the cream of society and the kind of contacts most PR companies can only dream about. You could dictate your own working hours, even go part-time.' Sebasten dropped that bait in the water and waited in hope of hearing it hooked.

'Quite a turnaround from my working conditions at Contaxis International,' Lizzie could not resist remarking while cringing with shame at the reality that she had almost leapt on that reference to part-time work. Wouldn't he be impressed if she took that easy way out at such speed?

His strong profile tensed. 'Blame me for that. I

wanted the spoilt little rich girl to learn what it was like to have to work for a living. Yet I would never have been attracted to you had you been what I believed you were.'

The Georgian town house he took her to see was only round the corner from his own London home and Lizzie did not comment on that reality when he did not, but her heart swelled with hope at the proximity he seemed keen to embrace. It was a lovely house, modernised with style and in wonderful decorative order. His lawyers, he explained, had negotiated a compensation agreement with the current tenants, who were prepared to vacate the house immediately. In a similar way, the owner had made a very substantial profit from agreeing to sell quickly.

'You always get what you want, don't you?' Lizzie muttered helplessly, struggling to admire the elegant, spacious rooms but increasingly chilled at the prospect of living there alone. She must have been crazy to demand such an eccentric lifestyle, she decided, close to panic. Feeling horribly guilty and confused by her own contrariness, she talked with gushing enthusiasm about how much she was looking forward to moving in.

Sebasten had been on keen watch for withdrawal pangs from the separate-house commitment. After all, the house would be a bit large perhaps but perfect in every other way for his future father-in-law, who had already mentioned a desire to sell the home he had shared with his estranged wife. As Lizzie complimented all that she saw, his hopes that she might never move into the house suffered a severe setback.

ON HER WEDDING DAY, Lizzie donned a gown fit for a fairy tale. The exquisite beaded, embroidered bodice bared her smooth shoulders and the flowing full skirt made the utmost of her tall, slender figure.

Surprise after wonderful surprise filled her day. A gorgeous sapphire and diamond necklace and earrings arrived from Sebasten as well as a blue velvet garter for good luck. Although she had never indicated any preference for certain flowers, her bouquet was a classic arrangement of her favourites. The equivalent of Cinderella's coach drawn by white horses came to ferry her the short distance to the church. Seeing everywhere the evidence of Sebasten's desire to make their wedding match her every possible fantasy, she was a radiant bride.

Her heart swelled when she walked down the aisle and Sebasten turned to watch her with a breathtaking smile on his lean dark features. Surely no guy marrying against his own will could manage a smile that brilliant? Hugging that belief to herself, she cherished every moment of the ceremony and sparkled with quicksilver energy in the photos taken afterwards.

'You look stunning,' Sebasten groaned in the limo that whisked them away from the church and, tugging her close, he ravished her soft raspberry-tinted mouth under his, awakening such a blaze of instant hunger in Lizzie that she clung to him.

'I'm wrecking your lipstick…your hair,' Sebasten sighed, setting her back from him with hands that he couldn't keep quite steady.

Loving his passion, Lizzie awarded him a provocative look of appreciation. 'It was worth it.'

There was an enormous number of guests at the reception. Introductions and polite conversations continually divided her and Sebasten and it was a relief for Lizzie to glide round the dance floor in the circle of his arms, safe from such interruptions.

'I feel awful...I just can't feel the same about friends who dropped me after Connor's death because of those stupid rumours,' Lizzie confided ruefully.

Sebasten stiffened, realising he disliked even the sound of his half-brother's name on her lips and discomfited by the discovery. 'Are there guests here who did that to you?'

'Loads of them. A good half of them I've known since I was a kid, and Dad's acquainted with their families too, so I didn't feel I had the option of leaving them off the guest list.'

'I wouldn't have given *one* of them an invite!' Shimmering dark golden eyes pinned to her in clear reproof. 'You're too soft. If someone crosses me once, they don't get a second chance.'

Lizzie tensed. 'Didn't I cross you too?'

Sebasten wrapped her even closer to his big, powerful frame, infuriated by the knowledge that she had been snubbed and ignored by people she had considered to be her friends and then been so forgiving. 'Continually...but then you inhabit a very special category, *pethi mou.*'

Lizzie looked up at him with her irreverent grin. 'Remind yourself of that the next time I cross you... you know,' she added impulsively, 'if I look very hard I can see that you *do* bear a slight resemblance to Connor.'

Taken aback by that sudden assurance, Sebasten's superb bone-structure tensed. 'Why are you even looking for a resemblance?'

At the coolness of that demand, Lizzie coloured in surprise. 'Only because you told me that you were half-brothers…and there is only a vague similarity. In your height and build, around the eyes, that's all.'

Without the smallest warning, Sebasten found himself wondering whether she had been drawn to him in the first instance because he reminded her of his younger brother. Until that same moment, he had not actually thought through what he had finally learned about his half-brother's relationship with Lizzie. Connor had cheated on her with another woman, Connor had essentially done the rejecting and wasn't it possible that Lizzie had been left carrying a torch?

'What's wrong?' Lizzie asked because Sebasten had fallen still in the middle of the dance.

'I should've warned you that Connor's true parentage is a secret. Ingrid had her own good reasons for successfully fooling my father into believing that Connor was another man's child. Connor himself never knew the truth.' His lean dark features were taut. 'Nor does his mother want it known even now.'

'I haven't mentioned it to anyone,' Lizzie swore, assuming that fear of her having already been indiscreet had roused his concern on Ingrid Morgan's behalf. 'To be frank, after what I had to put up with on his and Felicity's behalf, he wouldn't be my favourite conversational topic.'

Although Connor was most definitely not Sebasten's favourite topic either, Sebasten discovered that his thoughts continued to circle back in that direction. He sacked his memory in an effort to recall every word that Lizzie had said the night he took her out to dinner and she told him her side of the story on Connor. But he hadn't been listening, not the way he *should* have been listening, for at that point he had believed that her every word was a lie.

'So you can finally tell me where we're going for our honeymoon?' Lizzie carolled with rather contrived sparkle when they boarded his private jet some hours later.

'Greece.' Sebasten reflected that there had to be some evil fate at work, for he was taking her to the one place in the world that held once fond memories of Ingrid and Connor.

Still striving gamely not to react to his brooding aura, Lizzie smiled so wide her jaw ached. 'You're taking me to your home there?'

'A private island.' Not the brightest spark of inspiration he had had this century, Sebasten decided with grim irony.

'Whose island?'

'Mine.'

'You own your own island?'

'Doesn't every Greek tycoon?' Sebasten shrugged.

'So I'm being dead vulgar and I'm impressed!' Lizzie quipped, a glint of annoyance flaring in her green eyes.

They had enjoyed the most fabulous wedding. Sebasten had seemed to be in the best of humour and nothing had gone wrong that she knew of. So what was the matter with him? Was it only now sinking in on him that he was a married man? Was being married to her *that* depressing? Tears prickled at the backs of her eyes but her expressive mouth tightened and she lifted a magazine, enjoyed the superb meal she was served and said not another word.

Late evening, they arrived on the island of Isvos. The helicopter set them down within yards of a long, low, rambling house built of natural stone. Sebasten carried her over the threshold. 'Bet you're glad there isn't a flight of steps!' Lizzie giggled.

His brilliant gaze centred on her lovely laughing face and suddenly he smiled.

The interior enchanted Lizzie: polished terracotta floors, stone walls and rough-hewn support pillars of wood contrasted with glorious sheer draperies and pale contemporary furniture. In every main room, doors opened direct on to the beach and the whispering, soothing sound of the surf seemed to flow through the whole house.

'I love it,' Lizzie murmured with an appreciative smile. 'It's so peaceful.'

'Ingrid Morgan helped to design it.'

Lizzie glanced at him in surprise. 'I thought she used to be a very superior PA.'

'She was but she was also my father's mistress.'

Lizzie blinked and then her lush mouth rounded into a soft silent 'oh' of belated comprehension.

'She ended it before Connor got old enough to suspect the truth and moved back to England.'

'Has she ever come back here?' Lizzie asked.

'No. Ingrid's not into reliving the past.' His jacket cast on the chest at the foot of the handsome beech bed, Sebasten lounged back against the pale wood door frame, six feet four inches of glorious leashed male power and virility. 'Neither am I as a rule. But, as I'm sure you'll recognise, Connor is a subject we've never really discussed in any depth.'

'Connor...?' Lizzie repeated after a startled pause. 'You want me to talk about Connor...*in depth*?'

Lean, powerful face taut with determination, Sebasten shifted a broad shoulder in a fluid movement. 'We should get it out of the way.'

'Well, excuse me...' Green eyes wide with annoyance and discomfiture, Lizzie tilted her chin. 'I wasn't aware there *was* anything to get out of the way!'

'I know next to nothing about your relationship with him,' Sebasten countered with immovable cool.

'This is our wedding night and you want me to rehash unpleasant memories of another man...is that right?' Lizzie demanded, snatching in a sustaining breath in an effort to control the incredulous resentment splintering through her but failing. 'Go take a hike, Sebasten!'

Sebasten straightened, beautiful dark eyes flaring stormy gold. 'I might just do that.'

At that threat, fear touched Lizzie deep and that very fear that he might walk out only increased her fury. 'Wasn't it bad enough that you spent most of the trip here hardly speaking to me? I put up with that but I can't stand moody people. You never know where you are with them—'

'I am not moody,' Sebasten grated in an electrifying undertone. 'But when you admitted that you saw a likeness between me and Connor, yes, it did give me pause for thought. It made me wonder just what you *first* saw in me...'

Understanding came to Lizzie and she studied him with angry, hurt condemnation, for she could not change the reality that she had met his brother first. 'You have to be the most possessive guy I've ever met—'

Sebasten shot her a fulminating look. 'I'm not and I have never been possessive—'

'Volatile...possessive...jealous. Pick any one of them and they every one fit! If I'd just popped out of a little locked box somewhere the first night we met, you'd have loved it! How *could* you ask about Connor tonight of all nights? Do you honestly think I want to talk about how I found him and my stepmother in bed together?' Lizzie slung at him in furious reproach. 'You haven't got a romantic, sensitive bone in your body!'

The bathroom door slammed and locked on Lizzie's impassioned exit. Sebasten strode out onto the beach, angry with her, angry with himself, angrier still with Connor, now that he finally knew how brutal an awakening she had had to that affair. But he was not volatile. Nobody had ever accused him of that before. He was a very self-controlled guy. As for being possessive, what was wrong with that? *Theo mou*...she was his *wife*! A certain amount of possessiveness was a natural male instinct. As for that other tag, he wouldn't even dignify that suggestion with consideration.

Lizzie's frustration was overborne by tears of sheer tiredness. Where did Sebasten get the energy to be so volatile? At least though she now understood what had been riding him since the reception. She should never have mentioned that bit about there being a resemblance between him and his half-brother. She sank down on top of the comfortable bed, thinking that in just a moment she would go and track Sebasten down and smooth things over. After all, it was kind of sweet: Connor couldn't have held a candle to Sebasten in looks, personality or desirability.

When Sebasten strolled back in off the beach half an hour later, Lizzie was sound asleep. Clad in something filmy the colour of rich honey, she was curled up on top of the shot-silk spread. When he saw the faint track of a tear stain on her cheek, he suppressed a groan and raked long brown fingers through his tousled black hair. Why did he go off the rails with Lizzie? Connor had caused her a lot of grief. On the same score, his own conscience was hardly whiter than white *and* she was carrying his baby...

Lizzie wakened with a start and sat up. The doors on to the beach were still wide but now framed a spectacular crimson and gold sunrise over the bay. The indented pillow beside hers indicated that at some stage of the night Sebasten had joined her and she groaned out loud: she must have slept like a log. Sliding out of bed, she went into the *en suite* bathroom to freshen up and wondered where the heck Sebasten was.

When she returned to the bedroom, she stilled in relief. Sebasten was sprawled on the floor cushion by the doors watching the sun rise and her mouth ran dry. His strong brown back was bare and his well-worn jeans outlined every line of his narrow hips and long, powerful thighs. When he turned his arrogant dark head to look at her, deceptively sleepy golden eyes accentuated by the darkness of his lashes, he just took her breath away.

'Hi...' he said softly, extending a lean hand to her in welcome.

'You should've woken me up last night—'

Sebasten tugged her down beside him and pulled her back against him. 'Be honest…you were exhausted. A siren wouldn't have wakened you—'

'But *you* could have,' Lizzie whispered, curving back into the sun-warmed heat of him and tightening his arms round her for herself.

'Call it the first selfless act of a lifetime *pethi mou*,' Sebasten teased huskily, brushing her tumbled hair from one slim shoulder and pressing his expert mouth to her exposed skin in a caress that sent a helpless shiver of response coursing through her.

She twisted round in a sudden movement that took him by surprise and locked her lush lips to his with a hunger she couldn't hide.

'And this is the *second* unselfish act…' Sebasten shared with a ragged edge to his dark, deep drawl as he lifted her and set her back from him. 'Breakfast awaits you…'

'B-breakfast?' Lizzie stammered in total disconcertion.

'You can have me for dessert if you want,' Sebasten promised with husky amusement, vaulting upright with easy grace and pulling her with him to walk her out onto the terrace, where fresh rolls, cereal and fruit were already laid on the table.

'Are the staff invisible?' Lizzie asked as he tugged out a seat and tucked her into it.

'I made it. The staff will be very discreet and only show up when necessary—'

'And where do they hang out the rest of the time?'

'In the main house across that hill.' Sebasten nod-

ded in the direction of the thick pine grove that ran on
steep sloping ground right down to the edge of the sea.

'There's *another* house?'

'This place wasn't impressive enough to satisfy my
father's wives. I use the main house when I'm entertaining. When I'm on my own, I come here.'

That he had brought her with him made her smile.
When she had finished her tea, he peeled a peach for
her, fed her with it segment by segment. She collided
dizzily with smouldering golden eyes and licked his
fingers clean of the peach juice. He closed his hands
over hers and tugged her upright.

'Ready and willing,' Sebasten husked.

The well-worn denim of his jeans made that so obvious that her cheeks burned with colour but her awareness of his rampant arousal only heightened her own.
Driven by the taut sensitivity of her breasts and the ache
stirring at the very heart of her, she pushed into connection with every hard, muscular angle of his lean, powerful frame. He knotted his fingers into the tumbling
torrent of her hair and claimed her ready mouth with
explicit passion.

'I make a really *mean* breakfast,' he teased as he
swept her quivering body up into his arms and carried
her back to bed.

'But can you do it…every morning?' Lizzie mumbled, trying to hold her own in the breathless dialogue
while struggling with his zip.

'Try me…' Sebasten took care of that problem for
her by ripping off his jeans with single-minded purpose
and dexterity. 'You wouldn't believe how sexy it feels
to know that your woman carries your baby inside her.'

'Honestly?' Lizzie opened wide, uncertain eyes, met the fiery confirmation in his intent gaze, and relief and appreciation filled her.

'Honestly,' Sebasten confirmed with the slashing charismatic smile that always made her heart lurch inside her and he deprived her of her nightdress with smooth expertise.

Empowered by that declaration, Lizzie began, 'About last night, what you said about Con—'

'Shut up,' Sebasten warned without the smallest dip in that blazing smile. 'I was way out of line—'

'But—'

'Close your eyes and pretend we have only just arrived,' he urged, finding the tender peak of her breast with caressing fingers and depriving her of both breath and concentration.

He took her into a sensual world where all that mattered was the next sweet, drugging high of sensation. He let the heat of his mouth trail over her tender, pouting flesh and a long sigh was driven from her lungs. He lingered over the distended little buds until her sigh had become a moan she wasn't even aware of making and she was shifting her hips in a restive movement, unable to stay still.

'Sebasten…' she gasped as he worked his erotic passage down over the quivering muscles of her tummy. 'I want you…'

'Not yet,' he asserted, parting her slender thighs with ease and embarking on an intimacy that was new to her.

Shaken as she was, her eyes flew wide. 'No…'

But he transformed her negative into a helpless positive within seconds and drove her crazy with a pleasure that came close to torment. She was out of control, abandoned to the urgent need he had driven to an ever greater height. At the instant that her heart was a hammering thunder-beat in her ears and her whole quivering body was sensitised to an almost unbearable degree, he came over her and entered her in a single smooth-driving thrust. Excitement flung her so high, she couldn't catch her breath. She lifted herself up to him, moved against him in a helpless frenzy of need and then cried out as the shock waves of climax took her to an ecstatic peak and then released her again.

She felt soft with love, weak with fulfilment. Revelling in the peaceful aftermath of passion, she rubbed her cheek against a satin-smooth muscular brown shoulder. Happiness cocooned her as he hugged her close. He might not love her but he was very affectionate, she acknowledged, suppressing the inner sense of loss that that first acknowledgement threatened.

'Just to think, *pethi mou*,' Sebasten murmured with raw satisfaction as he gazed down into her warm green eyes, 'nobody but me is ever going to know how fantastic you really are.'

'Trust you to find a new slant on marriage,' Lizzie whispered with amusement.

Dark golden eyes welded to her, he brushed a kiss across her lush reddened mouth and breathed rather like a guy steeling himself to make a major statement. 'What we have is special...*really* special.'

'Is it?' she muttered, wanting more, striving to silence that need inside her and be happy with what they had.

'Yes.' Sebasten was just a little annoyed that she

seemed so indifferent to his attempt to impress on her how much he valued her. 'We're so close, I can *feel* it.'

'Oh…' Lizzie snuggled into him.

'I've never been that great at getting close to women,' Sebasten confided, soothed by the fact that she was now wrapped round him like a vine. 'But you're different. You're very open.'

'Have you ever been in love?' she muttered in as casual a tone as she could muster.

Sebasten tensed. 'No…'

And with that Lizzie had to be content.

TWO WEEKS LATER, LIZZIE shimmied into a dress the shade of copper and noted how well it became the very slight tan she had acquired in the heat of the Greek sun.

Emerald drop earrings dangled from her ears and an emerald and diamond necklace encircled her throat. Sebasten had given her the earrings at the end of the first week and the necklace just the night before. Lizzie smiled. She had never been so happy. Even the reality that her beautiful dress was just a tinge too neat in fit over breasts that had made an inconvenient gain in size as her body changed with early pregnancy couldn't cloud her good mood.

They had had lazy golden days on the beach, eating when they felt like it, swimming when they felt like it, staying in bed when they felt like it and talking long into the night over the exquisite dinners the staff served on the terrace in the evening. On a couple of occasions they had walked down to the sleepy little village at the harbour and dined in each of the two taverns, where they had been treated like guests of honour. Other days they had flown over to the bigger, busier islands like Corfu to shop or dine or dance.

She had learnt a lot about the male she married. She had also been both disconcerted and touched when he had said he would be cutting back on his trips abroad so that he would be able to spend more time with her and the baby.

'It'll be difficult for you,' she had remarked.

'It's my choice, just as it was my father's choice to be a stranger to me throughout my childhood. He was never there,' Sebasten had admitted, his strong jawline squaring as he voiced a truth that his sense of family loyalty had always forced him to repress. 'He expected his wives to do his job for him but they didn't. It was much easier to leave me in the care of the staff or pack me off to boarding school.'

For the first time, Lizzie had recognised the strength of his sense of responsibility towards their unborn baby and her heart had gone out to him as she understood that his own experiences had made him all the more determined to ensure that his own child would receive very different treatment. But for the early loss of her mother, her own childhood had been secure and loving and she began to grasp the source of Sebasten's innate complexity. He had been forced to depend on his own inner resources at too early an age.

Yet throughout those two glorious weeks they shared, Sebasten continually surprised and delighted her with the unexpected. The night that he found her eating sun-dried tomatoes with a fork direct from the jar she had brought out to Greece with her, he had laughed at her embarrassment over her secret craving and carried both jar and her back to bed. But within twenty-four hours a ready supply of Greek sun-dried tomatoes had been flown in.

'It's a Greek baby,' he had pointed out cheerfully.

She would never have dreamt of telling Sebasten but she truly believed he was a perfect husband. He was romantic, although without ever seeming to realise that he was being romantic. He was also incredibly passionate and tender as well as being the most entertaining male she had ever been with. In short, he was just wonderful. She could not credit that she had been so worried that he might not be ready for the commitment of marriage. She was convinced that at any moment he would open the subject of their living in separate houses when they returned to London and talk her out of what she had already decided had been a very stupid idea.

It was the last night of their honeymoon. Sebasten had selected it as the night they would cast off their newly married seclusion and host a party at the big white villa over the hill. He wanted to entertain all the Greek friends and business acquaintances who had not been able to make it to a wedding staged at such short notice.

'You look fantastic in that dress,' Sebasten informed her as he entered the bedroom.

Lizzie encountered the appreciative gleam in his gaze and just grinned. 'You picked it. The emeralds look spectacular with it too. Thank you.'

'Gratitude not required. Those emeralds accentuate your eyes and I had to have them, *pethi mou.*'

She looked so happy, Sebasten thought with a powerful sense of achievement and satisfaction. He could not believe that she would insist on living apart from him when they got back home again. If she had begun to care for him even a little again, she would surely change her mind.

'How did you get so friendly with Ingrid Morgan?' Lizzie asked as she kicked off her shoes to walk barefoot across the sand. The path that led up through the pine wood to the main house was on the other side of the beach. 'You never did explain that.'

'Between the ages of eight and eleven, I spent every vacation here with Ingrid and Connor. My father would just fly in for a few days here and there,' Sebasten explained wryly.

'*Every* vacation?' Lizzie queried in surprise.

'It suited Andros. He was between wives. Ingrid treated me the same way she treated Connor and I began to think of them as my family.' Sebasten grimaced as if to invite her scorn of such a weakness on his part. 'It ended the day I asked my father when he and Ingrid were getting married.'

'Was marriage so out of the question?'

'By that stage they had already had a stormy on-and-off relationship that spanned quite a few years. He never thought of her as anything other than a mistress and he'd convinced himself that I was too young to ask awkward questions. But he took me back to our home in Athens that same evening and I was an adult before I met Ingrid again.'

'That was so cruel!' Lizzie groaned.

No longer did she wonder why he had once admitted to not trusting her sex, for he had been let down by the only two women he had learned to love when he was a child. His mother had walked away through her own personal choice but Ingrid Morgan had had no choice, for she had had no rights over her lover's son.

Why the hell had he told her all that? Sebasten asked himself in strong exasperation. Lizzie's eyes were glistening with tears and, even as he was warmed by her emotional response on his behalf, he was embarrassed by it too.

Ahead of them lay the big, opulent white villa built by Andros Contaxis for his second wife. Lizzie had had a lengthy tour of the house the week before. While a hugely impressive dwelling with as many rooms as a hotel, it lacked character and appeal. Considering that problem and keen to change the subject to one less sensitive, she murmured in a bright upbeat tone, 'I've got so many plans for the house. I can hardly wait to get home to make a start. I really will need the advice of a good interior designer, maybe even an architect.'

Sebasten absorbed that admission in angry, startled bewilderment. He assumed she was referring to the house he had offered her for her own sole occupation in London. How the hell could she exude such enthusiasm for literally throwing him back out of her life again? Had nothing that they had shared in recent days made her reappraise that ambition? What was he? A negotiable part of the old sun, sea and sex vacation aboard? Or just a rebound affair after Connor that was now leading to its natural conclusion? Obviously not much more, for all that he was the father of the baby she carried!

Surprised by his silence, Lizzie coloured, for she had assumed that he would be pleased. But then possibly he believed that when they were only just married she had some nerve announcing that she planned to redesign one of his homes. After all, it should have been *his* suggestion, rather than hers, she thought in sudden mortification. Just because her own father had always preferred to let the women in his life take care of such matters did not mean that Sebasten had a similar outlook.

'Of course,' she added hurriedly, striving to backtrack from her stated intention without losing face, 'change doesn't always mean improvement and it could be a mistake to rush into a project that would be so expensive—'

'Spend what you like when you like,' Sebasten delivered in a derisive undertone. 'I couldn't care less.'

Shock sliced through Lizzie. As they entered the villa she stole a shaken glance at his lean, hard profile, wondering what on earth she had said to deserve such a response. Whatever, it was obvious that Sebasten was angry. Furthermore, once their guests began arriving in a flood, Sebasten roved far and wide from her side, leaving her more than once to assume the guise of a faithful follower. He also talked almost exclusively in Greek, which she supposed was understandable when he was mixing with other Greeks, but on several occasions when she was already aware that their companions spoke English he left her feeling superfluous to their conversations.

'You have all my sympathy,' Candice, a beautiful and elegant brunette, remarked to Lizzie out of the blue.

Having already been informed by Candice that she had once dated Sebasten, Lizzie tensed. 'Why?'

'Sebasten doesn't quite have the look of a male who

has taken to marriage like a duck to water.' Exotic dark eyes mocked Lizzie's flush of dismay at that crack. 'But then some men are just born to prefer freedom and it *is* early days yet, isn't it?'

That one stinging comment was sufficient to persuade Lizzie that Sebasten was making a public spectacle of her. Seeing him momentarily alone, she studied him. He looked grim without his social smile, pale beneath his usually vibrant olive skin tone, and concern overcame her annoyance. She hurried over to him and said ruefully, 'Are you going to tell me what's the matter with you?'

'Nothing's the matter.' Hard golden eyes clashed with hers in apparent astonishment.

'But I've hardly seen you this evening—'

'Do we need to stick together like superglue?' Sebasten elevated a sardonic ebony brow. 'I have to confess that after two weeks of round-the-clock togetherness, I'm in need of a breather and looking forward to leading more separate lives when we get home.'

The silence enclosed her like silent thunder.

'Believe me, you're not the only one,' Lizzie breathed, fighting to keep her voice level.

She walked away but inside herself she was tottering in shock and devastation. How could he turn on her like that when she had believed them so close? She loved him to distraction but how could she allow herself to love someone that ruthless in stating his own dissatisfaction with their marriage? What had gone wrong, how it had gone wrong without her noticing seemed unimportant. All that mattered was that once again she herself had been guilty of making a fatal misjudgement about how a man felt about her.

Oh, she knew he didn't love her but she had believed that they were incredibly close for all that. Hadn't he said so himself? But then, what did she believe? What Sebasten said *in* bed or what he said *out* of it? She knew which version her intelligence warned her to place most credence in. She gazed round the crowded room but all the faces were just a blur and the clink of glasses, the chatter and the music seemed distant and subdued. Then, without her even appreciating the fact, the most awful dizziness had taken hold of her. As she lurched in the direction of the nearest seat she was too late to prevent what was already happening, and she folded down on the carpet with a stifled moan of dismay.

Already striding towards her, alerted by her striking pallor and wavering stance, Sebasten was right on the spot to take charge but cool did not distinguish the moments that immediately followed Lizzie's fainting fit. Never an optimist at the best of times, in the guilt-stricken mood he was in, Sebasten was convinced he'd killed her stone-dead and the reality that there were at least three doctors present was of no consolation whatsoever.

Lizzie recovered consciousness to find herself lying on a sofa in another room. Three men were hovering but Sebasten was down on his knees, clutching one of her hands, much as if she were on her deathbed. She blinked, almost smiled as her bemused gaze closed in on his lean, strong face, and then she remembered his words of rejection and what colour she had regained receded again and she turned her head away, sucking in a deep, convulsive breath.

'Only a faint, nothing to really worry about,' Sebasten's best friend from university asserted in bracing Greek. 'A mother-to-be shouldn't be standing for hours on end on such a warm and humid evening—'

'And not without having eaten any supper,' chimed in another friend.

'She has a fragile look about her,' the third doctor remarked, his more pessimistic and cautious nature a perfect match for Sebasten's. 'Entertaining two hundred people tonight may well have been too much for her. This is a warning to you. She needs rest and tender care, and try to keep the stress to a minimum.'

Sebasten was feeling bad enough without the news that his lack of care on almost every possible count had contributed to Lizzie's condition. He scooped her up into his arms. 'I'm taking you up to bed.'

Lizzie made no protest. The more she thought about his rejection, the more anguished she felt, and what self-discipline she had was directed towards thanking the doctors for their assistance and striving to behave normally.

By the time Sebasten had carried Lizzie up to the master-bedroom suite and settled her down on the vast circular bed that had sent her into a fit of giggles when she first saw it, even he was a little out of breath. But so shattered had he been by her collapse and by the gut-wrenching punishment of having been forced to think of what life might be like without her that Sebasten was desperate to dig himself back out of the very deep hole that fierce pride had put him in.

'I was lying in my teeth when I said I was tired of us being together,' Sebasten confessed in a raw, driven undertone.

Thinking that now he felt sorry for her and blamed his own blunt honesty for causing her stupid faint, Lizzie flipped over and presented him with her back. 'I'd like to be on my own.'

'I'm sorry I was such a bastard,' Sebasten framed half under his breath, his dark, deep drawl thick with strain. 'I don't want to score points any more. I *do* want you to be happy—'

'Then go away,' she muttered tightly.

'But I *need* you in my life.' Sebasten forced that admission out with much the same gritty force as a male making a confession while facing a loaded gun.

A solitary tear rolled down Lizzie's taut cheek. Obviously he had recognised just how devastated she was at the concept of having to let go of her dream of a happy, normal marriage. 'I don't need you,' she mumbled flatly.

CHAPTER TWELVE

Sebasten had had a hell of a night.

Most of their guests had travelled home. Some who had had to stay overnight at the villa at least retired early, but those who did not kept him up until almost dawn. For what remained of the night he paced the room next to Lizzie's and fought the temptation to disturb her so that they could talk again. While Lizzie breakfasted in bed at his express instruction, he had to assume a cheerful-host act until the merciful moment that the last of their visitors had departed. However, by that stage it was time to embark on their return trip to London.

Lizzie came downstairs dressed in a dark green shift dress, her hair pulled back in a sophisticated style, all but her lush pink lips and the tip of her nose hidden behind a giant pair of sunglasses.

'How do you feel?' Sebasten asked, striving to suppress the recollection of finding her bedroom door locked when he had tried to make the same enquiry earlier in the day.

'Marvellous…can't wait to get home!' Lizzie declared, heading for the helicopter outside at speed.

Behind the sunglasses her reddened eyes were dull with misery but Lizzie had her pride to sustain her. When they boarded the Contaxis jet at Athens, she struck up an animated conversation with the stewardesses, went into several determined fits of laughter at the movie she chose to watch and enjoyed a second dessert after eating a hearty late lunch. And she called *him* insensitive, Sebasten reflected in receipt of that concerted display of indifference.

'I have to call into the office,' Sebasten announced after she had climbed into the limousine waiting to collect them in London. 'I'll see you back at the house... we have to talk.'

But what was there to talk about? Lizzie asked herself wretchedly. He had already spelt out how he felt. She had no option but to go to his London home, for the town house he had purchased had yet to be furnished. So, couldn't she buy some furniture? Surely camping out in bare rooms would be better than staying with Sebasten when her presence was no longer welcome?

How could he get bored with her between one moment and the next? Her throat ached and her rebellious memory served up a dozen images of intimacy that cut her like a knife when she could least bear it. Sebasten dragging her out of bed to breakfast at dawn and enjoy what he called 'the best part of the day' and her struggling to match his vibrant energy and conceal her yawns. Sebasten watching her try on clothes, a smouldering gleam of appreciation in his gaze letting her know exactly what to buy. Sebasten curving her into his arms last thing at night and making her feel so incredibly happy and secure.

No, camping out in bare rooms, she decided with a helpless shiver, would be more comfortable than the chilling prospect of sharing the same household even on a temporary basis, ever conscious of what they had had and then lost. Painful as it was, she knew that some men lost all interest in a woman once the excitement of the chase was over and that those same men could go from desire to uninterest almost overnight. Was that Sebasten's true nature? And had he not already achieved what he had said was most important? Their child would be born a Contaxis. The sad fact was that his parents did not have to live together nor even remain married to meet that requirement.

Infuriated at the crisis that had demanded his presence at Contaxis International, Sebasten got back home just before seven that evening. By then, Lizzie had already cleared out. The dressing room off the master bedroom looked as though a whirlwind by the name of Lizzie had gone through it and his staff had tactfully left the evidence for him to find. She had left a note on the bed. Seeing it, he froze, not wanting to read it.

'I borrowed some of your furniture but I'll return it soon. It's easier this way,' she wrote in her note. 'Stay in touch.'

Stay in touch? Sebasten crunched the note between his fingers. *Easier for whom?* He was in total shock. Nothing he had said the night before had made any impression on her. He had said 'I need you' to a woman who could break down in floods of tears over a sad film, but she had still walked out. Let her go, his stubborn pride urged.

WHEN SEBASTEN HIT THE bell on the front door, Lizzie mustered her courage and went to answer it.

Lean, bronzed features taut, he was sheathed in a formal dark business suit. She allowed her gaze to flick over him very fast. He looked sensational, but then he always did, she acknowledged painfully. Heart pounding like a road drill, she crossed the echoing hall and showed him into the only furnished room available.

'Look at me...' Sebasten urged in a roughened undertone.

She was shocked by the haunted strain in his dark gold gaze and the fierce tension stamped into every sculpted line of his hard bone-structure.

'Come home...*please*,' he breathed with fierce emphasis. 'We have to talk.'

'I think that all that needs to be said was said last night,' Lizzie said unevenly.

'No...I tried to give you space while we were in Greece. I went against my own nature.' Sebasten shifted a lean, forceful hand to emphasise that point. 'If I had that two weeks a second time, believe me, I wouldn't make the same mistake again.'

'But you went out of your way to hurt me last night.' Lizzie's mind was in angry, defensive turmoil, for she could no longer understand what he wanted from her.

Sebasten released a ragged laugh. 'What did you expect from me after I had to listen to you telling me that you couldn't *wait* to start renovating this house? How was I supposed to react? You were letting me know that nothing had changed, that you weren't prepared to live with me or even give our marriage a fighting chance!'

Lizzie stared back at him with wide, bewildered eyes. 'But I wasn't talking about *this* house...I was talking about your father's villa on the island!'

Sebasten stilled in his pacing track across the room and frowned in equal bemusement. 'You didn't make that clear. The villa on Isvos?'

'Yes.' Lizzie took in a slow, steadying breath as she grasped that they had been talking at cross purposes the previous night. His aggression had been fired by a simple misconception: his belief that she was still hell-bent on setting up a separate household. 'You picked me up wrong and leapt to the wrong conclusion.'

'I don't think so.' Sebasten had a different viewpoint. 'You've moved in here.'

'Only because I thought that was what *you* wanted!'

'Why would I want to live apart from my wife?' The fierce glitter in his intent golden eyes challenged her, his jawline clenching hard. 'I thought that I could accept that for a while if it meant that you married me but this feels more like the end of our marriage than the beginning. But I know that I can't force you to feel what I feel.'

'And what *do* you feel?' Lizzie almost whispered, so great was her tension, for what he was telling her was exactly what she had needed to hear from him.

'That maybe you haven't quite got over Connor yet. That maybe this situation is what I asked for when I screwed up our relationship from start to finish...but I still love you and I'll wait for as long as it takes,' Sebasten breathed with fierce conviction.

Lizzie was still as a statue. Shock had made her pale. 'You *love* me?'

Sebasten fixed level, strained golden eyes on her and nodded much as if he had just confessed to a terminal illness.

'Since when?' Lizzie could barely frame the question.

'Probably the first night we met. I did things that night that I would never have done in a normal state of mind,' Sebasten confessed with grim dark eyes, not appearing to register that she was fumbling her way down onto the edge of the sofa she had borrowed. 'I did take *huge* advantage of you. You were very vulnerable that night but I just couldn't let go of you. Love is supposed

to make people kinder but at that stage it only made me
more selfish and ruthless.'

'Sebasten…' Lizzie was wondering if she could dare
to credit what she was hearing when what he was saying was her every dream come true.

'No, I'm determined to tell it like it was, no stone left
unturned,' Sebasten asserted with a derision angled at
himself. 'After I sobered you up that night, I should've
put you in a guest room. On the other hand, if I *had*
done that you wouldn't have got pregnant and I could
never have persuaded you to marry me. So, I'm afraid
I can't even regret that we made love.'

Lizzie could not drag her mesmerised stare from his
lean, strong face. 'Yes, he was still very much the focused guy she had fallen in love with. But that he should
be grateful that she had conceived because that development had ultimately made her let him back into her
life again touched her to the heart.

'And when I suspected that you were a virgin, did I
feel guilty?' Sebasten spread rueful hands in emphasis. 'No, I didn't feel guilty even then. That made you
feel more like mine, and you're right—where you're
concerned I'm very possessive and jealous and I was
delighted that I was your first lover.'

'You're being so honest,' Lizzie managed in a shaky
voice. 'I really like that.'

'Then I saw your driver's licence and realised you
were Liza Denton and it all just blew up in my face.
From there on in, it only got worse,' Sebasten continued heavily.

'The night we met…you *honestly* didn't know who
I was?' Lizzie gasped.

'I told you I didn't! I saw you on the dance floor and

I couldn't take my eyes off you. I had not the smallest suspicion that you were Connor's ex.'

And she hadn't believed him, Lizzie thought in dismay.

'In fact I thought the little blonde I saw speaking to you was Liza Denton and I had no intention whatsoever of approaching her.'

'That was Jen,' Lizzie whispered, fully convinced that he was telling her the truth.

'Once I knew your true identity, I couldn't acknowledge how I felt about you. I wrecked everything trying to stay loyal as I believed to Connor's memory.'

'Why, though? You admitted you hardly knew him as an adult.'

Sebasten grimaced. 'The day of the funeral was also the day Ingrid told me that he was my half-brother.'

Lizzie absorbed that fact with a flash of anger in her expressive eyes. 'Oh, that was wicked...to finally tell you *that* when Connor was dead!'

'I wouldn't say it was wicked, but with hindsight I can see that it *was* very manipulative timing,' Sebasten conceded with wry regret. 'But Ingrid was out of her head with grief. It sent me haywire though. I felt a great sense of loss. I felt guilty that I had not made more effort to maintain contact with Connor.'

Lizzie did not believe he would have found very much common ground with his half-brother but she was too kind to say so. Her memory of the younger man had softened but she knew that he had been arrogant and self-centred right to the last in allowing his friends to go on believing that she had broken his heart and driven him to the heavy drinking sessions that finally contributed to his death.

'I've learnt more about Connor through what he did

to *you* than I probably ever wanted to know,' Sebasten confided with a grimace, as if he could read her mind. 'What I hate most is that I came along and I hurt you even more.'

'That's behind us now,' Lizzie assured him.

'Time and time again, I told myself that the secret of your incredible attraction was just sex,' Sebasten groaned. 'The minute I realised that you were Liza Denton, I swore to myself that I wouldn't ever sleep with you again...but I *did* and more than once.'

'I know.' Lizzie was trying hard not to smile.

'That episode in the basement just...' Sebasten threw up both hands in a speaking gesture of rare discomfiture. 'It was crass, crazy. I'm really sorry about that. Afterwards, I couldn't believe I'd lost control to that extent...I mean, I was fighting what I felt for you with everything I had! But I was a pushover every time.'

'That's when you realised how keen I was on you, wasn't it?' Lizzie prompted gently.

Dark colour scored his superb cheekbones. 'I felt like a total bastard and I didn't want to hurt you. So, I decided that I had to dump you because the entire situation had become more than I could handle.'

'You poor love...' Lizzie swallowed hard on the unexpected giggle that bubbled in her throat. 'You've had a really tough time.'

'You dumped me,' Sebasten reminded her. 'I couldn't even do that right!'

Lizzie got up and wrapped her arms round him.

'I thought you were angry with me. Why are you hugging me?' Sebasten asked, his Greek accent very thick.

'For making me feel as irresistible as Cleopatra... for letting me see that loving me has made you suffer a lot too…so now I can forgive you for having made me suffer,' Lizzie confided, locking both arms round his neck.

'You can forgive me?' Some of the raw tension in his big, powerful frame eased and he closed his own arms tightly round her. 'Give me a chance to make everything right from now on?'

'Loads of chances,' she promised, conscious of the anxiety still visible in his dark golden eyes. 'When did you realise you'd fallen in love with me?'

Sebasten tensed. 'I sort of suspected it in Greece but I didn't take those thoughts out and examine them because I didn't know what was going to happen when we came back to London. But when you collapsed last night I panicked and faced how much you meant to me. I had this nightmare vision of my life without you in it—'

'Traumatising? I hope so, because you're not getting a life without me in it.'

'I love you the way I never thought I would love any woman.' His possessive golden gaze pinned with appreciation to her, he framed her irreverent grin with gentle fingers. 'I love everything about you, *pethi mou*…even the way you annoy the hell out of me sometimes. So stop teasing me.'

She could not have doubted the rough sincerity in his every spoken syllable and the direct and steady onslaught of an adoring scrutiny that made her face warm with colour. 'I love you too…'

'*Still?*' Sebasten demanded. 'I thought you'd got over me…you wouldn't give an inch even when I practically begged you to come back to me!'

'I can be stubborn. But I never stopped loving you.'

His brilliant smile flashed across his lean, devastat-

ing features and he hugged her close. 'I feel a very uncool degree of happiness...say it again.'

She did.

And then he felt he had to match her with the same
words. He felt wonderful. He felt ten feet tall. Lizzie
was his, finally, absolutely his. His wedding ring on
her finger, his baby on the way. Freeing her just when
she was about to invite the kiss that every nerve in her
body craved, Sebasten closed his hand over hers and
walked her back out to the hall.

'Where are we going?' Lizzie muttered.

'Home...to where it all began. Any chance of me reliving the highlights?' Sebasten gave her a wicked look
of all-male anticipation.

As he flipped shut the door in their wake and then
tucked her into his car, Lizzie blushed and smiled. 'I
think that's very possible.'

An hour and more later, Sebasten lay back in what
now felt like a secure marital bed to him and held Lizzie
close. He was in a very upbeat mood, checking out her
freckles and discovering that, in spite of all his efforts
to keep her under sunhats and in the shade, the Greek
sun had blessed her with another half-dozen. He knew
she wasn't fond of her freckles, so he kept the news
to himself. He splayed his fingers over her still non-
existent tummy and grinned and secretly rejoiced in
feelings of intense possessiveness.

'What are you thinking about?' Lizzie whispered,
smiling up at him with complete contentment and trust.

'That you're the best investment I've ever made,'
Sebasten confided with quiet satisfaction. 'When you
have the baby, I'll have *two* of you.'

'We'll be a family. You'll be totally trapped because
I'm not letting go of you ever,' Lizzie teased.

'You'd be amazed how good that sounds to me.' Sebasten looked down at her with all the love he couldn't hide and she knew he meant every word of that assurance. 'As long as you don't expect me to buy any more houses for your sole occupation.'

Lizzie grimaced. 'I feel *so* bad about that.'

'Don't. Just remind yourself that we are the same two people who shared an incredible happy honeymoon and we talked about everything under the sun *but*...neither one of us had the guts to broach the sensitive subject of how we planned to live when we got home again,' Sebasten pointed out with wry amusement.

'I was waiting for you to try and persuade me to change my mind,' Lizzie complained. 'I wasn't expecting you to rush out and buy a house overnight either!'

Sebasten burst out laughing at that and kissed her breathless, and it was another hour before they had dinner and he dropped the bait about it having just occurred to him that perhaps her father might like to consider moving into the surplus dwelling they had acquired.

'That's a *fabulous* idea!' Lizzie exclaimed.

And Sebasten basked without conscience in her pleasure and admiration and knew that he would never own up to the truth that he had hoped for that conclusion all along.

A YEAR AND FOUR MONTHS LATER, Sebasten and Lizzie threw a party to celebrate their baby daughter, Gemma's, christening.

Ingrid Morgan attended and Lizzie and she talked at some length. They had made peace with each other months before: Ingrid had felt very guilty and had urged that meeting, but Lizzie had made the effort initially only for Sebasten's sake. However, when she had got to know the older woman better she had begun to relax and like Ingrid for herself. Ingrid had worked through her grief and admitted that she had had no cause to accuse any woman of driving her son to suicide. She had come to terms with the reality that Connor's death had just been an accident.

When all their guests had gone home, Lizzie changed Gemma into her cute bunny nightwear and laid her daughter with tender hands into her cot. She just adored the baby. Gemma had her father's colouring but was already showing signs of her mother's personality. She was a cheerful baby, who slept a lot and rarely cried. Elbows resting on the cot rail, Lizzie smiled down at Gemma, grateful that her baby girl had not inherited her freckles. It was all very well for Sebasten to have a positive *thing* about freckles but he had to appreciate that not everyone shared that outlook, Lizzie reflected with amusement.

It had been an eventful year for both her and her father. Maurice Denton was already divorced. Felicity had met another man and had been keen to speed up the legal proceedings. Her father's spirits had been low for quite a time but moving house had helped and he very much liked living so close to his daughter and was a regular visitor. His own friends had rallied round him in a very supportive way, but her father had also developed a wonderfully friendly and relaxed relationship with Sebasten.

At times during her pregnancy that closeness between her parent and her husband had been just a little irritating for Lizzie. Both Sebasten and her father had been prone to trying to gang up on her and wrap her up in cotton wool. Stubborn to the last, Lizzie had worked until she was seven months pregnant before deciding to tender her resignation. The PR job had been a lot of fun but it had taken her away from Sebasten too many evenings and it had exhausted her.

Gemma had been born without any fuss or complications but Sebasten had lived on his nerves for the last weeks of Lizzie's pregnancy, striving valiantly to conceal his terror that something might go wrong. But Lizzie herself had been an oasis of calm, secure in the knowledge that Sebasten was doing all her worrying for her. He had fallen instantly in love with Gemma and, if possible, Lizzie had fallen even more deeply in love with Sebasten just watching him with their daughter. The guy who had said he preferred children at a distance used every excuse that had ever been invented to lift his daughter and cuddle her.

'Don't you dare lift her,' Lizzie warned, hearing and recognising the footsteps behind her. 'She shouldn't be disturbed when she's ready to go to sleep.'

Sebasten strolled into view, and at one glimpse of his heartbreaking smile Lizzie's pulses speeded up.

'Just when did you get so bossy?' he mocked, brilliant golden eyes roaming over the very tempting vision Lizzie made in her sleek blue skirt suit with her glorious hair tumbling round her shoulders in sexy disarray.

Lizzie grinned. 'When I met you. Either I lay down and got walked on or I fought back.'

'But you're out of line on this occasion. I spent half the evening holding Gemma,' Sebasten pointed out with amusement. 'I'm in the nursery in search of you.'

Already well-aware of that just from the smouldering gleam in his vibrant gaze as he surveyed her, Lizzie eased forward in a sinuous move into the hard heat and muscularity of his lean, powerful frame and gave him the most welcoming look of invitation she could manage.

'You're an incredible flirt,' Sebasten commented with satisfaction, surrendering at speed and scooping her up into his arms with an efficiency that spoke of regular practice.

'You like that...' Lizzie was used to being carried off to bed and ravished and she encouraged him in that shameless pursuit of pleasure every step of the way.

'I do. And carrying you around does keep me in the peak of athletic condition,' Sebasten teased as he settled her down on their bed.

Lizzie just laughed and kicked off her shoes. 'Kiss me and prove it.'

Sebasten pitched his jacket aside, dropped his tie where he stood, demonstrating an untidy streak that had once been foreign to him, and came down on the bed to haul her back into his arms. 'You're a wanton hussy and I adore you...'

Lizzie battered her eyelashes but the glow of her own love was there in her softened eyes for his to see. Before she could even tell him she loved him like crazy too, he released an appreciative groan in response to that look and melded her lush mouth to his own.

* * * * *

*If you enjoyed this story from Lynne Graham,
here is an exclusive excerpt from her upcoming book
BRIDE FOR REAL.*

Available September 2011 from Harlequin Presents®.

"SANDER..." Shattered by that admission of continuing desire from the husband she was in the midst of divorcing, Tally stared at him, her emotions in turmoil.

"In fact, wanting you is driving me absolutely crazy, *yineka mou,*" Sander admitted darkly.

And for the first time in longer than Tally could remember, her body leaped with actual physical hunger. She was astonished as she had felt nothing for so long that she had believed that that side of her nature might be gone forever. Was it the dark chocolate luxury of his deep voice that provoked the sudden rise of those long-buried needs? Or the sinfully sexual charge of his dark golden eyes? Tally had no idea but she felt a sudden clenching tight sensation low in her pelvis and her mouth ran dry.

She gazed back at Sander, feeling as vulnerable as if he had stripped her naked and marched her out into a busy street. *Yineka mou,* my wife, he'd called her. And she *was* still his wife, she reminded herself helplessly.

"Any idea what I can do about it?" Sander husked that question, strolling closer with the silent elegant grace that was as much a part of him as his physical strength.

"No, no idea at all."

"You push me much too close to the edge, *yineka mou,*" Sander murmured, tilting down his darkly handsome head and running the angular side of his jaw back and forth over the smooth, soft line of her cheek like a jungle cat nuzzling for attention. The familiar sandalwood and jasmine scent of his expensive aftershave lotion made her nostrils flare while the faint rasp of his rougher skin scored her nerve endings into life.

Suddenly, Tally felt like someone pinned to a cliff edge, in danger and swaying far too close to a treacherous drop. She didn't want to be there; she didn't want to fall, either, but any concept of choice was wrested from her when Sander found her mouth and kissed her, strong hands firm on her slim shoulders to hold her still....

Make sure to pick up Lynne Graham's title
BRIDE FOR REAL
to find out what happens between Tally and Sander!

Available September 2011.

Exclusively from Harlequin Presents®.

REQUEST YOUR FREE BOOKS!

2 FREE NOVELS PLUS
2 FREE GIFTS!

PASSION GUARANTEED SEDUCTION

YES! Please send me 2 FREE Harlequin Presents® novels and my 2 FREE gifts (gifts are worth about $10). After receiving them, if I don't wish to receive any more books, I can return the shipping statement marked "cancel." If I don't cancel, I will receive 6 brand-new novels every month and be billed just $4.30 per book in the U.S. or $4.99 per book in Canada. That's a saving of at least 14% off the cover price! It's quite a bargain! Shipping and handling is just 50¢ per book in the U.S. and 75¢ per book in Canada.* I understand that accepting the 2 free books and gifts places me under no obligation to buy anything. I can always return a shipment and cancel at any time. Even if I never buy another book, the two free books and gifts are mine to keep forever.

106/306 HDN FERQ

Name _____ (PLEASE PRINT)

Address _____ Apt. #

City _____ State/Prov. _____ Zip/Postal Code

Signature (if under 18, a parent or guardian must sign)

Mail to the **Reader Service:**
IN U.S.A.: P.O. Box 1867, Buffalo, NY 14240-1867
IN CANADA: P.O. Box 609, Fort Erie, Ontario L2A 5X3

Not valid for current subscribers to Harlequin Presents books.

**Are you a current subscriber to Harlequin Presents books
and want to receive the larger-print edition?
Call 1-800-873-8635 or visit www.ReaderService.com**

* Terms and prices subject to change without notice. Prices do not include applicable taxes. Sales tax applicable in N.Y. Canadian residents will be charged applicable taxes. Offer not valid in Quebec. This offer is limited to one order per household. All orders subject to credit approval. Credit or debit balances in a customer's account(s) may be offset by any other outstanding balance owed by or to the customer. Please allow 4 to 6 weeks for delivery. Offer available while quantities last.

Your Privacy—The Reader Service is committed to protecting your privacy. Our Privacy Policy is available online at www.ReaderService.com or upon request from the Reader Service.

We make a portion of our mailing list available to reputable third parties that offer products we believe may interest you. If you prefer that we not exchange your name with third parties, or if you wish to clarify or modify your communication preferences, please visit us at www.ReaderService.com/consumerschoice or write to us at Reader Service Preference Service, P.O. Box 9062, Buffalo, NY 14269. Include your complete name and address.

HPI1B